Kir LUKOVKIN

The SECRET
of
ATLANTIS

Good Luck on your journey!

Yours, Kir Lukorkin

Citadel World
Book Two

Magic Dome Books

The Secret of Atlantis
Citadel World, Book Two
Copyright © Kir Lukovkin 2018
Cover Art © Vladimir Manyukhin 2018
English Translation Copyright ©
Petr Burov 2018
Published by Magic Dome Books, 2018
All Rights Reserved
ISBN: 978-80-88231-61-5

A

THE COLD WIND blew swathes of snow into Paul's face.

He closed his eyes and nearly fell to the ground from the blow he'd received.

"Where are you going!" someone growled in front of him.

Paul pulled on the reins of his bay horse. The other riders behind him followed suit. They shouted at each other, conveying the command to halt along the chain of riders. Paul rose in his saddle, trying to make out what was going on at the head of the column. Excited voices could be heard, sounding like they were arguing fiercely. Lanky Pete rode up on his old nag and asked him about what was going on ahead.

"I don't know," Paul muttered. "We wait."

Lanky Pete grimaced unhappily and rode on. Paul stared at his retreating back, dumbly. It was cold and all he wanted to do was to return to their Retreat, stretch his legs in front of the big fireplace and drink some hot ale. The horses snorted, flicking their ears and nervously looking around. Paul turned to see what his bay horse Duchess was looking at and started to examine the edge of the canal — a long depression that ran almost as far as the horizon. Nothing, just a gray line that grew misshapen as it stretched out in the haze. Duchess was clearly getting nervous.

"Now, now," Paul stroked the horse's neck.

Lanky Pete returned and rode back towards the tail end of the caravan without stopping. A cry came from the front for everyone to get ready as the caravan was about to continue on its way. Paul could not wait to get going. This was all because of the accursed cold. Everyone's hands had already gone blue from the freezing temperature, chilled down to the bone, their bodies barely obeying them. There was nothing you could wear to save you when you spent more than a day up on the surface.

The caravan crawled on, gradually twisting its way around some unknown obstacle. The reason for the stop became immediately obvious. Paul could not help but shake his head, thanking the Almighty for the fact that he was traveling on an empty stomach. A corpse lay in the middle of the canal, so disfigured that it was impossible to tell whether it was a man or a woman. As the column moved on past the body, Paul managed to overcome his disgust to have a closer look. The cadaver lay in a fetal position. The flesh had been gnawed all the way down to the bone. It was difficult to tell whether this was a righteous man or one of the possessed. Death is the great equalizer.

Paul stared at the edge of the canal ahead of him again. Everyone in their Retreat knew that the Great canal divided the plain in two. A shallow river flowed along it in summer, while the bottom was covered with a layer of ice and snow in winter. It was an umbilical cord that carried caravans to the Retreat from the Mainland. If anything was to happen to the canal, it would be the end of the Retreat.

Paul gloomily considered this every time the latest mission set off on its way. He thought about this the first time he joined one of the missions too...

The horse of the leading rider suddenly reared violently. The rider could not hold on and fell onto the ground, beneath the hooves of the horse behind him. There was a commotion up front for a few seconds, with pushing, shoving and shouts of frustration. Paul barely held on to Duchess, when she tried to bolt at a frantic gallop. He pulled on the reins with all his might and leaned towards the horse's head, patting her on the neck. Duchess' whole body trembled, and it was not because of the cold.

"What's wrong with you?" Paul exclaimed, trying to calm the mare down, but she whinnied loudly.

The other horses in the column replied, as they fidgeted nervously and attempted to rear or bolt. One horse managed to jump on top of a cart and knock it onto its side. There was a complete mess up ahead and some kind of serious obstacle.

The caravan stood still. A caravan master rushed past Paul, shouting commands and trying to impose order. Duchess finally calmed and that was when Paul looked up. The banks of the canal were covered with strange mounds under the snow. Duchess nearly stepped on one of these and immediately shied away, neighing wildly again.

Paul took a closer look and understood what the matter was. The horse's hoof had randomly swept some snow from a mound and a human hand appeared. It was as white as a block of salt.

The caravan master kept shouting, "Order! Order, you idiots! Get back into the column!"

And then Paul noticed *them*.

A human figure appeared far away upon the left-hand edge of the canal. It looked so small that it was barely the size of his little finger. Then, another tiny figure appeared by its side, as if it came from underground. One after another, they kept coming, until the edges were lined with silent watchers.

Paul felt the cold reach its tentacles right into his heart. His hands almost let go of the reins. He thought that he shouted, but only a weak croak emerged from his throat.

The figures did not move, but more and more of them appeared with every passing second. All the while, the people at the bottom of the canal were too preoccupied with getting everything under control as their horses trampled the frozen corpses underfoot.

Paul looked up at the sky for some reason, as if he was hoping for help from some unknown gods. A thick layer of clouds hung low and silent up above. He directed his gaze back down to look ahead and saw the figures start to move. It was as if a gray wave rapidly flowed down the edges of the canal in complete silence.

It was only then that a belated cry of "Possessed!" sounded nearby.

The cry was caught up by a multitude of voices along the body of the column, like a sudden convulsion. There was a glint of bared swords. Paul remembered that his blade was also sheathed by his saddle. It seemed to be a pathetic toy compared to the hordes bearing down from above.

"Here comes death," a thought flickered through his mind. The wave of possessed on the right reached the canal first and smashed into the side of the caravan. The howling, shouting, screaming of the horses and the clanging of steel got even louder. Barely a moment had passed when the same happened on the left-hand side.

The faces of the closest possessed were so near that it seemed that they could be touched with an outstretched hand. However, attracting their attention had to be avoided at all costs. Standing out among the crowd was also a recipe for disaster, as the possessed were predators that attacked the caravans to satisfy the only primitive and primal feeling that they had remaining.

Hunger!

Paul struck Duchess on her haunches and flew along the column at a gallop. The possessed smashed into the caravan behind his back. People screamed in terror as they swung their swords. Paul rode on ahead without looking back. It was obvious what was going on there anyway — the humans were entwined with beasts in human form in a bloody battle for their lives. The waves of attackers rolled down the slopes faster than Duchess could gallop. In a moment or two they would collide, crushing the column in a vice-like grip of death.

He had almost reached the end of the caravan, where he could already see Magister Choo and his escort, who had quickly separated themselves from the masses. It looked like the Magister was planning to slip away from the claws of the predators. However, the possessed were already rushing to cut them off from both sides. The first of them leapt with an unbelievable speed and threw one of the Magister's bodyguards off his horse.

Duchess reared again and there was a loud crunch as her front hooves smashed back into the ground. A braying scream rang out. Paul turned his horse towards the inside of the column, trying to hide from the possessed. Chaos was everywhere and death feasted as madness snorted with laughter. The Brothers of the Order fought back as hard as they could, but their experience as warriors was of no matter, as the enemy overwhelmed them with their numbers. For every possessed that fell, two rushed in to take its place. The monsters were chewing upon still living humans. They were filthy, they looked scrawny, but they were merciless beasts. Their strength was unbelievable. It seemed that they never got tired and that they were ready to engage in endless slaughter just to satisfy their hunger.

And then, Paul felt himself being dragged

from the saddle. He hacked away with his blade, but the grasping fingers kept dragging him to the ground even though he continued to desperately fight back. Duchess bolted, kicking through anything in her way. Two or three of the possessed had Paul in their deathly grip. His foot was stuck in the stirrup and he would have been torn apart if his boot had not slid off.

Duchess galloped away. A foul, blood-drenched maw hovered above Paul. He stabbed out with his blade and pierced the throat of the monster. A gushing stream of blood burst upon Paul's face and chest. The blood suddenly warmed him, giving him a moment of calm so he could look around. It would have been better if he had not — the furious battle had become a massacre, with the victorious possessed feasting on the bodies of their enemies with groups of them finishing off the few that still resisted. The horses had all fallen or run away. There were only a few people left that were still capable of screaming in pain and fear. The possessed growled and squealed. All of a sudden, Paul's shoulder was in agony.

He had no time to even turn his head when he felt another bite sink into his forearm. Paul screamed, trying to fight back without success and preparing to meet his death, when something inexplicable happened.

A strange hissing sound rang out, followed by a low drone, as if the air itself became thicker, twisting into a horizontal whirlwind. Paul's ears got blocked. The growls of the possessed changed to howls of terror. The monsters started to run away in a panic.

Paul could not gather the strength to rise so he just looked up again. The gray sky had turned pink. His head spun. It was as if he was starting to fall into the heavens but just could not do it. The possessed ran past, gesticulating and swinging their arms wildly — for some reason, they were engulfed by flames as if they were living torches. Gradually, the screams quieted down and the wind began to howl over the canal again. Paul felt the cold but he did not care, he was not afraid of freezing. He lay there and looked up at the sky and could not understand why he was not dying. Death should have come long ago, as well as a meeting with God, but neither seemed to be happening.

The snow crackled nearby and the sky was suddenly obscured by a face — a wide face, somewhat ungainly, with deep, dark eyes and raven-colored hair, adorned with a scraggly beard. It was very pale. The stranger examined Paul with a calm and uncaring gaze, as if he was an inanimate object.

"Where are you from?" the stranger asked

at last.

Paul could not answer. He tried to move his lips, but he was unable to. His strength had completely abandoned him.

"Blink if you want to say "yes". Do you understand?" the stranger instructed next.

Paul blinked slowly.

"All right. Where are you from? Are you from the west?"

Paul kept staring at the stranger.

"From the east?"

He blinked.

"The outpost at the foot of the mountain?"

Paul used his eyes to say "yes" yet again.

The stranger stood up, looking to the east and adjusted the unusual weapon on his belt — it looked similar to a crossbow, but instead of a bow and string, the stock featured a short tube with some sort of light blinking on the side.

Once he finished with his weapon, the stranger turned to Paul.

"Try not to die before the end of the day."

And then he vanished.

Paul thought that he would never manage to fulfill his request. However, the stranger returned after some time, pushing a cart. After performing some manipulations, the stranger picked Paul up and placed him inside. There was someone else in the cart but Paul could not see who it was as he could not turn his head.

The stranger left for a second time and did not come back for a while. When he did, he led a horse up to the cart, harnessed it and set off on his way.

Paul lay on the rough planks of the cart and gazed up into the pink clouds. Why were the clouds still pink? Why? He could not think of a coherent answer, probably because it had got very cold. Paul could not feel his arms and legs and could not stop himself from constantly drifting off to sleep. His mind became cloudy, his thoughts all jumbled up and repeating themselves as his eyelids became heavier with every passing moment.

His consciousness finally sank into the fog in its entirety and then faded to black, as if a candle had been blown out.

B

WHEN PAUL FINISHED telling his tale, the dark-skinned Abbot carefully topped up his cup with nectar and ordered him to drink it all. Paul obediently did so. The Abbot nodded, with obvious satisfaction.

"Excellent, brother. You have been of great

help to me."

Paul carefully lowered the cup onto a tray — he was slow and clumsy when he moved due to the bandages around his shoulders. It would take a long time until he was healthy again. The wounds and bruises would affect him for a while to come.

The Abbot turned towards the wall, which was covered with a curtain and gestured towards it.

"If you please."

Rick was relieved to get out from behind the curtain. The whole idea of hiding made him immediately uneasy, but he did not want to argue with the man in charge. As soon as Paul saw Rick, his exhausted face went white with fear. The young man's full lips trembled, while his fingers frantically gripped the arms of the chair.

The Abbot smiled, showing his complete control of the situation.

"Do you recognize your savior?"

Paul gave a quick nod. Rick carefully examined his face: the young man was thin, like many in the Retreat, with no distinguishing features apart from two. While the first one was a particularly intelligent gaze that could be explained through a natural astuteness, the second was so strikingly unusual that it made him stand out like a white crow. A literal white crow — Paul's hair looked as white as the moonlight. This was not just the hair of someone who went white with age or the pale straw color of a blond, but the milky white and pearly hair of an albino.

Rick had never seen people like that. He quietly lowered himself into an armchair.

"How is your shoulder doing?" the Abbot asked Paul.

"Thank you, Master Kiernan, it's much better."

Two weeks had passed since Rick brought Paul and another pair of brother monks to the gates of the dome which they called the Retreat. One of the brothers had died on the way. The other was disabled until the end of his days. For a time, Paul's life had also hung by a thread — the wounds turned out to be very severe. But he managed to drag himself out of it. It did come at a great cost, however — he had lost half of his weight, walked with a pronounced limp and lost a pair of toes to frostbite, according to the healers. Both of his arms were now tightly bandaged from shoulder to elbow. He could barely straighten them.

"That's good. We all prayed for you."

"Your mercy knows no bounds, my Abbot," Paul whispered reverently.

"Stop that. You are like a son to me. Glory

to the Holy Maus that you are still with us. The Almighty favors you and it was he that sent this good man to you in your time of need."

Rick glanced at Kiernan with reproach. But the Abbot continued with his line of thought, which smoothly grew into a grandiose speech about the Holy Maus and his teachings. Once he finished so he could wet his throat with a drink, Paul asked, "Abbot, what happened to the caravan?"

He had been isolated from any news while he recovered.

"We managed to save most of the supplies," Kiernan's eyes darted at Rick. "Again with a little help from our good friend..."

Rick moved in his chair, as it was time he broke his silence.

"That's right. This is why there's nothing threatening the Retreat."

The Abbot smiled with satisfaction. His tanned face had an oily shine to it in the light of the fire. The whites of his eyes stood out against his dusky skin, shining like a pair of fireflies. At the edge of his vision, Rick noticed some movement in the corner. It was a yellow canary in a cage. Rick could have sworn that the bird had shown no sign of life over the course of his lengthy conversation with the Abbot until the boy arrived.

Paul swallowed and asked, "Did anyone else survive?"

"Unfortunately not," Kiernan entwined his long fingers. "Had we known that the possessed would attack, this tragedy would never have happened. Accursed beasts! Their behavior is always unpredictable. We will need to look at the mission schedule and reinforce the guard detail."

The Abbot thought about something for a few moments and then continued, speaking with great conviction.

"It is all the devil's work. It is he that tempts man and turns him into an animal. His power over the possessed is great. We must thank the Almighty for having blessed us with intelligence and stopped us from the temptations of sin. Isn't that right, my good friend Rick?"

"I did not quite understand the last words you said, about the devil." Rick replied. "Do you consider those creatures to be possessed by evil powers?"

"That is exactly what I meant," the Abbot nodded with a satisfied air. "You have understood the very gist of it."

"I see," Rick paused. "I doubt that it is possession."

The Abbot's face changed to a strange expression, as if he had misheard something.

"It truly is demonic possession," he

countered.

"All right. Does that mean that a demon can be exorcised?"

"Precisely."

"Have you exorcised demons from the possessed?"

"It is extremely difficult to do," Kiernan began, caging his fingers. "Firstly, it is very difficult to capture one of the possessed and one that is captured dies in captivity very quickly..."

"Of course," Rick agreed. "But even being behind the walls of the Retreat does not guarantee salvation from the affliction."

The room sank into awkward silence for a while. Paul was even more afraid — he carefully glanced over at the Abbot. No one dared to doubt his teachings. Rick calmly weathered the grim stare of Kiernan. The Abbot turned to Paul.

"By the way, did you see anything unusual in the way they attacked? Perhaps they behaved in a strange or special way?"

Paul frowned, trying to think hard.

"No. Apart from the fact that there were so many of them."

"How many?"

"A couple of hundred. Maybe more."

Kiernan nodded.

"That's what I was discussing with our friend Rick as well. The beasts never gathered in packs of that size before."

"Maybe it is a migration," Rick suggested. "Or some other natural cause."

"That could be. As I already said, it is difficult to understand the ways of demons. Anyhow, Brother Paul, I invited you here to have a different conversation. Are you prepared to help me to resolve a certain issue?"

"Of course, Abbot," Paul nodded fervently.

"Good. You see, brother mine, while you were recovering me and our friend Rick spoke much about various subjects. I offered him to be a guest at our humble Retreat and our friend Rick acquiesced. It is an honor for us."

Kiernan paused, staring at Paul.

"Do you know which day it is?"

Paul bit his lip. His eyes suddenly shone with the realization.

"We are serving the Autumn Mass today."

"Yes. Our friend Rick wanted to see it before setting off to take care of his own business. This is why I would like to ask you to accompany him throughout this evening until its very end. Tell him everything you know, and you know a lot. Answer any questions he may have."

"I will perform the task you set me," Paul replied readily.

"Thank you, my young brother," Kiernan drawled ingratiatingly. "You may go now. My advisor will give you a ticket for a double dinner. Take a while to feed yourself properly."

Paul bowed clumsily and set off towards the exit. He stumbled a little as he passed through the doorway but kept his balance and confidently left the room.

"He was born under a lucky star," Kiernan said a minute later. "I would never have thought he'd make it."

"A young and strong body," Rick shrugged. "And a thirst for life."

Kiernan gave him an appraising glance.

"You are also rather young for such dangerous journeys."

"That's right. I am a victim of circumstance."

The Abbot nodded. Rick did not want to make his job any easier and waited for the new questions that immediately followed. First came the attempts to find out as much about the outside world as possible. However, Rick was in no hurry to tell him everything and mainly repeated the same things that he shared on his first day in the Retreat. That was obviously not enough for Kiernan — he wanted to know more and never stopped trying to glean just a little more information ever since. It was obvious that it was difficult for him to stop himself from applying pressure directly. Kiernan was a man used to issuing orders, but not in a situation where he was next to an outsider with a weapon who had managed to miraculously send a hundred possessed on the run.

They were both fully cognizant of this fact.

Kiernan kept smiling, showing two rows of magnificent, strong teeth and expressing his goodwill. Rick did so too, whilst keeping his hands on the stock of his blaster.

"You are never away from your weapon even for a minute," the Abbot noticed.

"This thing saved my life in the wastelands many times."

"But there is nothing threatening you here," Kiernan wheedled. "I vouch for every brother in the Retreat. I gave my word to do you no harm from the very beginning."

"I truly appreciate your concern, Abbot," Rick nodded. "However, carrying a personal weapon at all times is part of the culture of my people."

"The Holy Maus takes all of the peoples of the world as they are," Kiernan agreed. "It is your right to do so. Our teachings are the epitome of tolerance and peacefulness. We stand upon the foundation of several indomitable truths, but we are prepared to accept people as they are..."

Rick barely listened to him.

They conversed for about half an hour

more and then Rick left the Abbot's chamber. He came out into the inner courtyard of the Retreat and curled his lip at the sharp smell of paint. The locals were standing on scaffolding and painting some warehouse containers nearby. The stink tickled his nose and Rick could not help but sneeze.

What a vile odor! He tilted his head back, gazing sadly at the twilit sky above through the protective dome and dreaming of a breath of fresh air. The construction was well designed — arcing metallic struts covered a great area, with a clear material occupying the spaces in between them. The Ancients truly knew what they were doing. However, this place was as deathly cold as any of the expiring shelters occupied by mankind.

Even though the dome protected those inside from sudden temperature changes, the locals did not have sufficient fuel to heat the whole Retreat. They spoke of technology and generators with hatred, of course, using slaves for heavy labor. According to Kiernan, the people hid in the monastic cells of the temple and descended into the disused mine to sleep so they could find a warm corner.

Rick stood there for a while, looking at the metallic structure leading to the shaft which had been rent asunder by an explosion. Well... What must it be like for the slaves that live in the cages which stand in the yard? No wonder that one of them dies every day.

There were many cages and slaves in the yard. Rick's eyes met those of a dark-haired, brown-eyed boy that stood transfixed by the bars of his cage. They spent a while studying one another, until voices could be heard nearby. Rick turned his head and saw Paul standing nearby and chatting to one of the locals, so he slowly made his way towards them, remaining in the shadow of the Abbot's house. The local stranger quickly finished the conversation and left, while Paul remained with a pained expression on his face, trying to stretch the stiffness from his bandaged arms. Rick stepped out of the shadows and Paul flinched. Rick did not hurry to start talking, as he was interested in seeing Paul's reaction to his appearance. Paul shifted hesitantly, stepping back a little and coughed.

"Have you already had the time to explore the Retreat?"

"Yes."

Paul waited for Rick to continue, but he stayed silent.

"Hmm, in that case, there is no need to lead you around the yard and show you all the buildings, is there?"

Rick nodded.

"That's great, that's excellent," Paul

muttered, obviously avoiding looking straight into Rick's eyes.

Strange behavior. Rick gave the yard a quick once-over. It was as if the boy was afraid of something. Or someone.

"The Abbott says that you work as an archivist," he enquired.

"That's right."

"Are you literate?"

"Why?"

Rick waited for an answer.

"I know how to add up ancient letters into words. But I don't always understand their meaning. I know how to write and copy."

"That's sufficient," Rick concluded.

"For what?" Paul did not understand.

"To explain the meaning of your religion to me."

"Ah, oh, yes," Paul agreed and looked at the huge clock hanging from one of the separator struts under the dome. "Midnight approaches. The Mass will begin soon. It's best to come to the temple early."

He touched his chest by reflex to feel the item hanging on a string around his neck under his jacket.

"We'll do as you say," Rick nodded and bent his head forward a little to try to see what was so valuable about the item that Paul was hiding in the folds of his clothing.

"This is the medallion of the Holy Maus," Paul said when he saw the curiosity in Rick's eyes, reaching inside his jacket to take out a shiny round object, which was actually a universal electronic key of the kind used in Thermopolis. "A gift from the Abbot."

"Yeah," was Rick's only reply, as he added to himself that if the boy only knew the true purpose of this gift, he would never ever have shown it to him.

Paul started to hesitantly walk away from the house of the Abbot. Rick walked by his side. They walked around ten paces, when Paul asked, "Where did you come from?"

"Far away," Rick replied. "From the west."

"From the domed cities?"

"From far further away."

"There is nothing there, apart from the Abyss."

"How do you know?"

"This is what the Revelation of the Holy Maus teaches us."

Rick chuckled to himself bitterly. It was the same every time. They did a really good job at brainwashing them here.

"That's a lie," he said.

Paul was so shocked that he froze. His lower lip trembled. Finally, he managed to force himself to speak.

"If that's a joke, it is a very flat one, Master Rick. Otherwise, such words can lead to..."

"I know what such words can lead to," Rick brushed him aside. "Your Abbot told me. But this does not change the truth. And the truth is that there is no Abyss beyond the domed cities. If you like, I can tell you what is there."

"No," Paul cut him off in a hurry.

"As you want," Rick shrugged. "But remember, that if a man that looks at the sun closes his eyes, the sun will not disappear as a result."

They continued towards their midnight destination — a gallery of steel pillars that reached deep into the yard from the western side of the temple. The gallery gently arced in the direction of a structure that was roofed with a mesh-like spherical construction with a steeple at the top. The fires were already lit inside. People from the whole Retreat were beginning to congregate at the place of service. Their arrival was completely silent. Before Rick and Paul entered the gallery, Paul asked, "Could you please listen to me now? It is forbidden to speak during Mass, because it is the one and only Great Maus that speaks through his medium, the Abbot. You must stand, listen and obey everything that the priest orders."

"I understand."

"Your consciousness must be open for the sacred spirit of Maus. Do you understand?"

"Completely."

"Well, let's go then."

They ascended the stairs and entered a long rectangular hall. The congregation slowly progressed through it, removing their clothing and footwear on the way.

"It is customary to remove everything apart from your underwear," Paul whispered and started to take off his boots to set an example.

Rick watched him in confusion for a while, looked around and walked over to the wall. Paul was waiting for him with his boots in his hand. Rick thought it over for a moment or two and then made his decision. He deftly removed his robe, revealing his old jumpsuit underneath.

They undressed.

"No one will touch your things," Paul told him.

"Excellent."

"You will have to leave the weapon as well," Paul pointed out.

Rick looked around. It seemed that everyone was completely preoccupied with the preparations for the service. No one paid attention to him. Paul had already put some distance between them. Rick still gripped the barrel of the blaster. He hesitated, but then wrapped the weapon in his robe and put everything down by the wall next to his bag and hurriedly followed Paul.

The people were thin and scrawny to a man. It would be hard to call even the toughest of them healthy — their pale and filthy skin was covered with scars and abscesses. It seemed that the brotherhood rarely took care of its personal hygiene either — there was a strong smell of sweat and unwashed bodies in the air. Life was harsh here.

Rick thought this over as they passed through the hall and entered a spacious room covered with a mesh-like dome. Everything was already prepared for the ceremony. They walked to a free space behind the backs of the congregation so they could see everything that was going on. Paul silently pointed at the altar and the wide table. Rick enthusiastically examined the decorations — he was incredibly interested in who or what exactly was the Holy Maus.

A thick drapery hung behind the altar. The drapery concealed some sort of image on the wall. The altar itself was a stone plinth, carved with glyphs and writings. Kiernan was already here — the Abbot had changed into a long shirt made out of rough-spun wool. It was called a "hair-shirt",

Rick suddenly remembered.

All of a sudden, his temples felt as if he had been struck. Rick closed his eyes and shook his head — the seizure came at entirely the wrong time. His mind burned with pain, overloaded with the knowledge he gained through the Thermopolis rapid learning program, as dozens of fireflies danced in front of his eyes and he heard distant voices. That had not happened for quite a long time. It seemed that interaction with other people was having an effect as it was far less severe in the wastelands and the pain only overcame him when he was reading the books he found among the ruins.

Rick exhaled slowly, calming himself, and cast a sidelong glance at Paul. He was ogling Rick with fear, unable to understand what was going on. Rick looked ahead and saw Kiernan standing in front of the table with his eyes closed. At least that one did not notice anything. Complete silence fell.

Nothing happened for a couple of minutes. Kiernan slowly swayed from side to side and then upraised his hands and started to chant prayers. His voice carried itself up to the vaulted ceiling, reflecting off the walls. It was a high-pitched, somewhat gravelly voice dripping with mystical ecstasy. Kiernan started the service with a traditional prayer for cognition to be granted to humans from on high. He asked the Almighty to preserve the minds of men, so they could understand all of the grandeur of the designs of the divine and follow all the commandments that were given to the people. He also asked for the lives of his order to be prolonged, because it was the only fragile thing of value that remained after the dark centuries of chaos and ruin.

Kiernan asked for many different things, for mercy, for justice, for protection, but every time, his prayers somehow gravitated towards one thing — the desire to live a virtuous and intelligent life that was worthy of a human, not an animal. This was because animals in human form that were possessed by the devil prowled the earth, consuming the weak and tempting the strong. And this was the very reason that every commandment of the Holy Maus must be followed.

Kiernan climbed onto the table and started to perform a dance with complex, jerky movements. His mass had reached its second stage. Now he did not just ask, he thanked and praised God for all of the good things he did. The Abbot clapped his hands and his speech became rhythmical and terse, gradually turning into shamanic song. The smell of burning torches mingled with the smell of sweat.

"Let us praise the Holy Maus!" Kiernan

called out and the crowd that had so far been quietly observing the mass immediately reacted. People started to clap together with the Abbot and sing along. Rick carefully observed what was going on, feeling Paul's eyes upon himself.

An assistant gave the Abbot a large vessel full of yellowish fluid and a brush. Kiernan lowered the brush inside and used the liquid to asperse those present, swinging his arms wide. There was a spicy smell in the air. Everyone gladly put their bodies under this rain. They rubbed the elixir all over their skin, licked the drops from their fingers and made jerky movements as part of a rhythmic dance. Kiernan moved around the circle of worshipers, exclaiming invocations.

"Hail the Holy Maus! Let's praise the Holy Maus!"

"Let us praise him!" chorused the congregation.

Once the elixir had run out, Kiernan was unsteady on his feet and made another pronouncement.

"Holy Maus, protect us! Save us from the machinations of the dark powers!"

"Save us!" the congregation chorused in return.

"Keep your righteous sons safe from the evil eye, the evil word and the clouding of their minds!"

"Yes!" a chorus of voices answered him.

Kiernan accepted a new chalice of the liquid from his assistant.

"The mark of the Holy Maus!"

With these words, he started to dip his brush in the fluid and anointing everyone's foreheads, moving along the rows of the devout. The paint flowed down along people's brows and chins and their faces soon turned yellow. It was now Paul's turn. The hand anointed his brow and dripped the paint upon his clothing, as the youth closed his eyes in a paroxysm of transcendent languor. Kiernan continued to mark the flock, moving in Rick's direction.

When they came face to face, Rick firmly told him, "Don't do it, Abbot."

He wanted to step back, but then felt strong arms grip him on both sides. Kiernan hurriedly swung his hand, aiming for Rick's forehead, but Rick tilted his head back and pushed the Abbot back with a kick. Kiernan gasped and found himself landing on his posterior on the ground. The chalice rolled along the floor, splashing the spicy smelling viscous fluid.

For a second, everything stood still.

Everyone rushed towards the Abbot from all sides, helping him to get up. Someone picked up the chalice and brush. Kiernan passed his clouded gaze over all that were present until it stopped on Rick.

"Let him go," he ordered hoarsely.

The order was immediately obeyed.

"The Mass is over."

"I warned you," Rick told him.

Kiernan looked at him with an expression of stubborn righteousness. Rick needed to get out of there as soon as he could. The din of offended voices could be heard behind him.

When Rick reached the hall where he had left his possessions, there were three strangers busily looking around there. Rick found his clothing among the piles of rags and started to get dressed. After he put on his jumpsuit, he suddenly stood as still as if he had been struck by lightning

His weapon and his travel bag had disappeared.

He looked around. The three strangers looked back at him, silently. One of them walked right up to Rick, scuffing his feet on the floor and spoke, revealing a mouth full of crooked teeth and empty gaps.

"Lost something?"

"Yes. My weapon."

"None may enter the temple bearing weapons!" exclaimed the crook-toothed man.

"Return my effects to me," Rick forced out.

"Better go and air out your brain, pagan," the stranger answered with contempt.

He smirked again. Rick noticed one of the three strangers quickly slide out into the street with a bundle in his arms with the corner of his eye. That settled everything. Rick rushed after him, but the crook-tooth grabbed him by the shoulders.

"Let me go!"

The crook-tooth did not listen to him. Rick smashed him in the ear with his right hand, knocking him off his feet. However, other men who filled the hall blocked the way to the exit. Rick found himself surrounded. He managed to knock down another three, but could not fight his way to the exit as the crowd that poured out into the hall after the mass completely cut off all escape routes. Rick ended up on the floor in the ensuing melee, his legs and arms held tight against the stone. The crowd parted and Kiernan stood over him.

"What happened here?" he exclaimed.

"This pagan maimed Brother Jeremy, knocked Simon's teeth out and broke Blaze's jaw!"

Kiernan passed his cloudy gaze over the crowd and then stared at Rick.

"Take him away," he ordered.

32

Rick tried to break free, shouting that it was all a lie, but none listened to him. The crowd carried him out of the hall like a tidal wave.

C

THE SOUND OF STEPS rang out in the darkness of the corridor. Rick warily sat up on the bunk. His hearing was well developed, as it was a vital quality in the gloom of the world that birthed him. So, there were two people approaching the cell. One had a heavy step, while the other stepped lightly, limping along. The footsteps fell silent by the door to his cell.

Rick imagined how these two walked along the path he had taken down here on the day of the Mass. While he was being dragged to this place, he carefully memorized the way. He was lowered into the shaft which was under an explosion-ravaged structure. The shaft was twenty levels deep — a huge well, with walls comprised of residential blocks and places that had once been industrial units. Rick was taken down along a spiral corridor that circled the well down to the lowest levels. Once they reached level five, the convoy dragged him along a narrow corridor and threw him into a damp cell which was filled with empty wooden boxes.

There was a clang as the bolt slid open. The light of a lantern dazzled Rick's eyes and he saw the squat outline of a man in the doorway. The stranger waited for a moment before entering, as if he was afraid of his next step.

"Shout if anything happens," someone grumbled in the corridor.

There was a rustling noise, the clang of the bolt again and the sound of retreating steps.

Rick blinked after the bright light and looked at the door again. Paul was standing there. He looked around helplessly, getting used to the half-light. At last, he noticed Rick sitting on a bunk made out of a row of boxes.

"Come in," offered Rick, pushing an empty box towards him.

He actually knew that Paul would arrive ahead of time — he had requested the meeting himself.

Paul took a faltering step forward and stood stock still, staring at the box. Rick could not resist smiling — Paul was even more afraid of him now.

"I'm in no hurry," Rick told him. "I can wait."

Paul swallowed and got his breath back. He frowned, trying to make his face assume a severe expression, but the way he looked amused Rick even more. Paul carefully lowered himself onto the box, squinting in the gloom.

"A little dark, is it?" Rick smiled again. "I know what darkness is."

"I have no doubt," Paul blurted angrily. "What do you want from me?"

"Information."

"What sort of information?"

"What is in the east?"

Confusion rippled across Paul's face. He was so tense that his fingers contracted into fists. Of course, the Abbot had given him detailed instructions before his visit, so Paul was going along with the guidance from his mentor — be harsh and strict and aggressively provocative.

"Why do you want to know?"

"You're careful," Rick complimented him. "It's a good quality. A useful one. I observed you on that day. You were the only one that took your horse out of the column, while the rest were still trying to work things out. You were the first to notice the possessed."

Paul tensed up again, trying to look even more severe.

"I could stop interacting with you," he replied.

"Was that what Kiernan ordered you to do?" Rick enquired, leaning back against the wall. "That Abbot of yours is a cunning guy. He did a good job there."

"What job?"

"The Mass and all the rest. He used you as bait. He took advantage of my trust and sent his men to look at my possessions while we were listening to his howlings."

"That's not how it was..." Paul started to reply.

"I don't want to talk about it," Rick cut him off, suddenly leaning forward. "Tell me about the east. If you don't want to, leave."

There was a hard glint in Paul's eye for the first time. He jumped up, closing and opening his fists and breathed heavily as he looked for an insulting reply. But it was Rick who spoke.

"Hey, man, I did not want to offend you. I just spoke straight. Hard times require honest words and actions."

Paul calmed down somewhat, but did not sit back down on the box.

"A ruined canal leads to the east and there are the Tombs beyond that."

Some facts at last. Rick carefully pulled on the string to unravel the ball.

"And further along?"

"I don't know. None of the brothers ever went that far, of those that returned."

"So there were some expeditions?"

"Yes. Borislav, who was our previous

Abbott, left with three dozen men and vanished without a trace. That was almost twenty years ago. We have been wary of the east since then."

"I see. What about the north and south?"

"Mountains to the north, wastelands to the south."

"Did anyone come to visit you from those directions?"

Paul thought on it for a moment.

"Some sort of nomads," he tentatively ventured. "I think they were wild tribesmen. Pagans. Those that live at the edge of the Abyss."

"Did they try to attack you?"

"Some did, but many of them just went away."

Now it was Rick's turn to think about what he just heard. It seemed that his way lay in the direction of the Tombs. The canal was the main point of reference that he should not depart from. The canals were dug by the Ancients to connect the domes and the big cities. Over his weeks of wandering, Rick could count the number of domes inhabited by humans on his fingers. Most of the settlements were more like sepulchers. Coming across the caravan from the Retreat gave him a new hope.

"How long has the Retreat existed?" he asked.

"No one knows for sure. Ever since the first

adepts escaped here from the nearby cities."

"So the dome already existed," Rick muttered to himself. "Then everything matches... Was there anything left of those who inhabited the dome before?"

"Nearly nothing. The Abbot might keep some important things to himself, but no one knows what exactly they are. Only the Abbot's successor is initiated into all of the mysteries."

Rick thoughtfully scratched his chin through his unkempt beard.

"Do you know why you are going to help me?" he asked Paul.

Paul kept quiet.

"You are driven by curiosity. An inquisitive man can never calm down until they get to the bottom of things."

"You can say whatever you want," Paul looked past Rick into empty space with complete indifference, as if he did not even notice him.

"Fine. Then remember this: Kiernan is lying to you to maintain control of the Retreat and keep me here. It is all about my weapon. Did you see it in action at the canal?"

"No," Paul admitted.

"Well, the second survivor saw it all. He told Kiernan everything in detail. A sword can be used to kill one, two or three enemies, while my blaster can cut down dozens of enemies when it is set to wide beam dispersal. I see you don't understand some of the words I'm using?"

Paul was frowning, trying to pretend that he did.

"A blaster is a weapon created by the Ancients," Rick began to explain. "It was made in the ages when man could command machines and change this world. A blaster radiates energy similar to sunlight that has been intensified several thousand times. Do you understand what I am talking about?"

Paul ground his teeth. It seemed that he understood.

"When you own such a weapon, you can destroy the possessed and also make all of your enemies and all who disagree with you bow before you. It is absolute power." Rick accentuated the last word. "Have you ever thought about who built your Retreat and why people suddenly go insane?"

Paul's lips twitched, so Rick continued, having caught the initiative.

"Let me guess — the people of the Retreat are forbidden to go outside it when they wish to without escort. Because none of you have ever seen the outside world and gone beyond the domed cities. The majority of you are illiterate. The orders of the Abbot must be obeyed to the letter. No initiative, only discipline and obedience.

They indoctrinate you by saying that this is the way to get closer to God. Is that right? Touching ancient mechanisms and learning to read signs is forbidden under pain of death. Am I correct? You live in isolation, thinking that the universe is limited by the horizon, and that everything beyond is just emptiness."

"Do you have any more questions?" Paul almost shouted.

"You suffer from the cold," Rick concluded. "I know how to bring the heat back."

"Questions! Ask me questions!" Paul demanded.

"I can make it so that you will not have to travel along the canal to get supplies and risk your lives. You will no longer suffer from hunger and you will have a normal life."

"Questions!"

"But to do this, you will have to take a risk and get rid of your cult."

Paul staggered away, trying to hold his ears shut with his hands. He swayed towards the wall.

"I know that you regularly attend all of the Masses and services, Paul," Rick told him harshly. "But it isn't because you believe in your Maus so much."

Paul stared at him in horror.

"It's only because you need the holy elixir. You only feel well when you receive it."

"You are the spawn of hell," Paul whispered.

"I know," Rick laughed. "I have one last question."

Paul contracted, as if he was expecting to be struck.

"What does the Abbot intend to do to me?"

"I have no idea," Paul exhaled.

Rick tried to catch his wandering eye for a second. He failed.

"Then be on your way."

Paul glanced at Rick with distrust. He backed away towards the door.

"You should not have done that," he mumbled sadly. "You should have obeyed him."

"Obedience is the death of will," Rick replied with disgust. "Subservience is a sign of weakness. That is not my path."

"I must go. Unlike you, I have many matters to attend to." Paul turned towards the door and knocked, calling the guard. Unhurried steps rang out from the corridor again and Paul kept completely still as the guard approached. He just stood there, hunched over in silence.

"Paul," Rick called out. "The world is not the way you imagine it. Think about it."

There was no reply. Paul darted out of the cell and hurried back up above. Rick imagined the boy climbing up the stairs, constantly stopping to catch his breath like a wizened old man. Rick saw how he gradually returned to the world of light from the kingdom of darkness, but the pale light was but the shine of a cold November day that provided no warmth. A bleak and drab world spread out above.

That world had given someone a serious slap in the face today.

Rick turned to his side and fell asleep, feeling proud of himself.

D

THE DAY WAS COMING to its end, according to Rick's internal clock. Like the rest of the feelings enhanced by the darkness of his home, this one was rarely wrong. A bell rang somewhere far above. One peal, a second and a third...

The bell continued to ring — it was a special sign. When six men burst into the cell, Rick was already up and waiting for them.

"Hi!" he smiled at them.

They trussed him up and dragged him above. As soon as they reached the surface, they took him to the chapel where the local brotherhood had already begun to gather. By the time that his escorts led him up to it, there were many people packed inside. The doors of the chapel were left wide open, to allow the light and frosty breeze from outside to air it out. The convoy escorted Rick past the rows of worshipers towards the pulpit without stopping. Kiernan towered over it, dressed in a bright red robe with yellow sashes crossing over on his chest and a fur collar. The abbot clutched a paper scroll in his hands. His pale face showed a resolution to complete what he had started.

The bell finally fell silent, but the echo of its peals resonated through the chapel, reflected off the walls for a short while. Once the sound dissolved below the roof, a wave of whispers rolled through the crowd. Kiernan nodded curtly.

"My brethren!" he exclaimed, raising his hand up high.

Silence fell. The faces of the congregation turned towards the Abbot.

"My brothers in faith! We have gathered here today to resolve an important issue. It concerns a man named Rick, who recently arrived in out Retreat after a terrible battle at the canal. This man saved the lives of two of our people — Brother Paul and Brother Peter. He also helped to deliver the food supplies to our Retreat, which saved us all from starving to death."

Kiernan took a deep breath and continued.

"We welcomed our friend Rick with great

hospitality. We accepted him as our brother, gave him a roof over his head, a fire to warm him and out humble provender. Nothing was refused to him and he could freely move around the Retreat and do what he will. That is the proper way to treat a man that helped us. Our gratitude towards you for not leaving us in peril knows no bounds, friend Rick."

The Abbot paused again, slowly passing his long gaze over those present and then continued, "However, an incident has occurred that still confuses and saddens me. Because our friend Rick was really interested in our holy faith, I could never refuse his request and allowed him to attend the Autumn Mass, so he could fully understand the teachings and perhaps join our faith. I was leading the Mass and all was going as well as it could, until our friend Rick interrupted the ceremony in the crudest way possible. Many of you were here and saw everything with your own eyes. You know what happened. The Mass had never ever been interrupted like that throughout the history of the retreat. Any of you would suffer a harsh punishment for such a deed. But because we are good people by our very nature, I decided that this was a simple misunderstanding. If that was all, we would not be standing here now."

Kiernan flourished with his hand, pointing

44

at Rick, and started shouting.

"But this man did not stop there!" His voice got louder. "This man had the arrogance to accuse us of a foul, insidious and base crime — he accused us of theft! Yes, you heard that right! Theft! He dared to declare that one of us, brothers, one of us had stolen his weapons, supplies and his bag. Just stop and think a moment how badly he thinks of us. Think of how much one must despise people to throw such accusations in their faces. And again, these aren't just words; many of you were there when it happened. This outsider felt so arrogant here that he decided that he will push and order us around! Only the darkest, most ignorant and pagan peoples are capable of such things. Only barbarians! Brutes! Savages!"

The Abbot shook his fists as he finished. His cry rose up to the top and dissipated under the vaulted ceiling. The worshipers held their breaths, transfixed.

"But this was not enough for this barbarian!" Kiernan started again. "When we tried to talk some sense into him, he injured one of our brothers so badly that the poor man is still in the medical chambers. I had to lock up our friend Rick in the interest of safety so he would not harm any of you, my dear brothers. What happened that day was this." Kiernan started to count on his fingers. "The interruption of a ceremony, defamation of character and bodily injury. Even one of these deeds is sufficient to punish any of our flock to the full extent of the law. But we have a savage before us, so our laws do not apply to him. By the way, his equipment has been found. Here, look. It was lying around somewhere behind the temple. None of the brothers had laid a finger on it."

Kiernan nodded. His assistant placed the bandoleer and the combat blaster on the table before the crowd. He put the travel bag by their side.

The Abbot declared, "Brothers, I have thought about what to do for a long time. And I have reached a decision."

Rick chuckled loudly. Kiernan flinched as if he had been slapped in the face. The watching crowd showed signs of confusion.

The Abbot continued, "Crimes must be punished. However, because there is nothing he can offer us apart from his lost soul and considering his help as a mitigating factor, I have decided to take his bandoleer and weapon away. You accused us of the vile act of theft. You thought that you had lost your possessions because of us. Well, now we shall confiscate them from you!"

Kiernan's assistant threw Rick's bag on the

floor.

"Take your belongings and be gone from our holy land," Kiernan ordered, with a disgusted expression on his face. "Enough of you desecrating it with your presence!"

Rick clapped his hands and stepped forward.

"Bravo! What a beautiful speech," he slowly turned around. "I can see that there is no point in explaining myself and proving you wrong. You need to listen so you can understand, but your ears are full of wool." He shook his head. "All right then, I'm leaving."

Rick hooked the strap of the bag with the point of his boot, kicked it upwards and skillfully caught it, putting it over his shoulder. He quickly slid his hand inside and suddenly looked grim. Silence fell.

"Now this, this is going too far," Rick growled through his teeth.

He glanced over at Kiernan, who raised an eyebrow in pretend surprise.

"What are you talking about?"

Anger engulfed Rick. Did the Abbot think that he was an idiot? What arrogance!

He shouted, "You know full well, Kiernan! The map! Where is it the map?"

"What map?"

"There was a world map in my bag. It's no

longer there!"

"Are you trying to say that it was our fault it disappeared?" Kiernan hissed, stepping towards him.

Rick heard a noise behind his back, but did not show that he noticed.

"Come on then, say it!" Kiernan offered. "Maybe you will also dare to declare that we are trying to cheat you here and now? Maybe you want to accuse us of lying again?"

Rick took his time. It was their home, so it was their rules. And the cunning Abbot obviously counted on provoking aggression. Rick took a deep breath and laughed, sadly.

"I have nothing to say. When there's a fanatical belief in lies, they become the truth. I'm leaving."

He made a move to turn around, but the Abbot's assistant grabbed him by the shoulder. Rick's escorts suddenly appeared by his side.

"We haven't finished yet!" Kiernan shouted. The fire of vengeance smoldered in his eyes. "Did you think you will get away with it so easily? Did you think that you can insult the sacred Retreat and its flock and go unpunished?"

Rick tried to move, but his escorts held him fast. They had fed him almost nothing over the last few days, so he had no strength to fight back.

"I immediately saw your devilish nature,"

the Abbot shook his finger, "as soon as you entered the gates of the Retreat. I observed you. I saw how you mocked our faith. No one may laugh at us without punishment! You had the chance to leave hale and hearty, but you missed it, friend Rick! Look at him, brothers!" Kiernan raised his hands in exultation. "The beast has been trapped."

"I am a barbarian," Rick replied. "You cannot judge me."

"That's right. But we can convert you to our faith." Kiernan stretched out his hand and a brush covered with paint was placed in it. "I induct you in the name of the Holy Maus."

The guards threw Rick down onto his knees. He tried to fight back, but their strength was too much for him. Kiernan painted his forehead and cheeks yellow and then unfurled the scroll and started to read the ancient prayer of initiation. Rick thrashed around in a rage, spitting and swearing.

"You are now one of us! We can now exorcise the corruption from you!"

The congregation became noisy.

"By fire!" the Abbot exclaimed.

"Fire!" the crowd echoed as they made their religious gestures. "Cleansing fire!"

Rick went cold. If it was what he thought, it would have been better to die of cold and starvation like the slaves in the cages...

Suddenly, a burning torch flew through the window of the chapel. A desperate scream sounded from outside. A member of the congregation burst in through the open door. His face was covered in blood.

"Fire!" he shouted. "Over there! There's a fire! They started a fire!"

Everyone immediately started to run out of the building. There was noise coming from all sides. Another burning torch flew into the chapel and landed right in the middle of the crowd. Someone cried out in pain and the congregation panicked. People were running to and fro, knocking each other over while trying to put out the torches, but the fire quickly spread to the draperies hanging on the walls. The smell of smoke was in the air.

"Settle down!" Kiernan shouted, but there were few who heeded his order.

The majority rushed towards the exit in a panic, knocking over the prison guards and the armed bodyguards of the Abbot. Rick did not waste time. While his escorts were looking around, he knocked one of them out and grabbed his blaster and bandoleer from the table. The others tried to stop him from escaping, but Rick managed to get away from them and rushed towards the exit, pushing his way through the crowd.

"Get him!" Kiernan screamed, spittle flying from his mouth in fury.

The inside of the chapel was filled with thick smoke. The partitions and the wooden furnishings were already on fire.

"It's the slaves! They've started a fire in the Retreat!" came the shouts from outside.

The chapel was rapidly emptying. When Rick went outside, he saw a terrible sight. Several dozen slaves were fighting to the death against the followers of Maus. Some cages in the yard had been broken open, but others still held prisoners that the free were trying to release. The majority were women and old men, but they fought with such ferocity that the grown men of the congregation retreated before their furious onslaught.

Rick ran around the corner and then towards to an empty cart by the building on the opposite side, crouching to check his blaster — the weapon was in full working order and ready for battle. But he would always have time to use the blaster. Rick raised his head to watch the yard and soon understood that there was a certain order to the actions of the slaves, which meant that they had a plan and that their revolt had been planned in advance. He watched a woman run up to the stables with a torch at the far end of the yard. She paused for a moment, looked around, flashed a nasty grin and threw the torch inside.

Screams of pain and anger, the clang of steel, muffled thumping sounds and the crackle of burning beams came from all sides. There was a strong burning smell in the air. Over half of the buildings in the Retreat were on fire. The greedy, long tongues of flame howled as they consumed the fresh paint on the sides of warehouse containers, trying to reach the food supplies. This black smoke rose upwards to the edges of the dome so it could sneak through the air ducts.

The ferocious battle in the yard continued. Humans were fighting other humans.

The world never changed — Rick remembered similar battles with no mercy or compassion frequently take place back in his Thermopolis home.

Once they rallied after the surprise attack, the Mausites started to push the slaves back towards the containers. Rick angrily spat on the frozen ground and understood that he could not stay there anymore — the Mausites would take care of the slaves sooner or later and the fire would even reach his hiding place before the fight in the yard would stop. He had to go through the yard as it was the only way to get out of there!

Rick darted forward and this was the

moment when Paul stumbled out of the doorway of the chapel, rubbing soot and tears across his face as he could see nothing ahead of him as he coughed loudly because of the smoke he inhaled. A brown-eyed boy jumped towards Paul, brandishing a sickle. The gaze of the dark-haired slave burned with hatred. The boy raised his weapon, but Rick got there just in time. He grabbed the boy's arm and tore the sickle out of it. The boy hissed like a rat, twisted himself out of Rick's grip and darted away. Rick stepped towards Paul and put the sickle in his hand.

"Take it!"

"What for?" he moaned in reply.

By the great Expanse! Rick shook Paul by the shoulders.

"Wake up!" he shouted straight into Paul's face. "Take the weapon! If you want to live, follow me!" He ran towards the building which had been gutted by the explosion and which hid the entrance to the mine. Paul was breathing heavily and coughing behind his back, trying to keep pace. Rick kept looking around so that he would not miss a sudden attack from the slaves or the Mausites, but no one attacked him and Paul anymore.

The sounds of fighting and the howl of the fire were left behind them when Rick and Paul found themselves by the entrance to a stairway which spiraled downwards around the mineshaft. They could not help stopping for a moment — a guard and one of the women who started the fires were fighting at the edge of the platform in complete silence, as a torch which had been forced out of her hands lay burning beneath her feet. The guard was squeezing the woman's neck with his hands and she was trying to break his deadly grip.

Rick wanted to intervene, but he was not fast enough. The woman desperately thrust her fingers into the face of the guard, aiming for his eyes — there was a splash of blood, the guard howled in pain and flinched, but he never broke his hold as they fell upon the barrier. They kept fighting for a few moments longer but it was already too late once they realized what was happening — they both fell over the railings and disappeared down the mouth of the mineshaft.

Rick was used to seeing deaths. While he was not completely untouched by them, it was a long time since they made him dumbstruck the way Paul was now, so that he had to be shaken and directed where to go. Rick gathered the torch from the floor, grabbed hold of Paul's hand and dragged him down the stairway.

They went past several levels in this way until Rick stopped. His eyes feverishly searched the walls, floor and ceiling for a certain symbol.

An airlock was bound to be somewhere here!

Paul sniffled loudly and shivered by his side. Rick stared at him.

"Are there any passages here?"

"D-do you mean the corridor on this floor? Th-there are four of them, one for each point of the compass."

"Expanse take it, no! I need a corridor that will take us away from here!"

"I... I'm not sure th-that..."

Rick came close to Paul, looking into his eyes.

"Get your act together and answer. Do you know the way or not?"

Paul suddenly stopped shaking, with composure coming back to his eyes and silently pointed to a place on the wall where there were ledges covered in a thick lair of rust and moss. Rick touched the wall, brushed away the growths and smiled as he saw the symbol marking the exit with the label "A (III)" in the dim light of the torch. He stepped back, passed the torch to Paul, moved the intensity switch on his blaster, aimed it at the symbol and held his breath.

Rick's finger found and pulled the trigger on the grip of the weapon. The blaster spat out a ball of fire and a large hole with rough edges appeared in the wall. There was no time to wait for the smoke to clear, so Rick stepped through the opening and found himself in a tunnel.

He turned around and asked, "Did you think about what I said after we spoke in the cell?"

Paul was looking at him with a mixture of horror and awe. Valuable time was being lost, but Rick waited patiently.

"Thoughts cause pain," Paul said eventually.

"No one said that it would be easy."

The sounds of fighting at the top suddenly fell silent. There was a distant rumble. The roof of one of the buildings had probably collapsed. Rick stepped out of the opening and glanced upwards — it looked like there was not time to waste as the revolt had now been crushed and the Mausites could appear in the mine shaft any minute.

"I want to defeat the cold," Paul declared.

"Then get a move on," Rick replied.

Rick dove into the tunnel. Paul followed and they both set off at a run.

The torch soon burned out and they spent a while moving in complete darkness, feeling along the walls until Rick got used to the gloom. The smell of damp earth and rotting plants came from the direction they were moving in. They could feel hard stone under their feet. Rick noticed a panel on the wall, which he then tried to open, hoping to find some switches, but his efforts were in vain. It wasn't too much of a problem, they would get lucky eventually.

"Master Rick..." Paul called out fearfully.

Rick decided to wait before answering. Paul stood three steps away from him and could not see anything, while Rick had no problems orienting himself. It was amazing how blind people from the surface were whenever they found themselves in a dark place. Finally, Rick took pity on Paul and glanced back at him.

"Be quiet and make no sound until I tell you to. Do you understand?"

"Yes!"

They moved on ahead. The floor started to gradually slope downwards. After a while, the gloom started to clear and a weak light could be seen up ahead. Paul sighed with relief. They continued on their way. Rick tried to roughly determine the direction that they were moving in and decided that the corridor was leading them somewhere to the north-west. His assumption was soon confirmed as he could see part of the dome and the glint of the reflected rays of sunlight that shone through the distant clouds.

Rick decided that this was a good sign and picked up his pace, as the tunnel was obviously leading in the right direction which would take them outside the Retreat. He really did not want to end up in the place where the canal began, as they could come across the possessed. They soon had to stop as they found themselves at a fork in the tunnel. Rick looked at the tunnel openings stretching away into the darkness and tried to decide which one he should enter. The platform in front of him was incredibly clean — no sign of moss, spider webs, mold or rust. Paul crouched and slid his finger along the floor, coming away with a layer of gray dust.

"What are you looking at over there?"

"Nothing, Master Rick."

"We need to choose which way to go," Rick concluded. "What do you think?"

Paul shrugged. He saw no great difference between the corridors. This world was alien to him and it scared him. Rick understood that very well and carefully looked over the walls to look for signs. Nothing.

"Mother Darkness," he grumbled "We'll have to trust fate. Let's go down the right one."

They turned into the right-hand corridor which turned out to be taller and wider than the previous one.

"Ah-ha! The direction signs should be here somewhere. I think we've got into a maintenance section. That means that the power and water stations are nearby. Just as I thought!"

They stopped in front of a small square

projection from the wall that had some writing on it.

"Energy distributor," Paul read out.

There were also some letters and numbers that had been rubbed out by time there. Rick opened the hatch and flicked some of the switches.

"No power. Just as I thought," he turned to Paul. "The energy that provides heat and light goes through this box. The energy itself is produced at a station which is called a generator. Do you understand?"

"Is it something like a hearth?" Paul asked tentatively.

"Well done, you catch on to things immediately," Paul nodded and strode off down the corridor at a brisk pace.

Paul followed him.

"The space near the domes is full of corridors and levels," Rick explained, "where all the most important machines for human life are hidden. These devices were created a very long time ago, but many of them are out of power now, because people moved to the surface or died. The machines are still here, and they work. All we need to do is to supply them with energy and start them up again!"

"What for?"

"Don't you understand?"

"No," Paul confessed.

"What do you even know about this place?"

"The Scriptures of the Holy Maus state that the underground kingdom is the world of malevolent daemons that drag down the souls of sinners and consume them alive for all eternity."

Rick shook his head. The religions of all these small peoples were so different to each other, but they were always strikingly similar regarding the existence of hell.

"Right. In time, everything will be put in its place."

"Do you want to start up the ancient machines?" Paul asked with notes of fear in his voice.

Rick stared at him for a moment, but made no answer. Paul lowered his eyes.

"I'm sorry, Master Rick, it's hard for me to get used to things when everything is happening so fast and..."

"Can we agree that you will stop calling me Master? Just call me Rick."

They kept going.

"As you wish," Paul nodded obediently.

"You are driving me up the wall with your ceremonies," Rick grimaced. "Remember, that while you bow and say your pleases and thank yous, someone will take your head off and put it on a pike in the outside world."

Paul looked like he was in deep thought.

"Mast... Rick, may I ask you a question?"

"You're going to do that a lot in the near future, so go for it."

"Who are you?"

Rick did not give an immediate answer. It was a simple question, but... It was so hard to answer the simplest questions sometimes!

"Just another person, moving towards his goals. Satisfied?"

"Not really," Paul continued. "I mean, I understand that you are doing something extremely important, but what's the purpose of your journey?"

"It's a long story. Remind me to come back to it when things are quieter around us, if we survive that long."

They walked along the corridor until they found themselves in a hall which was two levels tall. Part of the hall was occupied by a pool of water, which was refilled from an inclined pipe. The water left the pool by way of another pipe that disappeared into the wall. Rick climbed up onto the edge, got a handful of water, sniffed it and poured the remainder into his mouth.

"I think it'll do," he declared.

They drank their fill. The water turned out to be a little salty, with a metallic aftertaste. Paul noted that it was a lot lighter where they were, even though he did not notice any light source, which he informed Rick about. It seemed like the dissipated light was coming from the ceiling.

"Well spotted," Rick said, as he filled his flask with water. "That's the mold fluorescing. It's a shame that your Abbot stole my papers. I had a map, a guide to universal codes, a dictionary and a list of computer passwords. It's all probably turned to ashes. It would have been so useful now."

He punched his hand in frustration.

"You are so sure about this..." Paul began, but cut himself short as soon as he met Rick's eye.

"You're as naive as a newborn! Haven't you understood anything yet?"

Paul kept silent.

"Kiernan played with you like a puppet, a doll that the Ancients used where they could tug on strings to make its arms, legs and head move around. He wanted to use you to find out everything I know. When that didn't work out for him, he just tried to get rid of me."

"Kiernan told me otherwise," Paul replied, looking hurt.

"Oh, really? So what did he tell you?"

"That your eyes are as dark as the guts of the devil and that it was impossible to look into them without a shudder. That you are the get of dark forces, created especially to deceive the righteous. First, you will help us to gain our trust and then, when we finally accept you, you will deliver a crushing blow. He also said that the disappearance of your belonging from the temple was a trick that you had set up. Another thing he told me is to be very careful and wary if you decide to speak to me. He warned me that you would try to lead me to temptation and ordered me to remember everything you said and report it to him word for word. And that we could only defeat you together."

Rick snorted.

"See, you were a puppet. I'm not even going to discuss it. Think for yourself and make your own conclusions."

"I have already concluded that Kiernan was mistaken," Paul admitted. "So what are those codes? Incantations or prayers?"

"Something like that. They help to control mechanisms and find out their purpose. There's a lot more you will find out about machines. Oh, take a look over there." Rick jumped off the railing around the pool and approached the doorway through which they entered the hall to point to a barely noticeable A (III) symbol. "We're on the right way."

They decided to take a short break. Paul was looking around the hall when Rick suddenly looked concerned and motioned to him to get his back to the wall by the doorway with the symbol. Rick stood on the other side, keeping completely still. Paul got noticeably tense as he listened out for any disturbances. Minutes of waiting passed. Paul sent a questioning look towards Rick. Suddenly, someone quietly padded into the hall. It was the dark-haired boy who had tried to attack Paul in the Retreat. As soon as he noticed the others, the teenager tried to escape as fast as he could. However, Rick managed to get in his way, push him back and level the blaster at him.

"Freeze or you die!"

The former slave stood stock still. His dark eyes glinted with anger and his gaze was full of resolve.

"Are you alone?" Rick asked. "Tell me the truth."

The dark-eyed boy nodded.

"Good." Rick stepped up to him and patted his clothes down, looking for weapons and then took a step back. "What do you want?"

The boy kept staring at him. Then, he noticed Paul and frowned, resting his eyes on each of them in turn.

Rick continued to question him.

"What is your name?"

Silence.

"Can you talk?"

Stubborn silence.

"Don't you have a tongue?" Rick started to lose his patience. He roughly grabbed the boy by the chin, forcing his mouth open. "Oh, you really don't. Who did this?"

The boy pointed at Paul. The teenager's face became a grimace of hatred.

"It wasn't me, it was the guards! The Abbot said that this was protection from possession," Paul mumbled rapidly.

"I see." Rick lowered his weapon and turned to the newcomer, "Thank their Holy Maus for this gift."

"I'm really sorry," Paul looked away from the boy.

He spat on the floor in disgust.

"Is anyone following us or tracking us?" Rick asked him.

The boy shook his head and made a noise in his throat. Then, he slunk over to the pool and spent a long time greedily drinking the water.

"We still need to keep moving," Rick concluded. "Let's go. Are you with us?"

He waved at the boy and stepped into the corridor. After they walked through a short connecting passage they reached a tunnel that was four levels high. Rick noted to himself that the underground spaces were becoming ever larger and more spacious. They stood upon the balcony and looked at the monorail strip that ran along the bottom of the tunnel. Walkways stretched out from the balcony along the walls on both sides and led to adjacent corridors. The ends of the tunnel disappeared into the darkness. This still made Rick happier.

The boy made a noise and pointed in the direction that Rick had supposed to be the north. Without waiting for an answer, the boy confidently strode off towards it. Rick agreed with the idea, so he followed.

"You're going to follow him?" Paul asked in surprise.

"Why not?" Paul shrugged as he walked.

"But..."

"We don't have any other options anyway, and it seems that this guy knows his way around well." Rick still glanced behind his shoulder. "What're you standing around for? Come on and catch up with us."

Paul had no choice, so he hurried along after them.

E

A LONG STRIP of sharpened steel pressed into Rick's side. If the makeshift weapon entered even an inch further, the scratch would have become a deep wound and Rick would bleed out. Not daring to move, he looked at the bearded man who stood in front of him, dressed in orange rags. He had narrow shoulders and thin arms, similar to those of the other people that they just came across, only the bearded man had many different chains around his neck. Judging by the smell, these people had not washed for a long time. Rick wanted to look around, but the shiv pressed deeper into his side and the bearded man growled threateningly. The brown-eyed boy was looking at him from behind the man's back with great interest, shamelessly picking his nose all the while.

So what did it all mean? They obviously knew each other. Only a few minutes ago, the boy had been quickly striding along the corridor ahead of them, when armed men suddenly jumped out from some hiding place and surrounded them. Rick immediately realized that resistance was futile, calmly lowered his blaster and raised his hands. Paul started to shake and quietly pray to his Maus for a merciful death.

The bearded man finally shifted his attention from Rick and stroked the brown-eyed boy on the shoulder, saying a few words to him quietly. The teenager demonstrated his open mouth to him. The injury made a great impression on the stranger. He glanced at Rick and Paul with complete hatred, hugging the boy and forgetting about the prisoners for a moment. Then he turned back towards them and bared his teeth, about to issue an order, but the boy stopped him and used sign language to indicate that Paul and Rick had come with him. The bearded man spent a while examining them with suspicion.

"Who are you?" he asked.

"We come from far away," Rick replied.

"From the surface?" Rick understood that the bearded man was in charge here. "Don't jackals in the skins of men prowl up there?"

Rick guessed that he was talking about the possessed.

"They passed us by," he said, patting the blaster that hung on the strap on his shoulder. "Thanks to this."

The bearded man narrowed his eyes and ordered the others to lower their shivs.

"I am White Worm. And this is my son, Black Ant."

Rick and Paul introduced themselves.

"Let us go to the lair of the White Worm," the bearded man commanded, and everyone followed him. No one uttered a word along the way.

White Worm's people led them through a web of corridors and split up, encircling them again once they reached a hall that had a similar setup to the central part of the temple in the Retreat, apart from being several times larger and more spacious. Lamps burned with orange light, pulsating like the embers in a bonfire. A myriad shadows danced upon the walls, which had numerous walkways and pipes stretching along them, as well as hanging bridges with ladders attached to them and masses of ugly constructions that were stuck together in the most unbelievable combinations. The prisoners were led to the platform in the center. The residents of this strange place stepped out of their dwellings, looking at the newcomers curiously. White Worm led the prisoners to an iron pillar, which was the height of two dozen men and had a huge chalice at the top of it. Metallic nets and protruding spikes of various lengths could be seen under the bottom of the chalice.

White Worm approached the pillar, opened the lid on an instrument panel and grabbed hold of a handle that slid out of it.

"We are upon the line again," he intoned.

"Upon the line," the men escorting the newcomers chorused.

White Worm pointed towards the handle.

"Connect to the great Network."

Paul stumbled back, but Rick grabbed him

by the scruff of his neck and dragged him towards the panel, whispering, "Don't even think about it, they will cut our throats if we won't do this."

Both of them took hold of the handle. Rick heard a noise in his ears and he prepared for another fit with dozens of voices in his head, but nothing happened and the headache and feeling of nausea receded.

"I am upon the line," he quickly declared.

White Worm nodded and looked at Paul.

"I am... On the line," he wheezed, his voice atremble.

"Now you are with us!" White Worm announced and clapped his hands.

An approving hubbub arose among the people who had gathered around to watch the proceedings. White Worm raised his hand, ordering silence.

"People of the Network, my son, Black Ant, has returned. The ones above took away his tongue, but my son has regained his mind."

"How can this be?" someone shouted from the crowd. "Didn't you banish him when he was turning into a jackal?"

"So I did. He and my wife became jackals and I banished them. But now he is one of us again!" White Worm declared and then turned to his son. "Show them."

The boy took a spear from the closest warrior and started to spin it around, Black Ant made shapes in the air with great skill. Shouts of approval came from the gathering. He stuck the spear into the corrugated floor.

"Good," White Worm continued. "These people came with him. My son's people are my people. My people are your people."

Rick could not quite understand what the chief was talking about. He was very perplexed now that he knew that his son had been possessed. Rick could not get his mind around the fact that Black Ant had somehow regained his mental faculties. Was that really possible? Could it be that Kiernan had taken the boy's tongue and cured him of possession that way? Unbelievable!

He felt eyes studying him and looked around. The newcomers were being carefully examined in silence, as if they were exotic trinkets. A large woman with missing patches of hair stepped forward.

"Have Black Ant's people come here forever?" she enquired.

White Worm turned towards Rick.

"No. We will go," Rick replied.

"Where?"

"To the east."

This was not understood. The people

started to whisper among themselves, trying to make sense of what they had just heard.

"What is the east?" White Worm asked.

Rick cursed himself inside his mind. How would they even know what that is anyway? These people only understood where above and below was.

Paul quickly answered in his stead.

"Above and even further."

White Worm mulled over what he heard for a moment or two and then burst out in wild laughter, joined by everyone else.

"The ones above will catch you and put you on a chain," White Worm guffawed. "They will make you pick at the dirt or drag around stones until you die. Even if you run away from them, the jackals will tear you to pieces. This is foolish. Let's eat."

Everyone immediately burst into movement. The residents of the underground city left for their decrepit hovels with surprising speed. The large and balding woman led Rick, Paul and the chief into a room, which was probably the home of White Worm and doubled as a place where all the important issues facing the tribe were resolved. Black Ant followed them inside. They were offered seats on a floor mat and gave them a bowl of steaming broth each. It smelled delicious. White Worm did not hesitate and started to eat, loudly smacking his lips and shoveling the food into his mouth with his bare hands. His son followed his example, and Rick decided to keep up. While Paul was sniffing at his portions, the rest of them quickly consumed their dinner. The woman was busy with the hearth, which emitted clouds of steam without a visible fire. Paul finally tasted the soup and quickly got stuck into the food. Rick asked for another portion without a moment of hesitation.

Once he was full, White Worm lay back on the bed and started to watch the way Rick and Paul finished off the remains of the dinner. Meanwhile, the fat cook collected the empty bowl.

"If you are going, let us trade," White Worm declared.

He took off one of his many chains and gave it to Rick. The chain consisted of small parts of ancient machines on a metallic string. Paul received a sharpened piece of graphite, carefully shaped like a human figure at its base. Rick took a folding knife from his bag. He showed White Worm how the blade was released using a button, which made a great impression on him. White Worm happily accepted the gift and then stared at Paul, who suddenly remembered that a gift was also expected from him. He looked around and then approached the light colored wall of the room and started to draw lines on the gray surface with the piece of graphite he had been gifted. Everyone looked on in silence. When Paul stepped back from the wall, there was an incredibly detailed picture of White Worm together with his son. The chief sprung up, and approached the wall, bending down with a furrowed brow, and stared at the drawing. He suddenly straightened and stepped really close to Paul.

Rick slowly got up, ready for any surprises. Black Ant stood still with his mouth open, his eyes fixed upon his portrait. White Worm took Paul's hand and started to examine his palm, squeezing his fingers, opening and closing them. Then he put his own palm against Paul's and compared them.

"Who are you?" he asked eventually.

"I..." Paul looked confused.

White Worm repeated his question and added, "Don't lie to me."

"I am a man from the surface. I was one of them, one of the ones above, but I have left them now. Rick isn't from their tribe, he came from far away. He saved me from the possessed... I mean, from those you call the jackals."

White Worm looked grim. Rick moved over to him.

"We are not going to do any harm," he assured.

"What do you think we do to the ones above?" The chief bared his teeth balefully. "Better you don't know."

"We respect your people and your laws."

White Worm looked deep in thought. Then, he headed for the exit.

"Follow me."

Rick and Paul looked at each other. There was no choice. Rick tried to look calm — there was no need for emotions now and Paul should not get too nervous, let him think that the situation is under control.

White Worm led them to the far corner of the encampment, where there was a pavilion assembled from steel poles covered with cloth. A leg stuck out from under the canopy in the front, which the chief kicked as hard as he could. The leg immediately disappeared, the canopy opened and an old man stuck his head outside, which was covered in deep wrinkles and framed by long gray hair, arranged in dozens of tiny braids.

"Hello," White Worm greeted him.

"What'd you want?" the old man grumbled.

"I have brought the one who had to come." White Worm pointed at Paul.

The old man looked him over with a measured glance and vanished into the hut. They could hear some rustling and coughing and soon the old man came outside again, leaning upon a stick. He had no leg, with a metal bar that had a horizontal movable plate and a rubber sole on the end in its place. The old man silently hobbled towards a wide opening that continued into a tunnel on the opposite wall.

White Worm beckoned his companions and followed the old man. Rick shrugged his shoulders and nodded at Paul — they needed to keep going. They passed through the tunnel, which led them to a hall with several pools of water. Rick was curiously looking around, trying to understand how and why did the Ancients build these installations. His temples started to throb unpleasantly and his head began to spin a little. There it was again! He had downloaded so much knowledge in Thermopolis that as soon as he tried to apply it his mind started to boil. It would not be good to collapse from exhaustion here — he fixed his eyes on the old man walking ahead of him, forcing himself to stop thinking about the hall full of pools. Otherwise he might fall, like he did in the wastelands once, twitching in the throes of his seizure as he foamed at the mouth and everyone would think that he was possessed and beat him to death...

The group followed the old man onto a walkway that was suspended above the pools, which were constantly supplied with water by sloping pipes. Rick walked onwards, as if on autopilot, looking at his reflection on the rippled surface. They passed the bridge and turned into a corridor between the pipes, finding themselves on a spacious balcony that hung over a black chasm.

The old man sat down on the edge, his leg and metallic prosthesis hanging down into the chasm and tiredly shut his eyes. White Worm tried to offer him some water, but the old man waved him away.

Everyone waited respectfully. It seemed that the old man had fallen asleep, but he finally opened his eyes and turned to his companions.

"This is Book of Faces," White Worm said, introducing the old man. "He is the eldest of all of us. He remembers all the people that he saw in his life and he has seen much because he was born up above."

White Worm nodded and thrust his finger upwards.

"Why him?" the old man asked the chief, pointing at Paul.

"Because he created a copy of me and Black Ant on the wall, looking like we were alive."

The mask of indifference slid off the old man's face and his eyes showed genuine interest mixed with amazement.

"You know how to draw?"

"A bit," Paul admitted.

"Where did you learn to do this?"

"I never learned. It just happens by itself."

"So it does," the old man agreed. "You can't even understand why it happens yourself. It comes from nowhere and seems to come alive. It wasn't there before and now it exists."

"Do you draw as well?"

"Now I don't. The Worm is right. I have many faces in my head and I can recognize any of them at first sight. I inherited this ability long ago..."

Rick was carefully listening to their conversation, hoping that the old man would continue. But Book of Faces fell silent, sinking into deep thought. A splash could be heard somewhere far down. Rick turned his head, trying to understand whether the splash had come from the chasm or somewhere from the corridor behind his back...

"They can smell us," Book of Faces laughed, "but they can't get us."

He turned to Rick and kept his eyes on him for a while.

"You! I have seen your face many times, more often than others," he suddenly exclaimed.

"Is that good or bad?" Rick asked.

"It is inevitable. And your face," the old man turned to Paul, "does not belong to you."

Chuckling, he moved his gaze from Rick to

Paul, watching their reactions. While this was going on, White Worm frowned a lot, but did not interrupt the conversation.

"I don't understand," Paul admitted. "What do you mean?"

"You will not understand until you find out what the Network is."

"How can I find out?" Paul breathed out.

"Here." The old man brushed his gray hair away from his temple to reveal a metallic socket which was implanted under the skin. "This is a very primitive method. You sit down in a machine and everything in the world goes right into your head. Everything that humans found out throughout their history. I have already forgotten half of it. But the faces stay with me to the very end."

Rick suddenly felt a chill in his very bones. The old man had been through the educational program the same as him once upon a time. But it looked like it all ended badly — Book of Faces had forgotten a lot.

Rick rubbed at his temple. His thoughts were mixed up in his head. Was this what awaited him too? Was there a difference whether he had gone through the educational program using his mind or by using a microprocessor implanted into his head?

"Worm!" the old man called out suddenly.

The chief rose.

"Leave!"

White Worm obeyed without complaint and disappeared down the corridor.

"So why did White Worm bring us here?" Rick decided to ask.

"Didn't you understand, man from the Citadel?"

"How do you know about..." Rick cut himself short.

There was no point in asking about it, Book of Faces knew what he was talking about.

"I am tortured by dreams of the future," the old man used his dirty nails to scratch his scrawny shoulder, which was covered in tattoos of red squares. "You are in those dreams. I had a dream about this conversation. Haven't you ever been visited by one of those visions?"

"No. But what I had was..." Rick glanced at Paul, but continued, "I have had pangs of pain."

"Oh," Book of Faces intoned. "You suffer from migraines more and more often. Any tremors so far? Have you had the cramps yet? Did you foam at the mouth?"

"Once," Rick nodded, "out in the wastelands".

The old man smiled with sympathy and returned to their previous subject.

"Haven't you worked out why you are

here?"

"I can only suppose. And ask questions." Rick glanced at Paul again.

"That's right." The old man sighed, and added, "There is no Network of any kind here because we are disconnected from the main server. The connection was destroyed a long time ago. However, human memory is a resilient thing. If you want to find everything out, you need to go beyond the canal, further down there." The old man waved his hand in the direction of the chasm. "This is why I ordered him to bring you. If people that know how to draw come here from afar, they must be shown the way."

"Is the whole world really covered with a network of caves like this?" Paul asked with surprise.

"Of course not." The old man looked at Rick. "Haven't you told him?"

"I didn't have time."

"Then tell him, before it's too late."

Rick turned to Paul. It was time for some revelations.

"There are underground cities around the world which were built in carefully selected locations. Our ancestors lived in them once upon a time. The underground chambers in which we are now, the domes on the surface and your Retreat are but a small part of one large city, parts of which can stretch out over many kilo... Many distances. We are standing at its very edge. I am looking for a path to the center of the city."

"What for?"

"The people that live on the surface are afraid of the underground, because it is full of ancient machines and mechanisms, the purpose of which they don't understand. You know this."

"Yes."

"Have you ever thought about the reasons that knowledge and communication were lost?"

"It was the will of..." Paul started and halted abruptly.

Rick waited.

"Everything was different. Is that right?" Paul looked at him with hope and then turned to Book of Faces, who smiled sadly and returned to staring into the chasm.

"It all started with the possessed," Rick explained. "The disease of possession appeared a long time ago and took many away. Those who survived hid from the diseased and waited for the disease to run its course, but it turned out to be stronger. People gradually lost their ancient knowledge and new generations started to be afraid of the past. That is how it happened."

"You want to resurrect ancient knowledge," Paul concluded.

Rick nodded. Paul kept watching him

carefully.

"Then how do you explain what happened to Black Ant? Does that mean that the disease is curable?"

"I don't know why that happened and I was just as surprised as you. We need to find the cause."

"Jackals turn back into humans?" Book of Faces joined the conversation. "How curious!" he grunted in surprise.

"Have you had some sort of dream about this, old man?" Rick enquired.

Book of Faces shook his head.

"What do you remember about your past? If you tell us, it will help."

"Very little, young man," the elder canted his head to one side and swung his legs, as if he was sitting on a tall stair, as opposed to an endless chasm.

"Everything has mixed together into one large picture, where there are many people, lines of people walking from one hall to another, transporter belts moving packages of cargo and huge lamps hanging over all of this, as bright as the sun. Oh, it's been so long since I last saw sunlight! I was born a slave and labored in a greenhouse farm for most of my life. Scrabbling around in the shit and the greenery from dawn till dusk. They kept assuring us that it wouldn't last long and we just needed to put up with it. Every year was supposed to be the last and it went on like this, harvest upon harvest, season upon season. They assured us that we will soon live under the open skies, with everyone in a home of their own, but we rarely saw the surface, while we lived in steel container-coffins that barely had enough space for everyone. And then people were struck by madness. People were turning into jackals in front of my own eyes. It was terrible! A man could start screaming with pain among the vegetable patches and swing his hoe at his fellow workers nearby. So we revolted, as we wanted to get out onto the surface. We wanted to speak to the government, but it turned out that they had run away long ago. And that is when the true insanity began. The jackals were destroying machinery and killing able-bodied men. Everyone tried to escape however they could. One scientist persuaded me to download all of human memory into myself from a machine. He was torn apart right before my eyes. I collected the remaining survivors and we ran down here."

"How did you manage to get in here? The canal is in ruins."

Book of Faces lowered his gaze. A minute passed, until he spoke again.

"Through the Tombs. Some never made it.

Those that did live here now. People from the domed cities think that we are infected and that the disease can spread, so they sealed the entrances that led below. We are lower than slime to them."

Paul and Rick nodded simultaneously.

"People are stupid," Book of Faces sighed. "But I believe that there is one person among a hundred idiots that is intelligent enough to think and ask the right questions and have them answered."

"Do you have a plan of the levels in this zone?"

"No. What are you talking about? We have nothing. Look at us. The people of the Network can't read or write and can barely count. Only I have some crumbs of knowledge left, but the children can't learn them, no matter how much I try to teach them. If you want to find a path, just follow the corridor with this sign." The old man drew a circle divided into four segments with dots in two of them.

"That looks like a highway sign," Rick suggested.

"Yes. Have you been to underground cities before?"

"I saw the remains of a city of this kind. Far to the west. But I never had the chance to investigate it, the radiation was too high."

"That's a familiar word," the old man's face twisted in a tortured grimace of pain as he tried to remember the word's meaning. "No. No, I can't."

"The product of the splitting of atoms during a chain reaction. Nuclear power," Rick reminded him. "A special ore serves as the fuel. And this ore..."

"Oh yes, that's right!" the old man exclaimed. "What were we talking about again?"

Paul stared blankly, as he understood nothing of what they said.

"About the map of the city," Rick reminded him. "I had a map copied from an ancient bas-relief, but I don't have it anymore."

He gave Paul a grim look, making him cringe as if he was about to be struck.

"If you studied the architecture of ancient cities, you probably know that everything is based on a circular shape. It is a very elegant system. There is a dome above and a well below. Ring corridors circle the well at various depths with separate blocks. There is a corridor from one of these zones to another and lots of utility installations. The zones are clustered together with a large dome surrounded by smaller ones. Highway tunnels connect them below ground and canals connect them on the surface. Altogether, it is like a conical frustum turned upside down, with a tough outer layer that is impervious to earthquakes and waters."

"What is this?" Paul asked, pointing to the red tattoos on the shoulder of the old man.

Book of Faces stared at the tattoos as if he had seen them for the first time.

"This... This is my passport. It identifies who I am."

"But..."

Rick did not let Paul speak, motioning for him to be silent. They all listened carefully — muffled shouts and screams could be heard through the whisper of the water pipes behind their backs. The noise gradually became louder — something unusual was definitely happening in White Worm's settlement. There was a loud bang. Then another. Rick anxiously grabbed his blaster and stepped into the corridor, looking into the gloom with concentration. Paul tried to walk ahead but Rick stopped him.

"So, it's happened know," said Book of Faces, as he examined the chasm. "They have come. They have become brave enough."

"What is he talking about?"

"Your Mausists decided to catch us, and they have come down here," Rick replied. "Time to make ourselves scarce."

"But aren't we going to help White Worm's people?" Paul asked.

"Go," the old man commanded harshly. "You must reach your destination!"

"What about the people?" Paul exclaimed. "They won't be able to defeat them!"

"Are you so sure?" The old man stood up and held his stick tighter.

Paul could not think of anything to say.

"Book of Faces, are you with us?" Rick asked. "Will you fight or run?"

The old man glanced at him ironically.

"I will accept my end."

"Thank you."

"Follow the sign, man from the Citadel," Book of Faces instructed. Looking at Paul, he added, "And you should draw this world. Create it again. Give it a chance to be reborn."

They parted ways with Book of Faces at the crossroads before the entrance to the hall of pools. They hurried to get away. Paul kept looking back, but he was unable to see anything in the darkness of the corridor. After a while, they heard the old man angrily exclaim something and other voices shouting back at him, then they heard a bang, a splash and then everything fell silent.

F

THEY QUICKLY MOVED along the corridor in the direction indicated by the old man. Rick's eyes followed the walls, confidently picking out familiar construction features — structural slabs, connecting seams and the way the communication lines were installed. Almost like home.

The corridor segments repeated at regular intervals. The walls were slightly convex, with a grooved grid-like surface. An external wall could be seen through this grid, with some space between it and the inner wall. There was probably something else behind it, some sort of other surface that isolated the corridor from the outside world — a many-layered cocoon, similar to the way that the outer layer of his native Thermopolis was arranged.

A rustle suddenly broke the silence. Rick raised his hand to signal Paul, slowed down his pace and bent forwards slightly, looking for the threat. Then, he crouched and put out his torch. Paul went quiet behind him.

They sat there in this way for around a minute. Once he got used to the darkness, Rick slowly raised the blaster, flicked the switch on the stock to raise the intensity and took aim.

Another tense minute of silence. Rick fired. The blaster coughed and the sound of a squeal followed by a thud on the floor came from ahead. Rick straightened out, quickly lit the torch and advanced, with Paul following in his steps. Once they reached the source of the sound, they stopped, staring at a pool of blood that had spread upon the gray slabs.

"What was that?" Paul asked.

"A rat. A rat the size of a child. When you hear squeaking, tell me."

They moved on. Rick gave the torch to Paul, so that he could comfortably hold the blaster with both hands.

"If I may say so, you're an excellent shot," Paul noted.

"Right. Lesson number two. Stop being so overly polite. How old are you?"

"Eighteen. My birthday was in spring," Paul proudly answered. "My initiation into the Brotherhood is coming soon."

Rick chuckled.

"I doubt it. How old do you think I am?"

He glanced back at him and noticed that Paul was no longer so quick to look away.

"Thirty?" Paul suggested.

Rick laughed. Did he really look that old? It was time to shave when he got the chance, it could be that his beard made him look a lot older.

"Wrong! I'm barely over twenty. So we're almost of an age. So stop being so obsequious."

"And these rats... How do you know that it's them?"

"I know, there's no doubt about that. If one of the creatures is around, the rest of the swarm is bound to be nearby," Rick assured him. "They never go around alone. But they are wary of people and larger aggressive animals. They're also afraid of fire."

"A kitchen rat once bit our cook on the nose," Paul offered.

"That's nice," Rick chuckled. "The one that we came across would have ripped his throat out. They can smell blood a kilometer away... I mean, from far away, many paces away. They will soon gather at the lair of the White Worm. Did you keep the sickle that I gave you in the Retreat?"

"Yeah."

"I would advise you to keep it handy."

"Tell me about the old world," Paul asked him.

"It used to take people years to learn all that I know." Rick slowed his pace, listening, but then quickened it again. "My words are unlikely to change much in your mind. You need time for that." He kept quiet, listening carefully again. "Of course, you need to know a lot and the more you know the better. Science, art, history and all the rest. Maybe we should start with the reasons you decided to follow me? How to defeat the cold? There are primitive methods, such as fire. But fire does not solve every problem and it is not possible to start a fire here, because there is not enough fuel."

"In the Retreat, every log is worth its weight in... gold."

"Gold?" Rick chuckled. "Do you understand the meaning of this saying? No one needs gold anymore, it has lost its value."

Paul blushed and explained, "I came across these words in the ancient books and I liked it a lot..."

"And you were waiting for a moment to use it?"

"Yes."

"Well, at least you're honest. Once upon a time, gold was one of the rare and expensive metals. It was used to make parts for various devices and for making jewelry, but gold does not interest anyone now, so it would be more correct to say that every log is worth its weight in food."

"I see."

Rick remembered Kiernan's tales about how the worshipers prepared wood for the winter in the nearest forest and returned to his previous subject.

"The heating of homes is an important issue. In order to resolve it, ancient humans invented machines for the production of heat which they got by burning coal, oil and gas, which are natural fuels. Nuclear power was discovered next — it would be difficult to explain the principles of the way it works to you because you do not know physics or chemistry. I was like that too, once upon a time and there were many things I did not know. I could barely count on my fingers."

"What is this Citadel that Book of Faces talked about?"

"A great fortress at the edge of the world. My former home."

"Is it bigger than the Retreat?"

"Much bigger. Its size is indescribable. Another creation of the Ancients."

"Did you leave it so you could restore knowledge?"

Rick said nothing, thinking about his answer. The faces of those that were left in Thermopolis arose before his eyes: Ahmed, Cornelius, Aurora, Kyoto... Maya.

"Yes," he replied at last.

Now it was Paul's turn to be silent as he thought on what he had just heard. After a few minutes passed, Rick decided to continue, omitting certain details about Thermopolis.

"When it became clear that people could also live beyond the bounds of the Citadel, I decided to find out if that was really true. My people also suffered from possession, which they called the plague. A lot of knowledge had been lost, but a disease must be studied in order to make a medicine to defeat it. However, this is impossible without knowledge. That is why I want to find an ancient city, as the science and everything else that is needed to save humanity from destruction might still be there. For all of the people in this worl

"That's a great goal!" Paul noted. "If we agree that possession is curable."

"So what is it that happened to Black Ant, in your opinion? He was cured, you heard it yourself."

"What if it wasn't permanent? Maybe a person's mind becomes clear for some time, but then they turn into an animal again?"

"That's what we will find out if we reach the city."

"All that happens must be seen as a trial..." Paul muttered.

"Stop that!" Rick interrupted. I have already heard these fairy tales. The trial is not the point. This sort of nonsense was made up for the uneducated and obedient in order to hold on to power. Where would you be now, if you had stayed in the Retreat? Would you be scrubbing frozen blood off the floor of the temple? Or would you update the records of the great Maus that nobody needs in the archive?"

Paul did not reply.

"Man has discovered much and became free as a result of curiosity and the violation of restrictions. Sometimes you need to go against the established order of things to make the world a better place."

Light glimmered ahead and Rick ordered for the torch to be put out. The bright spot at the end of the tunnel began to gradually increase in size.

"Keep your eyes peeled," Rick warned, as he slowed down and stepped as quietly as he could. "We can talk about everything later."

Paul was obviously nervous, breathing loudly behind Rick's back. Rick told him to quieten down again and raised his blaster. Fresh frost breathed into his face. They approached the opening, where the corridor ended in gray emptiness and stood still, taking in the sight before them.

The corridor had led them to the base of a giant crater, with the smooth ice of a frozen lake glittering at the bottom. Pieces of various constructions stuck out of the sides of the crater, covered in a thin layer of snow.

Rick surmised that something really powerful had exploded here, remembering how he had once seen something similar when he had come across an abandoned settlement with a ruined dome in the wastelands.

"We need to hurry up," he said, hoping that the explosion did not leave radiation behind and that it happened quite a long time ago.

He started to climb the slope, with Paul breathing heavily behind him. His feet kept slipping on the frozen ground. Rick tried to avoid looking up at the sky. His head still spun whenever he looked at that blue abyss, tinged with violet.

They got to the top and spent a long while standing on the edge of the crater and looking at the surrounding landscape. Rick used the rising sun to get his bearings and understood that they had wandered far to the northeast. The roofs of domed cities glittered on the horizon, the day was nearing its end and the shadows were getting longer.

Paul started to ask about camping for the night, but Rick ignored him, consumed by his own thoughts as he walked along the edge of the crater, carefully watching the horizon and trying to make out the details. He eventually stopped this pointless endeavor — it was too far away.

He stood there for some time and then

turned around and quickly strode away from the crater. He could hear Paul breathing raggedly behind him as the younger man caught up. Paul no longer tried to start up a conversation. They continued to walk along the plain in this way, in the light of the fading sunset. Once it got completely dark, Rick somehow came across some pieces of planks that had somehow ended up on the plain. He pointed the blaster forwards and burned a hole in the ground and started to take his gear out of his travel bag while the pit cooled from the heat. He unfolded and stretched out a piece of light but durable cloth over the hole, fixing it in place with pegs. Then, he took a thick metallic disk and pressed its middle to make a small pot, which he immediately gave to Paul, ordering him to gather some snow.

Paul turned the pot around in his hands in surprise and set off to do as he was bid. Meanwhile, Rick made a hearth out of rocks by the entrance to their dugout and used the planks to start a fire. Once Paul returned, he took a brick of dried concentrate from his bag, and broke it in half.

"Here you are. Eat. It tastes like rubber, but it gives you strength."

"What is it?" Paul asked with surprise as he passed Rick the pot full of snow.

"Food."

Rick put the pot onto the fire and started to chew the concentrate. The snow in the pot melted quickly, and when the water started to boil, Rick added some dark brown powder to it and took the pot from the fire. He waited a little and filled a glass that he had pushed out of another, smaller disk.

"It smells nice," Paul noted.

"You should drink some first."

"What is this?" Paul looked at the drink with suspicion.

"Coffee."

Paul brought the glass up to his face, smelled it and sneezed. Then, he took a sip and grimaced with disgust.

"It's bitter."

"Drink."

Rick put anything that he did not need back in the bag, pushed the embers around after adding the remains of the planks and took Paul's empty glass. He stopped for a moment, looking at his companion.

"You look terrible!"

He put his hand on Paul's forehead, which was covered in perspiration. Paul was obviously feverish.

"I am a bit tired," he complained.

"Are you cold?"

"No more than usual. My whole body is in

pain."

Rick poured him more coffee and forced him to drink it. While Paul was drinking out of the glass, Rick noticed that his companion had not finished his half of the briquette. After forcing himself to finish the coffee, Paul quietly crawled into the dugout, lying down in a fetal position, and laid there silently, shuddering occasionally.

"How often did you take the elixir?" Rick asked as the bent down to look in the dugout.

"A drop every two days," Paul answered reluctantly.

"I see. You're in withdrawal. It seems they got you on this horrible garbage to keep you on a short leash. Did they usually withhold the elixir from Mausites that had done sinful things?"

"Y-yes," Paul squeezed out.

"You are a drug addict, a man that is dependent on the ingredients of the elixir that cause euphoria, which is an illusion of happiness. Get ready to suffer."

Paul sniffed.

"Do you already regret that you came with me?" Paul had wrapped his hand with a piece of thick cloth and gathered the hot stones from the hearth, which he was now putting around the walls inside the dugout.

"Yes."

"That's right. Me too, for dragging you

along with me."

"It's a shame that I can't punch you in the face."

Rick chuckled. It was good if he was angry, that meant that he was fighting it. He climbed out of the dugout and put new stones around the hearth. There was not much firewood, but it would be enough for the night. He heard a quiet moan coming from the dugout.

"I am happy about your urge to fight," Rick said after he returned and sat down by Paul's side on the ground. "That means that all is not yet lost. You are pathetic and helpless now, Paul. The scrawniest rat could kill you now and all because you are not used to living in harsh conditions. You would not last a day on the surface on your own."

Paul started moaning again and twisted around, searching in the folds of his clothing with his hand.

"I have seen many people like you," Rick continued, "helpless slaves that live by their illusions that only care about their own well-being."

Paul turned around and lay still, blindly staring at Rick through the darkness.

"Your life is not worth spit," Rick whispered darkly. "You created nothing. All that interests you is your own precious hide and power. You bow and scrape before your teachers but you secretly hate them and dream of taking their place so that you can control the herd in exactly the same way, because you are all of one breed. You are soulless vermin, that's what you are. You are one of them too."

"Then why did you rescue me?" Paul's eyes glistened with anger.

"Exactly. Why did I? I don't know anymore. Maybe I believed in you for a moment, believed in your desire for knowledge. But everything turned out differently and now I think that I was wrong. You are a weakling."

Paul screamed with pain and struck out with his hand which was holding the sickle. The curved blade made a ripping noise as it tore the cloth above his head and got stuck in the ground as it landed. Paul swung blindly again, but then his chin felt the impact of a fist. Sparks danced before his eyes as his jaw cracked and Paul could not feel his body for a moment. When darkness filled his eyes and consumed the sparks, he heard someone say, "Nice try. But you should think about the fact that I was born and lived my entire life in the dark."

"Oh, god have mercy..."

"What are you complaining about?" Rick sneered. "Oh, all right, I think you've talked me into giving you another chance."

Paul groped about in front of himself and realized that he would lose anyway.

"You bastard!" he exclaimed and then gasped from the pain in his jaw. "Wasteland scum! Who are you? Who do you think you are?"

He found a stone, grabbed it, but immediately had to let it go — it was still too hot from the fire. He could not think of anything better than to start throwing handfuls of earth all around him and curse profusely. He was losing his breath from his helplessness until he completely ran out of energy. Then, he fell to the ground and groaned.

This was when Rick started to laugh.

"Not bad, my friend," he said. "I have finally understood that this is what Book of Faces meant when was talking about your face. You have been wearing a mask all your life and you have finally torn it off."

"What do you even know about me? You..." Paul muttered hoarsely.

"Believe me, I know enough." Rick sighed. "I knew a guy just like you. This guy lived his simple life, hoping for a better future. He just wanted to provide himself and his sister with everything they needed. Nothing special. He joined the guard in his Commune and honestly believed that he was doing the right thing. But everything turned out differently. He was the servant of liars and scoundrels that used him for their own criminal ends. They robbed the Commune and lied to the people, hiding the terrible truth from them. All of this was disguised as a great goal and the belief in a better future which would never come. The people suffered and thought that their suffering was justified. But one day, everything changed. This guy risked everything that was dear to him. He went on a dangerous journey where he could have perished. And when he violated the laws of the Commune it turned out that a new world opened to him and a new purpose appeared in his life. Just like you, he was the prisoner of many delusions. He was afraid, he made mistakes and he wanted to return. But he never lied to himself about who he really was. And when he chose a path, it meant that he would follow it to its very end."

Rick fell silent. His throat had gone dry and he took a swig from his flask.

"What happened to him next?" Paul asked.

"He had condemned himself to a long time of wandering. He lost those close to him and he must now do all he can to get them back. Are your parents still alive?"

"My father is. He lives in a domed settlement. My mother went away to the Almighty when I was very little."

"Any brothers or sisters?"

"No."

"Why did you go to the Mausites?"

"I had a talent for learning. Kiernan was looking for children like that in the settlements. My father fetched a good price for me. I think it's better to work with papers than to dig around in the dirt."

There was logic in Paul's words.

Rick took out some wire and used it to make some rough repairs to the hole made by the sickle and then started to make himself comfortable on the ground.

"I always liked it in the Retreat," Paul continued. "It has high walls, the rooms are clean and you get the chance to read there. I love reading. I like to work out the letters and see how they make up a word and then how words come together in a chain and how different words appear when you combine the same letters. There is a deeper meaning to it. The same as with drawing. You saw that I can draw. I could even draw you, Rick. It's not hard for me. I even like it. If I could, I would write and draw all day."

"Yes. You did a great job drawing White Worm and Black Ant."

"I used to draw on pieces of wood, on walls, on everything that was hard and smooth enough. I can draw all sorts of things — animals and birds, the sky and the earth, the sun and the stars. I can also draw people, trees, houses and various things. Sometimes, the drawings seem to come by themselves and something very unusual and special comes out — strange, bizarre creatures that couldn't exist in reality. I never showed drawings like that to anyone. There is something both unnerving and important at the same time about them. I don't understand what it is yet."

"Please describe one of these pictures."

After thinking for a moment, Paul said, "For instance, a creature with a horn on its head. It's a massive animal that looks like it is covered in armor. It has tiny eyes and giant, thick legs which it ambles along on. This animal is slow but it is incredibly strong."

Rick chuckled — it looked like he was talking about a rhinoceros.

"So you think that this animal is made up?"

"Of course!" Paul fell silent for a moment. "And do you know why I decided to come with you?"

"No, but it's obviously not because of the cold."

Paul breathed out as he gathered his thoughts.

"Something happened on the day that I went to your cell to talk to you. They had brought some captured possessed to the Retreat. There were many of them this time, five of them. Two females, a really old man and a pair of offspring. The females were very sick and obviously ill, while the children were emaciated. They were overgrown with hair, filthy, and they barely resembled humans at all. The hunters said that they dig themselves holes in the ground and live there like rats. The Abbott ordered for these possessed to be used instead of horses — he decided that they should pull carts until they fall down and die. Then, new ones would be caught to replace them.

I observed how the hunters stopped in the yard, fixed the cart with a cage on it in place and started to force the possessed to come out. They were whining and squealing. The hunters were merciless with them as they beat them with their whips. I wanted to look away and go and do my job, but something made me watch against my will. The adults were taken to the latrines and the children to the winter garden. The possessed started to howl louder.

One female stretched her arms out towards one of the children and the child tried to wrench himself away from the brothers' grip. They had almost been taken apart from each other in different directions when the boy twisted and slid out of their hands and ran towards his mother's embrace. The hunters then started to tear them away from each other, kicking and whipping them at will. It was a long struggle until they managed to separate them. The female became hysterical. The child was having a fit, fighting and kicking out with his feet. They knocked the female out with a club to the head and dragged her away from the yard. They took the child away as well. The blacksmith that stood nearby just said, "There's only one thing to call them — animals!" and went off on his own business."

Paul took a deep breath and added, "That child was Black Ant."

"Now I understand why he wants to kill you," Rick replied. "He saw how you were watching and did nothing. Sometimes, inaction is worse than violence. I understand him. I would have done the same in his place."

"Yes," Paul agreed, "I understand that now."

"Is that the reason? Have you begun to feel sorry for the possessed?"

"Yes, it is."

Rick decided against continuing and closed his eyes. After a while, he heard Paul's quiet voice.

"Drawing does not bring me any joy now. I wanted to draw a sparrow warming itself on the edge of the mine shaft. My hand refused to obey me. The lines were skewed and the features were all wrong. It was some sort of ugly chicken instead of a sparrow. I threw the coal away. And now I have something to draw with again..."

Rick drifted away to sleep for a moment. He woke up for a moment, saying "Let's talk about this tomorrow."

"My body is in pain," Paul complained. "I feel all twisted up inside."

"Just bear it and pray to your Maus. Who knows, it might help."

Rick turned away, hid the sickle that he confiscated in the folds of his clothing, gripped his blaster tight and fell asleep.

He was the first to wake up in the morning. Rick climbed out of the dugout and looked around. The ground around him was covered with a thin blanket of snow and he did not see anyone else's tracks on the ground. The sky was covered with thick clouds and a pale sun was rising in the west.

Rick listened to his feelings — his head seemed to be clear. He swung his arms energetically several times, warming up the muscles that had gone stiff from sleeping on the cold earth and started to blow on the glowing embers in the hearth so he could heat up some water. Rick picked up the pot and set off to gather some snow and get the lay of the land.

After about a minute, he understood that the plain was lifeless as far as the eye could see, with frozen ground strewn with boulders which had a dusting of snow on their shadow side. It was time to return and strike camp.

However, once he took two steps, he stopped and crouched behind a boulder, watching Paul get out of the tent. His recently awoken companion shivered, blindly looking around and started to rub the sleep from his eyes. Then he hesitantly called out, "Rick?"

Paul's eyes surveyed the landscape, without noticing Rick in his hiding place. He was stamped his feet as he stood there, rubbing at his shoulders in a futile attempt to get warm.

Silence. A frosty wind blew across the plain, carrying snow from stone to stone. Rick chuckled. Come on, you fool, sit down by the hearth, warm up and throw the remains of the wood into the fire. But Paul had other things to do — he walked around the dugout, had a look inside and then started to frantically look all around himself in fear. He finally thought of adding some fuel to the fire, warmed up a little and walked around their camp again.

"Rick!" he cried out in despair. "Rick, where are you?"

All he heard was silence again. Day had finally broken. Paul swore quietly, returned to the dugout and got inside. Rick shook his head. What an idiot.

Paul soon climbed back out and tried to roll up the cloth over the dugout. Rick was sick of watching him fumble around. He quietly sneaked up to Paul and pressed the sickle into his back. Paul froze.

"Rule number one," Rick declared. "Always be alert."

Paul swiftly turned around and his eyes were full of happiness and anger. Rick shoved the sickle into his hands.

"Just in case, you should have it at the ready. Let me help." He placed the pot on the fire, took hold of the edge of the cloth and started to carefully roll it up so that it would fit in the bag.

"Where did you appear from?" Paul finally wheezed. "You were not here at all!"

"I you opened your eyes wider, you would have seen me," Rick cackled. "I was here all of this time and looking right at you."

They finished with the sheet. Paul fixed the sickle behind his belt, his lips set in a line.

"I was walking through the wasteland once," Rick began, "and wolves started to follow me. A whole pack, around twelve of the beasts. They were lean but you could see that they were fierce. I was walking along the plain and they padded along after me. They were not in a hurry, they did not approach me and they kept their distance. They knew that their time would come. I kept walking and looking back, waiting for them to attack. That's how I walked for the whole day and when night came, I reached the edge of a forest. I started a fire, leaned with my back against a tree and watched them. Their eyes shone like embers in the darkness. And that was when I understood the foundation of their diabolical plan — they were waiting for me to fall asleep. I sat under the tree and stared into the darkness, until the darkness reached inside my head and I realized that I was lying on my side. I did not make any sudden movements. I just opened my eyes. The pack leader was right in front of me, saliva dripping off his fangs. I looked death straight in the eye."

"What do you want to say by that?"

"Nothing. Only a pair of seconds saved me from death. I was lucky enough to wake up just in time. I was off-guard and nearly paid for it."

Rick pushed the rolled up cloth into the travel bag, collected the rest of their belongings, filled the flask with warm water and they set off on their way.

"The wastelands are full of predators," Rick said. "If you do not kill them, they will kill you. Remember this."

"What happened to those wolves?"

"I killed them. Not all of them, to be honest. The most cowardly ones, or perhaps the most cunning and weak ones ran away. The ones that were at the back of the pack. Cowards are usually more cunning than those who are brave. They say that the strong survive, but somehow fail to mention that strength is sometimes in being careful and cunning. That's why the cowards survive sometimes."

They kept walking east along the plain and saw tall pillars appear ahead.

"Border markers," Paul said. "You can see them from the Retreat if you climb on the roof of the temple. The territory of the Tombs begins beyond them."

Rick and Paul reached the pillars by midday and saw that the surface was pitted with holes and iron reinforcing bars stuck out on every side. Each pillar was as tall as ten residential levels in Thermopolis. Rick touched the rough surface at the bottom of the pillar.

"Ancient concrete. Interesting."

"Concrete?" Paul asked.

"It's a mixture that fixes things together."

"Oh, I see. And the iron bars are there to reinforce the structure."

"That's right."

They both glanced upwards at the same time. It seemed that the pillar was supporting the clouded skies. The pillars stretched out in a line towards the edge of the horizon.

"I wonder, why did they put them here?" Paul muttered.

"I have no idea."

Rick took a Geiger counter out of the bag and switched it on, circling the pillar. The counter whispered and crackled weakly.

"What is that?" Paul enquired curiously. "What are you doing?"

"This device detects rays invisible to the eye that can kill anything that lives. But there are none of those rays here."

Rick turned off the counter and explained that the battery was almost at zero and that he did not know if he could find a new one anywhere.

They moved on and started to come across various odd shaped buildings — a half ruined stone pyramid, with a field of steel cones upon square bases behind it. Rick took out his Geiger counter once again and switched it on to check the background radiation levels. Once he was sure it was safe, he nodded and turned to Paul.

"Tell me what is known about the Tombs."

Paul did not reply immediately, thinking how to begin.

"This place is considered to be cursed. Animals give it a wide berth."

"Why?"

"They say that ghosts walk around here in the night. Sometimes, human voices were heard from here when the weather was calm."

"What, could they be heard in the Retreat?"

"Yes. I heard them a couple of times in the night. I woke up and listened to them. Someone laughed, sang, then laughed again and it went on for at least an hour."

"Right. What else?"

"They say that this is a cemetery of the Ancients. A single mass grave where countless people are buried. There are so many of them that the bones stick out of the ground."

"Why did this happen?"

"A great war. Or a disaster. Something like that."

"Did any of your people come here?"

"It is forbidden. Anathema awaits the violator."

"So you know about this place from other people's words?" Rick clarified. "But no one checked if it was true?"

Paul shrugged.

"Usually such things were taken on faith. It wouldn't cross anyone's mind to come here alone."

They passed a depression and once they got out of it, even rows of gray concrete blocks appeared before their sight. For a moment, the sun peeked out from behind the clouds, glinting on the glass of the windows that had miraculously remained intact in several buildings.

"It's a very ancient city," Rick reported. "This is the way people lived before the epidemic, before they started to build domes and underground shelters."

A road stretched out from the city to the east, snaking along the plain. Rick waved at Paul and they set off into the abandoned city, walking between the empty and deserted buildings and their gaping, empty windows. The wind blew trash around the street.

"What's that?" Paul pointed at a large, teardrop shaped metallic object, which had wheels on its sides. "Some sort of cart?"

"It's an automobile." Rick approached the machine and slid his hand along the bonnet, brushing away dust. "I have come across some of these before. This one is quite well-preserved. The Ancients used to ride these along the roads. It was very convenient."

Rick raised his blaster and adjusted the power switch, before shooting a weak charge into the door and climbing into the cabin to have a look around. However, he did not find anything useful inside. Once he climbed out, he looked at

Paul, who was examining the time-faded signs hanging above the bottom floors of the building.

"Tools and materials," Paul read out. "Hairdresser. Bar. What's a bar?"

"A place where people used to spend time. Like your temple, but without the prayers and much more fun."

"There are more signs there."

"Wait."

Rick walked through the door under the "Tools" sign. He was gone for several minutes and Paul could hear rattling and clanging noises coming from inside, until Rick appeared back out on to the street with a satisfied expression on his face.

"I found batteries for the radiation counter," he showed Paul some clear packages. "I will check them in the evening. What if there's some charge left?"

They moved on, looking around carefully. Paul read the signs out loud and Rick commented on them.

"Seeds."

"Hell with them."

"Furniture."

"No."

"Clothing."

"Now, that will be useful."

When they entered the building Rick took

everything that he thought they needed. In the end, Paul changed into a warm jumpsuit and got himself a backpack, where Rick put coils of rope, a flat box of tools and the same kind of folding pot and glass that he had, as well as attaching two rolled up blankets at the bottom.

It was not a big city, they noticed as they crossed a square with huge darkened screen panels along its sides. Rick told Paul that moving pictures had once been displayed on those kinds of panels. Paul listened with great interest and read what was written on every sign he came across.

"It seems that people left this place very suddenly," he noted. "I haven't seen any human remains."

"That does not mean anything," Rick stated. "However, I have to admit that it all looks quite strange. If we suppose that the bodies had been chewed on by animals from the wastelands, there should at least be some skeletons or at least separate bones left in their place, but there is nothing like that here. It really does look like a city which the Ancients suddenly abandoned. But it is nothing like any of the other ancient cities I came across on my travels. Not even close."

"Why?"

"The ancient cities of our ancestors were special. There were never even two buildings that looked the same. Every building was built in its own special style, while here everything follows the same model and the buildings look like identical twins."

Suddenly, Paul grabbed him by the sleeve and pointed to the edge of the square. A man was sitting with his back to them on one of the benches. The figure seemed immobile. Rick raised the blaster, Paul drew his sickle and they lowly approached the bench and started to circle around on both sides. The stranger calmly sat there, observing the dirty statue in the overgrown public garden behind the square. He turned his head towards them.

"Hi!" the stranger smiled.

"Hello," Rick replied, quickly looking around. He did not see anything dangerous, so he turned back to ask, "Who are you?"

"What a wonderful day," the stranger said with a pleasant and lively voice. "The weather is so lovely."

He was dressed in a clean long coat, dark trousers, polished black shoes and a... hat on his head. Rick could barely remember what the object was called.

"The weather?" Rick asked in surprise, exchanging glances with Paul. "It's not that great, but each to their own. Do you live here?"

"It's especially wonderful to breathe clean

air when the weather is so good," the stranger spoke again. "But my teeth used to hurt from the cold once upon a time."

Rick frowned and Paul looked confused.

"And I have solved this problem!" the stranger happily reported. "Yes! Yes! Now that I use Oriental toothpaste, I have no issues at all."

"What does this mean?" Paul exclaimed.

"So try it, what if it helps?" the stranger inclined his head and touched the brim of his head, blinked and disappeared.

Paul rushed over to the bench and started to prod it on every side.

"By the Holy Maus, what is this?"

"This is what you would call a ghost," Rick smiled. "In reality it's just a high quality hologram. What amazes me is something else. Why does it still work?"

He walked around the side of the bench and reported, "Well, here's the answer. Solar batteries!" He pointed at the other side of the back of the bench. "The light falls on them, feeds the processor and launches the hologram, which is a moving three dimensional picture. There are probably special devices called motion detectors nearby. We came near and the hologram switched on."

"Can this be of any use to us? I'm talking about the batteries."

"I think so."

They spent a quarter of an hour removing the small panel of photoelectric cells and carefully disconnecting the wires together with the current converter.

"Ugh..." Paul grunted when he felt the backpack get heavier.

"You suggested it yourself," Rick clapped his companion on the shoulder. "Once we make camp, we will go through our gear and I will take some of it, but you will still have to carry most of it. My hands must be free, with nothing restricting my movement so I can easily use weapons."

Paul nodded and they started to walk away from the square until they came across a partially collapsed wall at the edge of the city. The wastelands began again beyond it.

"There's another sign over there," Paul pointed at something the resembled an arch. "It's very big."

They approached the arch. Half of the letters on the sign were missing and the remainder formed the words " — a — t — ry XX — US — Bstn."

"What could this mean?" Paul asked.

The question hung in the air. Rick stayed quiet, going through possible words and their meanings in his head. Could it be a factory? But there were no large or industrial buildings in the city. Just in case, he wrote the letters down on a piece of paper and walked through the arch, stepping along a road of yellowish slabs which was slightly raised above the ground.

Once they were some distance from the city, he spoke, "The Ancients had special places where they stored items from the past to show how the lives of humans changed with time. Those places were called museums. Children went there to study history — they looked at all of these different objects and the museum staff, who were especially appointed people, made sure that all the objects were safe. I have a feeling that we just visited a place of this kind."

"These clothes are so warm," Paul noted with satisfaction. "If the Ancients knew how to make things like this, they deserve respect."

Rick did not reply, but he gave his companion an approving glance.

Surprisingly, the road was rather well-preserved. They occasionally came across mounds of earth and cracks with the twisted branches of bushes growing out of them, but it was generally easier to walk along it than the stony and frozen plain, which was covered with hillocks. There were signs placed along the edge of the road at even intervals with nearly faded inscriptions that were combinations of numbers.

Rick noticed that the numbers changed as they got further and further away from the city — "42-100", "42-000", "41-900".

"It looks like these number markers signify distances." he finally guessed. "So that you know how much is left until the place where you are going."

"What are the measures? Strides?"

"No, people used to have different measurement units — kilometers, miles, meters and feet. The first number could mean..." Rick thought for a moment. "The length of the road we are on in kilometers. The second one is probably the meters. One meter is around one stride and a kilometer is a thousand. Are you watching our surroundings?"

"Yes."

"And I think that you are getting distracted! Your eyes must be open all the time. You must see and notice everything that is unusual, every little thing, but you mustn't forget about your ears. So, you have seen the Tombs. What do you think?"

"They don't look like a graveyard."

"Great. Any other thoughts?"

"There's no sign of humans. Apart from that... ghost. As if something or some sort of power forced them to abandon all that they were doing at once and leave. Or disappear."

"I also thought so," Rick agreed. "The question is, what sort of power? Do you have any suggestions?"

"No," Paul shrugged. "Maybe they were possessed?"

"That's the version that first comes to mind," Rick nodded. "But... it's too obvious."

"That seems to trouble you. Is it too simple?"

"Yes. The answer lies on the surface, but I am used to getting to the bottom of things."

They kept walking along the road and came across the highway sign that old Book of Faces had described to them.

"We're going the right way!" Rick declared.

Paul smiled and nodded.

After the sign the road looked very well looked after — no cracks or bushes. Paul immediately noticed this because the color of the surface they walked on changed from yellowish to gray.

"Hmm, that's strange," Rick said as he crouched and touched the rough surface of the road. "It looks like plascrete — a special material that was used to construct the building I used to live in. It's a very durable and hard material that can withstand a lot of stress from high pressure to cold, heat, acids and alkalis. The buildings in that city were also built out of it. Stone would have cracked a long time ago and brick would have turned to sand."

"How much time would have had to pass?"

"A huge length of time." Rick looked at Paul. "I couldn't give you a number. And it is this mystery which never lets me rest. I have spent months trying to find out, but I still haven't established the exact date when the Ancients perished."

They walked for almost the whole day along the renovated highway which never turned, split or ended and kept stretching out smoothly into the distance until they saw a dark line of irregular sized constructions on the horizon. The setting sun made it difficult to make them out. Rick could feel that his goal was close and the lower the sun was in the sky the quicker he wanted to get to the legendary city. He hurried along, forgetting about his tiredness, but the rapidly approaching dusk made him stop. They left the road and prepared to spend the night.

And in the morning, the world around them was completely different.

G

THE PLAIN THAT SURROUNDED them had changed to a deep valley, but the road remained on the same level, upraised on a solid base and running into a long arched bridge over a swift and narrow river.

Rick walked up to the edge and looked down — it was a monumental construction, especially considering the amount of plascrete that had to be used for the base that supported it.

"Look," he told Paul, pointing with his hand.

There was a rocky ridge ahead, with a steep slope covered in trees. The road cut into the ridge, running along through the crevasse. Crying birds circled the tops of the trees nearby.

Rick looked back and realized what a long way they had traveled — the abandoned dead city could barely be seen in the morning twilight.

They soon reached the crevasse. The black cliffs hung over their heads and the intertwined roots of trees could be seen among the rocks in some places. The birds kept crying somewhere off to the side, but they could not be seen. There was a thickening mist ahead of them. The world seemed to melt into a milky white cloud. Rick glanced behind him — even the sun had turned into a pale spot.

"Keep close," he ordered, just in case.

They kept walking, carefully looking ahead. Step by step and trying to keep quiet. They could not hear the birds anymore and it became noticeably darker, with the cloying silence making them feel even more tense. Rick stopped. Paul went still by his side, his mouth open. There was a huge tunnel entrance up ahead. Rick quietly lit a torch and resolutely headed inside.

The light of the torch barely penetrated the thick mist. They almost walked into the wall a couple of times when there was a turn in the tunnel. Rick was afraid of walking in the wrong direction by missing a crossroads, but he did not show it, choosing the only tactic that he thought was right — keeping to the middle of the road.

The tunnel suddenly ended. It became noticeably lighter, but Rick and Paul did not start to talk and especially did not stop, quietly stepping ahead and trying to get as far away as possible from the oppressive cold and uncertainty of the mountain tunnel. The mist gradually cleared and it became markedly warmer. They soon started to see signs with numbers showing the distance they traveled. Once the "25-000" sign was behind them, they came across a crossroads where the road split into five directions.

"Here are the crossroads," Rick said thoughtfully. The looked around and ordered, "Read me the signs."

Paul obediently started to read, "It says "Sanctuary XX-US" on the one pointing where we came from. The one to the left of it says "Sanctuary XIX-UK", the one to the right says "Sanctuary XXI-FR" and even further to the right it says "Sanctuary XXII-GER." The very last one has no writing on it, just the sign that Book of Faces told us about."

Rick stared at the sign. A circle, divided up by a cross with dots in two of the four sections. But of course! They had been to the sanctuary of the ancient city. He looked around again and exclaimed, "Oh, there's another clue here!"

"Where?" Paul asked, looking around himself.

Rick nodded at the damp surface of the road where there was an inscription saying "A-III ATLANTIS." They re-read the signs and looked around the crossroads to see if they could find any more but did come across anything.

"What are we going to do?" Paul waited for his orders.

Rick took off his bag and took out an old piece of paper that had been rolled together. He found an empty sheet, put it on top of his toolbox and asked, "You can draw, can't you? I need a new map."

"But I never saw the original."

"I'm going to tell you what I remember and you just draw. Come on."

"But why me? There's nothing difficult about it."

"Trust me, you will do it better," Rick insisted. "Don't argue, get to it."

Paul muttered that he was at least better at something, bent over the page and took out his piece of graphite.

Rick began, "First things first, mark all the sides of the world. North at the top, south at the bottom, west on the left and east on the right. Excellent! Right. Now draw a dot right here. Put a "T" above it. That means Thermopolis, the building in which I was born..."

Paul drew all over five sheets until he came to the crossroads. He carefully transferred all that was written on the signs to the map and looked at Rick, waiting for further instructions.

"Not bad," Rick congratulated him and slapped his shoulder. "I definitely couldn't do it like that."

"You're not planning to go back, are you?" Paul asked in surprise, putting the remaining half of the piece of graphite into his pocket.

"I don't know," Rick shrugged. "Anything

can happen in this life."

He folded the sheets and started to put his equipment away. When he was done, he declared, "Great deeds await us. Shall we go on?"

Paul chuckled and nodded — he had no choice anyway. Rick confidently strode off in the direction the highway sign pointed. They soon started to feel hot because of their brisk pace, so they undid their jackets. Lone trees started to appear by the roadside — twisted and stunted, they stretched their branches towards the sun that had finally cleared the mist away. The rocky slopes by their sides were becoming less steep and Rick soon stopped to catch his breath and have a look around.

They came to the end of the defile and there was a new valley ahead, with low clouds moving slowly above it. The highway stopped at a pair of gates down in the valley which was built into a tall rampart made of earth. The ground in front of the rampart was black, as if it was burnt by fire. Here and there, lop-sided metallic structures glinted in the sun against the blackness, frozen in time by the side of the rampart.

Rick could not discern the purpose of the structures, but something suggested to him that these were ancient construction machines that may have been cranes. Why would they need supports otherwise?

Beyond the rampart, the rays of the sun played on domes similar to those that covered the settlements in the wastelands, but much larger. But this was not what surprised Rick.

He held his breath, standing motionless as he stared up into the clouds above the place where the thin yellow thread of the highway was leading... The road was visibly elevated there as it ran into the base of something... Something incredibly tall.

The top of the structure disappeared somewhere in the skies, but Rick knew for sure that this was it. A Citadel!

"Can you see that?" he grabbed Paul by the shoulder and pointed at the tower. "Can you?"

"I... I see something," Paul replied with a note of fear in his voice. "Even though I don't understand what it is..."

Rick tensely stayed rooted to his spot, trying to make out the details. The Citadel rose in the center of a gigantic disk that was broken into clearly defined segments which were bordered by the earthen rampart.

But how was he to understand this? Where was the city? According to what he once saw around Thermopolis, buildings, warehouses, vehicle hangars and roads should have been there... But there was only a gray, disk-shaped plateau which was split into segments.

"Let's go," he finally announced.

Paul did not dare to ask any questions and obediently fell in by his side.

Rick ran the last few meters before the gates, without looking around. Paul became seriously worried, as he remembered Rick's instructions and kept his eyes peeled, but everything was quiet around them. The sun shone softly through the clouds, stroking their skin with its warm rays.

The gates were extremely tall and seemed to have been cast in a single, huge mold. It would be impossible to move them, but Rick did not even try. He threw the things he was carrying down on the ground and readied his blaster as he walked to and fro touching the cavities and bulges on the metallic surface.

"Why are you standing around? Help me!" he turned to Paul.

"But how? We won't be able to move them!"

Look for secret hatches, control panel lids or levers. There surely must be something like that here; the gates must be openable from outside.

After a while, Rick became very angry. They had examined everything they could reach but still found nothing similar to control panel or console.

"Maybe they do actually open them from inside?" Paul suggested bravely.

"No!"

"But we looked at everything. There are no levers or secret compartments here."

"Look for them!"

"I think it would be better to walk along the rampart and look for another entrance or climb over it somehow..."

"Where? This is a rampart, it's an unbroken wall several stories high! How are we going to climb it?"

Paul stared at the leaning mast with steel supports in the distance.

"Don't even think about it," Rick cut him off. "We don't have any ropes that are long enough or any special hooks. The mast is way too far from the wall even if we manage to jump up high enough, and how would we get back down again?"

"You're right," Paul nodded.

"We need to look for the gate control panel."

"But there's nothing here." Paul leaned on an oblong bulge that protruded from the gates.

Something clicked underneath the steel skin, there was a faint buzzing noise and a secret opening appeared. Paul fell inside as he could not keep his balance.

Rick grabbed his bag from the ground and

jumped in after him, ready to use his weapon at any moment. But there was no need for that.

They found themselves in a cold rectangular hole. There was another pair of gates on the opposite size.

"It's an airlock," Rick guessed.

"What's an..." Paul sneezed and wiped his nose with his sleeve.

Rick helped him get up and then walked towards the gates.

"An airlock is a special room which separates one inhabitable space from another, which is needed because..."

It was too late when he realized what was happening.

There was a familiar buzzing noise behind them and the opening that they used to enter the airlock quickly sealed itself with its hidden hatch.

"Go! You've still got time!"

"No!"

Paul stayed in his place. The thin sliver of light was consumed by the dark. There was a click. They were in impenetrable darkness.

Paul rummaged around in his pocket and took out a lighter. The flint was struck and a small fire lit the face of his companion.

"All right. Well done, Paul," Rick patted him on the shoulder and walked over to the gates. "Let's think what we're going to do next."

Something crunched under his feet. Rick stopped and crouched, felt around the floor with his hand and immediately stood back up. Paul still managed to notice the rictus grin of a skull and other human remains.

"Come over here. Don't be afraid, the dead don't bite," Rick called him.

Paul finally got himself together and walked up to the gates.

"If we managed to get in here, then we will be able to get out," Rick declared. "Come on, remember what you touched. These gates are very similar and they might open in exactly the same way."

After walking along the gates and touching the metal surfaces, Paul shook his head.

"I don't know. I just leaned on it with my shoulder, like this," he repeated what he did the previous time in approximately the same place. "And that was it. See, nothing is happening."

Suddenly, a loud hissing sound came from the ceiling. They felt a gust of cold air and then a foamy liquid with a sharp chemical smell poured upon their heads.

They both cried out in surprise. Rick nearly dropped the lighter, which had just gone out. The liquid kept pouring down from somewhere on the ceiling in intense streams. Then, it suddenly stopped. There was another hissing sound and a gust of wind, but now the air was hot. Violet lines lit up on the walls and hurt their eyes. Rick and Paul shut their eyes, and when everything was quiet and they opened them again the gates slid apart with a clang, letting them into a tunnel that was as tall and wide as several men.

"The automatic systems kicked in," Rick explained. "The ancient machines switch on stage by stage according to their programming, which means the order in which their actions are performed. They let us into the airlock, then they washed us, covered us in some sort of solution that probably kills infections and now they are offering us to keep going. So what are you waiting for? Let's go."

Rick stepped into the tunnel and stopped, examining the slabs that covered the floor. Lamps flickered bleakly overhead, lighting up space to a distance of around twenty paces and another wide, gated opening could be made out ahead. Something made Rick stop. His feeling for danger had reached its very limit and he raised his hand, moving his blaster into firing position.

"What's wrong," Paul asked quietly.

"Wait. I'm thinking."

The experiences that he had in Thermopolis suggested that Rick should be on his guard. His journey between the levels and aeons came to his mind, with the various mechanical traps, mutants and the unknown and ever hungry beasts that lived in places of that kind. Without letting go of the blaster, Rick used his free hand to get a hammer out of his bag and threw it on the nearest slab.

Nothing happened. Then Rick crouched and pressed down on the slab with his hand.

Again, nothing.

"You see," he began, "each of these stone squares features a geometric symbol."

"Yeah," Paul replied. "This one has a triangle. And the one further along has a circle."

"I don't like any of this," Rick grumbled. "It looks like a puzzle."

"Why do you think so?"

"My instincts tell me this."

"I don't think so."

Before Rick could object, Paul stepped onto the slab with the triangle symbol.

There were several seconds of deafening silence.

Paul finally smiled.

"See? Nothing. I think we can go there," Paul decided and raised his foot to step on the next slab.

"No!" Rick exclaimed.

It worked. In the end, Paul did not step forward and waited, turning to his friend with annoyance. Rick offered the hammer to him. Paul crouched and struck the next slab, which disappeared under the ground in an instant. Rick barely managed to catch his companion by the sleeve in time before inertia carried him into the gaping hole that appeared in the floor.

"What was on the slab?" he asked, once Paul had got his breath back.

"A circle. There was a circle there."

They started to examine the slabs. Rick found a slab with a triangle nearby and carefully stepped on it. Nothing happened. Then he stepped onto another slab with a triangle ahead. Nothing.

"I think we have found the key," Rick declared.

"Why do you think the Ancients put this trap here?"

Paul tapped the nearest slab and moved onto it.

"It's a test. I am sure that anyone that gets here by accident will be afraid and turn back."

A minute later they both stood at the end of the tunnel in front of yet another pair of gates, getting their breath back. Rick drank from his flask with long, greedy gulps, wiping away the sweat from his brow. Paul was already curiously examining the gates.

"I still don't understand," Paul said as he probed around the gates. "The puzzle was way too simple. Think about how easily we found the solution."

"It's a test," Rick repeated stubbornly and stepped towards the gates. "Protection from idiots. It will probably be more complex further along."

"What do you mean?"

"We're about to find out."

The dim light of the lamps was barely sufficient, so Rick flicked the lighter again and slowly moved along the gates.

"Look!" Paul called out happily. "There's a triangle symbol here. Should I press it?"

"Well, go for it, but be careful."

Rick gripped the blaster tighter and stayed in his place. Paul pressed the triangle hard, ready to snap his hand back at any moment.

Nothing happened. Paul pressed it again and a small triangular segment receded into the gates. Something above made a loud crack, there was a low humming sound and a clang and the gates started to slide apart, sinking into the walls.

Rick immediately stepped towards the opening, thrusting his weapon in front of him and examining the part of the hall that was ahead of him. The mechanisms inside the walls fell silent.

"Let's keep going," Paul suggested

tentatively.

After quickly looking around, Rick nodded. They passed through the gates which immediately slid shut as soon as Paul stepped into the hall. They did it so fast that if they had paused for even a moment, they would have been crushed to a pulp.

Paul cried out and jumped up, almost about to sprint towards the center of the hall where a matte black steel column stretched out to the ceiling. Rick managed to grab his companion by the sleeve just in time and hold him in place.

"Calm down. Relax."

"B-but why did they c-close?" Paul was shaking violently.

"Take a deep breath. Here you are, drink some water," Rick offered him his flask, while standing still and studying the space around him.

The hall was round and the floor was concave like a saucer. The mysterious pillar was as tall as three men and had red dots flickering on its surface near the top. It felt like it almost became brighter in the hall because of these pulsating lights.

"How are you?" Rick asked.

"I seem to be okay."

Paul returned the flask to him and stared

at the pillar.

Rick gripped the blaster tight and slowly approached the pillar. Whatever lived here had awoken and it was watching them. The top of the pillar changed to a red color and the pillar itself started to turn upon its axis. Rick froze. A low hum rung out. Suddenly it fell silent, and a pleasant male voice rand out from the ceiling, "One, two, three."

The words seemed to appear out of thin air. Rick tried and failed to determine the source of the sound. The voice counted again and then fell silent.

"And what does this mean?" Paul whispered.

"They are examining us."

"What for?"

"I have no idea." Rick waited, as he did not want to risk approaching.

"Hello," the stranger said suddenly.

Paul flinched.

"Greetings!" Paul replied loudly and clearly. "Whoever you are, we come in peace and we won't cause you harm!"

"I am an it, not a he. Not a human. However, the paradox is that my main function is to detect Homo sapiens."

The friends exchanged glances.

"What for?" Rick enquired.

"This place was created for humans," the voice declared. "It would be logical to suppose that only humans should be able to get inside. Do you agree?"

"Yes," Rick answered.

"Does the second creature possess the power of speech?" the voice asked.

"I do," Paul hurriedly replied.

"Wonderful."

"How are you planning to test us?" Rick spoke again.

"I am already testing you. But you should answer a series of questions before I stop."

"Why make it so complicated?" Rick feigned surprise, trying to look as natural as he could. "If you are a machine, that means you can scan us and determine that we are part of the human race by our skeletal structure."

"You are completely right," the voice agreed. "This has already done. Biologically, you are part of the human species."

"So why all this talk?" Rick swung the blaster behind his back.

"A reasonable question. I shall explain: my task is to determine your cognitive ability. It is possible to have a human body while not being a human."

"Possession," Paul muttered.

"Pardon me, what did you say?"

"Nothing, I wasn't addressing you," Paul assured, afraid of unforeseen consequences.

Rick looked at him with disapproval and said, "All right. Ask your questions, machine."

"I shall start. But first, a technical disclaimer."

Paul and Rick exchanged glances and then quietly watched the pillar.

"There are two of you," the voice continued. "This means that there will be twice as many questions, issued to you separately. Determine the order in which you will answer."

"You could have let us in long ago," Rick grumbled. "I will answer first."

"Excellent. Question one. There's a pear hanging there, that to eat you'd never dare. What is it?"

Rick thought that he had misheard.

"Are you mocking me?"

"Should I consider that an answer?"

"No!" Rick hurried to reply, angry at himself for choosing to go first.

He rubbed at his chin and glanced around the hall. He breathed out.

"Now then..." he turned to Paul and shook his head. "By the great Expanse!"

"Help is forbidden," the voice warned.

"I understand," Rick replied.

The task of the machine is to understand

that sentients had entered the hall, creatures capable of abstract thought. Abstract thought. Mathematics. Logic. The ancient machines were programmed with algorithms of sequential operations.

"The pear tree is a fruit tree," Rick deliberated out loud. "I remember what pears look like. If the fruit is not edible, that means it is not a fruit."

The machine kept silent. Paul stood still, fraught with tension and holding his breath.

"How much time do I have to think?"

"I can wait until the passage of time makes me fall apart or until your biological death. Due to the fact that the probability of the latter event is several times higher, the time you have for deliberation is limited to your lifetime."

"In other words, we will be stuck here until we die of hunger or thirst."

"Yes."

"Must the answer be exact?"

"Preferably. However, considering your level of education, approximate analogues are permitted."

"All right." A picture from a documentary that was part of his accelerated education course sprung into Rick's mind. "The answer is that it is just a light bulb!"

A few moments passed when it seemed that

the machine had forgotten about the new arrivals.

Then, the voice uttered, "Correct. Here is the second question. You have entered a room and there are two dogs and three cats lying on the floor, while two chickens are walking around the room and one goat is standing there. How many legs are there in the room?"

"Two," Rick replied without hesitation.

Another pause until the voice spoke again.

"Correct. Now for the last question. This creature moves around all four legs when you, on two legs when it is mature and three legs when it is old. What is it?"

"A human."

"Explain why."

"Explaining my reasoning was not part of the question!" Rick replied with indignation. However, as there was no reaction from the machine, he hurriedly added, "Only a human crawls around on all fours in childhood, then walks around on their own two legs and uses a stick so they do not fall when they get old. Time is an allegory. And this riddle is thousands of years old."

If he wanted, Rick could have told the story of the Theban Sphinx, as well as listing the whole pantheon of Ancient Greek gods. All of this knowledge was securely stored in his head. The machine was silent. This time, the pause was extended.

"Correct answer. You have been determined to be human. The other creature must answer the questions now."

"His name is Paul," Rick told the machine.

"Nice to meet you, Paul," the machine replied. "Are you ready?"

Paul nodded.

"Three people have been asked to describe one creature. The first man said that it was a tree, the second said that it was a snake and the third called the creature a seashell. None of them were correct. Why did this happen?"

Paul started to think. A film of perspiration formed on his forehead, the veins bulged on his neck and his eyes were wide open and intense. Then, he suddenly relaxed and stared into space with an unseeing gaze. He took a deep breath and said, "Those people were blind. They were describing an animal that they touched."

"Correct. Next question. It crawls in the morning, keeps still at midday and flies in the evening. What is this creature?"

A weak smile appeared on his face. Paul was deep in thought again, but his face was calm this time and only his lips moved a little. A minute passed and then another. Even more minutes passed. It seemed that Paul had gone somewhere deep inside himself with his thoughts.

"It's a butterfly," he suddenly said.

There was a pause.

"Correct. And now the last question."

Paul wiped the sweat from his brow.

"Once upon a time there lived two twins. One day, one of the twins went on a long journey for several years. When he came back it turned out that he had turned into an old man, while his brother became only a little older. How did that happen?"

Mother Darkness! Rick stared at the pillar, frowning. The machine was asking a man who lived in the Middle Ages questions about the space-time continuum!

Paul breathed out. His eyes darted over at Rick. A loud signal immediately rang out.

"No assistance. Answer the question."

Rick gritted his teeth. There was nothing worse than watching someone else die when you are powerless to stop it. Paul sighed and shook his head.

"A journey over which one twin got old and the other one didn't..." he pronounced. "A man gets old over many years. This means that a very long time has passed. On the other side, however, the second brother only got a little older. How is that possible? It turns out that one day that one brother lived was like several days for the other."

"Your answer?"

"I don't know for sure. I think it's something to do with time."

"Explain yourself."

"Time passed differently for each one of them."

"Why?"

"I don't know. Maybe one of them was bored while the other one was busy with work all the time. Maybe one suffered from loneliness while the other had a family. Everyone perceives time in their own way."

The machine stayed silent. Paul gulped nervously. Rick adjusted his blaster, trying to seem innocuous. If that piece of scrap decided to destroy them, he would give it a final salute.

"Answer accepted. You have been determined to be human. You may continue on your way."

"And what would have happened if we did not answer the questions?" Rick asked with genuine curiosity.

"You would not be able to continue on your way."

"What if we tried?" he brandished his weapon.

"This entire hall is an autonomous matter disintegrator."

"What does that mean?" Paul did not understand.

Rick did not answer, he just nodded. No, there would not have been a chance for a final salute. Before his synapses could convey the command for his finger to squeeze the trigger, anything alive would have been reduced to its component atoms.

"Let's get out of here," he hissed.

A door opened at the end of the hall. They hurried towards the rectangle of light and got out. There were no new rooms this time — they stood upon an open platform, which rose above the yellow-gray disk at the bottom of the tower. Rick approached the railings and stopped, amazed by the view in front of him.

All of the space before the tower was occupied by a sector that was an incredibly complex structure that had suddenly appeared from some unknown place that had been erected by unknown architects. Rick would swear upon anything in his life that when they had first noticed the tower and the disk at its base they saw nothing like this at all. So where did it come from?

In wonder, he looked at the blocks of identical buildings, domes, the needles of the pillars that intertwined in rows along road intersections, the deep holes of the wells and canals which were filled with water in some places.

The sector before his eyes was surrounded with high walls. Now this was a familiar sight — the territory by his Thermopolis homeland had a similar architecture, similar to a cake that had been cut into even slices. The bed of a wide and very deep canal stretched out from underneath the observation platform.

What is this?

"Where?" Paul suddenly asked.

Rick shook his head. It seems that he had asked his question out loud. He pointed at the canal.

"This. What do you think?"

Paul shrugged and said, "It's an unbelievable structure! I'm talking about all of it. I can't even imagine how long people labored here."

"Not people. Machines. Mainly machines, but not without some help from humans."

Paul nodded in agreement.

"It looks like a highway," Rick pointed at the canal again. "Like some sort of special highway. See how it stretches out through the sector past most of the intersections to the bottom of the tower?"

"Yes"

"That's it," Rick shielded his eyes from the

sun with his hand.

He was still tortured by the question of how a whole sector with a city suddenly appeared in front of the tower and where it came from.

"What?" Paul asked, also looking out ahead.

"The third Thermopolis."

"There were ruins at the location of the second one," Rick was looking ahead intently, but the top of the tower was hidden by clouds.

"I don't understand," Paul said with irritation. "It's time for some explanations. Stop speaking in riddles, Rick. Where did we finally come and what for? What is Thermopolis? What is this unusual city? What do the possessed have to do with it? What is going on, anyway?" he demanded.

Rick glanced at his companion and then continued to stare intently at the faraway citadel. He could understand Paul.

"See this?" he gestured at the view before them.

"Yes..."

"This is our future. I really hope that I won't be mistaken this time around."

H

WHEN THE FRIENDS DESCENDED to the bed of the highway, Rick immediately noticed the narrow metal plates that had been pressed into the plascrete. Paul was also interested in them, as they did not see anything like that on the way here. Rick supposed that the plates were elements that conducted the energy that would be supplied to car engines to enable them to travel in the direction required.

Paul was very impressed with what he heard and declared that he wants to study various sciences and resurrect cars so he could travel in them all around the city. Rick smiled with amusement, but said nothing and they continued on their way.

The decision to travel along the highway seemed to be correct. Firstly, it was a path straight towards the citadel. Secondly, they could easily change direction if they found themselves in danger, because there were many tunnels connected to the wide canal, the ladders and flues of industrial units could be seen along the walls, bridges and arches stretched out above casting a latticework of shadows upon the bottom, and the flyovers and the roofs of tall buildings could be seen above its tall edges.

Rick felt like an ant that was trapped in a rain gutter compared to all of these structures.

"So it turns out that you don't even know exactly where we are?" Paul asked with interest.

"That's right. This is the first time I have seen architecture and structures of this kind."

"That's good." Paul nodded at the distant citadel. "Then explain what Thermopolis is."

"A giant tower that contains a city. A whole city in one fortress. A thousand floors."

Paul whistled.

"That's unbelievable!"

"I was born and raised in a tower like that, but my homeland is far behind me now. To add to it, the fortress did not quite turn out to be a fortress at all."

"What do you mean? I'm confused."

"No wonder. It's difficult for me to understand it myself, but I saw it with my own eyes," Rick chuckled. "The Citadel turned out to be a huge air transportation device, a machine that flew up into the sky."

"By the almighty," Paul muttered. "But what for?"

"I think it was for the salvation of humanity. To be honest, I haven't entirely worked out the plans of the Ancients yet."

"What do you mean?"

Rick sighed, and told him about the

Uranus program that he had launched when the Citadel was taken over by rebels from the Omicron sector. Then he understood that he did not start at the right point and told Rick the story of his escape from his home in the Commune in the search for phantom generators that would have defeated the darkness and cold which had engulfed his world. Rick told him about the sectors and their inhabitants, about the manlike proles, about the internal design of the tower, about their journey on the external shell and finished his story by describing the way that the ark was launched.

"I should have been up there," he pointed up at the sky, "but as you can see, I am here. After the transport left, I spent a long time searching the Command Center for important information, but I did not find much. That's when I made the decision to set off and try to find some sort of traces and answers here on Old Earth so that I could try and work out what was going on. This is the third month that I have been wondering on the surface. I came across a huge city similar to this one once, but everything was destroyed there, including the citadel. None of the buildings were intact and everything was irradiated. I got away from there as fast as I could as I did not want to sentence myself to a long and wasting disease and eventual death. And then I saw you caravan when I came across the canal that led from your Retreat to the domed settlements. The possessed appeared, and you know the rest of the story."

"I see..."

They walked along in silence for several minutes, each lost in their own thoughts.

"So what do you think about this place?" Paul asked at last.

"It's too early to come to any conclusions," Rick admitted. "But some of the details give me certain ideas. Look over there, at the walls of the highway. Pay attention to the joints between the segments. What do they look like?"

"They look like scars and welts that appear at equal distances along the way."

"Now, look at the floor. Especially at the way the floor slabs are connected."

"The same sort of seams. Wait... something is inscribed on the slabs. It looks like a series of signs."

"Yes, they are called glyphs. The walls of my fortress were covered in similar glyphs and had similar seams."

"So what does this mean?"

"At the very least it means that the same technology was used to construct these structures."

"Then why wasn't there a city around your

tower?"

"Well done, that's a good question. You're thinking, Paul. I also ask myself this question. But I swear by the Darkness that I will find the answer! The main thing is to reach the tower and get inside. That's our main goal and then..."

Rick spun around aiming his blaster in front of him. Paul also turned and saw a silvery sphere about the height of a human in diameter standing still behind them. Two intersecting lines could be seen on its surface following its circumference — a horizontal and a vertical line that divided the object into four equal parts. The sphere emitted a muffled hum and it seemed to Rick that the highway under their feet was vibrating slightly. He guessed at the distance to the object — it was around half a hundred paces.

Suddenly, the sphere started to move forward.

"Run!" Paul shouted and dashed away from it.

Rick only stopped for a moment — the sphere had moved, but it did not roll along. The horizontal and vertical lines around its circumference stayed in place, while an unknown force accelerated the movement of the sphere.

A crossroads could be seen ahead, with narrower canals that joined the highway. The humming noise behind their backs grew louder.

Rick glanced over his shoulder and saw that the sphere was covered with sparks that it was discharging. He turned to face it, walking backwards and raising his blaster as he flicked the power switch to maximum to blast their pursuer.

A wave of heat swept through the air, but the sphere consumed the ball of energy without any visible effect.

"Damn it!" Rick exclaimed. "That piece of scrap is tougher than I thought!"

He sprinted after Paul.

"Let's split up!" Rick shouted at his back. "You go left, I go right!"

Without thinking, Rick rushed into the side canal. It was darker here, but he had no time to look at the details, so he ran, trying to keep his breathing under control. He could hear a drawn out hum behind him.

Rick understood that he was getting tired and would soon be out of breath. The canal turned a few times and led him onto a spacious square, surrounded by high walls with girders above and a rope hanging down from one of them. Higher up, everything drowned in the gloom under a dome that barely admitted light. In his distraction, Rick slipped and twisted his ankle, nearly flying onto the floor and letting go of the blaster, its strap sliding and burning his neck as the weapon flew to the side.

He heard the hum behind his back again. Rick took a look over his shoulder. The sphere slowly emerged from the canal. At first, he tried to go for the blaster, understanding that even though the weapon was useless, he should not surrender. What if he was lucky and found a weak spot? But then, blindingly bright lights lit on the upper sections of the sphere and two red rays quickly darted towards Rick as he froze, holding his breath.

He felt a chill run down his spine and his shoulders and knees trembled. This demonic machine would turn him to ashes now.

The red rays transfixed Rick's chest and there was nowhere to run. He retreated until his back was to the wall. The sphere remained calm, sparkling with its charges and continued to hum.

A moment later, two new spheres that looked like copies of the first emerged from the canal. They released more rays that clustered on Rick's chest. Was everything about to end here and now?

He swallowed loudly, squeezing his fists tight. Mother Darkness. By the great Expanse, why?

Rick quickly took in the walls — they were smooth and even, with no ladders or handholds to grab, nothing at all. Nothing apart from the rope hanging down near him. The spheres had blocked the way into the canal — another one, then two and then more and more of them emerged.

If they were not attacking, it meant that they were waiting for something, Rick decided. He started to slowly move towards the rope. More and more spheres pushed themselves through the canal, gradually filling up the square. Their numbers grew — there were already nine of them, ten... twelve. The rays were blinding him with their bright red light. The first sphere shuddered a little and rushed forward. Rick jumped towards it with his remaining strength. His hands grabbed at the rope, the inertia carrying him forward, swinging as he managed to quickly pull himself upwards. Like a pendulum, he swung back towards the wall, turning around and continuing to climb, putting one hand over the other as he rose higher and higher. Only the thought of escape reverberated around his head — the main thing was to hold on and that the old rope would not break.

When his feet finally rested on the wall, the sphere below him crashed into the barrier. Rick stopped, trying to get some rest. The sphere had struck so hard that dust rained down from above. The rest of the spheres followed and the square was full of humming and the sound of discharging electricity. More and more spheres appeared from the canal, pressing on their neighbors and pushing them upwards.

Rick pulled himself up higher, glanced downwards again and almost let go of the rope — the diabolical spheres were rolling on top of each other, filling up the space below him and trying to reach their quarry. He gritted his teeth and finally managed to clamber up onto the wall. He immediately rolled away from the edge and lay there on his back, breathing heavily.

"And we thought you wouldn't make it," a jovial female voice sounded out of the darkness.

Rick rolled onto his stomach, his hand automatically going down to his hip to look for the blaster, but then he stopped as he rose onto his knees. Around a dozen people stood in front of him on the edge of the wall, dressed in drab green camouflage. Many of them wore protective goggles with wide lenses set in a soft and thick frame. Some wore helmets with opaque visors. One of the strangers took off their helmet and...

"They usually just have a little left to go," said a woman with dark hair plaited into dozens of little braids and a friendly and attractive face.

Her eyes, or rather the look in her gray eyes was cold and harsh, which spoiled the first impression. But Rick had learned not to trust his emotions.

The rest of the group quickly surrounded him and took off and emptied his travel bag, quickly distributing its contents among themselves. One of them started to skillfully coil the rope that saved him.

"And then they fall," the woman kept looking at Rick, as before. "I wonder why."

"I imagined that the wall was even taller and that I needed to climb just a little more," he replied. "But the end of the wall was nearer."

He did not mention that he had a wealth of experience of testing situations in his home citadel. What was the point of telling too many people about it? His journey through Thermopolis taught him many things, mainly not to trust people.

Strong hands helped him to rise up from his knees, but they did not let him go. The metallic clang of colliding spheres could be heard from below. Rick thought of the blaster that he left below with regret.

"So then, Olivia," a tall bearded man asked the woman. "Shall we let him fly?"

"No," she replied calmly, glancing at Rick intently again. "He will always have time to do that. Do you want to tell us something?"

"No," Rick immediately answered, as he wanted to first see what was going on and avoid mentioning his companion yet.

At the end of the day, the spheres did not go after Paul, so he could have easily survived and could be somewhere nearby. Maybe he could come back and rescue Rick in case of serious trouble with the locals.

"That means you're coming with us, little birdie," the bearded man laughed out loud. "Move your little feet!"

They pushed him in the back and led him along the wide girders. The movements of this group were quick and nimble, so it was immediately obvious that they had lived here for a long time and knew the environment that surrounded them very well. Olivia issued a short order as they traveled and three figures armed with sharpened disks separated themselves from the group and disappeared in the labyrinth of structures under the dome. The group kept going, along girders and roofs, walking from one building to another along narrow walkways and constantly changing direction. The walls and roofs of the buildings were mainly constructed of pale yellow plascrete. They emerged into the light from under the dome and descended by a metallic ladder into a sector filled with pipelines and industrial service lines. It was humid and oppressive here, with clouds of caustic fumes and a blue mist filling the space around them.

The group walked through the mist for

some time until they reached a dirty gray wall, which had a phosphorescent purple circle with a yellow dot in the center.

"The Cluster," Olivia announced.

Rick would have given her forty years of age, but when he remembered how wrong Paul had got his own age, he decided against guessing. He was roughly shoved in the ribs and made to hurry up. They walked along the wall and found themselves in an open space — the service line zone had ended and a huge sporting arena appeared in front of them, just like the one that Rick had seen in the Thermopolis documentary chronicle, but surrounded by a very tall barrier wall. Assemblages of boxlike structures piled on top of each other rose in the middle of the arena, with some having see-through walls. All of this partly reminded him of the underground settlement of the people of the Network, but with the difference of everything being larger, more spacious, better lit and much cleaner. People were going about their business everywhere. Each person was engaged in their own tasks. Rick noticed that there were hatches and wells in the floor of the arena and people kept going in and out of them. He could see stairways and walkways here and there on the barrier wall which led to platforms on its upper edges where observers stood watch. Part of the arena was lit by the sun and something glittered there, so bright that it hurt his eyes. The facade of the nearest residential block had "ESCALATORS" written on it in large letters, together with a signpost pointing in their direction.

An elderly man wearing dark overalls came out to meet the returning party. His hair was burning copper, with freckles covering his face so thickly that they looked like droplets of pain.

"What's happening?" he asked, stroking his fiery red and carefully dressed beard.

"The rollers tracked down two runners. One of them ran off." Olivia nodded at Rick. "And this one turned out to be quite nimble."

Rick got tense. It turned out that Olivia was testing him when she asked him a question before they came to the Cluster. The locals had noticed him and Paul even before they came across those accursed balls that they called rollers. And now she obviously let him know that she knows about Paul, who had never been mentioned before.

"He isn't rabid, is he?" the red-haired man glanced at Rick sideways. "The rabid are strong."

Olivia approached Rick and took him by the chin, turning his head and examining it in the light.

"No. Say something!"

"What for?" Rick asked. "Why did you bring

me he..."

"Be silent." She let him go and turned around. "See, Igor? He can be formatted and placed on the perimeter."

"He seems quite scrawny," the red-haired man called Igor replied, as he considered Rick with doubt in his eyes.

"It'll be fine. He'll get bigger on the synthetics. We need ersatzes."

"All right," Igor agreed reluctantly.

"Send him for digitization," Olivia ordered.

They started to lead Rick away. He took a couple of steps, but then stopped and loudly asked, "Who are you?"

Olivia and Igor looked at him dismissively and turned away, continuing their conversation. Rick was prodded in the back and then someone grabbed him by the shoulders.

"Hey, let me go!" he shouted, but his arms got twisted behind his back, making him bend over.

He was punched painfully in the ribs a few times and once in the face, making him choke and feel a surge of fury. After spitting blood onto the floor, he glanced at the tall bearded man who had offered to throw him back into the square with those diabolical spheres.

"What're you looking at, rat?" the man barked, smirking crookedly. "Want some more?

Get a move on!"

"Scum!" Rick hissed.

The large man was taken aback. The other guard also froze in expectation. Silence hung over the platform. The people surrounding them stared at Rick with obvious interest. Olivia and Igor stopped talking and turned around.

"What? You little rat!" the bearded man raised his fist.

But Olivia called out, "Hornet."

The man twitched as if he had been slapped and stopped. Only his lips trembled nervously and the hand he had raised to strike shook.

"You would never have survived a minute down below!" Rick told him clearly.

Hornet's whole body flinched, but he did not dare to disobey Olivia. He obviously did not understand what was going on. His pockmarked face went red. More gawkers started to gather around the altercation. Igor looked at Rick as something interesting instead of an object for the first time.

"Would you survive, runner?" he asked.

"Perhaps!" Rick replied, with a note of challenge in his voice. "Want to test me?"

Igor frowned. Olivia chuckled, "The runner obviously hungers for the ordeal."

"Well, why not?" Igor suddenly looked

cheerful. "Do you agree?"

"What awaits me?"

"You have challenged Hornet, which means you have challenged the whole Cluster. This is only washed away with blood. A runner that dares to do such a thing is unworthy of even maintaining the perimeter."

"All right," Rick replied hoarsely.

He immediately remembered his homeland of Thermopolis and the sector which was ruled over by Cornelius. History was repeating itself. Everything really was the same all around the world.

"If it is my fate, I will die free. What are you suggesting?"

"You said it all yourself. Go down into the canal."

Rick wanted to agree, but then Olivia interrupted, "He has already been there and proven that he can get through it. It would be unfair to do such a thing. The fords value honor. We need something else."

"As you wish," Igor gestured, showing that he had no objection to any alternative.

"Wall. Ring. Tunnels. Choose," Olivia offered.

"What are all of these things?"

"Choose."

"Ring."

The inhabitants of the Cluster clapped their hands approvingly.

"The fords like your choice. Let's go."

They let Rick go. He noticed that the convoy had taken a couple of steps away as if there was an invisible barrier around him. Everyone present slowly followed Olivia, who let them to a small platform, bordered by low transparent walls on two sides and pointed at the middle of it.

"Go there," she ordered.

Rick obeyed.

"Who will go for the Cluster?" Olivia turned to the people.

"I will!" Hornet bounded forth and grabbed a whip twined from a thin line with a slim blade on the end from the pile of iron bars, clubs and chains at the edge of the platform.

"Of course."

Olivia waved her hand and two translucent green barriers appeared on the two sides of the platform that did not have walls. "Resolve your dispute. Only one of your will leave the ring, and he will be a ford."

As soon as she finished, Hornet went on the attack. The whip whistled through the air. Rick did not react in time and the blade sliced his shoulder, while Hornet was already preparing to strike again, growling with excitement. Rick ducked and the whip whistled over his head and cracked, only brushing past his hair.

Rick needed to get a weapon — he threw himself towards the edge of the platform, but he miscalculated. As soon as he stretched his hand out towards the pile of metal bars, the green energy barrier turned on and the energy wave threw him backwards, making him fall onto his back and saving him from another strike of the whip. As soon as he got up, the whip cut into his upper arm, shearing through the skin.

"Dance, rat!" Hornet guffawed as he swung the whip yet again.

Rick understood that he had to get closer, but Hornet was not bad at this and did not let him close the distance. Rick started to dodge and feint at his opponent, jumping back as soon as he raised his hand to strike. He managed to catch Rick another couple of times, wounding his hip and the right side of his torso, but he never managed to make him fall or cut his face with the blade. The denizens of the Cluster silently watched the fight. Time dragged on and Hornet started to run out of breath, his movements becoming slower and his strikes getting weaker, but Rick was also slower and less agile than before.

When he jumped away again to put more distance between them, Hornet lost his self-control and roared, "Come here, rat! Come!"

Rick was waiting for this moment — his opponent did not even raise his whip hand to strike but rushed forward with a twisted expression on his face. Rick lunged forward to meet him head on. The whip whistled through the air. There was a crack, but the strike never reached its target. Rick's fist flew into Hornet's chin, making him stumble. His opponent grunted in surprise and fury and threw down the whip, grabbing Rick by the neck with his hands.

Hornet was almost a head taller, had much wider shoulders and his eyes were filled with hate and anger. Rick tried to struggle, but Hornet had an iron grip that squeezed his neck like a vice. His vision started to go dark and his body went limp as his legs went out from under him. Hornet was glaring in Rick's face as he strangled him, slowly forcing him back onto the floor.

In desperation, Rick grabbed and tore out a clump of Hornet's beard. However, his opponent did not even make a sound — his anger about being humiliated before the residents of the Cluster only gave him strength. Rick tried to get free again. He twisted himself around, hit his opponent with his knee and tried to push himself away from the floor with his hands... He suddenly felt a piece of rope under his hand. No, it was the whip!

"Filthy vermin," Hornet hissed. "You're going to die now!"

The thought of salvation was so clear in his fading consciousness that Rick did not even have to see. Rick gripped the blade at the end of the whip in his hand and stuck it into Hornet's neck and face several times. There was a gurgling sound and a gasp and the strangler's grip weakened abruptly. Rick coughed and wheezed and then rolled away with great difficulty, breathing heavily. The mist in front of his eyes cleared and he turned his head — Hornet was holding his face and neck, trying to close the wounds that were gushing red blood.

That was it. Another test had been passed. Rick wanted to get up onto his feet when the platform suddenly shuddered. Frightened shouts could be heard from the gathered crowd. A great rumbling sound followed and the air started to vibrate. Many people fell to the ground, but some remained standing, including Olivia. She stood there, looking at the barrier wall that surrounded the arena. Rick also cast his gaze in that direction and he could not believe his eyes — buildings were moving beyond the wall, with glass domes, sections of roads and service lines and whole districts sliding by.

"It's a shift!"

People darted in every direction as if they

had been stung.

"Shift!" could be heard coming from every side.

The energy barrier at the borders of the platform flashed and went out. Rick made an uncertain step towards the edge when the Cluster itself started to move. The arena with the buildings began to slowly rise like a giant transportation platform, crushing the structures on the barrier wall with its edges. Many of those who ran upwards along the stairs and walkways on the walls were out of luck. Desperate cries for help came from everywhere at once, mixed with the final screams of the dying. The air shivered, saturated with pain, death and fear.

The arena rose to the edge of the barrier and stood still. Rick tried to step to the edge of the platform again, but the floor shook under his feet, even though it was not so noticeable this time and everything started to move horizontally. Rick finally realized that it was not the buildings to the side of the arena that were moving, but the whole of the Cluster.

Where?

Why?

For what reason?

The arena was getting covered by a giant shadow, as if the sun had descended below the horizon. The city at the edge of the Cluster was raised to a significant height and the districts of the Cluster gradually lowered as they moved horizontally and it was an ordered movement, subject to the algorithms programmed into the mechanisms. A network of intertwined tunnels, halls, corridors and spaces opened before his eyes, where everything was also rearranging itself, putting itself into blocks and being rebuilt in a predetermined order.

Mother darkness! What was happening?

District after district descended into the darkness under the surface of a new segment of the city that grew before his eyes. The sky turned into a gradually constricting rectangle.

Thirty seconds...

A minute...

The rectangle of light turned into a narrow strip.

At last, the sky disappeared and the world was covered in darkness.

Well, at least here was something he did not have to get used to. Falling to his knee, Rick looked ahead, quickly getting his bearings in the dark. Gradually, the shapes of walls, ceiling and floor became clearer around him and a constellation of glimmering lights appeared above like stars.

A shadow moved close by, so Rick quickly rose to his feet and sidestepped, clenching his fists.

"A ford has come out of the circle!" Olivia declared.

Other people surrounded them.

"What happened?"

"A shift," Olivia replied calmly, as if that explained everything. "Absolute night usually falls once very eight years, but then everything goes back to its previous place after about a day or two. The shift happened earlier than usual this time."

"Why did that happen?"

She shrugged.

"That's the way the world works. We didn't make it up. Let's go."

When he was brought to a residential block with transparent walls, where shell cases full of flammable fluid were used for lighting, the first thing that Rick asked for was for some water so he could wash as his face and hands were covered with Hornet's blood. Olivia issued an order and he was brought a little water and then given a brick of dry concentrate to satisfy his hunger. While he ate, he noted that most of the people had gone back to their usual activities. They started to climb in and out of the hatches on the floor. Sometimes, someone would visit the block and quietly make a report on the situation to Olivia, going away after receiving their orders.

"Thanks for the food," Rick told her as he finished his concentrate.

Olivia nodded.

"Have you seen the other runner?" he enquired.

"Runner? Oh, you're talking about your companion. Yes, he set off towards the freezers and the rollers followed him."

"Those strange spheres?"

"That's right."

Red-haired Igor entered the block and glared at Rick.

"The newbie wants to find his companion," Olivia reported.

"Forget about him," Igor replied.

"Why?"

"Consider him dead already. No one has managed to run away from the rollers in the freezer sector yet." Igor sat down on a box by the entrance, smoothing out his overalls and then asked, "Who are you?"

Rick briefly told them about his and Paul's expedition to the citadel.

"All of this is unimportant. You are a ford now," Igor concluded.

"What does that mean?" Rick did not understand.

"A ford..." Olivia spoke up. "Everyone who is strong and intelligent is a ford. Those who are weaker are ersatzes, who are our servants. What is your name?"

"You already heard," Igor interrupted. "His name is Rat."

Rick wanted to object but a man he did not know entered the block and asked, "Igor, can you come outside for a minute. Something is happening."

Rick's stomach growled and he cast a worried glance at the corridor where the men were talking to each other. There was obviously something going on in the Cluster. The people had returned to their usual way of life as the shift was nothing new to many of them, so everyone had calmed down, but not the leaders or the watchers. It would be a good idea to fill himself with food in advance.

"Where does the food come from," Rick asked Olivia.

"From the synthesizer barrels," she answered, without emotion as usual. "Rat, you saw them when we were approaching the Cluster. Everything is simple in our world — food from barrels, water from the pipes and air from the world. Light from darkness. Do you want to eat again?"

She threw him another briquette.

Rick quietly chewed what she gave him and washed it down with the rest of the water from his cup. All of this time, Olivia watched him indifferently.

"Why were you going towards the center?" she enquired.

"We were going towards the tower. Do you know what's inside?"

"Death is there. Many fords have gone there and not returned."

"Because of the rollers?"

"Not only them."

"The possessed? Is that what you call them too?"

"Yes. But there is something else as well." She paused. "Well, it doesn't matter, it's too dangerous there. We're fine here as we are. We maintain the perimeter around the walls and take everything we need in our lives from the world, no more, no less. Exactly as much as we need."

"I see. So you have lived here for a long time."

"For many years. It has always been this way. The Cluster has lived, it lives and it will keep living."

Rick thought for a while and asked another question, "What are the rollers?"

"We don't know. They are very fast and they live in the canals and that's it." Olivia undid her jacket, dragged up her shirt and showed him an ugly scar on her stomach. "See that? Once, we found a dead roller in the canals of the Cluster. It did not shine and it was covered in rust. One of the fords decided to come closer. I stood further away than everyone else, but even I got caught. I was young and inexperienced then and always stuck my nose where it did not belong."

"What, don't you even leave the boundaries of the Cluster?" Rick asked in surprise.

"Why would we? Everything is the same everywhere."

Igor stepped into the block again and beckoned Olivia. Rick rose as well.

"You stay here," Igor ordered.

Rick decided against arguing. He came up to the transparent wall and looked out into the Cluster, which was shrouded in darkness. The ceiling was quite distant — it was two or three Thermopolis levels in height. Lights glittered at even intervals, with barely perceptible communication hubs and pipes underneath. The arena had barely changed apart from the steel pillars that appeared between the floor and ceiling. They were obviously there to reinforce the structure and probably extended when the Cluster stopped under the city segment that had grown on the surface. The segment was pressing down on the Cluster with incredible force.

The pillars could be seen everywhere beyond the arena as well, even in places where the standard, low buildings stood. There were impenetrable walls at the outer boundaries of the Cluster. Rick was used to enclosed spaces, but his was still worried as he did not understand what was going on. He needed to work out what the situation was.

The residents of the Cluster were setting up their life in their world, which had sunk under the surface of a new city. They were lighting shell lamps, carrying water and changing into lighter clothing. Surprisingly, it became noticeably warmer with every passing hour. The rumble of gigantic machines had long quietened down and there was only the noise of machines moving around deep underground coming from far away. Rick remembered the view that he saw from the hill when they approached the city gates and understood how infinitesimally small the Cluster was compared to the area of the gray disk around the citadel.

He looked around. Igor and Olivia were not in the corridor anymore. Ignoring his orders, he left the block and looked around, but his new acquaintances had disappeared somewhere. Rick felt a growing unease. He pointlessly wandered around the arena, until he found himself by the border — a standard, squat building which was obviously empty was ten paces away.

Hmm, that was strange, why did the fords

stay in the arena and not use the buildings? Rick approached the metal ladder on the wall of the building, climbed up onto the roof and looked out at the arena from his high vantage point, trying to find Olivia and Igor. He noticed a bright light off to the side and turned in that direction — people were busily working by the entrances into the dark tunnels, which were the height of three people.

Rick moved to the other edge of the roof, carefully looking ahead of him — several fords were trying to do something at the edges of the entrances to the wide tunnels that had a platform fixed above them crowned with shining searchlights. People were shouting, swearing and waving their arms, sometimes pointing at the edges of the tunnels and into the darkness.

What could this all mean? Rick frowned. Were they arguing about the way to close the gates? He stepped forward.

Suddenly, a scrawny human jumped out of the tunnel. It was impossible to determine If it was a man or a woman because the hair of the new arrival was long and matted and it hid their face, while their clothing consisted of torn and filthy rags. The fords recoiled. The creature shouted incomprehensibly and ran away from the tunnel, from which more ragged wretches emerged. The fords tried to stop them and quickly mixed into a large and noisy crowd. The space of the Cluster was filled with worried exclamations, which changed into screams of pain and terror. Rick froze, trying to decide what he should do as he could not understand whether those that arrived in the Cluster were possessed or just the people from some clan that had lived nearby where the living conditions were far worse, considering the appearance of the newcomers.

The wretches kept on coming and Cluster residents armed with steel bars and sharpened disks rushed out to meet them. However, the wretches did not try to resist them for some reason, dodging them and trying to run deeper into the Cluster instead...

A loud noise came from the tunnel and a powerful torrent of water suddenly burst out of the tunnel on the right. The water struck the people, washing them away as if they were pieces of trash and carried them through the passageways between the housing blocks. The sound of the torrent drowned out the screams for help.

Suddenly, the noise intensified and a new torrent came from the other tunnel. A few moments later, water was pouring in from different sides of the arena and quickly rose, flooding the residential blocks and coming closer to the roof of the building where Rick was standing. The foaming streams of water were full of struggling people and lifeless bodies.

Rick rushed to the ladder, descended one floor down and tried to grab a man from the water streaming by. He grabbed him by the hair, pulled him in, but then let him go — the eyes of the man were full of madness. A light-haired youth swimming after him shouted for help and stretched out his hand, so Rick dragged him onto the platform.

"What's happening?" he exclaimed.

"Water!" the youth pleaded, coughing and spitting.

"Where from?"

"The... The underground sea!" the youth swallowed, coughed again and continued, "The valves had always been closed! And now they are open!"

"Do you know how to get out of here?"

The boy just stood there, blinking aimlessly. Then he shouted and pointed at a long walkway that stretched out above the tunnels of the collector which was still lit up by searchlights. Sealed black pipeline hatches could be seen in some places above the walkway. Rick guessed at the distance to it — it was at least fifty paces and there was a current there, which had become weaker as the torrents burst in from the other side but they were still dangerous. The water whirled, drowning everything around it.

He turned to the boy again.

"Do you know how to swim?"

"No!"

"Then hold on to me. We are about to jump."

"Wait!" the boy sniffled. "I'm scared!"

"Me too. But I want to live. Jump!"

He bounded over the railings into the cold water, which was covered in filthy foam. There was a splash nearby. Rick turned and grabbed the boy by the scruff of his neck, ordering him to stay still and swam with his free hand and legs.

The boy did not listen to his words, he spat and screamed, hammering at the water with his hands which made their swim slower than Rick expected, so he quickly started to tire. All of a sudden, the boy fell silent and then turned around forcefully, his eyes shining with exactly the same madness that Rick saw in the eyes of the man that Rick wanted to save a couple of minutes beforehand. The boy pushed down on Rick's shoulder, pushing down at him and forcing him under the water. At the last moment, Rick took a gulp of air, twisted around and pushed the youth away with his legs. Once he broke the surface, the boy was gone.

He did not waste time on thinking about what happened and swam towards the walkway with wide strokes. The current was weaning noticeably, but his strength was running out too. Rick still managed to grab at the edge of the walkway, but did not manage to climb higher as his cold fingers did not obey him and his muscles were completely stiff. Suddenly, the searchlights on the railing started to blink furiously, the generators sparked and there were popping and crackling noises. Rick suddenly felt cramps throughout his body and he started to shake uncontrollable as he realised that he had been electrocuted, which helped him, unexpectedly. Feeling unusually invigorated, he pulled himself up after two attempts and found himself on the walkway, where he leaned on the railing, trying to catch his breath.

The Cluster was now full of water which covered the residential blocks. The shouting had almost quietened down, as only the few survivors sat on the roofs of buildings called out to those who struggled in the water nearby to swim towards them.

Rick quickly undressed down to his waist and started to rub himself all over with his hands so that the blood would flow faster in his veins. Too many experiences in one day. He really wanted to lie down right there and then and try to fall asleep after getting warm first. But all of this could wait, because the water kept coming and would soon flood the walkway.

He looked up — the massive hatches had reliable locking mechanisms based on wheels and levers. Rick pulled on one of the wheels and tried to turn, but it would not budge. He reluctantly put his wet clothes back on and considered what to do. He had seen similar hatches before, but they did not have wheels. Then he pulled on the levers, which easily gave way. Right, this was better. He tried to turn the wheel again but to no avail.

There was some sort of trick to it. Rick narrowed his eyes, noticing the faded pictures above the levers — bright, semicircular arrows. He grabbed the levers, pressed down on them and they both went downwards. Now for the wheel. One turn and another. It worked!

Rick pulled the heavy hatch towards himself and it opened with a drawn out grating sound. It seemed that the fords did not pay particular attention to the collector and never opened the hatches. He was in luck. He was very fortunate that the hatch had not fused with its frame.

He pulled himself up inside the pipeline, closed the hatch behind him and crawled forwards on all fours.

Rick crawled on in complete darkness, losing all sense of time and distance. He warmed up and even his clothes became a lot drier. He had no time to celebrate though, as he heard a noise behind him. He was overcome by a premonition of danger. Rick sped up as the noise intensified. A few moments later, he was caught in a cold stream and spun around inside the pipe. It was pointless to resist, the main thing was to try to avoid suffocating or hitting his head so he would not lose consciousness.

The stream carried him, twisting and turning through the pipe and keeping up the pressure, sometimes carrying him into uncovered channels where Rick once tried to grab at the edges, but could not hold on as he cut his hand, so he did not make any more attempts. Once, when he was carried through a channel that led through a spacious hall that was lit by purple light, he noticed squat human-like creatures with contorted facial features. They had pale, gleaming bodies and their eyes were pure black, without whites.

The soon changed back into a pipe which bent downwards steeply. Rick spent a pair of seconds falling down head first and then the pipe ended, as he inadvertently threw his arms upwards, somersaulted through the air and fell into a pool, splashing a myriad droplets all around him.

It seemed that his journey had come to its

end.

He had hit his back hard as he fell. When he broke the surface and looked around, he saw that he was in a hall with a faraway light under the ceiling with another visible to the side. The pool was huge, but he was lucky, as the pipe that threw him out was almost by the edge. Rick swam over to the wide edge of the pool and climbed out of the water.

He had no strength to undress left. The hall was warm and the light of the lamps weakly reflected off the rippling water to dance upon the walls. Rick moved away from the edge, lying prone by the wall.

He was alive!

The lids of his eyes were glued together from fatigue, as his consciousness became clouded and he barely heard a distant splash that interrupted the monotonous sound of the water falling from the pipeline. But Rick did not give it any further notice. A moment later, he was fast asleep.

I

RICK WOKE UP from the pain in his back. He tried to get up and gasped. His muscles had gone numb and his waist hurt from him hitting the water. Rick somehow brought himself up onto his knees and looked around. He was in a great stone enclosure. Judging by the water level, the pool was almost full. He looked upwards and saw that the water was barely flowing out of the pipe under the ceiling. At least that was good, one less thing to worry about.

His clothes had completely dried while he slept, as he must have been lying here for a long time. He got a handful of water and washed his face. Then, Rick stood up, checked how he felt and carefully bent down twice to warm up his stiff muscles.

Everything seemed fine. His back hurt, but bruises were nothing new. It would sort itself out.

His stomach growled plaintively. Yes, of course, he always wanted to eat. Hunger was nothing new either, but it was very bad that his gear had been lost forever. He needed to arm himself with something, as he remembered the strange pale creatures and their black eyes. He shrugged and walked along the wall towards a wide platform where he could see the entrance to a maintenance corridor.

The corridor led him in to an oblong hall, full of pipes and noisy machines. Rick was examining the entwined different colored wires and the panels with levers and buttons until he came across a sizable operations console and the words "Pumping Station 32-54" written on the wall. He cleared his throat and looked over the pumps — the machines were purring along evenly in automatic mode. Rick looked at the manometer readings, trembling indicator arrows and flashing lights. Amazingly, it all still worked!

He kept going, slowly looking for an exit or a ventilation shaft and soon stopped in front of another control console, where the monitor displayed a diagram of two circles, with one inside the other and the space between them divided into many sectors of different sizes that fanned out all around them. One of the sectors was lit up in red, with a message full of incomprehensible numbers and abbreviations blinking by its side. A rectangle underneath said "Information."

Rick tapped the rectangle and the diagram on the monitor changed to become three dimensional, the red sector growing in size to be displayed as a complex diagram. More labels began to appear, some of which were entirely understandable. "Main Highway", "Generators" and "Pumps", for instance. Rick thoughtfully looked at the picture, trying to guess at its purpose. He finally realized that it was a plan of the water connections in the sector! He touched the rectangle labeled "Back" on the monitor and the picture became flat again, showing two circles with the space between them divided into segments. It turned out that all of these sectors were separate autonomous regions equipped with ancient machines that were built around the citadel. The sectors were labeled with letters from the Latin alphabet. Rick counted twenty-five sectors in total. The circular structure in the middle was marked with the letter "A".

Well then, everything was clear and simple with the letters and he just needed to remember this rule so that it would be easier to orient himself.

He set off. A spacious corridor served as the exit to the pumping station, with one of the walls replaced by a panoramic window with an icy blue-lit cave beyond. Rick walked along the corridor, glancing through the glass at the cage occasionally. Doors were positioned on the wall on the opposite side to the window and he looked inside those which were unlocked, but saw nothing apart from empty shelves inside. Sometimes, he saw entrances to side corridors, but they all looked the same and it would have been easy to get lost, so Rick decided to keep going in the direction he had chosen as he had a feeling inside that it was the right one. The way the sector was arranged actually reminded of his native Thermopolis quite a lot — although Rick believed that this was no wonder, considering that similar designs and technologies were used when it was being built. He just wanted to understand the intentions of the builder. That shift, as the fords called it. Especially because it happened every eight years before.

He sighed, as he understood that one of the life support programs was active here just like in Thermopolis. If only he could get to the city control center...

The cave behind the glass came to its end and he found himself at an intersection where the corridor met another wider passage that had landings and stairways on its side. There were also direction signs hanging here: Branch F-01001, Highway T-331 and Radial No. 42001.

He decided to turn and walk along the highway. There was not as much light here as the illumination from the cage barely reached beyond the turn and emergency lamps blinked red ahead. Rick walked along the wall, tensely watching the gloom and regretting the loss of his blaster. He also glanced upwards as he went, in case he came across a ladder or the grille of a ventilation shaft so he could try to get out onto the surface.

Rails ran along the floor of the highway and the tunnel was shaped like a rectangle with ribbed walls made out of an unfamiliar bright colored material. It was similar to metal, but the surface was too rough, with no sign of rust.

A droning sound came from the depths of the tunnel far ahead. Rick stopped. The droning sound continued at the same frequency, as the floor started to vibrate slightly. It looked like some part of the city started to move again. Rick started walking again when the drone quietened down. It soon disappeared completely.

Around a quarter of an hour had passed when Rick reached the blinking red emergency lamps and found a sign on the wall with the label 13-500. It was probably the distance that he had walked from a point unknown to him, or maybe it was the other way round and it was the distance left until he reached an unknown destination.

The highway soon made a gentle turn and Rick entered a large hall, bisected into two parts by the rail. Mold fluoresced on the walls and ceiling and a rail carriage stood on the rails up ahead.

Rick climbed onto the ramp and walked along the carriage, which was attached to a locomotive that featured a wide metallic blade vertically fixed to its front. An open platform could barely be seen ten paces in front of the locomotive and rick walked past it to discover another locomotive which was equipped with a huge drill.

He looked around, searching through his

memories — it seemed that this was a small depot. The unusual word was simple and understandable. Suddenly, he was twisted with pain. His whole body cramped and his legs went out from under him. Rick cried out, grabbing his head in his hands and fell to the floor.

His consciousness came back slowly and circles swam in front of his eyes for a long time, until Rick managed to make out the fluorescent green mold on the walls and carefully stood up.

Rick's head spun a little and he did not know how long he had spent unconscious. Mother Darkness! He felt his forehead, where a sizable lump had grown. He probably hit his head when he had the fit. Good that there wasn't some beast that came upon him and ate him.

He noticed a crowbar lying on the platform and armed himself.

Now he was calmer, even though he was reassuring himself. It was not a great weapon, but it would be all right for close combat.

Listening to his feelings, Rick continued on his way. After an hour had passed, the tunnel came to its end and highway stretched out as a bridge spanning a huge open space. The ceiling with its air vents letting in the weak ray of the sun was far away, the walls even further and the floor furthest of all, as deep as ten levels. This was just like Thermopolis!

Rick confidently strode onwards. The familiar architecture of this space cheered him up. It was incredible that this was only a small part of the city around the citadel. How many people could have lived here once? This world was probably vibrant and full of light, warmth and color once upon a time. But now it was just a huge and artificial dead space.

He crossed the bridge and entered a tunnel again. He heard a rustle somewhere over his head. Rick stopped, listening. It was probably his ears playing tricks on him. He started to walk on, but then he stopped again. He slowly turned around, carefully examining the mold-covered ceiling and suddenly felt very small and helpless.

He had to get out of here! He sped up his pace, feeling someone's intent gaze on his back. Goosebumps run down his neck and the hair on his head twitched as Rick walked even faster, afraid to look behind him and start running. At the same time, he heard the sound of his own steps which was soon intertwined with an echo as if Rick was not walking alone. He stopped, even though he understood that he should not do it and listened again.

"Go forward!" and inner voice insisted. "Why are you standing there? The longer you stand there the less chance you have to survive! *It* is coming..."

Rick heard a series of rapid taps behind his back and looked over his shoulder. A multi-legged fat monster with a striped tail which pulsated yellow was running along the wall towards him. Its head featured several pairs of glowing red eyes and mandibles covered with long moving whiskers. The creature was as long as a human.

The terror that engulfed him immobilized his body. Rick watched the insect run towards him, squat down towards the floor and raise its tail, preparing to strike. It was only then that Rick came to his senses and quickly backed away, slipping on the damp floor and falling down. The tail snapped and its sting rang out as it hit the place where its victim's foot had been but a second ago.

Rick jumped up and started to run. The insect chittered piercingly behind his back and tapped its feet along the floor, chasing him. Rick ran as fast as he could just so that he could put a distance between himself and the monster. His lungs were burning, his face was flushed with blood and it was getting more and more difficult to move and breathe. However, he held on as he had to escape the beast and put some distance between them so that he could quickly hide in a niche or room...

When his breath finally run out and he

whirled around, swinging the crowbar in his hand, there was nothing in the tunnel. Rick fell onto the floor, unable to suck in enough breath — he had spent too much strength on his sprint and his heart beat too fast. Multicolored circles swam before his eyes as his body convulsed in spasms from the overload.

However, the feeling of danger still did not go away but rose to the maximum instead. He did not understand why. The empty walls radiated danger. It was as if they shouted at him, "Run!"

Rick slowly raised his head and looked at the ceiling. The sting of the insect that hung above him was about to pierce his forehead. But a shadow bolted nearby, there was the whistling sound of something cutting through the air and one of the mandibles on the head of the creature suddenly fell to the floor. Cloudy liquid poured out of the stump and Rick automatically drew back, covering his face with his arm. The creature chittered, hit the wall hard with its tail and disappeared in an opening on the ceiling, swaying from side to side.

The shorn mandible was still twitching when a human figure appeared out of the darkness in front of rick. The stranger crushed the mandible with their foot and turned around. It was Olivia. She wiped the thick blade of a cleaver on her sleeve and chuckled, whispering a command loudly, "Let's go!"

"But..." Rick started as he got up.

Olivia silently pointed behind her back with her thumb. Rick looked over her shoulder and almost screamed — there was a yellow light in the depth of the tunnel and it was full of long-tailed creatures that had smelt their prey. The tapping sound of their long legs and the snap of tails grew ever louder, coming towards them from afar.

Olivia rushed forward, uncoiling a rope as she ran.

"Get ready!" she shouted to Rick as he caught up with her.

The tunnel ended abruptly and they were on a bridge that stretched over the mouth of a huge shaft.

"Fight back!" Olivia thrust the cleaver into Rick's head as she started to fix the rope to the side of the bridge, using a complex knot to fix it to the hook.

Rick chopped at one of the monsters that approached them and chose the right moment to cut off its head. He lunged to scare away another one when he heard a voice behind his back.

"What're you waiting for? Climb down!"

Olivia was nowhere to be seen as she was somewhere under the bridge. Rick put the cleaver behind his belt and went over the side, holding on to the rope.

"Be quick! It's not far!" came from below.

Rick swung like a pendulum, almost making him release the rope, but he looked down just in time. A wide channel of water was going past below him — if he let go of the rope, he would have swung past it!

He found the right moment when he had swung back and jumped. His feet slid on the inclined wall of the channel so Rick fell onto his posterior. Olivia helped him to rise and they both glanced upwards — the insects were staring at them over the edge of the bridge, chittering, moving their whiskers and mandibles and pushed each other around. However, they did not try to descend.

Olivia grabbed the rope, made a circular motion with her upraised arm and tugged hard. The end of the rope fell into the channel, causing the creatures to squeal loudly again.

"We need to go. We are provoking them," Olivia told Rick, as she quickly coiled the rope.

Rick nodded and they hurried away.

"How did you find me?" he asked as they walked.

"I swim well. I saw how you opened the ancient entrance to the waterways. None of the fords could open one of them before. How did you manage to do it?"

"It's hard to explain. It would be easier to show you. So what happened in the Cluster?"

"I have no idea. The great water usually goes around it."

"But not this time."

"That's right," Olivia glanced at him. "You fought Hornet well. He removed a dozen fords from the circle before you."

"But the fords have the protection of the Cluster!" Rick countered.

"Why do you think so?" she chuckled. "We are vulnerable. Several of us are taken over by madness every year. The ford loses their mind and attacks everything that lives, with the sole aim of tearing them to pieces. A ford like that stops understanding human speech and becomes a beast. We watch each other, so if a ford is afflicted by madness, there are those like Hornet that are there to deal with them. If the rabid one has not had time to do harm, we just get rid of them or lower them into the canal."

"And if they kill someone who is healthy, they get executed," Rick guessed.

"Correct. The runners are usually the rabid, as they are still around in some of the empty segments of the world. This is why when you escaped the rollers and started to speak, I decided to risk it and give you a chance." Olivia sighed. "Now there's no Cluster and my people are no more."

"Do you know where we're going?"

"No. We need to get to the top."

"But those creatures could still be waiting for us."

"Better them than the things that live here. Look! See what's on the walls and ceilings?" Olivia pointed at the white ragged strands hanging down at the entrance to the tunnel where the channel was leading them. "I wouldn't advise touching them. Our ersatzes sometimes walked into this horrible stuff at the lower levels. Fords do not like catacombs and darkness. The underground radiates death."

Paul nodded curtly. He was familiar with webs, as there were predatory spiders in Thermopolis as well.

"What does "ford" mean?" he asked, as he carefully walked ahead.

"I don't understand what you are talking about."

"Where I come from, they usually say "human". Why a ford?"

"I don't know. That's the way it is in the Cluster."

"So why is it called a Cluster, as opposed to a commune or settlement?"

"They have always spoken that way," Olivia shrugged. "I have no idea why."

Rick decided to stop asking questions. They walked out into a space which was lit by a faraway clear light, with walkways joined by a connecting bridge running along the walls. Garlands of white strands hung off the bridge, coming together in a large ball over the floor, which contained something formless and dark that was stuck in it forever.

Olivia carefully moved ahead, crouched and climbed through the gap between the wall and the hanging garlands. Rick followed her example, and they quietly hurried towards a ladder so that they could get up to the walkway. Once there, they quickly found another ladder that led them into a dark corridor.

After Rick got used to the darkness, he suggested that they walk towards the source of the slight breath of wind that he felt upon his face. Olivia did not object and they soon managed to get out onto a highway that led them into a deep rift, where the walls stretched out up high towards the blue sky. The rift was crossed by the lines of faraway bridges far above, which may have been other highways.

Rick and Olivia stood around for a while, breathing their fill and enjoying the light and the cool air and then followed the highway into the mouth of another tunnel. More strands of web hung down from the ceiling, but they were torn and obviously old, which suggested that the creatures did not hunt here anymore.

The highway soon went through an open space, where the ceiling was lost high up in the darkness, mold fluoresced on the far walls and unusually shaped machines, intersections of pipes and metallic buildings could be seen to the sides. They were all probably a part of the complex mechanism that changed the city landscape. Finally, they saw giant gears that were attached to a pulley with a chain mechanism, where each link of the chain was as tall as two people.

Olivia and Rick stopped, open-mouthed as they examined the gigantic turning devices. This must be the landscape shifter, Rick decided. He already wanted to tell his companion about his supposition, but froze when he turned his head and saw a vile and fury beast that hung below a girder over the highway. The many legs of the creature twitched convulsively and gathered under its belly. The giant spider turned on its own axis with admirable agility in complete silence, frozen in expectation.

Rick still managed to slowly turn towards Olivia and understood that he had touched a translucent strand that hung by his shoulder.

"Don't move," he whispered, warning his companion and gripping the handle of the cleaver behind his belt. "A creature is right above us."

Olivia did not react as she stopped still, she just started to breathe more rapidly.

The furry beast that hid half of the view over their heads also stayed still. Rick slowly stepped back, but the sticky strand was stuck fast to his shoulder. He drew his cleaver from behind his belt and gave it to Olivia, asking her to cut through the web strand on his shoulder.

It seemed that this task took her forever. But then the strand fell away and hung down on the side, swinging in the drought. The creature above trembled and started to move — its legs worked fast as it drew in the strand they had just released.

"Run," Olivia whispered, and they dashed forward.

They both turned onto a small bridge that led to a walkway along the walls and then turned into a corridor from it. Olivia kept looking over her shoulder and hissed, cursing the memories of the filthy rats of the Cluster. The corridor was a gentle incline leading upwards — they were approaching the exit, which was lit with a glimmering light up ahead. There were more and more white strands on the walls. Olivia overtook him and hacked at them with the cleaver, warning him whether she was dodging or jumping over them.

"Let's head back!" Rick shouted when he noticed that the opening in front of them was covered with webs.

"No! The mark of the Cluster is there!" Olivia exclaimed, pointing at a gap in the web through which a familiar symbol could be made out.

She hacked at the strands powerfully — once, twice and more, freeing up the way and continuing to move. Rick followed her, with a quick glance at the glyph, which was a triangle inside a circle. He caught up with his companion.

"Everywhere where there is the sign of the cluster," Olivia rummaged around the folds of her clothing as she walked, "the amulet can be used to activate ancient machines."

She finally extracted a medallion key and Rick grabbed her hand.

"What're you doing?" Olivia exclaimed, afraid that Rick was going to rob her.

"I am familiar with this sign," he said as he let go of her hand. "I saw it on the neck of my friend. The one who I came here with."

"You lie!"

Rick choked with indignation, caught his foot on a protrusion on the floor and nearly fell.

"I can..." he quickly glanced over his shoulder and spat, noticing the beast following them. "I swear upon all the gods you believe in and on my own life!"

"But where would he have got a Cluster amulet?"

"He called it by the name of his god."

"It doesn't matter," Olivia waved her hand. "We will discuss it later!"

She stopped abruptly and touched the medallion key to the slot in the wall. The outline of the glyph lit up with a blue light.

Rick heard a rustle and looked into the corridor again — the creature was approaching them. Rick sidestepped inadvertently and heard something crunch below his feet. He stepped away again and heard another squelching and crunching noise. Finally, he looked down under his feet — he had crushed several white eggs which were the size of a fist.

"We better hurry," he hissed, once he realized where they ended up in. "This is her nest!"

Olivia was busy with wall. The spider inexorably approached. Rick gathered himself, clenching his fists and understanding that there was nothing he could do against the beast that approached them.

"Hurry up!" he shouted.

The wall suddenly cracked along an even vertical line and opened, displaying a niche and a console covered in flickering lights.

"Follow me!" Olivia commanded as she took the medallion out of the slot.

Rick did not need to be asked twice. The spider had almost caught them and stretched its legs into the niche, but the secret doors closed again and cut the appendages stretching towards them. Rick exhaled loudly and lowered himself onto the floor, watching how Olivia worked with the panel of blinking lights on the console.

It was only know when he understood that he was in the cabin of an elevator and that it was rising. The darkness beyond the transparent wall changed to glimmers of light — it was the mold fluorescing on the walls of the giant shaft. Rick's eye caught some movement to their side and he gasped — the spider was following the cabin, nimbly climbing up along the wall and did not look like it was going to give up any time soon.

"I chose the highest floor," Olivia said.

"Where did you learn how to control an elevator?" Rick stood up by her side, watching the spider.

"It is the first thing all children of the Cluster get taught! We would never have survived without ancient knowledge. The Cluster takes souls but it gives a lot as well. We respect the ancients. Now how did a Cluster amulet end up with your friend, tell me."

"There are settlements and fortresses

outside," Rick did not like her commanding tone, but he had no strength left for arguments and resolving issues, especially considering Olivia had now saved him twice. "I met him in one of those places. They had a sect there, where the locals worshiped Maus. That is the name of their godling, while this sign upon your amulet," he pointed at the medallion key on Olivia's neck, "is the symbol of their deity."

"But..." Olivia was obviously taken aback. "How is that possible?"

"The elders..." For some reason, Rick suddenly thought of Kyoto and Book of Faces. "Anyway, they told us that people had run away from the cities once upon a time. That could have been the way that the amulets ended up in the cluster. Oh!"

The sight took his breath away as the cabin came out of the shaft and ascended along the wall under the open sky.

"Yes, it's impressive!" Olivia turned towards the glass and looked at the segment of the city beneath their feet. A high wall was before their eyes, with the main transportation highway visible in the distance as it stretched from the west to the east like a wide yellow strip. There were identical box-shaped buildings between the highway and the walls, empty streets and the lines of the pipelines and another wall further away.

The higher the cabin rose, the clearer the structure of the city built around the tower became. Rick had carefully memorized the plan that he saw in the pumping station control room and finally realized that the tower was surrounded with rings of sectors which were themselves subdivided into clusters of different shapes and sizes. That is where the fords got this word from. For them, the cluster was their territory. It turned out that it was necessary to go along the main highway to get to the tower quickly, but it was controlled by rollers that were almost impossible to escape. The way through the city districts was not much better as danger was everywhere, with various beasts, mutants and the possessed, as well as a changing landscape so you could never guess what would start to shift and when. If only he could see what was behind the wall that the elevator rose along...

He stared into the distance, where a row of thick pillars had just towered, but disappeared from the surface rather quickly to be replaced by a dome which reflected the sun.

Judging by the distance, the pillars and the dome were rather sizable. It would be curious to visit that place... He wanted to bring Olivia's attention to that location, but the cabin smoothly slid into an opaque pipe in the wall. The light immediately came on and the cabin came to a complete stop after a few moments.

"We're here, let's get out!" Olivia tugged Rick by the sleeve.

"Oh? Oh yes," he realized as he heard a grinding sound and a rustle underneath the cabin.

It looked like that relentless spider would not stop until it would catch up with them!

Olivia dragged Rick onto the wall, which had something resembling a low railing along one side. The wall was around two paces wide, but the height... The height was so mind-blowing, that he inadvertently shivered.

"Don't approach the edges! The wind is treacherous!"

Rick glanced back at the cabin, which was suddenly pushed upwards with a piercing screech. The spider was probably pushing with its head from below, and trying to squeeze itself through the gap. The monster was strong!

"Let's go," Olivia dragged Rick after her, but moved forward without hurrying, stepping carefully and turning her face away from the cold wind that blew in her ace.

Getting as far away as possible seemed to be a logical choice. Rick looked back again. They would not be able to go far this way, as the spider was bound to catch up with them after it had pushed the cabin all the way up and it did not care about the height.

"Everything looks different from up here!" Olivia suddenly shouted over the whistling wind. "It's so small!"

"Yes!" Rick started to realize that Olivia had some sort of plan and that here was a reason that she was dragging him in a particular direction. "Did any of you try to find out what is that tower at the center of the city?"

"The axis of the world! It's crystal clear anyway!" Olivia glanced back. Her expression darkened. "Get a move on!"

Rick did not turn around as it was obvious that the spider had climbed up onto the wall anyway. Olivia ended up switching from a walk to a run. The railings ended up ahead, the platform widened, turning into an overhang, which ended with a sheer channeled slope that ran somewhere far down, towards the faraway streets between the city buildings.

"Over there!" Olivia shouted. "Be quick!"

When they ran out onto the overhang, the wind struck them from the side. Olivia cried out and crouched as if she had twisted her ankle and almost got blown off the wall. Rick held on to her and roughly pulled her to her feet.

"Thank you," Olivia breathed out. "Slide down with me, don't wait around!"

They both stared at the approaching spider.

Rick nodded. They had no choice, but the height...

"Here!" she thrust her medallion into his pocket. "Take it!"

"What for?"

"Don't argue! Come on then! Let's jump!"

She squeezed his shoulder painfully and shouted, "Don't disappoint me!" into his face.

"Wait!"

But Olivia already slipped downwards and started to slide along the channel on her back.

Mother Darkness! Rick glanced over his shoulder again, to see the spider raise itself on its forelegs and spit out sticky strand. That was when Rick jumped.

When he landed on his belly, he understood that he should have listened to Olivia instead of waiting. The spider stood still on the lip of the overhang, not daring to follow him and its shape quickly receded. Rick drew his knees up to his chest and turned himself onto his back. He was just in time, as he had picked up an impressive speed, so he had to constantly hold his head up and keep his arms crossed on his chest, otherwise the fiction would have burned the hair at the back of his neck and the skin of his palms.

The channel through the slope glittered silver in the rays of the midday sun, looking like an endless, blinding strip. Rick felt his back get hotter and hotter as his speed became dangerously high. The noise of the wind in his ears changed to a howl, his neck was in pain and he really wanted to lower his head, but he could not, he had to endure it and look ahead so that he would see the end of the slope. He saw a dark spot ahead of him through the tears that welled up in his eyes. This must be Olivia, it could not be anyone else. If she was sliding down along the right way and holding herself together, it meant that everything was still fine.

Suddenly, the channel ahead of him bent and Olivia flew into a spin, followed by Rick. The channel ended. He heard a loud scream. Rick understood that he was flying too, waving his arms and screaming as he spun through the air. A wall, some walkways, the roofs of the buildings and the sky flashed before him and then a dark strip covered with ripples suddenly appeared in front of him and then disappeared.

Impact!

A splash!

He was very lucky to have entered the water feet first. Once he came up to the surface, he swam to the concrete edge of the canal in a couple of strokes, finally breathed out and fell on his back throwing his arms to the sides and greedily sucking in air.

Olivia lay in a similar pose nearby, breathing heavily.

Then they both laughed loudly. But their joy was short lived. Olivia abruptly went quiet. A shadow blocked the sun above Rick and he sat up quickly.

Armed men in gray jumpsuits stood at the edge of the canal. One of them raised his blaster, putting the barrel to Rick's head and said, "Pray to your gods."

Rick would have considered this good advice. But he no longer believed in the gods.

J

THE MAN IN GRAY pulled the trigger and the weapon emitted a dry click. The stranger chuckled and lowered his weapon, carefully observing Rick.

"Fritz, there's something strange about this one," he said to someone behind his back.

Another man separated himself form the line of gray strangers. He was a tall man with a square jaw, thin lips, a straight nose and light colored hair. He approached, towering over Rick like a mountain and asked, "Who are you?"

"Rick."

"Where are you from?"

"The wall."

"I see. Rick from the wall."

The blond man examined him for a while and then suddenly swung his blaster, aiming the stock at Rick's face. Rick instinctively flinched, covering himself up with his arm.

"Everything's fine with him, corporal," the blond man smirked. "Take him to the rest of them."

The corporal that had tried to shoot Rick grabbed him by the collar and roughly pulled him up, making him get onto his feet. Another man put Olivia on her feet in the same unceremonious way and another two men joined him to take her into a lane between the buildings in a completely different direction.

"We'll catch up with you," they snickered.

"Eyes forward," the corporal rewarded Rick with a cuff.

And now Rick could not take it any longer. Olivia, who was being taken away by those three, the blond man who was grinning after swinging his stock at him, the barrel that the corporal had shoved in his face — all of these images jumbled together before his eyes. He was full of anger. Rick balled his fists and turned, punching the corporal in the nose, followed by a swift uppercut. The corporal's head twitched from the two impacts, his eyes faded and rolled back in his head and he fell with his back onto the concrete.

Rick spun on his heels, as he heard a sound behind him but could not do anything before something hard struck him in the face, his head rang and the world went dark...

However, once he opened his eyes he immediately understood that he had not been knocked out for long.

"The wild one has woken up, Fritz!" called out the stranger in gray that stood nearby.

For some reason, he was holding a bucket in his hands.

"Get him in line," the blond man ordered.

A strong pair of hands grabbed Rick by the shoulders and it was only now that he realized that he was all wet and immediately worked out that the stranger with the bucket poured water on him to make him come to his senses.

"Line up, soldiers!" the blond man commanded loudly.

Rick was shoved into a row of people he did not know. It was easy to see that they were all prisoners — most of them were filthy, dressed in different colors and unarmed, unlike the soldiers in the gray jumpsuits. All of them stood straight as rods, with wide shoulders like their commander Fritz, looking tough with their harsh unfriendly eyes and tense facial expressions.

One of the subordinates made some sort of report to Fritz, who nodded and issued an order, "We're going back."

Angry shouts telling people to move and pokes from the weapons came from all sides. Rick turned his head to and fro, seeking out Olivia among the prisoners, but did not manage to see her. However, he did notice one of the three that had taken the woman down the side lane. The soldier had a darkening purple bruise on his cheek. The soldiers that walked behind him were laughing and mocking him. Rick nodded to himself and stopped looking around, really hoping that Olivia had managed to run away.

They walked through many blocks. They canal was now far to the side and the column was already moving along the hanging steel walkways between the buildings, soon finding themselves on a wide road with a surface textured with small bumps that led them to a pair of huge steel gates.

The gates stood out among the architecture of the roadway and the city blocks along it. It was likely that the gates had been built here relatively recently, brutishly forced into the landscape and supported by firing positions reinforced with thick armor plating by their sides.

When the gates were opened, a plaza appeared before their eyes, surrounded by squat, identically patterned buildings with boarded up windows.

Everything looked drab and monotonous here. Patrolmen with their weapons ready walked the streets. Watchmen sat on the roofs and sometimes one of the soldiers up above would greet their friends among those that returned with the prisoners. A large building which was similar to the Mausite temple towered in the center of the plaza, its dome shining in the rays of the setting sun. Container modules used for command and residence were arranged in row in front of the building. This was a camp, a military camp.

Rick shook his head, ridding himself of the pieces of information giving him hints that came up from his subconscious. Damn it, not now, he could not have a fit!

His head stopped swimming and his heart rate slowed down and his breath became even again. It looked like it let him go. Rick quickly looked around him. The order and the strict calculation with which the modules were arranged immediately caught the eye. Light could be seen behind the narrow firing port windows, but all of them without exception had armored shutters many of which were closed. The prisoners were stopped as they approached the camp. A small unit of armed soldiers marched past in three ideally regular columns. The movements of the soldiers looked like the workings of a well-oiled machine.

"Lucio, take them to the distribution unit," Fritz ordered the soldier at the head of the convoy as soon as their unit entered the territory of the camp.

"After me!" barked black-haired Lucio and waved his hand.

They were led to the far end towards barracks assembled of red stone, which were surrounded with a fence made of barbed wire. Further along, there was a wall as tall as two and a half men beyond which nothing could be seen. Rick soon understood the reason they were being led towards the barracks — prisoners just like themselves were looking out of the windows and looked at the new arrivals with curiosity. They had almost been led to the furthest barrack when a lanky young man jumped out of their group. He was quick and wiry and he gave one of the soldiers a hard push, running towards the wall with the obvious intention of getting over it. Rick thought that this was a stupid idea.

"On your knees!" Lucio shouted.

The majority of them obeyed. The runaway deftly vaulted over the barbed wire fence and almost reached the wall. Lucio calmly drew his combat knife, aimed and threw it after him. The steel glinted in the sun and entered the back of the lanky man, so he fell as if his legs had been cut from under him, raising a cloud of dust. Lucio gestured towards the soldiers and they dragged the runner back and laid him at his feet. Calmly and impassively, Lucio pulled his knife out of the back of the groaning wounded man, wiped it on his own clothes and put it back in its sheath. As he did this, the man tried to croak something as his hands clawed at the ground and he still tried to move towards the wall which he had been unable to reach.

"Remember, I am sergeant Lucio and I have just cut through his spine," Lucio announced and continued in an instructive tone of voice, "and now he cannot walk. All of you, look at that! This is what will happen to everyone that dares to run away from the division."

With these words, the sergeant stamped down on the neck of the wounded man — there was a loud crack and he fell silent. Following this, orders rang out and the prisoners were forced into the barrack where they were made to undress and hosed down with cold water. They were then led naked to another barrack, where they were dusted with some sort of sharp smelling powder and hosed down again. At the exit they were issued with gray jumpsuits, had their heads shaved and were given a bowl of soup of unknown provenance as well as a piece of pressed concentrate each.

Rick quickly put away the soup, without thinking about its unpleasant smell and taste and hid the concentrate in his trouser pocket, as he was thinking about escaping soon.

When they finished with the food, they were taken into a residential barrack, full of people that had gone through a similar treatment. Many of the newcomers were afraid and looked around apprehensively, expecting some sort of trick from the locals.

A soldier bearing silvery patches came closer to the evening and introduced himself as a staff intendant and recorded the names of all those who were admitted to the barracks on that day. After this the "lights out" command sounded and people started to lie down on the multi-leveled bunk beds along the walls.

Rick climbed into the top bunk in the corner and stared at the dim light under the ceiling, thinking about how he would make his escape and the events of the last two days, until sleep overtook him.

However, he did not get to have an uninterrupted sleep — it happened in the middle of the night. He felt how someone's hand was searching around his body and looking for something to steal. He waited until the fingers of the thief got to the trouser pocket where the piece of concentrate lay and quickly grabbed the wrist of his hand, and sat up, saying "Do this again and I will tear your throat out."

A thug with a hooked nose stared at him from the gloom.

"You wouldn't have the guts for it, whelp," the stranger squeezed out as he grimaced from the pain in his wrist.

Then Rick changed his grip to the man's thumb and twisted it against the back of his palm.

Something snapped.

The thug paled and almost collapsed to the floor, spitting out a quiet curse and hurrying to disappear in the darkness of the barracks.

On the following day, they were divided into groups according to their age. Rick and his companions were put together in a platoon with a mix of young men and women and then all of the new arrivals were lined up in front of the barracks. The sergeants spent a long time swearing and hitting people around the head as they lined up the new recruits. Finally, when everyone stood still in silence, Fritz approached the lines. He spent several minutes quietly walking past the rows of people and examining their faces.

Then he came back to stand in front of them and declared, "Welcome to the division! You are all soldiers now! I am your commander! You may only address me as "commander" from this moment onwards!"

His words reverberated through the camp and echoed off the wall. The morning was overcast and sparse snow fell from the skies. Rick stared straight ahead: he could make out the barely perceptible silhouette of the citadel through the low-hanging clouds. The snow kept falling on the gray people and the gray container modules, the gray identical buildings with boarded up windows and the tall gray wall that surrounded the sector where the division was located. The commander continued to spit out words before the line of recruits.

"This place is your home now! It is your homeland until the end of your days! You can never get out of here alive, but it is better here than in the holes where you were hiding before! The division will provide you with all you need: a roof, a home, clothing and service! You will give your all to the division! You are the new blood of our great brotherhood, which is headed by Enlightened Landmaster Vasilevs! From this day, the preparation for your service in the division begins!"

Fritz went red and lost his voice by the end. With a wave of his hand, he left them, walking towards the HQ container module that had the black flag of the division streaming in the wind above it. The platoon commanders led the new recruits to their barracks according to the numbering of the units. Rick's platoon was assigned to barrack no. 7. When they were inside they were all ordered to sit on the floor. The platoon commander was a man of uncertain age with narrow eyes and high cheekbones.

"My name is Lee," he declared. "Over the next month, I will be your master and I will command you however I want. If I so desire, I will stick any of you degenerates like a pig, and no one will do anything to me for it."

He nodded, once he was sure that everyone listened attentively and continued.

"Excellent. Now, I will tell you the primary rule of the brotherhood: one is nothing and the brotherhood is everything! None of you are worth as much as my little finger. I will soon prove this to you. But if you survive and become part of the division, then you will feel its whole strength and power. You will never be the same again. Is that clear?"

The recruits carefully exchanged glances, hesitant to answer.

"I thought I asked, is that clear?" Lee

shouted, with spittle flying out of his mouth.

"Yes!"

"Of course!"

"Clear!" came many voices from all sides.

"I can't hear you!" Lee shouted again, so loudly that the veins stood out on his neck and forehead. "When you answer your commander, you must shout, "yes sir!" All together now!"

"Yes sir!" the platoon answered.

"Whoresons!" Lee spat angrily. "Remember — I am not your nanny and I will not wipe your shit after you. Eat it yourselves. We have a simple regime. Wake up when ordered, marching and physical drills, hygiene, work, military exercises, special missions and lights out. I will soon mold you into real soldiers. Only those that can take the regime will survive until they join the ranks of the division. Fight or die. I don't care. Any questions?"

"No!" the platoon chorused in reply.

Lee fiercely moved his jaw and left the barracks. His assistant corporals made the platoon come out onto the street and started to discipline them, teach the recruits how to march in line and shout the correct replies to their orders. By the end of the day Rick could not feel his feet. He was tired. His body ached and his breathing was hoarse, the same as many of those who had to shout their replies to the questions of the platoon commanders. But that was nothing compared to those who fell down when they had no more strength left. The corporals dragged them up and kicked them back into line. But one still fell down again, and then the corporals did not touch them. Platoon Commander Lee drew his knife and approached the man lying on the ground and the recruit suddenly dashed back among the others before Lee even had the chance to open his mouth. He just chuckled at his retreating back, baring his strong and even teeth.

After their dinner in the evening, the platoon lay in their bunks in their barracks, talking halfheartedly among themselves. An orderly stood on duty at the entrance, his eyes bulging with excitement. He was very lucky — he did not have to take part in the training, but he understood what awaited him on the next day.

"I'm going to die soon," a thin man on the bunk near Rick complained.

"I'll do it earlier," his neighbor below answered. "One more day and that'll be the end of me."

"Stop whining," he heard from somewhere in the depths of the barracks. Rick recognized the voice; the man's name was Marek, as far as Rick could remember. "It's always hard at first. We will get used to it, in time."

"How do you know?" the thin recruit

224

exclaimed.

"I just know and that's all."

"He's lying," a voice sounded from another corner.

"I'd break your face in," someone promised from the depths of the barracks, "but I'm exhausted."

The duty officer walked into the barracks with a list and shouted, "Gareth, to the exit!"

The man in the bunk beneath Rick groaned as he got down onto the floor and ambled after the duty officer.

"Why are they doing this just before nightfall?" someone muttered nearby.

An excited whisper ran through the barracks.

Gareth returned ten minutes later. He did not look anything out of the ordinary, apart from perhaps his ears which looked so red that it seemed they were used to drag him around the yard. The duty officer called out another name and another recruit headed towards the exit.

"What did they want from you?" everyone asked Gareth, but he just waved them away.

"They are going to torture us," the grim neighbor in the corner bank stated and chuckled.

No one found his joke funny. An oppressive silence suddenly hung over the barracks. When it came to Rick's turn, everyone's eyes followed him to the exit. The duty officer took him to the container module in which the platoon commander was located.

Lee was sitting behind a desk and using the point of his knife to clean out the dirt under his nails.

"Sit down," he ordered, without looking at Rick.

Rick sat down on a stool.

"Get up."

Rick got up. Lee smirked and glanced at him with disgust.

"They say they caught you with some sort of woman. Is that right?"

Rick nodded.

"Are you dumb or something?" Lee turned the point of his blade towards Rick. "Don't make me angry."

Rick would have shown him what anger was, but he decided that his time would come yet.

"The woman's name was Olivia. We walked through the city together for a while."

"Walked? They say you fell down from the sky. Lucio saw it."

"Not from the sky, we slid down a slope from the wall," Rick explained.

"What were you doing there?"

"Running away from a huge spider with

Olivia. We barely survived."

"What sort of spider?"

Rick told him everything exactly how it was. Lee frowned with distrust.

"That means you are fortunate guy," he concluded finally.

"We were just lucky."

"Really?" Lee moved the knife to the edge of the desk and spread his hands, sitting back in his chair. "Take the blade."

Without hesitation, Rick stretched out his hand towards the weapon, when Lee added, "But know that if you take it, I will kill you."

Rick froze, deep in though.

"What're you waiting for?" Lee smiled condescendingly. "Take the knife."

Rick stared him straight in the eye and his hand darted out a moment later. Lee turned out to be quicker, grabbing the knife first and elbowing Rick in the chest.

It was painful. Very painful. He barreled into the wall with his back and grimaced, rubbing his aching ribs.

"Get out," Lee ordered him in a calm and everyday tone of voice, as he slid the knife into its sheath.

Rick stood up straight, but he was in no hurry to get out. Lee glanced at him with annoyance.

"May I ask a question, Commander Lee?"

"Hmm," Lee's expression changed, and there was a glimmer of curiosity in his eyes. "Give it a try."

"What happened to the woman?"

Lee grinned.

"The same that will happen to you soon, flyboy."

Rick nodded and enquired whether he could go now.

"Wait." Lee took out the medallion key that Olivia had given to Rick from a drawer in his desk. "Where did you get this?"

"It's my personal medallion."

"You're lying, you scrawny whoreson."

"Not at all."

"Want me to make you bleed?" The knife appeared in Lee's hand again.

"It's your right, commander," Rick replied calmly.

"Fine." Lee put the medallion away into the desk. "Get out of here."

Rick came back to the barracks and could not get to sleep for a long time, staring at the ceiling. He was thinking about Olivia.

K

"THIS PLACE IS CALLED the Pit!" Lee announced loudly.

The recruits were lined up on the edge of a huge hole in the middle of a concrete square. There were boxes with open lids lying on the bottom, with clothing, boxes of dry rations, flasks which were probably filled with water or something stronger and various pieces of military equipment and even weapons. Rick saw a pair of familiar looking blaster stocks sticking out among the gear. There were four boxes altogether.

Lee walked along the opposite side and pontificated, "Every recruit must pass the selection by Pit. I went through it too and today it is your turn. The rules are simple — everyone takes what they can. The one who is left with nothing, leaves the contest. You have exactly an hour for this test. Are the rules clear?"

"Sir, yes, sir!" the recruits shouted, having trained their throats for the past week.

Many had learned a hard lesson — the platoon commander does not forgive those that keep quiet and some of those that avoided answering the commander's question still had bruises and welts which were yet to heal.

"Excellent." Lee slowed down and asked with interest, "Perhaps someone has some complaints about their health? Is anyone tired?"

The platoon kept their silence. Everyone knew what would follow a complaint. Then Lee pulled back on his sleeve, looked at his watch and shouted, "Forward!"

Everyone dashed into the hole. Two immediately tripped up, or maybe they were helped and a jumbled up pile of bodies suddenly appeared at the edge. Rick jumped over the bodies after those that had rushed to the fore and found himself near the boxes. However, he did not have time to grab anything before a fight broke out. He managed to knock one of his opponents down with a punch to the jaw and another fell down by himself — someone had struck him on the back of his head from behind. Rick threw himself towards the boxes again, almost running into the arms of a stocky red haired man, dodged and reached another box.

"Stop, you bastard!" the stocky man exclaimed.

It was too late. Rick grabbed the first thing his hand brushed past in the box and bounded off to the side, avoiding the approaching runners. A melee broke out by the boxes again — the strongest were already dividing up their booty on the side while the weak clambered over each

230

other, trying to find at least something to grab hold of. There was no mercy for anyone and the women had to fight as hard as the men.

Suddenly, they heard the call of a bugle. Everyone stopped and looked up.

"Excellent!" Lee shouted and clapped his hands. "And now, the gear has all been taken and we have an unlucky loser!"

A thin young man darted around among the recruits, the one who had complained about life in the barracks after the first day of exercises. Rick remembered him well. The young man was dashing from box to box, trying to find something, but they were empty.

"The loser is eliminated!" Lee declared. "Recruit, to me!"

"Give me another chance!" the unfortunate shouted.

"All right," Lee nodded. "Come here, soldier! You have five seconds for this task. The time has started!"

The recruit froze with indecision, but in a moment he was clambering upwards, tearing the skin of his hands. Lee watched him with narrowed eyes, his mouth twisted in as smirk.

When the man appeared at the top, armed soldiers came to stand by Lee's sides.

"I'm begging you!" the poor man cried, stretching out his hands. "Please don't!"

"Only one mistake is allowed here!" Lee cut him off coldly. "But I gave you a chance. You need to meet the time standards!"

He waved his hand.

The blasters crackled dryly and the man fell onto the concrete, his chest burned through with the charges. The platoon stood there, looking up and holding their breaths. Rick felt his throat go dry. He lowered his head and saw that he was gripping the handle of a knife that was hidden in a plastic sheath. Rick bared the blade and the steel glinted in the light and then misted up from the breath that reached it from his mouth.

"But that isn't all!" Lee declared from above. "There are thirty of you in the platoon now. There is one less now. The division requires for only twenty of the best to remain. The selection happens in the Pit."

"What does that mean?" Gareth shouted.

"Thirty went it and twenty will get out, you idiot," the grim-faced recruit muttered quietly.

Yet Lee had heard him.

"Well spotted, soldier!" the commander chuckled. "Whoever starts climbing out without my order will end the same way as that loser." He spat on the back of the murdered man. "Let the selection begin!"

Turning on his heels, he disappeared from

sight. The armed soldiers stayed on the edge of the hole. Rick pressed his back into the rough and cold wall and looked over the remaining recruits.

"All right," Gareth suddenly said and adjusted his grip on the blaster that he had got out of one of the boxes. "Playtime is over."

It looked like he knew how to use weapons well as he was holding it correctly. Rick noticed how Gareth's fingers automatically released the safety catch and immediately moved the charge power switch to maximum output.

"What are you talking about?" the grim recruit asked.

"You know it yourself," Gareth replied confidently.

"Hey, you," a blonde girl called out to them. "Maybe we can think of some way to get out of the situation?"

"You heard everything loud and clear," Gareth cut her off. "The selection has begun."

"This is madness," said a dark-skinned man, stepping forward. "We are humans, we aren't possessed!"

"This is the selection," the large red-haired man stepped forward to meet him, holding a compact shovel which was very well sharpened and nodded at Gareth.

Gareth returned his greeting and declared,

"You will be the first. I need another eighteen people."

"How come you're choosing people?" the grim recruit asked him.

"Want to argue about my rights? Go for it," Gareth aimed the weapon at him with a smile.

They exchanged piercing stares for a while, and then the grim recruit surrendered and raised his hands, "All right. Let's do it your way, you're in charge now."

"Excellent, go and stand by his side. And you," Gareth pointed at the girl. "And you."

He motioned at the black man with his weapon.

The girl said nothing as she joined them, but the black man was still hesitant,

"Hey!" they heard from the other end of the pit, as a bald man with a deep and crooked scar on his face came towards the boxes. "Who do you think you are?"

He had the same kind of blaster in his hands as Gareth. But Rick noted that the weapon's safety was on and that the charge indicator was set to minimum.

Gareth silently pulled the trigger, and there was a crackle, some surprised shouts and a dead body on the ground.

"She is not right for me," Gareth noted and looked over everyone else with a tense appraising gaze. "You — come here. You too. And you..."

He selected those who held something resembling a weapon in his hands. Rick hid hiss knife behind his back, attaching the sheath to his belt. When the new group had been joined by around a dozen people, there was a popping noise similar to the shot of a blaster, just not as powerful.

A charge fell past Gareth and hit someone nearby. Gareth turned abruptly and shot back. A tall woman by the boxes shuddered and grasped her own neck, dropping a short-barreled compact blaster.

An instant later, went fell down on her knees, but did not manage to stay up and collapsed on the ground. The grim recruit by Gareth's side fell, holding his stomach.

As if nothing had happened, Gareth pointed at the man who was standing by the woman who was shot and who had backed away in surprise, "You. Come here."

When Gareth's unit reached eighteen strong including him, two of the remaining women started to shout, interrupting each other.

"Choose me!"

"No, me!"

One of them had a flask in her hand and the other was holding a torch. Gareth cast his mocking glance at each one in turn and then said, "You are both so lovely that I don't know who to choose. Decide among yourselves."

It took the women a few seconds to digest what they had heard and then they attacked each other, screaming ferociously. Gareth and the others watched the fight between the candidates for the place in the unit with interest. The woman with the flask immediately put it to use, smashing her opponent in the face and crushing her nose, but got shoved with the end of a torch in the stomach, which made her fold over and get hit with the thick part of the torch on the back of her head. She groaned and dropped the flask, falling to the ground where her opponent turned her onto her back and started to smash her repeatedly with top of the torch, turning her face into a bloody mess. Once she was satisfied, she wiped the blood from her broken nose and nonchalantly approached Gareth.

Impressed by what he had just seen, he announced, "You have earned your place among us." The amusement was gone from his eyes, which shone with excitement. "Stand with the others."

When the woman took her place among their ranks, Gareth looked over the remaining four recruits, including Rick.

"You all saw what happened. We have one more place, so decide who gets it for yourselves."

"You won't do that!" a broad faced man said and put a green box labeled "grenades" in front of himself. "Either you take me, or I will blow up everyone sky high!"

"You're not going to do that," Gareth disagreed calmly.

"Want a bet?" the man quickly opened the lid of the box and grabbed a grenade. He had no time to pull the pin as the remaining recruits jumped on him and started beating him with their fists.

A moment later those who were selected for Gareth's squad joined in. They kicked the blackmailer in the ribs until they broke as well as crushing his nose and dislocating his jaw. He was alive, even though he was barely breathing when Gareth ordered them to stop.

One of the attackers tried to go for Rick in his excitement, but immediately backed away as he had almost gutted himself on the knife that Rick held out.

"Don't come near me," Rick shook his head.

Both stood there tensely in their fighting stances.

"Leave him to me," a voice came from the side.

Rick glanced over and recognized the hook-nosed thug who had recently tried to steal a piece of concentrate from his pocket at night.

"His own mother won't recognize him when I'm done with him."

The thug got a better grip on the heavy monkey wrench he was holding, slapping it against his other palm.

The confused recruit that was between them stepped out of the way. This was enough for the thug to jump on him and crush his larynx with a single strike. With a short gurgle, the surprised recruit was dead before he fell.

"Just like that," the big man concluded, glaring at Rick with a bloodthirsty smile. "Except that I will kill you slowly."

As soon as he said that, he rushed forward. But Rick was ready for him — he sidestepped to let this huge and furious tank past him, so that the oaf would barrel into a hard wall.

He struck.

The empty ring of a wrench which was nearly lost.

A growl.

The big man turned around and howled, tried to move sideways as Rick sliced him with his knife on the inside of the crook of his arm.

"I thought you wanted it slow," Rick told him sarcastically.

Somewhere at the edge of his awareness Rick understood that it was only a little separating him from becoming no better than this thug, but he was also overcome by a thirst for revenge — he wanted to punish this oafish murderer, punish Gareth and punish all those that bring people to this state and turn them into animals!

There was a pop and the head of the thug exploded like a pierced pustule. By reflex, Rick drew back as the pieces of skull and brain flew into his face and spun around so he could see the shooter better. He wiped the filth from his face.

"I chose you," Gareth declared.

"Why?"

"You are a strong fighter but you could have been injured."

Rick was looking at Gareth, thinking whether to jump on him and kill him now, or resolve everything later. If he thought about it logically, Gareth was right, as he could have been harmed if he did not kill the big man but only wounded his arm.

"You did not surrender," Gareth continued, "you have an iron will. And..."

"The selection is over!" they heard from above.

Everyone looked up. Lee stood on the edge of the pit. The platoon commander was not alone — Commander Fritz was by his side.

"That's it for today, you can go and rest.

And you," Lee pointed at Rick, "will come and see me this evening."

"Yes, sir!" Rick shouted and walked through the ranks, deliberately shoving Gareth with his shoulder so that he almost fell and started to climb the steep wall of the pit.

Once he was up above, it started to snow heavily. Lee and Fritz were already on their way, accompanied by armed soldiers and their figures receded into the white fog...

L

"YOU HAD AN INTERESTING selection today." Lee was not even looking at Rick, who was standing to attention as he sat at his desk and cleaned the dirt from fingernails using the end of his combat knife. "Everything is usually decided in the first few minutes. But it all got drawn out with you. Why did you hide the knife? You could have immediately shown it to Gareth, I'm sure you would have been one of the first people he chose."

"I wanted to test you, commander." Rick stared straight ahead, because Lee stopped digging into his nails and looked up at him in astonishment.

"You should not lie to me. I can smell lies a

mile off, like the stench of a corpse." Lee got up and walked around the table, standing in front of Rick. "I know what you're thinking. Of course, killing those like you in stupid arguments is disgusting. But there's no other way in our line of work, believe me. There's no place for the weak here. It's better that they die than the strong die because of them when the time will come to fight for the division. Cowards always run from the battlefield. But you're no coward."

Lee looked like he was about to sit down, but he spun around and shouted "Am I right?" in Rick's face.

"Yes, Commander Lee!"

The platoon commander nodded, sat back behind the table and continued, "We sort the wheat from the chaff. We select those who truly are the best and the most able to survive in difficult conditions. That's the only way to protect society from internal and external threats. Now, answer me. Why did you hide the knife when Gareth began the selection?"

"I did not want to show my advantages."

"That's cleaver for those who are watching, but not for you in that situation."

Rick blindly stared straight ahead.

"Commander Fritz said the same thing, as well as some of the highest ranking officers. And these people don't make mistakes. Do you agree?”

“What about?” Rick moved his eyes to look at Lee.

The platoon commander raised an eyebrow and chuckled.

“Have you even worked out where you are, son?”

Rick did not answer.

“This is the Division!” Lee stood up ramrod straight. “The first fully operational military organization, which was created after the Great Departure out of wild bands of scavengers who hid in the depths of the landscape. This is a new world! Do you understand? Our new world, our homeland, created through blood, sweat and tears, the hope of humanity!”

“Then why are they making people fight like animals in the pit?” Rick could not resist bursting out. “Anything for the cause.”

Lee looked at him for a while with his jaw hanging open, then gathered himself together and continued, in a surprisingly calm tone of voice.

“I will give you some leeway for being young and stupid. If an experienced soldier had said something like this, then he would be hanged inside a quarter of an hour. But that's not what we're talking about now. The Division is preparing for an important expedition to the sector of the inner ring by the tower. We are collecting resources for the performance of this important task — getting inside the core of the world. We could not get inside the inner ring for many years. No one knows what happens there. The gates were open many years ago, even before the Great Departure and the citizens of this city could freely go in any direction they wished. But when the rabid ones arrived, everything changed. Our ancestors almost disappeared off the face of the earth. The remainder of those who miraculously kept their sanity spent an age hiding in the twists and turns of the quarters until it was time for us to unite. Do you understand why you're needed now?"

"Yes, because I came from the outer limits. I managed to survive there and I am sure I will be useful here."

Lee nodded approvingly.

"But doesn't the highway lead to the tower?" Rick asked. "Wouldn't it be easier to cleanse it with fire and achieve your goals?"

"Do you think we haven't tried? The spheres are unkillable! There is no salvation from them. Haven't you seen them in action?"

"I ran away from them in the Cluster of the fords," Rick admitted.

"Ran away? But..." Lee suddenly took a notepad out of his desk and quickly wrote something in it. "You ran away, so they did not touch you and you got away without consequences?" he clarified.

"That's exactly how it was, commander. What's the matter?"

"You're lucky," Lee nodded. "Usually, when a sphere catches a man, they burn up like gunpowder from a spark from the smallest touch."

He snapped his fingers, deep in thought and made another note, shook his head and continued, "They say that the scientific corps of the Division has managed to solve the secret of the lock on the gates and will be able to unlock them. We are going to go through the quarters avoiding the highway zone. The tower is just a step away there." His eyes glinted strangely. "Do you understand what that mean?"

"Not exactly, commander Lee."

"The tower is the key to the past. The answers to every question are there. We can reanimate the ancient machines and find a cure for rabies. And that is only a small part of the power we will have." Lee waved his hand in an uncertain direction. "As you said, you survived in the outer limits. That's the sort of people we need. This is why I will close my eyes to your lapses in discipline. Understood?"

"Yes, commander!"

Lee carefully looked into Rick's face and then asked, "Why did you suddenly run away from the outer circle?"

"There was a shift."

Lee frowned, not understanding.

"The movement of city segments," Rick started to explain. "The city is divided by walls into rings, which are divided into clusters. The rings sometimes turn and the landscape inside the clusters changes. One of the segments goes underground and another rises above at certain intervals, taking up the space that opens up. These events follow a program that was assigned to the mechanisms of the city. But the program had an error and the cluster in which I was when the shift took place got flooded. I managed to escape together with Olivia, the female ford. We left through the collector which filled up with water later too. We barely survived. We found ourselves by the territory of the Division and walked until we came across the nest of a gigantic spider.

"Are you saying that you went through the termite nests?" Lee asked in amazement. "But that's a dead zone."

"Yes, sir." Rick decided to keep the fact that they had used the medallion key and rose to the surface in an elevator to himself.

"And then you climbed the wall and slid

down it along the channel."

"That's exactly what happened, commander."

"You're lying again."

"If you doubt me, put me into the pit with another platoon," Rick pronounced dispassionately.

Lee hummed and bent down over his notepad again, writing something down. Once he finished, he said, "You should understand that everything you are telling me, it's all too... too unusual. Even though we came across people from the outer limits in the past, such things never happened before. For someone to get over the barrier and the space between the outer and middle rings..." He shook his head. "There are only wild and predatory beasts out there and no normal person can survive. We though that there were no more people beyond the walls of the rings. And now you have appeared..."

The way he looked at Rick changed and his eyes lost their military demeanor. It was only now that Rick noticed that Lee's voice was also different and that it had lost its edge of steel. What was that all about?

"That's exactly how it is, commander," Rick replied automatically.

Lee acted as if he never heard him, as he thought about something and then snapped out of it.

"All right, say we believe you. Tell me, how did you get onto the highway from the outer ring?"

"I just went there."

"Aren't the passages between them closed?"

Rick felt that he was missing some important detail, but could not understand what it was.

"I opened them," he replied.

"How?"

"The same as any other door. Is there something difficult about that?"

Lee frowned and his eyes and expression became intimidating again. He stepped towards the exit of the residential module, commanding, "Follow me, soldier."

Rick obeyed. They walked onto the concrete square in front of the camp and Lee stopped.

"Look at this," he pointed to the concrete beneath his feet.

Rick lowered his gaze and noticed a symbol that had been pressed into the concrete — a square which was diagonally split into three equal triangles. There was a small circle where the lines crossed at the center, as if it was absorbing the crossed lines into itself.

"Open this passage," Lee ordered.

Rick crouched and touched the rough

surface. Was this square depression really a hatch? He touched the hollows and then pressed the point where the lines crossed with his palm but nothing happened."

"It's not working," he announced, glancing at Lee.

"What if you have a think about it?"

"About what exactly?"

"You're cleverer than you look." Lee folded his hands behind his back. "But you don't know how to lie."

Rick stayed silent, as Lee continued, "I am not trying to terrorize you, I just want to know, will you be able to open this passage or not?"

Rick let out a deep breath and bent over the symbol again, carefully examining the little hollows in the concrete. There were no locking mechanisms on the surface, so there was no doubt that the passage was opened using a key. Rick asked Lee for a knife and cleaned the dirt out of the special slot where the key card had to be inserted. Then he looked around — there was a transformer box near the concrete square, which was more proof that he was right.

"No," he said at last. "There is no way to open it without a key and without energy."

Lee nodded in satisfaction and ordered him to go to the barracks.

"Attention!" the duty officer shouted as

soon as the commander crossed the threshold.

"Form up," Lee commanded.

"Platoon! Line up in the central passage!"

The recruits swore under their breaths as they noisily rolled off their bunks and rushed towards the exit. A minute later, they arranged themselves in a ragged line, pushing each other in their underwear.

"Platoon!" Lee paused for effect. "I just came to wish you good night."

There was a deafening silence in the barracks.

"I also wanted to report to you that I have promoted Recruit Rick to be my deputy."

Lee gave Rick a friendly slap on the shoulder.

"Commander, are you serious?" Rick burst out.

"Of course. Did you all hear? Rick is my deputy from this very moment. That means that his orders must be obeyed without question, just like mine."

"Commander Lee," Rick had no intention of commanding anyone. "I refuse this appointment."

"It's an order," Lee flashed a crooked smile. "And what do we say about orders, platoon?"

"Orders are not discussed, commander Lee!" two dozen throats chorused in reply.

"At ease!"

Once the door closed behind the commander Rick went to his bunk quietly. He felt the tense eyes of others on his back but he did not turn around because he did not want to talk to anyone.

But people were not going back to their bunks and they were discussing him.

Rick could not bear it and shouted, "Orderly, issue the lights out command! And if anyone is not in their bunk in the space of a minute, they will be off to clean the latrines all night. All clear, platoon?"

An instant later, a chorus of voices answered reluctantly, "Yes, Deputy Commander Rick.

m

THE PLATOON ADVANCED along the empty streets of the dead city. The sun was at its zenith, a washed out, cold blotch shining through the cloud cover as rare snowflakes circled between the buildings, lay on the walls and the cracked concrete and immediately melted.

The camp had been struck at the break of dawn in the early morning. By midday, the joint Division expeditionary group had passed around a dozen quarters on their way to the citadel.

There were almost no incidents, but the tension of the previous day still kept its hold over them — a platoon near them had gone too far to the east of their planned route, coming right up to the main highway. The lookouts had lost visual contact with this squad, and when they realized. Rick was trying to work out, where could twenty well prepared soldiers have disappeared? It was as if they had vanished into thin air. The scouts that had been sent to find them came back empty-handed, apart from a spoon with the sigil of the unit commander that they found at the nearest crossroads. Discussion of the missing unit was forbidden under pain of execution by firing squad but Rick could see that many of the soldiers wanted to talk about it written on their faces. It was only fear that made them keep their mouths shut and push onwards. The oppressive silence and the wind howling between the blocks kept up pressure on their minds, making their hearing and eyesight especially acute. Their eyes constantly teared up from the stress and the cold and any sound coming from around them seemed to be alien and threatening. Just to add to it, commander Lee had gone back to the center of the column for an officer's meeting, leaving Rick in command.

Another unusual even was the reason that the officers were called together. Around an hour ago, one of the soldiers in the next platoon became rabid. Rick did not see how the fit began and when he came to the location with the others, the afflicted man was running around in a circle of his fellow soldiers and desperate howled with pain as he tore his own hair out. At first, they tried to speak to him and even called a medic, but the unfortunate continued screaming. His eyes soon lost their lively gloss and glazed over, as he collapsed on the ground and started to convulse and thrash around. He eventually lay still, gathering his legs to his stomach in a fetal position.

Sharp-tongued Gareth immediately declared that he was "done". The platoon sergeant, who was a large, mustachioed man tried to touch the soldier on the ground. Rick and some of the other soldiers crowding around shouted at him, but it was too late — the madman jumped up and sunk his teeth into the sergeant's neck so quickly that everyone just froze in place as they watched what was going on. When blood sprayed out in a stream from the neck of the sergeant and he started to scream, Commander Lee raised his blaster and put a charge in each of them. But that did not stop the scene, as the madman put down the dead sergeant as if he did not have a hole burnt by the blaster through his chest and turned around slowly, looking over the soldiers with his dead eyes. Rick felt that the gaze stopped on him for a second, which caused an ice cold drop of terror to run down his spine, so furious were those eyes.

The madman laughed and then this human laughter changed to a bark as there was no longer a person but some other creature in human form standing before them. However, it did change quickly — it lowered itself to the ground like an animal and musculature grew under its clothing. The creature stopped barking and let out a piercing howl like a pack leader calling for help. A moment later, it jumped on Commander Lee.

The platoon commander was no slouch as he immediately discharged his blaster into the creature. A charred corpse fell beneath Lee's feet.

An hour passed but Rick still felt the vile smell of burning skin and no washing with water or attempts to breathe through a cloth could help dull the strength of these sensations. He had to walk on and bear it in silence.

The citadel had grown larger before them as time passed, which calmed him down as it meant that their goal was closer than before. Rick walked without looking back at the platoon. Every soldier was given a charged shocker which would be enough for a pair of shots but the experienced soldiers and commanders still carried deadly blasters with them.

The column soon entered an enormous plaza. It was surprising, but Rick had never seen so much space that was free of buildings in the city as the plaza was the size of the fords' Cluster. They decided to make temporary camp there, consume some nutritional concentrate and plan the rest of their route.

Over the short time he had spent in the Division, Rick had learned that everything was done according to a strict timetable — they even had to go to the toilet at a particular time. That was why he had postponed his escape until better days. Even though this was an appropriate time as it was a military expedition with less attention from the commanders, it was actually traveling as part of an armed group that lessened his desire to escape. The small army was still successfully moving towards the place where Rick wanted to get to so much.

At first, he was very surprised that the commanders had not taken any food supplies with them, but then he discovered that the concentrate was produced by synthesizers which were located in semicircular buildings at the end of each quarter. The most interesting thing was that the synthesizers, which were twin cylinders as high as two men, still worked. The taste of the concentrate was similar to the briquettes that

Rick had already eaten his full of in his native Thermopolis. What amazed him though, was the fact that many of the experienced soldiers never even thought about the source of the food they consumed as it was a natural and familiar process for them.

Rick kept waiting for them to come across a synthesizer that did not work. When it finally happened, it turned out that the Division had mechanical engineers capable of starting up a broken concentrate producing machine. This was an entirely commonplace event for many of the soldiers.

A messenger arrived with an order from Commander Lee before they sat down to eat — they had to reconnoiter the local area. Rick received three portions of concentrate ahead of the queue and took Gareth and Diana with him. They climbed to the top of the nearest three story building, where they could see the gigantic symbol of the sector on the surface of the plaza — a circle with crossed lines in the middle. Rick did not know what the symbol meant and he did not want to engage in guesswork. As ordered, they looked around the surrounding area, but did not discover any dangers or anything that aroused suspicion, so he sat down on the edge of the roof to chew the concentrate they had crumbled into a pot.

"Deputy Commander Rick," Gareth called out behind his back.

Rick did not react as he continued to consume the gray mass, watching the citadel which was mostly hidden by the clouds.

"Is it true that people eat each other beyond the outer limits?" Gareth chuckled loudly.

Diana was about to burst out laughing, but immediately went quiet, realizing that Gareth had decided to mock someone who was in command of them now.

Rick did not reply.

"It looks like they do," Gareth continued. "No, I don't judge them. Life is probably hard out there. The poor wretches have to fight for survival. I also heard that there are territories where there are people with two heads or with three arms. Is that true?"

"I never met any," Rick replied.

"I wonder, what is it that is beyond the outer limits of the city..." Gareth continued. "There are probably truly terrible beasts out there. They..."

"Just shut up already!" Diana hissed.

For a while, Rick heard their spoons scrape against the travel pots as they squashed the concentrate and the way Gareth chewed loudly as he put away the soft and tasteless mass.

"I never liked this shit," Gareth suddenly

told them. "They prefer rats in our quarters. The meat is a bit tough, but it is real. You can also catch larvae in the summer and..."

"By the sky gods!" Diana moved over to Rick. "Can I sit down here please?"

"Of course. Just hurry up..." He got up and nodded at the approaching sergeant Lucio. "They are about to ask us to leave."

He was right. Lucio ordered them to come down and be quick about it.

When the three of them were down on the plaza, the sergeant made an announcement.

"All right then. The task set to your platoon is not to let anyone out of that block," he waved at a tall building at the beginning of the neighboring quarter. "If they manage to get through, hit them with the shockers at maximum power. Let none of the lowlifes get away."

"It won't work," Rick disagreed and took his shocker out of the holster. "This is a toy, not a weapon against the rabid."

"Did I say a single word about the rabid?" Lucio frowned angrily and Rick understood that he was talking about something else. "The lowlifes are local scum that have gone wild here without us, but haven't lost their minds yet, so they can help us find out how to get inside the tower and if our senior commanders so desire, the most loyal of them will get the right to join

257

the Division."

Rick nodded. He liked this plan less and less — someone obviously wanted to test the recruits.

"Commander Fritz's recon troops are working in that building right now, so look out and be careful when you surround it. Only shoot when you are certain! That's all." Lucio slapped Rick on the shoulder. "If anything, we'll cover you."

The sergeant demonstratively brayed with laughter.

Once Lucio left, Rick gathered the platoon around him and explained their task.

"Surround the building," he ordered.

The soldiers slowly moved to take their positions.

"Your troops are slow," Lucio shouted from afar as he watched, surrounded by his subordinates. "They'd be jumping like fried fleas if it was up to me."

Rick made no reply as he was looking for Lee among the people in the Plaza but he had chosen exactly the wrong time to have disappeared somewhere.

Around a quarter of an hour later, Rick's platoon had occupied their assigned positioned. Rick checked on every soldier. This was not because he strove to do his duty; he just did not want someone to suffer because of making mistakes. While he traveled he learned an important lesson — the locals often fight to the death for their territory. He did not know what to expect of the feral ones that had established themselves in the high-rise.

The silence was pregnant. Rick was looking at the front of the buildings, with its faded glyphs above the wide doors of the entrance. A row of empty windows started at around the height of three men from the ground, with a white rag hanging out of one of them. It fluttered in the wind, as if it was the banner of a division, carried by a standard bearer that accompanied high-ranking officers.

Rick carefully looked over his soldiers, who stood there alert and ready to use their shockers. Oddly enough, many of them liked being in the Division. Rick understood that there were certain positives in the army way of life — they were people who were always full and in good physical shape who were obliged to look after themselves and their clothes and equipment, banded together in grounds ready to stand up for each other, they had something to do and the main thing was that they had the chance for a long and well provisioned life. However, there are other sides to every picture, as old Kyoto said sometimes. The Division was gathered by force, their personalities were broken and those who did not obey were exterminated.

"Deputy Commander Rick," blond Marek called over in a whisper, as he silently appeared behind his back. "Gareth is planning something against you, but nothing too bad."

Rick turned his head slightly. It seemed that he had his own informers now. Everyone does what they want with their life.

"It's the grief that's inside him," Marek continued quietly. "They say that he had an older brother that was torn apart by the rabid." Marek paused. "There are more and more of them, those filthy beasts. You never know who'll be next. Maybe me. Or maybe Diana."

Rick had long noticed that Marek liked her.

"So that's why Gareth wanted to be a commander, so he could get a blaster and kill the rabid ones, but Lee suddenly made you his deputy."

Time passed. They stood there, maintaining the cordon and observing the windows and the entrances to the high-rise but nothing was happening. Rick looked back at the positions occupied by Lucio's people some way away — the experienced soldiers showed no emotion, while the new recruits were visibly nervous, with some of them chewing their nails, fidgeting and whispering to each other as they thought no one could hear them. Anyway, it did not matter. It was the uncertainty that was tired. It also started to snow, just to add to the misery.

Rick was about to shout at the ones who were chattering when they heard noise coming from the high-rise. A loud popping sound, followed by a staccato tapping noise and human cries, which then changed to rustling and scrabbling.

"Platoon!" Rick shouted. "Attention!"

Gareth grumbled something over to the right, but Rick could not hear him.

The window above the entrance suddenly exploded in a spray of shards and a glass rain fell upon the ground. A ragged wretch stuck his head out of the window, squealed loudly but then quickly went quiet and disappeared.

Right at that moment, two tall figures in gray jumpsuits came out of the high-rise. Two more were dragging another who was wounded.

"What's happening there?" Rick asked, stepping forward to meet them, but received no reply.

One more recon scout appeared in the doors, followed by seven of the wretches, one of which was a really young snub-nosed boy with a shaven head. The rest of the scouts followed out of the high-rise.

"That's it," Lucio said behind Rick's back as

he quietly approached. "The clean-up is complete. Lift the cordon."

Rick commanded the platoon to leave their positions and oversaw his subordinates lining themselves up in a column, but did not make a move himself. He stared at the open doors of the building — something called him there, something that others could not hear.

He put his hand on the handle of the shocker and quickly walked up to the doors, looking inside. A gloomy, quiet, foul-smelling hall — there was probably a place used as a toilet nearby. Rick wanted to leave it and come back to his subordinates, when someone jumped out from behind the nearest pillar, making him draw back. Rick almost fell, hitting his shoulder on the corner of the door, but managed to catch the stranger by the elbow momentarily, but they burst out of his grasp. It was a teenager, a girl dressed in rags, her long hair clumped and eyes full of pain and despair.

"Stop!"

She froze, noticing the soldiers in front of the building, looked back at Rick and then dashed directly away from the plaza towards the neighboring quarter.

Rick was about to run after her, but the girl was running as fast as she could and she turned into a small lane to disappear from sight. Rick stopped at the intersection as he did not want to go deeper into unfamiliar territory, but then swore at himself — what was happening to him? He had completely lost his mind, he was chasing children. He turned around to get away from there as soon as he could and nearly walked into Lucio.

"What're you waiting for?" the sergeant growled. "She's about to escape! After her!"

He was accompanied by two experienced scouts and Marek from the new recruits.

Lucio snapped his fingers.

"Help them," he ordered the scouts.

Rick sprinted forwards and heard the sound of running feet behind him. He remembered the place where the girl had disappeared and he was going there now. On the way, he pulled out his shocker and took the weapon off the safety. Once he reached his destination, he looked around — there was no one there, not a soul. Marek and the scouts caught up and stopped nearby. One of them crouched and pointed to some marks on the melting snow.

"Tracks. She ran over there."

"Let's go," another scout nodded in agreement.

The chain of tracks led to a turn to the neighboring street and ended on a small square between two squat structures made of gray plastic.

"Hear that?" the scout that noticed the track suddenly said.

He was pointing at the corner of the building on the right.

"Yes," the other scout nodded and raised his blaster. "Let's approach it from different sides."

Rick did not ask what it was that they heard and hurried forward, with Marek following him. After they ran around the building, they found themselves in another small square with a statue of a man with his hands upraised to the sky standing proud in the middle. The runaway was rummaging around under its pedestal with her back to them.

The scouts went to the sides while Rick went directly towards the girl.

She heard the sound of their steps and turned around. Once she realized who they were, she tried to dash one way and another and then she returned and put her back to the pedestal, eyeing Rick like a hunted animal as he stopped a pair of paces away from her.

Marek breathed loudly behind his back. It was only now that Rick realized what the girl was doing — she was trying to repair a doll and attach its arm which was torn off, but she saw the men and dropped the doll in her fright.

Rick picked up the toy, carefully attached its arm and gave it to the girl.

"Who are you? What is your name?" he asked her.

The girl was silent, looking at Rick with her deep eyes that looked like a pair of melting pieces of ice.

"Take it, I don't bite," Rick smiled.

The girl hesitated, trembling a little like a scared mouse.

"Come on," Rick stepped towards her, but the girl moved away. "Don't be afraid."

She quickly shook her head. Then Rick threw the doll under her feet and told her, "Come with me, I don't let anyone harm you."

When she bent down to pick up the toy, he tried to take her by the hand. But the girl cried out, scratching his hand and jumped away.

She crouched, gathering herself into a ball and started babbling something in an unknown language. The sounds mostly sounded like incoherent noises.

"There's no point," one of the scouts said suddenly. "Finish her."

"She could be useful," Rick turned to him.

"No," the scout cut him off. "I am sure Lucio would find it very funny if he heard that."

He raised his blaster, preparing to pull the

trigger.

"Wait!" Rick stepped towards the scout, putting himself in front of the girl. "I will do it myself."

Rick turned around, gripping the shocker in his hand. The girl went quiet, looking at them fearfully. Rick suddenly realized how loudly his heart beat in his chest. The child was not guilty of anything, this girl could not cause anyone any harm... He desperately looked for a way out of the situation, but to no avail.

"Deputy Platoon Commander Rick," Marek suddenly said. "Allow me."

Rick glanced at him with surprise. Marek was not looking at him — he was looking at his victim with a determined gaze.

"I'd advise you to hurry up," one of the scouts spoke again. "We are in a dangerous zone. Other lowlifes or creatures we don't know about could be hiding here too."

He spat in the direction of the girl, whose eyes suddenly blazed with anger as she stood up straight and launched the doll at his head. The scout did not dodge in time, so the doll struck him on the forehead.

"Oh, you little shit!" He added another pair of choice expressions and raised the blaster. "Recruits, out of the way! I'll sort her out with an interesting death."

"No!" Rick stood in the way, protecting the girl with his arms spread.

The scout was taken aback. His team-mate said, "Hey, youngster, maybe you shouldn't open your mouth so much. Get out of the way, or you might swallow a stray bullet!"

Rick gritted his teeth. He was furious, but he restrained himself and said, "I am the senior officer here. That means that you must obey me."

"Oh, really?" the scouts glanced at each other, grinning crookedly. "Perhaps you will assume command of the division?"

They both laughed. Rick kept standing there, breathing heavily and covering the girl. Finally, he could not take their mockery anymore and shouted, "Enough!"

"Shut up, you little shit and get out of the way," one of the scouts told him and then turned to Marek, "Get some sense into his head. We need to finish up here and leave."

"Yes, of course," Marek replied readily and stepped towards Rick.

Rick was about to put a charge into Marek's chest, but he suddenly drew his shocker turned around and pointed behind the backs of the scouts.

"Look out!"

The scouts turned around. Rick also involuntarily became alarmed, looking around for danger and discovered a scrawny teen standing by the stunted plastic building at the edge of the square. The scouts immediately pointed the barrels of their blasters at him.

"Hey, you, keep your hands where we can see them! Don't do anything stupid!" one of them told the stranger as he moved in an arc to see what was going on behind the building.

The other scout glanced at Marek and said, "Didn't I tell you what to do? Why're you standing around? Act!"

He nodded at the girl.

Marek raised his shocker. Rick understood that he would not be able to stop him but something entirely different to what he expected happened next. Marek pulled the trigger, discharging the shocker at the nearest scout and turning him into a pale blue candle for an instant.

When the scout who was already dead started to fall down to the concrete, the other one shot at Marek. He shuddered once and then again when the second charge hit him. And then the scout shone with the same pale blue light and fell down dead.

Rick did not look any further, as he threw away the empty shocker and caught Marek, carefully laying him on the ground.

"Why?" he asked incredulously.

"The soldiers took away my parents." It was hard for Marek to talk as the charges had ruined his shoulder and his chest. It was amazing that he was still alive. "They came... came to our home. They... they took all the men and I hid. They don't touch you if you.... you obey. But... father... he refused. They killed him immediately and when mother..." Marek coughed and blood started to seep out of his mouth. "I have no regrets. Go, while you... you have time."

He smiled weakly as his face went as white as snow. His eyes went still.

Rick nodded and closed Marek's glassy eyes. A shadow moved by his side. Rick turned his head. It was the scrawny teenager...

"Mother Darkness!" Rick whispered as he made out his face. "Black Ant."

His old acquaintance nodded.

"How did you end up here? How did you survive after the attack on your settlement?"

Black Ant smiled victoriously and shook his head, showing Rick that they really had to get out of there with his whole demeanor

Rick looked around. The girl was nowhere to be seen. They could hear voices coming from the street they used to come to the square with the gray buildings, one of which Rick knew very well.

"Here! They went here! Hurry up!" Lucio

loudly and clearly commanded.

Rick grabbed Black Ant by the arm and started to run. Then he stopped, returned to pick up a dead scout's blaster and glanced at Marek, mentally thanking him for all that he did and returned to the teenager.

When they started running again, they heard shouting and the pops of gunshots behind them.

"I see them!"

"Go!"

"Take them alive! Shoot at their legs!"

Black Ant took Rick into a building that had its doors wide open. They had turned right on time — carefully aimed blaster charges whizzed through the air behind them.

Black Ant led him through the dark corridors on that floor and then jumped out onto the street through a broken window and immediately went sideways and turned the corner. Rick could barely keep up with him, but they could still hear running feet and the voices of their pursuers as they were close behind.

Suddenly, the street ended, taking them into a dead end. There were only the smooth walls of extremely tall buildings around them. They had no time to return and hide in buildings and their pursuers were about to appear from behind the corner of the nearest structure.

Rick put the stock of his weapon against his shoulder and moved the power indicator to the maximum setting — he was sure to kill several of them and it would be great if Lucio was among their number.

But it never got to that point as the boy did something that caused a creaking and jingling sound behind his back and forcefully pulled Rick by the sleeve.

"What..." Rick did not finish as he suddenly found himself staring into the opening of a smooth walled well.

Black Ant smiled with satisfaction, showed Rick a medallion key which he used to open a secret hatch in the floor and then put his hands to his sides and jumped down the well.

Rick did not wait around as he hung the blaster over his chest, held it tight and followed the boy.

As soon as he fell into the darkness he heard a whooshing sound above his head, as the charge from the blaster of one of their pursuers hit the wall of the dead end with a bang, showering sparks into the well.

The shaft of the well bent smoothly. Rick was sliding down on his side and slowed down somewhat. Suddenly he was surrounded by light — they were swept out into an open space somewhere above the transportation highway.

Far away they saw figures in gray jumpsuits on an open balcony walkway.

"What..." Rick did not finish, as the opening of a well with smooth walls appeared before his eyes.

Black Ant showed Rick the medallion key that he had used to open the secret hatch in the floor with a satisfied smile, put his hands along his sides and jumped into the well.

Rick did not think twice and hung his blaster on his chest, hugging it tight and followed the boy.

As soon as he fell into the darkness, there was a whizzing sound about his head. A blaster charge from one of his pursuers hit the wall of the dead end and emitted a loud bang, showering the well with sparks.

The well shaft bent gently. Rick slid down it on his side, as his speed decreased and he was brought into the light. They were taken to an outside space with a view over the transportation highway. They saw figures in black jumpsuits far off on the open balcony walkway.

Those were not their pursuers, but they were definitely soldiers, who might have been lookout or another unit searching for them in a different area. They saw the escapees so they would soon report it to their commanders.

Darkness surrounded Rick again as he slid

went back into the open mouth of the tunnel on his back. The tunnel almost became horizontal, so he climbed out onto a small concrete platform, where he saw Black Ant in the gloom, digging around inside a control panel on the wall.

He was getting used to running away by sliding down channels. Rick went on one knee and raised his blaster, but he could not see his pursuers. It seemed that Lucio did not want to risk a journey into the unknown, however great was his anger and his desire to have revenge for his murdered comrades.

There was a lout creak, so Rick glanced over his shoulder. The boy waved at him to follow him through an open circular door.

"Yes, you're right, we should not stay here."

However, he did stop to listen for a second. Some sort of barely perceptible vibrations that he noticed at the last moment made him take pause, and when Black Ant grabbed him by the arm to pull him along, gesticulation wildly Rick understood that they were being threatened by another very serious danger. The round door led them to the highway, and they set off at a run.

Black Ant did not look back anymore and ran as fast as he could, followed by Rick who could hear a rumble and feel a growing vibration in the floor. There was no mistake; they were being followed by a roller, possibly more than one.

The boy soon started to run out of breath. He tripped, so Rick caught him and dragged him along, looking for some sort of side street or passage where they could hide like rats to escape their pursuers. However, the highway went on, stretching out as it rose at an incline above the quarters of the city, with the roofs of buildings and aerial masts sprawled out on both sides. They could have climbed onto the barrier at the side of the highway, but where would they go next? The height was so great that they would fall to their deaths and trusting fate in the same way as they did with Olivia when they were escaping the spider was definitely a bad idea. The chances of there being an open body of water below them were slim.

The rhythmic vibration suddenly changed to a weak humming noise. Rick let go of the boy's hand, checked the blaster as he ran and took a look over his shoulder. Three silvery spheres were following them. That was too many — he could not stop three at the same time.

Black Ant wheezed loudly and fell, almost smashing his face into the rough surface of the highway. Rick stopped, quickly took aim at the first of the approaching rollers, but did not pull the trigger. Suddenly, teardrop-shaped cars came tearing around the bend, one after the other.

As silvery as the rollers, the teardrop cars easily overtook the spheres at high speed, with one making a tight turn to block the road and the other stopping by the runaways. The rounded canopy at the top of the car slid to the side.

"Do you want to live?" asked a bald man in a light colored and tight fitting jumpsuit from the cabin. He had a good-natured face with a serious expression and looked Rick straight in the eye.

"Yes!" Rick replied without pause.

"Then get in!"

The closest roller increased its speed. Rick stared at the unusual car which had no wheels and just hung above the road, with air currents weakly moving below.

"Hurry up!" the stranger ordered.

The escapees got inside the cabin, which was so tight that there was barely enough space for the two of them in the compartment behind the cabin. They still had a great feeling of confidence and safety once the canopy slid shut.

The cars immediately took off, but there was a sudden vibration that ran through the hull.

This was not the rollers, but something else.

"What's happening?" Rick leaned forwards towards the pilot.

"The canal!" he replied, as he ran his fingers through a three dimensional projection schematic that appeared in front of him. "The canal is filling up! It's happened again! Hold on!"

With an unbelievable burst of speed, their teardrop-shaped car raced upwards along one of the flyovers. Rick looked back and saw that there were a lot more spheres, with some rolling out of side passages and hidden hatches in the walls. This was not what scared him, however — it was the foaming wall of water that filled the flyover to the edges that followed them.

The wall easily crushed all of the rollers and almost caught the car that was following them. It was only now that Rick realized at how high the speed at which they were flying over the road was, but the wall of water was still gradually catching up with them.

"Fasten your seatbelts!" the pilot shouted. "We're about to change our angle of incidence!"

Rick was experienced in the piloting of ancient flying machines, so he was quick to work out how to use the seatbelts, first ensuring the safety of the boy and then himself.

Their car and then the other quickly came close to the edge of the flyover and rose high up, sliding along with one side in parallel with the floor.

Rick guessed that gravitational compensation plates that interacted with the surface of the highway which was covered with a special layer of conductive materials were installed in the bottom of the cars. This knowledge somehow appeared in his head, which made him feel a sudden headache and dozens of voices began speaking inside his consciousness, making him grimace and grit his teeth so that he would not cry out. Rick barely managed to control himself and choked as the pain receded.

Ouch... He wiped the sweat from his brow and looked at the water which was only an arm's length away from the side of the car, overtaking it.

It was incredible, but the pilots had saved everyone's lives with their sudden maneuver. The pilot touched the hologram in front of his face again and the car lurched to the right, as it stopped being inclined and continued along the flyover that rose up and to the side of the main highway which was under the deadly stream of water.

Rick almost cheered up, but then the flyover arced downwards to rejoin the highway and they almost collided with the rushing water. The pilots managed to keep the cars on the edge at the outer border of the canal, dangerously close to the border. The stream of water eventually touched the canopy and gave their car a push, but the pilot managed to maintain their previous course. There was another push which was stronger, almost pressing the car into the wall. Something howled beneath the bottom of the car and started emitting irritating clicking noises. Rick held on to his seat, gripping so tight that his knuckles went white. The highway suddenly divided into many branches that went in different directions and the pressure of the water became significantly weaker as a great mass of water went downwards along the flyovers with only a little going on ahead and disappearing through the grilles of the drains.

The pilots lowered their speed, driving the cars along the highway that stopped at a dark and sheer wall in the distance. Rick became worried again, but a secret opening in the wall slid open and let the car into a well-lit and spacious tunnel, closing immediately afterwards. Rick and Black Ant let out a breath of relief as they got out of the cabin.

Rick looked around. They were in a huge hangar with a high ceiling and sturdy walls. Dim lights hung overhead. Rick jumped off onto the floor and inadvertently rested his hands on his weapons as he carefully observed the people approaching them. He did not point the blaster at them, but he noticed that the strangers slowed down when they saw the way he moved the weapon. After a brief pause, they continued confidently walking towards him.

The people meeting them were dressed in the same type of form-fitting jumpsuits as the pilots. Their heads were completely shaven, with smooth skulls, smooth faces and no sign of growth on their pale skin.

"Who did you bring, Hans?" a woman with large blue eyes stepped forward and asked strictly.

"I had no time to look at them," the pilot replied, uncertainty creeping into his voice. "I thought that they were shamblers and almost took their heads off. And then..."

"It looks like our guests are gray rats," the pilot of the other car interrupted. "Put the weapon down," he turned to Rick and demanded.

The strangers looked at the newcomers carefully. Rick nodded, slid the strap of his weapon over his head and put the blaster on the floor, showing his hands palms upward to demonstrate his good intentions.

"We don't want to do you evil," he added, stepping back a pace.

"Those are the words that precede the darkest evil," the pilot of the second car noted.

He had a hard, elongated face and narrow brown eyes. He stepped up to Rick and tore the Division patch from his shoulder.

"I am being honest with you!" Rick exclaimed indignantly. "I have nothing to hide and nothing to lose! I have risked so much over the past few days that I am not afraid of anything. I am tired of running."

Silence fell.

"There is not fear in his eyes," the woman agreed.

Some of those standing behind her nodded approvingly.

"And why is the boy silent?" she asked, pointing at Black Ant.

"He can't speak," Rick told her. "Some narrow minded and stupid people tore out his tongue, thinking that they will cure him of possession. You call those who lost their mind "shamblers", is that right?"

The woman nodded.

"We are not shamblers and we are not possessed. The boy is called Black Ant, his settlement has been destroyed and his parents have died."

The woman looked at Black Ant with calm indifference and then turned to the pilots and said, "Hans, upload the information into the database. We will speak to the newcomers later."

Π

RICK TURNED the Cluster medallion key around in his hands — it was an exact copy of the one that Paul from the Maus worshiping Retreat had. Black Ant had brought this thing with him. It was unknown whether this was Paul's medallion or not, as there was no external difference between them.

Yet again, they were awaiting the decision of the leaders of a commune. Rick had not found out its name yet, but he did not particularly want to. Why hurry if these people live outside the confines of the tower? They possessed ancient knowledge and unusual high-speed cars, but they were not living in the tower for some reason, which meant that something was preventing them from getting inside or there was some sort of mysterious reason that stopped them.

The room where they brought Rick and Black Ant was small — a pair of beds, a plastic bedside table and nothing more. They were fed with synthesized concentrate. Black Ant ate two portions at once and now sat one the bed, trying to use gestures to explain how he managed to get into the city.

Rick did not understand anything. Sign language was like the programming language which he sometimes saw on the monitors in Thermopolis. However, Rick still tried to clarify what happened by asking probing questions. Suddenly, he had a moment of inspiration so he took the piece of graphite pencil he had saved back in the Division and offered it to Black Ant.

"Here you are. Draw your path on the wall."

Black Ant got up off the bed and turned to the wall, deep in thought. And then the rough and clumsy drawing of a stick man appeared from underneath his hand. Then the boy drew two long parallel lines above him. Black Ant pointed to the man and to himself and then at the lines.

"The highway?" Rick asked. "You walked here along a wide yellow road."

Black Ant nodded.

"I see. Please continue."

Rick sat more comfortably on his bed. It seemed that it was working. Black Ant was drawing a new picture on the wall with the pencil. He continued the lines of the highway but made them wavy, then turned around and pointed at himself, then at the wavy lines, running his fingers up and down them.

"The rocky hills!" Rick exclaimed. "You traveled through the rocky hills."

Black Ant nodded again and smiled, feeling proud of himself. Then he climbed onto the bed and continued drawing. A sizable oval appeared on the wall and Black Ant drew another inside it and then another. Rick almost whistled in surprise. It turns out that Black Ant knew the way the city was arranged in rings around the tower. But the boy did not stop, as he filled the space inside the ovals, separating it into clusters and segments, marking them with letters and numbered symbols. He did not draw particularly well, but it turned out that he had a fantastic memory — Rick would never have remembered this number of symbols and markings.

Interesting, where could the boy have seen a plant like that?

Suddenly, Black Ant was still, turning to Rick with disappointment written on his face and showing his dirty fingers.

"Did the graphite run out?" Rick asked.

"Uh-huh," the boy replied.

He was not to be deterred, so he wet his finger with saliva and drew a line from the stick man figure to the large oval. Rick was watching the route and the further the stick man went, the more his eyebrows shot up and the more his mouth hung open in surprise. Black Ant then took the medallion from Rick's hand, approached the door, placed the medallion against it and pushed.

"You did it!" Rick exclaimed.

"What exactly?" The pilot of the second car appeared in the doorway, accompanied by Hans and another man unfamiliar to them.

Black Ant deftly hid the medallion in his wide sleeve in such a way that no one noticed it. However, the strict pilot had not been looking at him for a long time.

"By the great wheel!" he exclaimed, looking at the drawings on the wall. "What's going on here?"

The surprise on his narrow face changed to suspicion.

"We are trying to figure out where we are," Rick explained, nodding at the diagram.

Hans entered the room and looked at the wall.

"Hmm, this is rather detailed. Isn't it, Klaus?" he said to the other pilot. "Especially this," he pointed at segment F.

"Where do you have this information from?" Klaus asked harshly, scaring the boy.

Black Ant moved closer to Rick.

"You forgot that he can't speak," Rick told them, "you're scaring him."

"Then the question is for you," Klaus moved his intense gaze to Rick.

"It seems that he saw this diagram somewhere before."

"He did? I thought you traveled together."

"Not quite." Rick understood that he would need to tell them everything from the very beginning in order to avoid needless suspicion and overcomplicating the situation. "I doubt that you will believe us, but we came here from the outer limits."

Klaus and Hans looked at each other.

"Where from?" the stranger standing in the doors asked.

"What does that mean?" Klaus asked. "Are you trying to say that you came from the outer ring?" pointed at the biggest oval on the diagram.

"No, even further away," Rick got up and pointed at the stick man at the beginning of the highway. "We went here, along the road through the wastelands and the rocky hills."

"That's impossible!" all three men declared simultaneously.

"It's still true."

"How do we know that you're not lying?" Klaus looked at Rick with suspicion.

"You will have to trust me," he replied.

"Trust is too much of an expensive pleasure in our times. Do you know how many infiltrators we caught over the last two dozen days? Twelve! Do you know how to count? Do you know what that number means? They were all gray" He poked Rick in the shoulder that once had the Division patch. "All armed and wearing this uniform. They were also telling us all sorts of fantastic tales and swore that they said the truth."

"They changed their opinions when they had a meeting with the shamblers," the stranger in the doorway added. "Maybe..."

"It's too early," Klaus interrupted.

"Hear me out," Rick replied. "Take me to the woman that met us in the hangar and then decide what to do next. If you let us go, we will travel on towards the tower. If you want to kill us, we will fight."

"Iron logic," Hans nodded.

"Rather well said," Klaus confirmed. "Let's go and see Margaret."

They left the room and rode an elevator to an open walkway, where Black Ant shivered in the cold wind and rubbed his shoulders with his hands. Rick strode after him, looking around curiously. It looked like they were on the roof of one of the hangars as rows of oblong dark structures that were connected with similar walkways stretched out as far as the eye could see. It looked like one gigantic covered cluster.

"Our segment does not have the structures you would be used to seeing," Hans confirmed as he walked behind Rick. "We only have transport vehicle hangars here. The gray ones don't know how to open the gates, but sometimes get in here through the utility ducts. That's how we live our lives."

Rick wanted to ask about the transports, but Klaus turned and told Hans to be quiet. They found themselves in an elevator again and descended into another hangar, where they were brought up to a wall that showed a relatively clear map of the city with the same markings, symbols and numbers that Black Ant used in his drawings. The diagram was several times better and more detailed.

Several men stood here waiting, lined up in a semicircle with the woman that Rick had met before in the center.

"May I have a word, Margaret," Klaus asked her, taking the woman to the side.

He whispered something to her for some time, and then the woman exclaimed, "Are you serious?" and stared at the outsiders.

Klaus nodded and started to whisper something again. Rick stopped trying to listen in and stared at the diagram. Three concentric rings, divided up into segments and clusters. The circle with a cross in the middle and the adjacent sectors were the Citadel.

"We have diagrams of this kind everywhere," Hans quietly explained as he stood by Rick's side.

"It looks like a world map," Rick

remembered the diagrams of his native Thermopolis and looked for the Omega sector.

"It seems that you wanted to tell us something," the woman called out as she joined the rest of the men together with Klaus. "I'm all ears."

Rick looked at them for a while, gathering his thoughts together and then cleared his throat and told them a very abridged version of everything that happened to him over the past several weeks, only omitting any mention of his native Thermopolis. Black Ant stood by his side and listened with interest. When Rick reached the point of telling them how he entered the city, he turned to the diagram on the wall and continued to explain and clarify which clusters he had visited and what he saw there. As he talked, he suddenly realized that the letters on the cluster walls that he saw along his travels throughout the city were arranged in reverse alphabetical order. He and Paul first traveled along the area of the great external ring marked as cluster Z. Then they came across the rollers and Paul escaped into the neighboring segment while Rick ended up in the cluster of the fords. He had no way of explaining why the people living there called themselves fords but he easily determined from the diagram that the letter of their cluster was O. His path went through the second inner ring next, through cluster E, which was by cluster F where they were now.

Rick fell silent, those listening to him staying silent as well. Most of their faces expressed surprise and amazement and only Klaus regaled Rick with a grim look.

Hans was the first of them to speak.

"It sounds too crazy to be a lie. I don't think I know anyone who could make something so complicated up. This is why we are going to have to believe it."

"I wouldn't rush to any conclusions," Klaus countered. "Did you hear what they said about the gray ones? They are advancing towards the core! Or at least they want us to think so. Isn't that right?"

He stared at Rick with disapproval again.

"Think what you want," Rick calmly replied. He was sick of the endless suspicion and arguments and there was just one thing he wanted. "I need to get to the core."

"What for? What's there that we don't know?"

Rick gathered his thoughts together. They really did not know anything about the purpose of the tower.

"I... The place where I lived was very cold and dark."

"So what?" Klaus grinned. "Are you

counting on finding a large oven inside the core?"

"No, not just that." Rick had very little desire to explain his true goals to these people. "There are secret floors in the core from which you can control the city."

"How do you know that?" Klaus immediately asked, his eyes suddenly shining like a bright lamp, as if he had caught Rick in a lie.

Rick suddenly understood how strange his words sounded. He restrained himself from shouting at Klaus because of his sudden feeling of powerlessness to persuade anyone of anything. He forced himself to forgive his ignorance and spoke as calmly as he could.

"From the archives beyond the outer limits. I know how to read the ancient language and I especially prepared for a far journey to make this city come alive again. All I need to do is launch the ancient machines."

There was a hubbub as people started to exchange glances and discuss what they just heard.

"What would you say, Margaret?" Even Klaus seemed to have suddenly taken his side. It was as if he had quickly lost his aggression and probably believed Rick about the machines.

"Stupidity and madness," the woman coldly replied, making everyone go quiet. "The ancient machines of the core are dead. There's nothing that could breathe life back into them."

"Then why did the water start to flow?" Rick asked.

Margaret remained calm as she gave her answer.

"We expected this to happen. It already occurred once upon a time, many years ago. It always happened before us too. We prepared for it this time and we will keep preparing for the coming of the water in the future. The city lives according to its own laws. We just need to adapt ourselves to them." She spread her hands. "You know, I heard many stories about this city, with some even saying it did not have any walls. Others tell that long caterpillar-shaped machines used to go along the highways and tunnels of the city which could be used to get from one end of the city to another, while other machines were winged contraptions that flew through the air like birds. Can you even imagine such a thing?"

"Yes. I have seen all of these machines and they exist. I believe that this is the way it was in your city. But that's now important right now. You still haven't explained why the water comes."

"Does the sun need a reason to rise? It just appears in the morning, and that it all."

"The city was created by ancient humans. That means that it's possible to understand how it works and learn how to control it," Rick insisted.

He saw doubt mixed with the desire to believe him in the eyes of the others and saw that friendly Hans wanted to say something but seemed afraid of something.

Margaret chuckled coldly.

"We have heard all of this before. I have seen fools like this in the past. However, if you're so clever, on you go to the core and command the machines."

Rick wanted to reply but there was a sudden distant rumble. The floor started to shake under their feet.

"Another shift!" Hans exclaimed. "We shouldn't be underground when this is happening."

Everyone silently climbed to the roof of the hangar and watched the movement of the neighboring segment from the walkway. Faraway buildings crawled along the wall that divided the clusters.

"Is this something you can understand too?" Margaret asked Rick.

He had nothing to say to her. The Citadel held all the answers.

"Just as I thought."

The buildings disappeared under the ground to be replaced by white domes and satellite dishes.

Margaret and the rest of her people set off along the walkway to the elevator. Hans noticed that Rick and Black Ant stayed where they were and decided to come back.

"Don't get offended by Margaret," he told them, standing by their side. "She is our leader and she is responsible for the safety of the clan."

"She is very forgiving with you for some reason," Rick squinted as he looked at the tower in the rays of the setting sun. "Klaus is also less harsh, even though he's strict. Why is that?"

"Margaret is my wife."

Rick turned to Hans — now everything was clear.

"Yes," the pilot nodded. "And Klaus is her brother."

Hans offered a friendly smile. Rick looked at the tower again. Black Ant shivered from the wind, but waited patiently by his side.

"So," Hans started speaking again, "you want to get inside the core?"

"Yes, over there," Rick pointed at the tower.

Hans stopped smiling.

"It's a damn complex task."

"Why?"

"Nobody has been able to overcome the last wall yet."

"We will try."

Hans looked from Rick to Black Ant and said, "You are very strange people. Do you know that?"

"No," Rick shrugged. "What's so strange about us?"

"Both of your eyes are alight in an unusual way. Especially yours."

"You have fast cars. Are they from these hangars?" Rick asked, nodding at the nearest roofs. "The gray ones have no car and they walk through the city on foot."

"The gray ones could also learn to use the silver arrows," Hans explained, "but they are afraid of drones."

"Yes, the large metal spheres."

"Ah, that's what you call them. They call the spheres "rollers" in the cluster of the fords."

"I see." Hans nodded and continued, "Our arrows are useless outside the highways because the surfaces of the streets do not have gravitational code detection. It came about that our clan ended up owning the hangars. We know how to use all of the vehicles we found, but we can't understand what's inside or how it works. It's too complex."

"Have you tried to study the blueprints and instructions?"

"Yes, many times. We even took the vehicles apart but we could not put them back together so they would work again. When we come back from our missions, we save the graphs and technical status data in the database of the main navigation computer, but we don't know and can't work out why. If we don't save it, the control system will issue a warning and will block the interface after this happens three times. Sometimes we have accidents on our trips and sometimes the gray ones catch us by surprise and shoot at the cars, so pilots die and the cars are put out of commission. Sometimes they just break down and we can't repair them."

"Let's get away from here, Black Ant is really cold," Rick offered.

They went descended into the hangar, where the lamps glowed dimly and not a soul was around.

"This world is an interesting place," Hans continued, as he unhurriedly crossed the hangar. "All the time that I have been living here I have been finding something new. The patrolmen drive along the radial canal from one wall to another. Sometimes we go on a long trip along the ring highway. When we go along this great circle, we stop and we observe and study the city."

"What have you seen?"

Hans smiled mysteriously and answered, "People."

"Shamblers? Those that lost their minds?"

"Not only them. Normal people. Some hide inside the buildings, while some of the braver ones try to attack us. The gray ones actually hunt us. The city seems empty, but it is not true. You saw for yourself that the segments have their own clans, tribes and groups, each one living by their own laws."

They crossed the hangar and stopped in front of a pair of gates with "MAINTENANCE" written on them in faded lettering. Hans sat down on the striped railing that bordered the fire point zone, took out a clear plastic box full of little white pellets and put one in his mouth.

"Why don't people unite?" Rick asked. "They used to all be together before."

Hans slowly swallowed his little white pellet. He sat for a while, trying to work out his feelings. Then his eyes went distant, as he answered, "We are used to living in danger. When death awaits you at every corner, no one wants to play fair, especially with outsiders. You told us yourself that you ran away from the gray ones."

"I don't share their principles. The society of the Division is built on violence and the very idea of that disgusts me."

"Hmm, the strong eat the weak is the principle of every creature."

"No," Rick said with determination.

"Then I'm really surprised how you

managed to survive this far. You are either unimaginably clever or just very lucky."

"But your clan is nothing like the gray ones," Rick ignored Hans' words.

"You haven't even spent a day among us."

"All right. What if I offer you to come with me?"

Hans hiccupped loudly in surprise.

"What for?"

"It doesn't matter. To achieve any kind of goal. Would you go?"

"I don't see the point. We have everything we need."

"Oh, yes. Cars that constantly grow fewer in number. What are you going to do when the last one breaks down? Try to take it apart?"

Hans looked at him carefully.

"Some of us also think this way. But you know what the problem is? We can't change anything. This world is greater than our understanding. We have food, highways, arrows and lots of living space." Hans spread his hands. "We don't need anything more. If the last car breaks down one day, then we will come up with something. But no earlier. This is why and expedition to the core won't give us anything. Let's go."

"Where?"

"Are you leaving or will you spend the night

in warm beds?"

"That depends on whether we are guests or prisoners."

"You're stubborn and principled," Hans nodded with approval. "Consider yourselves guests. It's pure lunacy to walk around the surface at night anyway. Let's go, I will treat you to a strong drink you're sure to like, but it's a bit too early for the boy."

Rick and Black Ant exchanged glances, as Black Ant smiled with condescension.

"We're in."

0

THEY DID NOT MANAGE to get a good night's sleep. They were awakened by a stranger that ordered Rick to follow him and for Black Ant to stay in the room.

It was noisy in the hangar where the strange took him as people crowded around a car that had been singed by fire in many places. Some of the people were engaged in an excited discussion while others were trying to open the canopy of the car. Once they finally managed to do this, they extracted a nearly dead and wounded pilot out, lifted him in their arms and carried him away. The voices immediately quietened down. The wounded man muttered something and then suddenly cried out, "...we had to! Do you understand?"

"Rocky," Hans stepped out of the crowd near Rick and asked a tall young man who was following the procession with the wounded man with a dark glare, "Those bastards hunted you, didn't they? Tell me what happened to Kamensky, please."

The man did not reply, so Hans touched him on the shoulder, "Rocky, did you hear me?|"

"Ah, yes, Hans... Of course... We... We stopped in segment C, in the branches that were not filled with water." He nodded at the wounded man that was already being carried into the brightly lit doorway of the medical unit. "Fraser left the cabin to stretch and look around that section of the canal. Me and Kamensky stayed in the cabin according to instructions."

Rocky went quiet, looking at Hans and obviously expecting approval.

"Keep going!" Klaus demanded, as he pushed his way through the crowd towards them.

"Then we... When Fraser was walking back towards the car, we saw a man at the edge of the flyover in the pedestrian zone. He was wearing gray... And looking at us." Rocky swallowed and continued, "He waved his hand and shouted to us that he wanted to talk. Fraser got into the cabin, but we... We decided to stay. The gray one was unarmed. Yes, and he was far away and no one else was around. I swear it! The scanners were silent, and we decided that the stranger would not cause any harm."

"What else did the gray one say?" Klaus clarified.

His face became even stricter than before. Hans shook his head with disappointment by his side.

"That he wants to come down into the canal and if we could wait for him."

A disapproving hubbub spread through the crowd.

"However, we decided against delaying any longer, and started up the cars," Rocky continued.

He went silent again, looking at the gathering as if he was counting on their support and approval, until he understood that everyone wanted him to continue.

"At first, I did not understand what happened. There was a flash, a roar and a sharp jolt. I immediately switched to the rear camera display and there was a strange wheeled car with a long horizontal tube protruding from its hull with gray ones all around it. When we started up, it was nowhere to be seen. They were probably hiding in the drainage tunnel, as it has wide gates that would let a vehicle through. Kamensky's arrow lay there on the side covered smoking and covered in soot, while Kamensky had somehow climbed out of the car but..." Rocky looked down for a moment. "The gray ones took him. Then they followed us and shot at Fraser's arrow. By then, we had accelerated and managed to turn onto a parallel flyover and get away."

"How fast did the car of the gray ones move?" Hans asked.

Rocky shrugged his shoulders with a guilty look and it was obvious he did not know. A lot of people shook their heads with disapproval.

"So, now we know for sure that the gray ones can move around along the highways in armed transport vehicles." Klaus gritted his teeth. "And they have Kamensky."

He grimly looked over the gathering, stopping when he found Rick but did not have time to say anything.

"We must get away immediately!" Margaret declared behind their backs, so everyone turned around. "Announce the evacuation. There is one hour to get ready. Tell the people in the neighboring hangars. We are going to a safe hideaway."

The hangar came alive and only Rick and Klaus stayed in place, looking at each other tensely and waiting for someone to start first.

"This is all your fault," Klaus finally squeezed out. "That's exactly how it is! It was calmer before, and then you came and..."

"What have we got to do with it?"

"Do you know what they will do to Kamensky?" Klaus stepped up to Rick and took him by the front of his jumpsuit. "What they do after they torture the information out of him? Do you know?"

"I can imagine," Rick replied calmly and immediately added, "We will definitely leave today."

"Oh no," Klaus' lips twisted in an ominous grin. "You did not understand. Whoever you are, we are going to exchange you or trade you for Kamensky with advantageous conditions."

"What if it doesn't work?"

"And what if you are even more valuable than I think and you hold a strong card in your hands?" Klaus shook Rick.

"What if the gray ones don't care about our fate at all?"

"That's possible, but they do care about us!" he gave him another shake, a harder one this time.

"You are just standing in their way. Their main target is the core!"

"So is it the core again? Then why did the gray ones lay an ambush on the highway?" spittle

---

flew out of Klaus' mouth as he almost started to shout.

"Don't you understand? They think we have access to the core. The pilots of arrows that can move along the roads of the city with unbelievable speed are bound to know how to cross the barriers that divide the city up in to clusters. That's the way they think!"

"Enough arguing, Klaus," Hans appeared by their side. "Time to get down to business."

He took the angry pilot by the hands and made him let Rick go, with some force.

"Margaret ordered to take them with us," Hans told him and turned to Rick. "Go to your room and collect your gear. Rocky will show you where to go."

Rick was about to argue and stay to explain everything, but Hans suddenly gave him a strict look, showing that it would be best to obey.

He was soon in his room and quickly told Black Ant about everything was happened. Rocky, who had escorted him, paid no attention and waited by the entrance. They did not have anything with them anyway, so they decided to immediately set off for the hangar to be closer to the others. Their attempts to start a conversation with Rocky were unsuccessful as the pilot was probably no fan of newcomers. As soon as they returned to the hangar, Rocky immediately gave the outsiders to the people from Hans' circle and went over to the maintenance crew to help them prepare the arrows for the journey. An hour later everyone was gathered in front of a massive pair of extremely tall gates, or external locks, as the maintenance crews referred to them.

A low rumbling noise came from somewhere above and the floor vibrated. Rick and Black Ant started to look around nervously, but everyone stood there waiting silently. The gates shuddered and started to spread apart so a strip of bright sunlight poured into the hangar.

The silver arrows were the first to go through the opening and sped away along the flyover towards the wall that ringed the tower nearby. The people walked on foot after them, with the technicians rolling along charge batteries for the cars in electric carts and the women carrying some basic supplies in bags and leading children by the hands.

Rick and Black Ant kept looking around, trying to work out where they were and what was going on. It seemed that the movement of the clan into an emergency hideout was nothing new. The people looked ready for this turn of events and acted without any undue haste, without looking particularly nervous and silently following Margaret, who was accompanied by Hans striding along by her side.

Surprisingly, Rick did not notice Klaus among the technicians. Why didn't he leave with the pilots? Rick pointed at Klaus and whispered to Black Ant, "Keep away from him. I feel that we will have problems with him yet."

The boy nodded.

"Do you still have the medallion that you showed me in the room?" Rick asked quietly.

Another nod.

"When you see signs like those on the medallion, or a door with similar symbols, tell me."

Black Ant made an affirmative sound and they continued on their way in silence.

There was a light layer of snow dusting the gray slabs under their feet and it was cold. The vague outline of the sun shone with a pale light before their eyes. Rick noticed a giant letter F which had almost completely faded on the wall, labeling the cluster where they were. "ATTENTION! Sector border. When the shift occurs, keep behind the line of the canal," was inscribed alongside the letter. Rick whispered to Black Ant, drawing his attention to this and asking whether he understood what line they were talking about, but the boy only shrugged in response.

Margaret led the people along the flyover

towards the barrier wall that had the Citadel towering behind it. Rick kept turning his head, getting the lay of the land and soon noticed a straight canal that stretched along to the side of the flyover. It was not deep, but it was wide and it diagonally crossed their way ahead of them.

Perhaps this was the canal referred to by the inscription? He slowed down, looking at the canal cutting through the open space. Black Ant also held back, standing by him. The slabs under their feet suddenly shuddered violently and some people cried out in fear. Hans turned around and shouted at them all to hurry up.

Rick was about to suggest to Black Ant to go faster, when the slabs shook again and the world split in half.

Just a moment ago, the slabs where the technicians rolled along their electric carts were lying flat. A break suddenly appeared, with a dark, rusted section of wall rising out of it with a screech, covered in riveted metal squares with fresh blood spattered on them. Margaret, Hans and several other people had probably been crushed by the underground mechanisms in an instant. Rick was not sure of that, but that was what he thought, for some reason.

By accident, a woman and a child ended up at the edge of this section and both were screaming. Screams came from all around, from those who had fallen into the crack, to those that ended up on the other side of the section and everyone who was ahead because they did not know what to do. More and more new wall fragments rose out of the crack, fencing off a new city segment.

This was when Rick finally understood what the inscription on the wall had meant, so he grabbed Black Ant by the hand and pulled him forwards, towards the place where the barrier had not risen yet and where it was still possible to get to the other side.

They ran up to the crack and stopped because it was impossible to jump over it as the distance was too great. Then Rick shouted to Black Ant that they will run along over the edge of a rising section of the wall, but it needed to be done fast and without pause upon his order. Rick told him to get ready and when the fragment appeared from the crack commanded, "Run!"

Black Ant threw himself towards the other side. Rick hesitated for a moment as he felt someone's presence behind his back and almost fell in the opening between the slabs and the growing wall when someone's strong hands gripped him by the shoulders and pulled him back. Rick tried to turn around, but he did not manage to do it in time as he was hit on the back of his head and on his legs and thrown to the side. He barely managed to put up his hands so that he would not fall on the floor face first, drew his legs up to roll to the side and he was right on time. Klaus stamped down hard on the place where he had just been.

"Why?" Rick bounded up and clenched his feet.

Klaus made no reply — his face was twisted and insanity was in his eyes. He tried to attack Rick again, who managed to dodge out of the way and start running away from the crack so that he could get to the other side where the wall had not risen yet. He only managed to go for a few paces, when he was struck on the legs and rolled along the slabs. Klaus caught up with him and fell on top of him, grabbing hold of his neck and started to strangle him.

Rick's vision swam as he tried to loosen Klaus' grip but he was not strong enough. Then he tried to knee Klaus in the back and push him off himself, but he failed again.

Suddenly, the grip on his neck weakened. Rick twisted to the side, wheezing and coughing. He saw two silhouettes through the mist in front of his eyes — one was dark and lying on the slabs in torn clothing and the other silhouette in a light jumpsuit kicking the one on the ground.

Rick managed to get up and lean on one knee, as his eyes finally focused on the figure and growled in fury when he realized that the insane Klaus was beating Black Ant.

"Over here!" Rick grunted with difficulty. "Come to me!"

Klaus turned to the sound of his voice and walked towards Rick clumsily, his limbs machine-like as he moved them. His face had become even more twisted, his eyes staring wide as he let out a scream of pain. Before he reached Rick he swung his fist through the air and then did it again and again.

Rick straightened out as he waited, watching how Klaus, who had lost the last dregs of his sanity and sense of space swung his fists at an invisible opponent and how he started to foam at the mouth, his screams merging into an incomprehensible howl. His movements became jerky and twitchy. He fell to his knees, clawing at his bald head with his fingernail.

The rumbling around them started to quieten down as the last section of the wall rose at the line where the crack touched the walls of the neighboring cluster. The slabs under their feet shuddered, as if there was a gigantic monster moving around below and everything went quiet.

Rick felt incredibly tired and empty and he could barely stand up on his feet. Klaus stopped tearing off the head on his head, fell down face first onto the floor and did not move anymore.

"Are you all right?" Rick called out to Black Ant, who had stood up on his feet.

He only grunted, nodding in agreement as he spat out a piece of his tooth and smiled.

"Why did you come back?" Rick asked, even though he understood anyway — they became close friends with the boy of late. He would also have come back for Black Ant if something similar happened to him.

Black Ant only shrugged and glanced over his shoulder. The wall had cut them off from the others forever. They needed to find another way. People were scrabbling around, crying and arguing nearby. Around fifteen of them were left by the walls, some elders, a pair of grown men, women and children.

One of the women noticed them looking at her, turned around and exclaimed, "Look, they have left us behind!"

"They left!" another lamented.

"It's all your fault!" a third one shouted.

She was supported by an elder. The two men stepped forward resolutely, raising their fists.

Rick shook his head unhappily. The world never changed.

"Hey, relax," he replied firmly.

Something in his eyes, voice or appearance stopped them.

"Anyone who will try and accuse me and my friend of their problems again will die."

"You're lying!" the elder said as he stepped forward.

"Want to try me, like Klaus did?" he nodded at the body lying motionless in front of him.

The old man immediately stepped back behind the other men.

"Have you calmed down?" Rick looked into the unfamiliar faces carefully. "Now listen to me, because many things depend on your answers. Did the slabs that we are on now ever move before?"

"No," the first woman replied confidently. "Nothing of the sort ever happened before."

"Yes, this is the first time," answered another.

"They say that this is the sign of the end of the world," the third one added immediately. "Hans and Margaret promised to save us. They lied!"

She sniffed and burst into tears.

"Enough of that!" Rick told her off. "Give me quick answers without any of your speculations when I ask questions. Is that clear?"

Everyone looked at each other for a while and then an uneven chorus of voices made an affirmative sound.

"Hans and Margaret are no longer," Rick

declared. "There is also no direct path to the emergency hideout. This is why I am going towards the core. If you want, you can follow me."

People waited for him to continue, but then Rick turned around and set off towards the eastern wall of the segment. Black Ant fell in alongside.

"There's no way out over there!" someone shouted after him.

"I know, but I will find it!" Rick replied without turning around.

"No, that's the wrong way!" a hoarse voice sounded.

The women gasped with fear. Rick and Black Ant turned around.

"It's the wrong direction," Klaus wheezed as he rose to his feet.

Klaus looked terrible. There were bloody welts on his head, his left eye twitched visibly and his nose and jaw looked broken. It seems that he received these wounds when he fell on the slabs. The main thing was that there was sanity and fear in his eyes.

"It's as if I was enshrouded in mist," Klaus muttered guiltily as he wiped his mouth. Everything went blank in my head. I remember how I heard the noise and then how I was lying on the ground as this wall..."

"A shambler!" one of the people standing off

to the side exclaimed. "Klaus has become a shambler!"

Rick did not think so. He glanced at Black Ant and they both approached Klaus.

"Does your head hurt?" Rick asked.

"I have a splitting headache."

That was bad. Rick suffered from such fits himself, but it never got as bad as this.

"We are looking for a way through," Rick told him, without wasting time on explanations. "I must get to the core. Do you know how to get in there?"

"I know who can help us."

"Speak straight."

"Here," Klaus stumbled as he went into his jumpsuit pocket. Rick held him up by his elbow. "This is the key."

He took a familiar looking medallion out of his pocket. Only the symbols on that medallion were different to the one that Black Ant had with him.

"Let me guess," Rick said, "we just need to find the door which this key opens."

"You know a lot," Klaus chuckled crookedly and motioned for Rick to stand away. "You need to go over there," he pointed westwards, "there is a hidden passage."

"Why should I trust you?"

"I don't know, decide for yourself."

"Well... All right," Rick nodded. "Show us where to go."

Grimacing with pain, Klaus slowly strode off in the direction he had shown, followed by Rick and Black Ant.

They heard voices and then the sound of steps behind them — the people had quickly made their choice. There had nowhere else to go.

P

THE LOUD ECHO of the boots upon the steps spread throughout the shaft. They were descending into a gigantic, dark well along a metal stairway which circled along the wall. Rick walked at the very back, but he took a quick look to the south before he slid downwards, pulling the hatch tight.

What if his eyes had just played tricks on him? Rick stopped on the platform, watching how the torches of the people below shone on the walls and steps. Perhaps he should have checked? To do that, he would have to climb back outside and... No, it was best to just assume that the gray ones were following their tracks and that they would soon be here.

He closed his eyes, bringing up the picture

in his memory. A faraway dark wall and the immense half-open gates of the hangar with gray figures walking out of them. Yes, these were the soldiers of the division and no one else. Rick nodded to himself and activated the electronic lock panel by touching it with Klaus' medallion. He made sure that the hatch was locked, grabbed the railings and hurried down the stairs after the others. Now, he was more concerned about what awaited them below as opposed to what went on above.

Klaus only knew the way to the shaft where he had descended with the pilots a couple of times. There was a branching network of corridors and tunnels below which the people were afraid to enter, so Rick had to choose the only correct direction so that they would not get lose their way and their valuable time. He knew how to do that — the main thing was for the markings on the walls to still be preserved, and there was no chance for the gray ones to catch up with them if he managed to reach a terminal and get information up on the monitor.

The descent took a long time and Rick counted forty landings, with each of them as deep as one residential level in Thermopolis, by his reckoning. It was incredibly deep. At last, they reached a hangar, similar in shape to those where Klaus' clan had recently lived.

One of the men turned out to be a technician, so he had no problem finding the instrument panel and switching on the emergency lighting. However, there were only two working lights that turned on under the ceiling. Two was not bad either, so Rick walked around the hangar, reading the inscriptions above the exits to the corridors and stopped by the three of them which had attracted his attention: "Cargo Section", "Waiting Halls" and "Control Room."

"That way," he said decisively, pointing at the last exit.

Everyone went after him, following the tunnel to a spacious hall with rows of seats before dead black monitors. Rick tried to switch on at least one of them, but it did not work as there was no power. He asked the technician for help, but he could not do anything either as they could not find the main power supply control panel and the smaller ones they came across did not provide them with the results they needed.

"Let's keep going," Rick decided. "We need to start up at least one of the terminals so we get a diagram of the city by the core so we can plan our route."

He headed for the side exit that had a "Hangar No. 1" sign above it.

"So you want to say that these terminals store information, just like the database of our main navigation computer?" asked Klaus. He looked noticeably better overall, even though his breathing was still labored and he spoke with a hoarse edge to his voice.

"That's right," Rick stopped abruptly.

Black Ant had not expected it and walked into him from behind.

"Sorry. Are you all right?" Rick ruffled his hair and turned back to Klaus. "Did your main navigation computer only store data about the cluster or did it also include the other territories?"

Klaus thought for a while and then pronounced, "I am not that great with electronic machines. Margaret and Hans were the ones who understood them well, but I can tell you one thing for sure — the database contained information about all the places which we ever visited in our arrows."

"Would you be able to connect to the main navigation computer is we manage to start up a terminal?"

Klaus shrugged and replied, "You need a unique access code. Only Margaret had one."

"An access code..." Rick repeated to himself. "All right, we will discuss this once we launch at least some kind of terminal."

The corridor led them to a balcony with rows of seats, but there were no lifeless monitors.

There was a view into a huge hall with glass walls where the shapes of flying machines could be seen in the weak glow of mold. Rick immediately recognized them, but he could only use one of them if he knew how to raise them to the surface.

"Do you know where we are?" Klaus asked, lowering his voice to a whisper for some reason as he looked down into the hall, completely mesmerized.

"I have an idea," Rick shone the torch at the signs in front of the stairways that led downwards from the balcony. "Do you see those signs? The Ancients called a place like this a transport hub. Judging by the sign, you can get to the city, the core and the outer ring from here."

He pointed the torch upwards and they all looked up.

"Notices used to appear on the big information screens up here that people used to find out where they should go and when so that they get into the flying machine on time," Rick continued.

"How do you know?" Klaus asked.

"There are many other interesting things in the ancient archives," Rick chuckled. "Once we'll get inside the core, this will be the least of the things you find out. Let's head below and take a look at the machines."

They went down into the hall and walked

towards the glass wall which had several exits, but never managed to reach it.

In the space of a second, there was a barely perceptible change around them. Either the mass of air moved or some invisible force touched his mind, but Rick and everyone with him suddenly stopped when they felt *it*.

Squat figures stepped out from underneath the flying machines. They appeared silently out of the dark, moving out onto the balcony and sneaking out of hidden passages in the gloom. Dozens of emaciated, hairy and filthy creatures in human form with ash-gray hair and shining pale eyes that only expressed the feeling of hunger.

Rick's hands went up by reflex to protect Black Ant, while the other people clustered together in fear. They did not make any sudden moves as there was nowhere to run. The possessed slowly converged from all sides, closing the distance to the people more and more. There were two hundred of them or more and Rick clenched his fists so hard that they hurt as he regretted that there was no way to reach the core anymore and that Black Ant does not deserve a death like this.

All of a sudden, the possessed halted, as if some invisible barrier had stopped them, leaving a narrow passage into a small corridor with an exit onto a railway platform by the side of shining rails at the end.

The twisted and dead faces of the creatures suddenly had a very subtle change to them, as curiosity was added to their animalistic pain and anger. They stopped and seemed to be waiting for something.

Somebody hiccupped loudly behind Rick's back and then giggled. Klaus reacted to this very quickly and calmly, as he turned a shook a clan-mate who had almost lost his sanity to bring him back to his senses. This was when Rick made his decision.

"Follow me," he whispered. "And no sudden movements."

Their group carefully set off towards the passage into the corridor. The possessed stayed in their places, only turning their heads after them, stretching their neck as if they were trying to smell them.

With Rick at its head, the group passed through the corridor to come out onto the platform and stepped off onto the rails that led into a wall with a massive pair of gates after fifty paces with a gigantic letter A inscribed upon them.

This was the way to the core! Only a little remained. Rick turned around and froze with the rest of them when one of the women slipped on the stairs and cried out as she fell on the rails.

For a minute, everyone tensely stared through the corridor into the hall full of possessed, but they stood there without moving, with their heads turned towards the people and their necks stretched out.

They got away with it. Rick whispered for everyone to be as careful as they can and avoid making noise and sudden movements for any reason. They had to open the gates, no matter what. It was only now that he noticed that the stress had made him sweat profusely. He wiped the sweat from his face and headed towards his ultimate goal.

The gate control panel was nearby, its terminal awakening and shining pale green under a coat of dust as the people approached. Rick blew at the screen and touched it with his fingers, activating the menu.

"You need more than the key," Klaus whispered as he came to stand by his side. "See, they require a unique code!"

He pointed at the scanner where a hand had to be placed.

"I'll manage."

Rick slid the medallion into the slot on the device and the words "confirm identity" appeared on the screen.

"But you're an outsider..." Klaus looked genuinely scared. "Margaret warned that machines of this kind can kill an outsider if the code doesn't match."

Rick placed his palm upon the scanner and nodded, without looking at Klaus.

One second...

And then another...

"Code recognized" the screen informed. With a rumble and a creak, the ancient mechanism turned and the gates slid open.

That was close. Rick went to pull the key out of the slot on the reading device, but nothing happened. The key was stuck and a warning appeared on the screen about the gates being blocked within thirty seconds.

"Let's go."

Rick looked over his shoulder. The possessed stood still. Then he stepped into the opening and decided that he would not stop anymore. The tunnel ahead was brightly lit and led them to a glass bridge over a gigantic pool full of water, with huge gears breaking the surface. He had come across them on his way to the tower. It was probably these gears that were responsible for the movement of the shift mechanisms of the city segment above. Wisps of steam rose upwards to be sucked in through wide ventilation grilles by the sides of the bridge.

Rick looked up and saw the distant sky. This was why it was so light, even though they were almost at the bottom of yet another deep shaft.

The gates closed behind them with an echoing rumble and Klaus could not resist asking, "Are you sure that you did the right thing?"

"Yes."

"But the key has been left behind there!" he waved backwards with his hand.

"Don't worry, this is how it must be."

"And what if we get stuck in here?"

Rick turned abruptly, looked Klaus in the eye and told him harshly, "If we remained, we wouldn't have survived."

He did not waste any more time on conversation and strode off. There was another tunnel beyond the bridge and another pair of gates with a terminal that required a key and a unique code.

Klaus stood there, open-mouthed, observing how Black Ant took out the medallion key that he had hidden in the folds of his clothing to put it into the slot on the device and how Rick placed his palm on the scanner yet again and a repeat of what happened before.

They went through. They did it at last. Rick wanted to shout for joy, but he did now show it. The people following him were whispering to each other and thanking fate for sending them these outsiders that saved their lived. Black Ant looked proud of himself as he felt the attention and friendly eyes upon him and smiled.

They soon entered a transport hub similar to the one they left. The same railway platform and corridors were here, but there was no hall full of flying machines. They were not even needed, as Rick worked out where they were by shining his torch at the signs and took everyone to the stairwell.

Half the job was done. He was tired, but proud of himself and happy that he did not have to die and the rest of the people with him were safe too. He just felt really good — it was a feeling that he had not felt for a long time.

"Let's go upwards," he declared.

His followers nodded their approval and chorused their support.

It started to get dark when they reached the surface. His companions were noticeably tired and almost all the women were out of breath. Only Black Ant smiled, showing the way nothing could faze him.

"We need to hurry." Rick was thinking well — if they did not manage to find shelter in a place that was not open to the wind, they would freeze. It would be good to find somewhere where the generators worked and they could turn on the light.

Soon enough, luck smiled upon them again as the first terminal they came across accepted the code from Rick's palm and let them into a squat boxlike metal structure with buzzing transformers inside where they could turn on the light and where there was heating, which was the main thing.

"We are too tired to walk on," the women immediately voiced their concerns, having noticed that Rick stayed by the doors and was about to leave.

"Stay here," he nodded.

"And you?"

"I have to go." He understood why they were worried, so he added, "but I will be back soon."

Black Ant was about to follow him, but Rick shook his head, bent down towards him and whispered, "Not this time. Look after them, I have no one to entrust these poor people to."

Black Ant nodded and cast a questioning glance at Rick, motioning with his head towards the exit to ask him why he was leaving.

"Don't worry," Rick smiled. "I need to quickly find the archive, the place where ancient knowledge is stored. I am the only one of you that knows how to read and understands the language of the Ancients."

Black Ant nodded again. Rick looked at

Klaus who was helping to sort through the few items that they managed to bring with them.

"Keep watching him," Rick warned Black Ant. "All right?"

The boy hit himself on the chest with his fist and waved his hand for Rick to leave.

"Lock yourself in from inside," Rick ordered as he stepped out onto the street.

He could not waste time now. If he managed to get here then the gray ones would be able to overcome the same distance. His only relief was that they would have several hundred of the possessed, darkness and the cold night to overcome. However, he still felt unease deep down inside. Rick switched on his torch and gathered his pace.

He walked along the street and read every sign that he saw along the way one after another until he found the sign he needed. Once he got his bearings and memorized the street that he came from, he took a turn in the direction of the sign and entered a square after passing through a quarter where the hemisphere of the core informatorium was located.

Rick had not problems finding the entrance, which had no terminal by its side, to his surprise. The stood around by the sliding doors, touched them several times and even tried to break them with a kick but all of his attempts to get inside the building were in vain. The transparent material was as hard as steel and was not affected by his ministrations.

A stupid thought that someone was watching him and deliberately not letting him in crept into his mind. Rick looked around himself, shining the torch around the street, found what he was looking for and went towards the drainage well.

It took a long time to get the grille open, but once he managed to get inside he descended to the bottom of the well using the handholds built into the wall, walked around a dozen paces underground towards the hemisphere and then climbed back up, using the handholds of another well. He found himself in the basement of the informatorium where the well was also covered by a grille, but he did not have to scratch up his fingers this time as the basement was not so cold and the grille had not frozen to the floor.

His eyes immediately found an evacuation plan hanging on the wall. Rick worked out the plan of the basement and climbed up, entering a spacious hall.

The moonlight reflected off the walls. The space around him was empty apart from the bundles of rags that lay on different sides of the exits. Rick walked up to one of them and shook his head with a loud sigh. What he thought was a bundle of rags were the remains of a person. He did not approach the one on the other side. The sight reminded him of what he saw in his native Thermopolis — these dead people had lain there for many years.

He walked up to a wide staircase that led to the upper floors and flinched when the lamps started to blink weakly under the ceiling. An unobtrusive flat panel stand came to life to his right. Rick wanted to come up to it, but then a human figure appeared behind it, making him step back and clench his fists.

"Who are you?" Rick exclaimed.

"Hello," the stranger replied with a sonorous voice and smiled.

He was clean and well presented, with dark hair, blue eyes and milky white teeth.

Rick took a closer look at the stranger and lowered his hands. This was a hologram, similar to the one they came across with Paul on the way here. Something he already knew but he could not get used to.

Rick sighed when he thought of Paul and a second later, the hologram started to speak.

"Welcome to the informatorium." The light above became more intense. "I am glad that you have decided to visit us at such a late hour. May I ask if you have a permanent pass?"

"No," Rick breathed out.

"No problem," the hologram smiled. "Would you like to use a single-access pass?"

Rick nodded and immediately heard, "What are you interested in?"

The program offered him to use the informatorium only once. He needed to select the correct section.

"History," Rick answered at last.

"No problem. Which period are you interested in?"

"The period after the hibernation of Thermopolis."

"Forgive me, but I don't understand. There was no hibernation."

Rick frowned. He had to make his requests more carefully. However, the program came to his aid.

"There was a reconstruction."

"Exactly!" Rick grasped at his chance. "That's what I wanted to say."

"What format would you like to receive the materials in? Text, interactive files or artifacts?"

This time Rick did not get confused.

"I would like to watch documentary films on the subject. Choose the most informative ones as I don't have much time."

"I understand," the hologram smiled. "Time is a valuable commodity."

Rick nodded in reply. The stand hummed

quietly and a small plastic rectangle with a black strip on one side and a five figure number on the other slid out of it.

"Cubicle 1005, floor five, right wing," the hologram told him. "The instructions are attached. Happy watching!"

Rick took the card, muttered some words of thanks and hurried over to the stairs, ignoring the offer to use the elevator.

He did not want to take risks and use a mechanical cabin at such an important moment as it could break down. Once he had climbed up top, Rick found the right cubicle and slid the card into the terminal, lowering himself into a soft armchair. He slid the interactive helmet onto his head and lowered the visor.

The world disappeared.

Q

"THE RECONSTRUCTION PERIOD was one of the most important periods in human history," a pleasant and calm voice sounded in Rick's head. *"All that you hear and see is only educational material reflecting the part of the past selected by the user."*

Rick felt like he was flying through a dark

sky full of stars. He did not feel his body at all and there was nothing in the space around him to orient himself, only his own being and a disembodied voice.

"Man, so great in his power," the voice continued, *"had to face the most serious challenge of recent times. It was not a world war or a natural disaster. It was not even hunger or socioeconomic issues. Humanity was under the threat of annihilation as a result of a virus which was unknown to science. A virus which was called "Mindstorm"."*

Rick suddenly found himself in the middle of a clean and brightly lit street full of pedestrians. He would have jumped in surprise, but he still could not fell his own body, so he could just observe and listen. Buildings of glass and concrete towered around him, flying cars raced through the sky and the people hurried along somewhere on their own business, almost never looking around.

"It took only a few days for the epidemic to engulf the planet. It was not possible to establish the source and origin of the virus. Mindstorm symptoms included memory disorders, dyslexia, attention deficit disorder, reaction slowdown, headaches, depression, fear, aggression, hatred and complete insanity at the terminal stage, expressed through the complete loss of sentience.

The affected person would enter an animalistic state. They would become a beast, driven by the most primitive instincts and requirements."

One of the passer-by in the street suddenly fell to one knee and grabbed his own head, twisting around and tearing out his own hair. He then bounded up and threw himself at Rick...

"Sometimes, the symptoms would manifest themselves strongly, with a terrible migraine that blocked the neocortex and causing an explosion of the hormonal system and the creation of large portions of cortisol and noradrenaline. The patient would be engulfed with anger that they expressed through aggression towards those close to them. Such patients were overcome by an unstoppable desire to crush and destroy everything around them and kill any living being if it happened to get in their way. The afflicted also displayed excellent reflexes, unbelievable strength and a heightened pain barrier. There is a great number of documented incidences of immediate Mindstorm affliction."

Rick watched them one after another, standing in the street among a crowd which had gone insane and letting the possessed through himself one after another as well as those that were still alive and trying to save themselves.

"The infected were studied. However, all attempts at finding the harmful virus failed. The

mindless infected also did not react to the effect of synthetic physical activity blockers, but did exactly the opposite, with miraculous feats of inventiveness. They would break free, unite into groups and attack humans again. The medical practitioners built up an image of the appearance of a Mindstorm carrier — accelerated breathing, a high heart rate, explosive reactions to irritants, unexplained aggression and a wandering gaze.

At first, the epidemic spread through the cities, then the provinces, then the entire countries and eventually, it consumed entire continents. The number of healthy humans was falling rapidly. Enclaves numbering thousands rose and fell. The Mindstorm virus was everywhere. It was then that they remembered about the Thermopoli of the architect Spanidis. Thousands of those who were still sentient set off to hide away in the gigantic towers. However, the entrances to these shelters were closed to them.

It was then when the great architect made his address to humanity, before the storming of the Citadels.

"Citizens of the world," a familiar old man with sad eyes was looking at Rick. "The Mindstorm virus is affecting the citizens of Thermopolis just as much as the other people that live upon this planet. This is why you should not look to us for salvation. The disease will take you if that is your fate. And now, I would like to talk about the ultimatum from the Secretary of the Security Council of Nations. My answer is no. Please, don't try to take the citadel by force. You will fail anyway. We do not want to do evil against anyone and would only like to ask to be left alone. When I was constructing the first Thermopolis, the whole world was laughing at me. Now that you look at me with hope, you must know that nothing will save us."

Spanidis let out a sad sigh.

"We are entering a new ear. The greatest moment in the history of humanity has come. It is now that our future is being decided as the Reconstruction Period begins. It will take the survivors a long time to carefully restore everything that we managed to destroy and remember all that we have forgotten. To learn that which we did not know." The architect went quiet for a while, looking ahead of himself intently, and then continued, "The Thermopolis project is entering a new stage. I will make an announcement about our work if the right time comes."

The architect disappeared and Rick watched the gigantic Thermopolis from above. The picture was so familiar, as he had once descended from the top of the tower to its bottom in a flying machine. But this time, there was a flowering plain around Thermopolis, which gathered thousands of people and dozens of deadly machines.

The disembodied voice began to speak again.

"The Security Council of Nations and the International Armed Forces decided to put their plan for the "liberation of the Thermopoli from an authoritarian regime" into action and sent military detachments to the citadels. Following a short period of negotiations, the soldiers attempted to capture the outer perimeters but came across an energy field of unknown provenance. Archimedes Spanidis was accused of resistance to the world government, but there was no reaction from the architect. The armies then launched a coordinated rocket strike at the perimeters of the towers. The explosions did not harm the walls because the rockets struck the defensive force fields, but they damaged the natural zones and the spaces around the Thermopoli, causing great damage to the environment, so Spanidis openly warned the coalition of retaliatory action. However, the Security Council of Nations only redoubled their efforts, gathering all of their reserves around the towers, but it never got to the stage of active measures. A simultaneous targeted electromagnetic pulse caused the malfunction of all military equipment. The soldiers left the

battlefield in shock. All the citadels had stood fast.

The population of the planet had numbered twenty billion at the beginning of the epidemic, but it was reduced to three by the end of the year.

The population dropped to one hundred million by the end of the following year.

Another year after that, and it was reduced to a mere two hundred thousand that had found shelter in the Thermopoli.

It seemed that the time of humanity had passed. However, once yet another had passed there was not a single incidence of infection. This is the moment which is considered to be a turning point in human history. The Era of Reconstruction was nigh. However, the successful launch of the program required..."

R

FIRST, RICK STARTED to feel his body again, but there were multicolored circles swimming before his eyes. He blinked and finally realized that the transmission had been interrupted. He blindly stared ahead of himself, but then he removed his helmet, got out of the char and stood up, getting used to having feelings again. Finally, he pressed the activation button on the terminal, which still had the plastic card issued by the hologram sticking out of it. He had to find out what was required to launch the Reconstruction program.

However, the terminal only informed him that his session was over.

"Hey!" Rick exclaimed, slapping the screen.

No reaction, apart from a message saying "Session interrupted." Rick breathed heavily and tried to activate the terminal again, but to no avail. Then he tried to switch on the neighboring terminals, but the screens showed messages that access had been blocked. He headed downstairs in frustration. The light in the hall switched on when Rick approached the stand where the hologram appeared.

"Hey, there was an error up there," Rick said to the hologram and pointed behind his back. "The session was interrupted. Switch it back on."

The hologram silently blinked and smiled, like it did the first time around.

"Hey!" Rick exclaimed with growing irritation. "Switch it on."

"I can't," the three dimensional projection over the stand shrugged its shoulders in a very natural way.

"But why?"

"Because the validity period of your pass has run out."

"So what? Issue a new one."

"That's not possible."

Rick went behind the stand and the hologram started to flicker, but when he took a step back it became clear and turned its face to him. The body of the hologram had no bottom half, with a projection from the stand that emitted a barely perceptible light."

"All right," Rick grunted, deep in thought. "And what if I turn this stand into scrap right now?"

He demonstratively looked around for something heavy.

"Don't even think about it!" the hologram replied immediately. "That is against the law!"

"Oh, really?" Rick made a surprised face. "Come on, I will just write myself a new pass and that'll be that."

"You are violating the rules of the Archive!" Panicky notes suddenly appeared in the voice of the hologram. Rick kicked the stand and dug around in the plastic card slot with his fingernail.

"You will not be successful. A pass is given a unique number which only I can generate."

"Then generate it," Rick demanded, walking back in front of the stand.

"No," the hologram replied firmly.

"Do what I tell you," Rick hissed, "or I will disassemble you for spare parts!"

"No. You do not have the requisite authorization. You can destroy me, but you cannot make me break the rules."

Rick considered the situation. This only a program, and artificial image of a human loaded with a particular set of algorithms.

"Do you obey a strict set of rules?" he asked calmly.

"Yes."

"Who is it that programmed you with them?"

"I do not divulge information of this kind. You are not a citizen of Atlantis, which means that you do not have full access to the archive."

"Atlantis..." Rick muttered, trying to remember the word. "What does that mean?"

"The validity period of your pass has run out, which is why I can't provide information related to this request."

"Can't you just open the question?" Rick shouted, unable to restrain himself again.

He was answered with a curt "No".

"All right," Rick looked at the hologram angrily. "Then tell me, can I speak to your superiors?"

The hologram canted its head to the side, studying Rick as it stared at him.

"Hey!" he waved his hand in front of himself. "Can you hear me or not?"

"My sensors indicate that you have raised arterial blood pressure and you are breathing at an excessively rapid rate. Please, do not be so stressed out."

Rick started to feel concerned — what was this electronic dolt talking about? Why are the pauses between the answers becoming longer? What if the machine was sending requests to an invisible operator and receiving instructions about how to act and what to say? He slowly backed away to the corridor that led to the steps into the basement.

"Are you leaving already?" the hologram asked in surprise, smiling pleasantly. "I apologize if I was unable to help."

"It's nothing," Rick waved it away, glancing over his shoulder occasionally.

"Are you still experiencing feelings of anger and aggression?"

Rick increased his pace, but still tried to keep an eye on the hologram.

"Are you being overcome with rage and anger towards those that are around you?" the words kept coming from the stand. "Do you feel the desire to destroy something, causing irreparable harm? Didn't you want to destroy me? Are you suffering from a headache? Do you have a prickling feeling in the region of your..."

Rick did not listen to any more of this and

ran out into the corridor, descending into the basement and getting out into the street the same way as he entered the informatorium.

The sliver of sky between the buildings had become noticeably brighter. That meant that morning was coming and he had to be quick and return to the place where he had left his companions. He set off at a run down the street — he had to move fast so that he would not lose warmth.

The night had been freezing so the wet snow that had fallen was covered with an icy layer and steam came out of his mouth. Rick ran to the end of the quarter, noticed his own tracks and turned onto another street, turning yet again when he reached the crossroads, stopping to look around again once he had passed two buildings.

Mother Darkness, the tracks were no longer there. The area looked familiar, but... The building he saw there did not exist when he was walking towards the informatorium. He came back to the previous crossroads and looked for the signs, which had disappeared somewhere.

Right... Getting lost was all he needed. What would Black Ant and the rest of them think?

The sky painted itself red, so the day promised to be clear and frosty. Rick rubbed his hands, jumped up in down in place and then stood still. The Citadel! How could he not have guessed? He ran between the buildings and oriented himself by looking at the Citadel, which towered majestically over the city.

Now, everything was fine. Rick clapped his hands happily, clenched his fists and ran into the lane, which led him to a familiar street where he immediately noticed the places he had been to before. It was just around the corner from the place where his companions had made camp.

He soon ran onto the small square that had the squat structure on the edge. Rick let out a deep breath happily, as he hurried over the square, but he stopped stock still after he took two steps. The smell of smoke hung in the air. Rick looked around and noticed the remains of a bonfire in the other corner of the square.

How was he to understand this? It was fine if someone started a fire in the wastelands, and it as quite natural, but how was he to understand this happening in the city where there is no firewood or any need for it?

An unpleasant chill ran down his spine. Rick slowly turned around, looking for anything unusual that did not fit into the usual picture of the world and his eye stopped at the door to the structure where his companions had spent that night. It was slightly ajar.

Only a moment before, the door had been

closed.

"Hey, Black Ant!" Rick called out. "Klaus!"

The head of the boy poked out of the open door. His face looked as if he had just been sleeping, with a tired look on his face. Why did he not walk outside, why did he only look out, as if someone was holding him behind the wall?

Rick felt something hard poke into his back and turned around sharply.

Paul was standing in front of him.

"Rule number one," the former acolyte stated. "Always be alert."

"You? But..."

"How?" Paul finished his question for him and put his shocker away in its holster. "Very easily. I learn fast."

His white hair shone in the rays of the rising sun and his eyes glistened with excitement. He was dressed in the gray uniform of the Division with a corporal's insignia.

"How did you get here?" Rick never noticed the mocking tone of Paul's voice. "Why are you wearing the uniform of the Division?"

Paul canted his head to the side. Rick noticed how much his appearance had changed. His facial features, which had once been smooth and childlike had become more defined and rough and the greatest difference was in his eyes, which were hard and imperious, like those of the commanders of the...

This was when Rick finally realized that the Division uniform that Paul was wearing was no random trophy and that the former acolyte who used to be a confused and scared boy was now a corporal of the Division and a deputy platoon commander, like Rick before him.

With the edge of his gaze, he noticed movement in the square. He turned his head and saw soldiers coming out of the buildings and side streets. More and more of them came, tough looking men with grim faces and hard eyes.

Black Ant was pushed outside, followed by Lucio who had a twisted smirk on his face as he saluted theatrically. Rick gritted his teeth in impotent anger and looked at Paul again.

"You know," Paul said, "I used to think that you were an envoy of the devil. What a stupid boy I was."

"What are you trying to say?"

"Rick, you were absolutely right about the outside world. It isn't the way I imagined it at all!" Paul moved his head to indicate all around him. "It is much greater and more interesting. All of these buildings and mechanisms of the Ancients, their machines and their weapons..." He patted the holster with the shocker on his hip. "You were asking how I... how we got here? Simple. We just walked in here. We followed you, clearing our way with fire! But how did you get in here? How did you open the passage? That's the question that concerns me."

Rick stayed silent. Paul waited awhile and then prodded him, "I am waiting for an answer."

Rick kept looking at him, waiting to see how it would all end.

"Answer me!" Paul shouted. "Don't make me use force against you!"

"Oh! I'm impressed," Rick said with surprise. "I believe the Division has made a man out of you."

Paul choked with rage and drew his shocker.

"You're mocking me!" He waved the weapon in front of Rick's face, but then lowered his hand and added, "No matter. You won't even think about joking soon."

"Listen, Paul," Rick glanced back at Black Ant and Lucio. "Do you really think that I..."

"Silence!" Paul ordered furiously. "I have understood it all from the very beginning now. You were leading me on and using me for your own purposes. Yes! You were using me as a shield and manipulating me just as well as Kiernan. You abandoned me to be torn apart by those metal spheres at the first sign of danger!"

"Are you talking about the rollers on the highway? It all happened too quickly and..."

"Oh, leave me out of it!" Paul grimaced. "What happened, happened and I am even glad that this is the way it turned out. I've got rid of my fear and I can now look any enemy in the eye."

"Are we actually enemies?"

Paul looked at Rick angrily for a while and then declared, "Right then, you don't want to answer." He nodded to Lucio and he brought Black Ant up to them. "What about this?"

Paul put the shocker to the temple of the boy.

"Don't touch him!" Rick clenched his fists, tried to move towards them, but he was grabbed by the arms from behind by the soldiers. "We... we went through the gates of the lower levels using the keys of the people from segment F."

Paul immediately became animated.

"See? That's better already. Looks like you know how to give clear answers. Here's a new question — why did you leave your companions here? Where was it you went yourself?"

"I was looking for the answers to my questions in the informatorium."

"Did you find them?"

"No, a faulty ghost-machine sent me away."

"Hmm, a ghost-machine. You mean a hologram like the one we saw on the way to the city?"

Rick nodded.

"I see." Paul scratched his forehead with the barrel of the shocker. "So where were you off to with a group of these lowlifes?" he nodded at the Black Ant.

"I think that you know. My goal is the core and these people you call lowlifes lost their homes because of the soldiers. I promised to help them and I am true to my word. What about you? How do you explain your behavior?"

"You're a deserter. You have no right to question me."

"Is that the way it is?" Rick chuckled. "That's a shame. I really wanted to know what your Holy Maus looked like in your Retreat to understand why you believe in him. Especially you. Maybe you can draw him? You haven't forgotten how to draw yet, have you?"

Paul gritted his teeth and his face got flushed red with blood.

"Follow me," he ordered.

They gray ones surrounded Rick and Black Ant. Paul turned on his heels and strode off down the street, holding his back straight.

"How are you, young man?" Rick asked Black Ant.

He did not like the way Black Ant looked. They might have punished the boy somehow and drugged him with some sort of substance as he looked ill, still weak and sleepy.

"Where are the others? Did the gray ones..."

Rick was struck hard on the back with the stock of a blaster and he nearly fell. When he looked around, Lucio promised that if he opened his mouth again, they would beat the boy to death.

They walked in the direction opposite to the informatorium, escorted by the soldiers. Rick had no other reference points, but at least he had something so he would not have explain himself if the soldiers decided to check his words and send him into the archive to speak to the hologram.

They soon heard a rumble ahead. Rick became alarmed, trying to determine the source of the noise, but the soldiers were calm. Several minutes later, they came out onto the main highway, which streamed upwards on support pillars to the base of the Citadel. Wheeled vehicles growled and chugged on the highway. Some of the vehicles had multi-barreled weapons mounted on them. Their ammunition belts glinted in the sun and loud orders came from all sides. Everything was ordered according to the will of the commanders.

"Move it!" Paul shouted, without turning around and waved his hand, hurrying his followers along.

The amount of equipment was impressive, as Rick counted five cargo trucks with heavy weapons and three angular armored cars. He could see another somewhere behind his back by the turn, but it was too far away so he could not make it out clearly.

When Paul led the group across the highway and turned towards a high-rise building, the engines of the cargo trucks roared, blew caustic black exhaust fumes into the air and started to crawl along to the base of the tower, aiming their weapons at it.

Paul entered the building and they brought Rick inside after him. Black Ant and the rest of the convoy stayed in the street. Following a short elevator ride, Rick and Paul entered and open balcony with a view of the tower and the city. A broad shouldered officer stood by the balustrade with his back turned to them and gold star insignia on one of his shoulders.

Paul stepped up to him, saying, "Leopold Vasilevs, permission to report?"

The officer turned his head slightly and nodded. His profile seemed familiar to Rick, but the glare of the sunlight made it hard to make out his features.

"Armed opposition was not encountered in the course of the reconnaissance mission," Paul continued enthusiastically. "Thirty aborigines and two savages from the outer limits have been apprehended. One is approximately twelve years of age and incapable of speech. The other is... approximately twenty years of age, in possession of his faculties, a deserter."

"What?"

Paul hesitated and then declared, "He is wearing the uniform of the division, Landmaster!"

The officer turned around slowly and Rick gaped in surprise. "This is the one I was telling you about. Rick from the Omicron sector of the Thermopolis citadel, a man from the outside world. I immediately recognized him," Paul quickly added,

The officer stepped towards Rick.

"We meet again. Welcome to the core, soldier."

Rick was facing Platoon Commander Lee.

S

"I SEE THAT YOU seem to be surprised," Lee-Vasilevs noted. "I agree, it's quite unusual to wear a mask, but the ends justify the means when we want to achieve our goals of being equals with our soldiers and to know the Division inside out as we bring everyone to perfection."

Lee, who was also Vasilevs, was unusually excited. His eyes glinted feverishly. Paul made a move and the Landmaster told him over his shoulder, "Bring commander Lucio."

Paul set off to obey the order. Rick glanced after him — it seemed that the lad had a new holy man to follow.

"Now we can talk in peace." Vasilevs stood at the edge of the balcony, facing the tower again. "Come here."

Rick stepped up to the balustrade to stand by his side.

"Look," Vasilevs pointed at the highway, which was filled with human figures and military vehicles which emitted fumes into the sky. "This is my army. What do you think?"

"It's an impressive force," Rick admitted.

"I gathered everyone here. All five thousand troops plus the mechanized battalion of segment O, with twenty four military vehicles in total." Vasilevs looked at his creation with pride. "I have spent half my life building a new order and finally, the day has come when we will impose it upon the entire city."

The noise of engines and the voices of marching soldiers united in song came from the highway.

Vasilevs turned towards Rick and looked at him carefully for a while.

"I know what you're thinking," Vasilevs bared his even white teeth, "You think we won't manage to do it."

"The use of force alone is not enough to take over the city," Rick nodded.

"You're right," the Landmaster understood Rick's words in his own way. "The machines of the Ancients require knowledge. It will take some time to study them, but I am prepared to wait as long as required. Some time ago, I created a department for the decipherment of ancient glyphs. I was right to do so, as the members of this department found the keys to open the western gates. It was them that managed to switch on the machines and find warehouses full of weapons and supplies on the map." He nodded at the exit from the balcony. "Your key and your friend Paul helped us in this. He's a talented young man, just like you. I need people like that."

Vasilevs glanced at Rick.

"That's clear," Rick answered.

"Excellent. What have you decided?"

Rick looked into the dark, narrow eyes of Vasilevs and remembered a part of human history which he could never forget as it was about a military dictator that thought he was god and decided to rule the world.

"My answer does not mean anything, as I have no choice anyway."

"You say things the way they are. I like people who are understanding. Yes, you don't get much of a choice. Paul is right — you are a deserter. Which means that I can sentence you right here and now." Vasilevs put his hand upon his holster and looked at Rick questioningly. "Or..."

Rick looked away.

"Or we can organize an expedition to the Citadel," Vasilevs nodded in the direction of the tower. "We will send all the best, including yourself. Paul told me something of the outside world, of the other Citadel and your abilities. I guess he only knows a small part of it?"

Rick sighed. If he did not obey, Vasilevs would kill him. Shoot him without any doubt or feeling of guilt like a rat in a drain. Maybe he should not waste his chance to get inside the tower?

"All right," Rick replied with a chuckle.

Vasilevs grabbed and turned Rick to face him.

"That doesn't sound the way I expected." He looked into Rick's eyes intently and continued, "There is no place for the weak here. You can stay and reach the rank of commander or even higher. You can have a proud place in my army. Your place is here Rick. You are one of us. Look over there. Look hard. Look at my soldiers, they are happy. Isn't that enough to have the right to power and the imposition of order? Just tell me, don't these people deserve that? Haven't you ever wanted to be part of a great power? Look at them march in step. Power in its purest form. Order and might. No chaos, barbarity, lawlessness, discipline is paramount. Our society will be completely equal. Isn't that something worth fighting for?"

Vasilevs clenched his fist and shook it in the air. The vehicles kept growling on the highway below, as orders and the sound of marching rang out. The sun shone over it all and it was unusually bright today. Rick looked up to the sky. It seemed that a star glinted somewhere high up there. Rick's head spun and he grabbed hold of the balustrade.

"I was once part of a power like this," he replied calmly, "and I almost lost myself. I have a different goal now."

Vasilevs stepped back and laid his hand upon the holster again. His cheeks shook with tension. He was about to say something, but a piercing scream suddenly rent the air from below. One of the platoon formations broke up around a man rolling around the floor as if he was having a fit.

The soldier kept screaming. Medics with white armbands ran up to him. The soldier disappeared behind their backs for a moment, but then new screams of pain and terror started to sound. The medics backed away. The maddened soldier had sunk his teeth into one of their neck.

Blaster shots rang out.

The madman shuddered and fell to the floor, followed by the wounded medic. The bodies were immediately dragged to one side and covered with a tarp. Only a few seconds passed, when more screams came from the other end of the army column on the highway. No one tried to help the madman this time. Shots immediately rung out and his cry of pain drowned in the general noise.

The Division continued on its way, but its ordered rhythm had been interrupted. A minute later there was yet another scream of pain over the highway. Rick looked at Vasilevs, who had a stony expression on his face. His dark, narrow eyes stared into the space in front of him intently.

"Landmaster," a familiar voice sounded behind them. "Commander Lucio reporting, as per your order."

Rick and Vasilevs turned around. Paul and Lucio, whose right arm was bandaged and hung in a sling, stood in the doorway.

"What happened?" Vasilevs enquired.

"A madman," Lucio replied readily, trying to

stand up even straighter. "It's nothing, my commander. I await your orders."

Vasilevs looked at the bandaged arm with an empty gaze.

"What's going on with the cordon, where's Commander Fritz?"

"He is establishing positions in the quarters to the east of the tower. He will have the base encircled in around two hours."

"Good. Any emergencies or conflicts with the locals?"

"No, my commander. The territory is under our control."

Vasilevs nodded and was about to turn away, but Lucio looked hesitant, like he was struck with indecision, which did not slip the Landmaster's attention.

"Out with it!" Vasilevs ordered.

"Landmaster... Something is going on." Lucio sniffed like a soldier who had broken discipline. "Something is wrong with the soldiers."

Vasilevs was waiting.

"They are going insane," Lucio finally declared.

"You know what to do," Vasilevs sneered.

"Yes, we do, but there are more and more of them," Lucio's eyes flicked to the side nervously, as if he had talked too much.

"It doesn't matter!" Vasilevs cut him off. "Do what you must."

"Yes, my commander!" Lucio clicked his heels.

More screams came from the street, followed by gunshots, but Vasilevs was not concerned with the issue anymore, so he switched to something else.

"We have a deserter here," Vasilevs nodded at Rick. "And he is burning with desire to atone for his crimes."

Lucio stood ramrod straight, with his chin raised.

"This is why he will be included in the team for the expedition to the tower," Vasilevs ordered. "Lucio, you will go there, as well as Paul and several others from among my best soldiers. You move out within the hour. Your mission is to reconnoiter the inside perimeter of the tower. Rick and Paul know how to read the ancient glyphs and will help you find your bearings on location. Rick will obey your orders. He is to be terminated at the slightest disobedience. You have exactly twenty four hours. If you do not return, I will send out another party."

"My commander," Lucio's voice trembled with worry, "this deserted is not going to help us. He is more likely to incite a mutiny and try to run away."

"I have no doubt," Vasilevs smirked predatorily. "But he is not going to do that. Do you want to know why? Well, I will tell you. We are now all in the same boat."

Confusion was written on Paul and Lucio's faces.

"There are reports from the middle ring that the outer ring has been entirely taken over by the possessed. They are already on the wall. They are all the inhabitants of the segments as well as outsiders that keep coming every hour. There are thousands of them. They are coming from the north, south, east and west. I have lost communication with almost every group of lookouts. The city is under siege. We have no way back, only ahead!"

He pointed at the tower.

Rick suddenly realized that he could not hear the noise of the vehicles and the marching soldiers anymore. They could only hear the weak sound of voices from below, as the highway emptied with the main forces of the division occupying positions at the base of the tower.

"Is there something in particular that we need to look for?" Lucio came to his senses first.

"Yes. You must find any ancient high-tech means of defense I am not confident about the perimeter of the core. Any wall can be overcome or the perimeter can be passed under the ground.

Isn't that right, Rick from Omicron?"

"This expedition is an act of desperation," Rick replied.

"We have nothing to lose apart from our lives," the Landmaster concluded.

Rick did not argue his point.

"The mission is clear, my commander," Lucio declared.

He did not have time to click his heels as an unfamiliar officer appeared on the balcony and reported, "Landmaster, a man has come to us, saying that he is an envoy."

"Where is he? What does he look like?"

"He is under guard in the next room. He looks possessed, but he is somehow able to speak clearly. He says that he has a message just for you. We are concerned that his might be some kind of enemy ploy to get to you. This is why..."

"Bring him."

"Bring in the envoy!"

The officer stepped aside, taking his heavy blaster off his shoulder, moving the safety catch and raised the weapon, ready to fire. Soldiers brought a dark-skinned man wearing long fur-lined rags onto the balcony. He had a shining golden medallion on his neck, hanging on a thick chain which was rusted through with time. He wore worn shoes on his feet. The man moved his head, as if he was trying to find someone with his inner gaze, as his eyes were entirely white. He stopped and turned to Vasilevs.

"Who are you?" the Landmaster asked tensely.

"I am a man."

"And that's all? Do you have a name?"

"I do not need one. Names mean nothing."

Vasilevs frowned grimly.

"Do you even understand where you are?"

The envoy suddenly burst out laughing. Rick heard something familiar in that laugh, but he could not quite put his finger on where he had heard it before.

"Of course. Otherwise, I wouldn't be here."

"And do you know who I am?"

"An outcast, that has imagined himself to be a king."

Vasilevs' face changed, with fury and panic glinting at his eyes at the same time. His nostrils moved as he breathed heavily.

"And what do you need?"

"I was sent..." the man's face suddenly twisted into a tormented grimace as he forced himself to continue, "Sent to tell you just one thing."

"Who sent you?"

"They..." the envoy waved behind his back and closed his eyes. "We are telling you to stop. Stop!"

Vasilevs waited, but the envoy stood there with his eyes closed, swaying form side to side and barely moving his lips.

"Anything else?" Vasilevs burst out.

The envoy suddenly opened his eyes, which suddenly had pupils and irises and looked around in surprise.

"I had a dream," he suddenly told them. "In that dream, I was a priest and I served a pointless god. We held masses, shivered from the cold and believed in a better world. But one day, the god died right in front of my eyes and a man came from the tower and woke me up. Since then, I..." His eyes rolled back in his head and his pupils disappeared as his voice became heavy and drawn out. "We... speak. We say, it is time to awaken."

"Enough!" Vasilevs decided. "Take him away!"

The escorts took the envoy under the arms, but suddenly, he easily pushed them away and shouted, "Stop, outcast! Stop, before your dream becomes a nightmare!"

Vasilevs snatched his short-barreled blaster out of his pocket and shot three charges in the head and chest of the envoy.

There was a burst of flesh. Rick could not help staggering away, as he covered himself from the pieces of skull. When he turned back, a smoking corpse hit the floor like a stone pillar.

Vasilevs put away his weapon and ordered calmly, "Take this away from hear. And you," he turned towards Lucio, "must prepare for the expedition. Hurry up, time is not on your side."

Lucio and Paul clicked their heels.

"Landmaster," Rick asked, "if we are going to do this, please include Black Ant in the unit as well."

Vasilevs quizzically raised an eyebrow.

"It's a boy who managed to get here unarmed and by himself from the outer limits and got inside the city without help from anyone."

"Give me at least one reason for me to agree," Vasilevs smirked.

"I actually have several." Rick started to count on his fingers. "He is careful and quick-witted. He cleverer than Lucio thinks and he has a phenomenal memory. He is agile and supple, so he can get into places that even the most experienced fighter can reach."

"All right," the Landmaster said after a pause and sent a pointed look Lucio's way.

T

THEY WERE QUICKLY rising up to the base of the tower. Rick activated an elevator on an inclined monorail and now looked at their surroundings through a clear wall. He did not speak to the others almost at all since the beginning of the expedition. Black Ant stayed close, preferring to look at the same things as Rick.

As a result of some sort of malicious intent or perhaps by random chance, they had included Gareth in the group. This could have been the work of Lucio, or Gareth may have volunteered himself. Rick did not want to think about it, as that would not make it any easier.

The cabin shuddered a little as it passed a rusty joint. The fiftieth floor of the base of the tower receded below them. This was no great height for one who had grown up in a citadel, but everyone else apart from Black Ant seemed to think otherwise, judging by their facial expression.

"We will be there soon," Rick calmed them down.

The cabin slowed and came to a complete halt soon after. The doors hissed as they slid open and everyone quickly got out. A glass-walled terrace that followed the rounded base of the tower stretched out to both sides of the elevator. Rick looked around. There were other exits from the terrace at every hundred paces.

"Go first," Lucio ordered. "The boy will come with me."

Rick looked back at them. Lucio pulled Black Ant's sleeve, bringing the boy closer to himself.

"All right." As Rick expected, the boy was made a hostage.

There was another side to it though — Black Ant managed to survive before so he would manage it again. Rick also knew the plan of the tower in which he was born and bred — he doubted that outsiders would be immediately able to understand its complex architecture without a guide.

They all stood still in silence and waited. Rick slowly tuned around, looking at the familiar shapes of the aeons through the clear ceiling and almost believed that he was back home for a moment.

"Hey, are you going to stand around and gawp for much longer?" Lucio could not contain himself. "Maybe we should move on?"

Rick just nodded and pushed back against the wave of memories as he set off towards a wide stone stairway.

They got to the first aeon without any

problems. All that was left was to pass through a wide archway that framed a tunnel with a high ceiling. Rick turned to look back at the city.

"What do you see there?" Lucio asked him, understanding his behavior in his own way. Some sort of trouble?

"No. None yet."

Lucio did not calm down so easily, so he hid behind Black Ant's back, crouched and raised his heavy army blaster. The others, including Paul, followed his example. Rick and Black Ant had obviously not been issued with weapons.

Rick chuckled and walked under the arch. His eyes quickly got used to the gloom. When the group had gone a significant distance into the tunnel, the soldiers turned on their torches. Rick soon asked them to turn the lights off so that they would not attract the attention of any possible denizens of the Citadel.

They soon found themselves in a vaulted hall with the Chorda rising up high in the center. He choked up again from his memories of Thermopolis, but he did not make a stop this time. Once he oriented himself, he determined the direction where the elevator niches were located and calmly set off there. They were under no threat here. Back when he was in his native Thermopolis, Rick learned to distinguish between different types of silence and he knew that this was the silence of abandonment.

"Where are we going?" Gareth asked, catching up to him.

"Towards the transport hub," Rick explained.

He approached a terminal, activated the screen by touching it with his palm and called an elevator. A cargo cabin appeared a minute later.

"Are you sure that it's safe here?" Lucio kept himself at a distance from the wall, gripping Black's Ants shoulder hard with his hand.

"Absolutely," Rick replied nonchalantly. "Otherwise, they would have already stopped us on the terrace at the foot of the stairway."

Rick entered the cabin and asked, "So are you coming with me or waiting here?"

Paul was the first to come inside and another four soldiers followed. Gareth, Lucio and Black Ant entered last. Rick touched the control keys on the panel and the cabin started to crawl upwards, accelerating gradually.

The elevator quickly passed through the levels an entered a shaft through an opening in the barrier wall between the aeons. The cabin sunk into darkness for an instant, until one of the three lamps under the ceiling blinked and switched on. Everyone was tense, watching the outside through the clear wall. Thick girders, rows of pipelines and the grilles of a hundred ventilation shafts on the walls swam past as they sped upwards. The light in the cabin suddenly blinked again and then went out for a couple of seconds, before lighting up again. No one had the time to panic as the cabin passed the barrier and continue rising through a new aeon. Rick did not like what he saw at all. He stepped up to the control panel, typed something in with his fingers on the buttons and stopped their ascent.

There was nothing apart from empty space above their heads.

A huge, empty well with only a silent Chorda and the vertical rails of the elevator stretching upwards. The Citadel was empty inside — there were only bare walls with slots prepared for the installation of horizontal girders.

"Why did we stop?" Lucio asked warily.

Everyone looked at Rick expectantly.

"It's empty here," he replied, "and the Chorda is not alight."

"What should it have here?"

"It should have levels, whole floors full of various equipment, residential units, warehouses, sections full of machinery..."

"You are lying to us!" Lucio shouted, drawing his knife and putting it against Black Ant's throat. "Tell us the truth right now!"

"It's the truth!" Rick threw his hands up in

desperation. "I don't understand why a whole aeon of the citadel is empty or why there is no energy in the Chorda! My world is an exact copy of this one, with the difference that all the space inside the tower was occupied with floors that had everything needed for maintaining life."

"Is that even possible?" Gareth asked in surprise. "Are you trying to say that machines and a lot of things you need to maintain life can be raised to such a height? You're delirious! Why are you doing this?"

He glanced at Paul who seemed to trust Rick more judging by the expression on his face.

Rick did not want to waste time on pointless arguments and look for someone's support as he was worried by what he saw. He was overcome with questions but could not find the answers to them.

"All right, let's say you're not lying," Lucio spoke up again. "What do we do now?"

"We have two options," Rick finally offered. "We can go up or down."

"But there is nothing up there, am I right?" Gareth interrupted.

"It's possible that all the aeons are empty," Rick nodded.

"That means we should have gone downwards," Paul concluded.

"Isn't it empty there too, with a barely

glowing pillar and nothing else?" Lucio asked.

"No," Paul said, looking at Rick carefully. "We should go even further down."

"That's right," Rick confirmed. "There is probably a sector zero down below with the maintenance floors. But there could be a command center up above. It was located inside the fifth aeon in my citadel, on the floors at the very top."

"I don't like the idea of climbing up there," Gareth said, pointing the barrel of his blaster at Rick. "This scumbag is leading us into a trap."

They all turned to Lucio, who had to make a decision.

"First we go up," he finally said. "And then down."

Rick turned to the control panel, but Lucio stepped up to him and ordered, "You will first explain how to me how to control this thing. You will show me everything and hide nothing."

"All right," Rick nodded and told Lucio about the purpose of all the keys and commands displayed on the panel.

Lucio sent the cabin upwards by himself and seemed to be very satisfied.

They soon rose through the aeon and found themselves in the space inside the barrier again. Following a few moments of waiting, they entered yet another empty aeon. Rick sighed in disappointment, furrowed his brow and told everyone, "There will be another three of these sections that go through the barriers."

No one said a word. The cabin kept rising along the dark and lifeless Chorda. Rick was carefully examining its surface, as he could not understand why the Chorda glowed below but stayed dead here.

A while later, they passed another aeon, where the situation as similar. The darkness hid the distance from then and no one could orient themselves in the space, as they could not even imagine the unbelievable height they were at. However, once the cabin reached the cold and open platform at the top that was buffeted by the ice cold wind under the shining sun, everyone held on to the railings and did not want to get out.

Only Rick, Paul and Gareth stepped outside, shivering from the cold that pierced them down to their very bones, brought upon them by the freezing wind.

Rick looked back when he heard a sob behind him. Gareth had vomited, which was no wonder at this height, as this world was alien for people from the surface. Paul held himself together rather well, apart from being as pale as the snow which gusted into their face when the wind picked up pace.

The platform they saw around them was empty. There was only a thin metallic rod protruding in the center at the top of the Chorda, as well as a few vertical rails that stuck out from sealed elevator openings. That was all.

Rick walked towards the edge of the platform, which had no railing. He stopped a pair of paces away, looking out into the space below. There was an incredibly simple and understandable picture around the tower stretching out below — three concentric rings of city buildings separated from each other with tall and dark walls. He could clearly see the main highway and the branching roads that led to it. The fine details of the segments were impossible to make out, but Rick got a general impression of the city.

He shifted his gaze to the east and gasped with surprise. An endless and calm ocean rippled with its dark waters in the distance. There was a glittering strip of sunlight that stretched towards the horizon, as the shore gently undulated as it followed the edge of the water.

"Look at that!" Paul's excited voice rang out behind Rick's back.

Gareth and Rick hurried over to him.

Paul was standing on all fours in dangerous proximity to the edge and pointing to the city. A weak and drawn out rumble came from below as the outer ring slowly turned together with the city buildings.

"Unbelievable!" Paul exclaimed. "Can you see that?"

Rick nodded and glanced over at the elevator cabin where Lucio still stood holding onto Black Ant's shoulder together with the other soldiers who were afraid to get out onto the platform.

The outer ring turned slowly and resolutely together with the segments that filled it. The buildings and the channels of the roads, the translucent domes, the threads of the pipelines and the black boxes of the hangars were all moving. Rick carefully observed the city, forgetting the height and the cold wind and a picture gradually started to come together inside his head. The city was rebuilding itself in such a way that the programmed mechanisms grouped the structures along the wide highways that met the supports by the base of the citadel that had the gigantic stabilizer fins of the future spaceship hanging over them.

Rick closed his eyes, trying to remember the scientific chapter which he had studied back when he was still in Thermopolis, but unfortunately his memory refused to provide him with information.

Could this be a mistake? Were things

different to the way he just imagined them? He backed away from the edge as his head started spinning and looked upwards, where a dot that slowly moved towards the horizon glittered in the dark sky. The rumble below became louder and Rick looked back at the city, noticing the middle ring start to move.

"What is going on over there?" Lucio shouted from the elevator cabin.

No one answered him. Rick was staring at what was going on below, hoping that his guess was correct.

"Hey!" he heard from behind. "Look out!"

Rick did not react immediately as it was Paul who moved first, surprisingly. It first seemed that he had thrown himself at him but then there was a shadow that moved by his side. Paul knocked Rick off his feet before Gareth struck Paul on the back with the stock of his blaster, falling down to the floor as well.

Rick had to push Paul to the side and waste valuable time. Gareth raised his blaster to strike again, his face twisted and his eyes shining as he bared his teeth. Rick barely managed to move to the side and got hit by stock on the shoulder.

Gareth howled and it was unclear whether it was anger or disappointment. He threw away his blaster and rushed at Rick, grabbing him around the neck.

Lucio and the soldiers shouted at Gareth to stop and threatening to shoot from the elevator cabin, but they did not see that Gareth had gone insane and did not understand anything, so they hesitated to open fire.

Rick managed to hit Gareth around the ear, punch him in the ribs and pull him under himself. Both men rolled along the platform. The madman still did not loosen his grip as he hissed and shouted, squeezing Rick's neck tighter.

"Look out for the edge!" Lucio shouted.

It was too late when Rick realized where they were rolling and punched Gareth with all his strength. Gareth shuddered for a moment and seemed to come to his senses, as his eyes flashed in panic and recognition. He was still carried to the side by inertia and he dragged Rick after him until they both fell onto the edge of the platform.

Gareth screamed as a current of air immediately blew him away. Rick managed to gather his legs to him, but then he spread his arms and realized that he is falling right onto the inclined stabilizing fin. He moved his hands to change the position of his body again. An instant later, his back touched the sloping surface.

His eyes teared up from the air streaming into his face. Rick could not see anything as it all merged into a huge white spot. He slid along the stabilizer on his back, praying to Mother Darkness that he would not hit some projection.

He slowed down soon after, but his speed was still great enough for him to be crushed if he hit a hard object or tear his back apart if there was a rough surface.

Through the mist in his eyes he somehow made out the highway nearby, where men in gray clothing were moving around and it seemed that he heard gunshots and shouting. He did not manage to understand what was going on though, as the fin ended abruptly and Rick found himself flying through the air again and waving his arms, screaming...

The last thing he saw was a snow-covered roof. He flew into a snowdrift feet first. A terrible pain pierced his foot and then his side.

He went out like a light.

U

IT WAS LIGHT in the street when Rick came to and climbed out of the snowdrift. Rick decided that this meant that he must have spent the whole night in his snowy cave which saved him from freezing. His side burned with pain, but his foot was even more painful and he could barely stand on it.

Once he got his bearings, Rick came down from the roof and limped towards the Citadel, picking up a steel rod on the way that he could conveniently lean on and use as a weapon if needed. He had no idea what was going on around him and did not know whether the soldiers managed to take the core under their control. He doubted they did, anyway. As he walked, he occasionally came across bodies in gray uniforms lying in the streets. Some lay there with their throats turned out, gripping their weapons, while the others had coagulated wounds on their bodies. Sometimes, dead bodies dressed in rags lay among them, who Rick thought were probably possessed. However, it looked like the soldiers had killed each other without help from the possessed in most cases. The question was, what made them do it?

Rick's head rang and he constantly grimaced with pain.

However, pain was much better than cold and death. He walked along for around a quarter, when his way to the square before the base of the Citadel was blocked by one of the possessed, who wore a torn brown jumpsuit and had long hair which had stuck together hanging down onto his face. Rick could not see his eyes, but it seemed that the madman standing in his way was carefully examining the newcomer.

Rick took a pair of steps and said, "Get out of the way."

No reaction. The madman made no move. Several other possessed poured out into the street from the buildings and side-streets. They also stood still nearby, staring at Rick as if they had seen something amazing and unusual.

"What do you want?"

He was answered with silence. Rick set his mouth in a grim line and advanced on the hairy possessed who did not even think of moving out of the way. When Rick raised his rod to strike and crush the madman's skull, he suddenly spoke.

"The key for the start."

"What?" Rick froze with his rod still raised to strike. "What did you say?"

"The Uranus program," he heard from the side.

Rick turned towards the voice.

"Could all passengers get into their places," came from another direction.

Then the voices came from all around him.

"Secure all movable objects..."

"Put on your oxygen masks..."

"The countdown is about to begin"

"Ten, nine. Three squared equals nine."

"Eight, seven. Two times tow equals four."

"Weight is connected to the substance of the elements so much that they always keep the same weight when they turn from one into another."

"Let it be necessary to find the magnetic induction module at the center of a very thin spool that has a number of coils equal to..."

"The mass of a substance appearing on the electrode is directly proportional to the electrical charge that passes through the electrolyte..."

"The sum of the squared lengths of the legs is equal to the square of the length of the hypotenuse..."

Interrupting each other, the possessed spoke of genetic codes, cryogenic chambers and the colonization program, constantly mentioning the planet of Terra Nova. They reported the physical constants and parts of formulae and listed the numbers related to the necessary fuel and life support supplies. Rick shut his eyes in disbelief as to what was going on. He would have kept standing there like that and waiting for the madmen to shut their mouths, but then the loud report of a heavy military blaster interrupted their unstoppable squall of voices.

Rick opened his eyes when the hairy possessed was already lying on the ground, half of his skull caved in by a blaster charge.

The possessed all turned their backs to

Rick as one, growled and charged at the soldiers that appeared in the street, as if obeying someone's invisible command. They had turned into wild and starving animals in an instant.

Rick had to quickly get out of the way so that he would not get accidentally hit by a blaster charge. He stumbled along to the wall of a building and he was about to go through the door but he stopped at the entrance, as he watched a bloodied woman crawl out.

The woman stretched out her hand towards him, saying, "Charles the King, our great Emperor, has been in Spain for seven full years..."

The woman was dressed in the greenish jumpsuit of the cluster of the fords and Rick suddenly recognized Olivia's face. She kept crawling towards him with her hand stretch out. Rick crouched and touched her cold fingers. Something changed in the woman's eyes and she whispered, "A Threshold. This is a Threshold. The instructions require..."

A blaster shot rang out nearby and Olivia shuddered, stretching out on the floor as she kept her glassy eyes on Rick. Her lips were still moving when he heard a second shot. Rick turned his head and saw Landmaster Vasilevs standing before him. A dozen and a half soldiers stood behind him, blasters at the ready.

"You?" the Landmaster exclaimed in surprise.

"Yes, it's me."

"Why didn't they touch you?"

"I have no idea..."

"Where's everyone else?"

Rick realized that the unit headed by Lucio did not establish communications and gave Vasilevs a brief overview of their elevator trip to the top of the tower, his fight with Gareth and his speedy descent.

"Do you think I'll believe you?" Vasilevs asked.

"Possibly. I'm still alive and you need me."

"That's right," Vasilevs nodded and called a soldier with a medical armband. "Examine him and do everything so he can walk," he ordered.

Rick was injected with some sort of vaccine and his foot was fixed in place with a bandage. The boot had to be sliced open to take out his foot, but the pain went away after several minutes and he managed to somehow put another boot back on and stand up straight.

Vasilevs nodded with satisfaction and he waved at the soldiers to move through the square towards the tower. Rick walked by his side, with the soldiers surrounding them in a ring. Circles swam before his eyes from the drug, but he breathed easily and even seemed refreshed. Rick knew that this was a temporary narcotic effect which would soon make him feel sick. The image of Olivia as she died and her last words appeared in his mind. What could those words have meant?

Rick followed Vasilevs, thinking awhile and then told him, "Only the underground sector remains. If it is empty, we are done for."

Vasilevs turned around and looked at Rick questioningly.

"We must descend and explore the underground floors of the Citadel," Rick explained. "I think that is where the main secret if hidden."

"Excellent," Vasilevs replied with a predatory smile. "Let it be so."

"Aren't you afraid of possession?"

"What about you? Aren't you afraid?"

Rick only chuckled in reply and shook his head.

"See? The main thing is to believe in yourself. By the way, what is it they were mumbling at you?"

"Formulae," Rick did not look at Vasilevs as he answered automatically, deep in thought. "Formulae and poetry."

"What? Poetry? But why?"

"I have no answer," Rick shrugged. "I wonder, how did they retain this ancient knowledge? And why did the possessed start to talk anyway?"

They walked through the square, which had groups of possessed at its edge. They had assembled a cross from steel girders, upon which they tied a dead soldier with his eyes torn out.

They saw a square granite monument that was along their way with a madman by its side, who had drawn a woman in a toga on the stone with a torch in one hand and a tablet in the other. The woman had a sharp pointed wreath upon her head. The drawing was very realistic and it was painted in blood. The madman was adding the finishing touches, wetting his finger in an open would on his own wrist.

One of the soldiers surrounding Vasilevs quickly raised his blaster to shoot the unfortunate artists, but the Landmaster forbid him to do so. Rick nodded approvingly — they did not need any extra noise right now as there were several of the possessed off to the side of the monument who circled in a silent dance, holding each other's hands. They were howling and growling a simple three note melody and were quite successful at that.

They came across several other groups of possessed on their way to the tower, but none of them paid any attention to the quietly advancing soldiers. Finally, Rick and Vasilevs were by the cabin on the inclined rail that led to the clear terrace at the base of the tower.

"Symbols," Vasilevs suddenly said, pointing at the pictograms on the control panel of the elevator. "They are on every device here. My scientists spent a long time trying to decipher them. They tried many different methods, but their efforts were in vain until Paul showed them how to open the airlock using the medallion. His medallion was what we had to start with. We actually had several of them. I used to think that it was some sort of decoration, a useless bauble, but it turned out that it was a most valuable object."

Vasilevs grinned and activated the panel to open the doors and Rick and the rest of their group entered the cabin.

"We started to try out the medallions on the ancient machines," Vasilevs continued. "Sometimes they would work and sometimes they wouldn't. We understood that a medallion has a set of standard codes. For instance, it would open the doors to any maintenance room. However, there were mechanisms that Paul's medallion did not work on, but ours suddenly activated. It then became clear that each medallion was tied to a particular city segment. Medallions from other segments were brought to me. We managed to gather several dozen of them in total, but this was enough to get us into places, which people had never reached before. We descended below the ground and found whole floors and roads, streets and city quarters all dark and dead. There are gigantic mechanisms there below the surface of the city. Machines that occupy gigantic spaces. We found warehouses full of clothing, supplies, weapons and unusual devices. We managed to launch some of them, understand their purpose and the way they were controlled. We also found fragments of information about super-weapons in the archives and…"

"You wanted to get into the core," Rick said sadly.

"And we did it!" Vasilevs exclaimed. "Of course, we had to go through some trouble, but we managed. I was only mistaken about one thing as I never knew that the Division will get infected during the attack. But we are by the tower and we will soon see what's going on. Isn't that right?"

"I guess so," Rick replied, even though he was rather doubtful.

At least he knew the reason that the soldiers were killing each other now. They became possessed like Gareth did up top and attacked normal humans in their pain, anger and hunger, only the animal instincts that tore their minds apart.

The cabin delivered them to the terrace and Rick showed where they had to go.

"We have practically won." Vasilevs' eyes glinted with excitement. "All of these savages have lost their minds and they are incapable of anything. We will reach the super-weapons and the defensive systems of the citadel and easily destroy all of these madmen." They entered the hall with the glowing Chorda. "We will cleanse them from the city, restart the ancient machines and restore order. The main thing is..."

His speech was interrupted by a scream of pain. Rick and Vasilevs looked around. The soldiers that were escorting them stepped away from one of their number who was on his knees, hitting his head upon the floor.

Rick flinched when he heard the report of a blaster by his side.

"We shouldn't delay," Vasilevs said as he put the weapon away in the holster on his hip.

He turned around and strode off towards the Chorda. Rick and the rest of the soldiers spent a while looking at the Landmaster's retreating back, but then followed him.

"What sort of place is this?" Vasilevs asked as if nothing had happened.

"The first sector," Rick responded. "Its central part, to be more precise."

"Excellent!" Vasilevs stopped two paces

away from the Chorda then turned to Rick and nodded. "Go for it."

"What do you want?"

"Start up the ancient machines," Vasilevs raised his hands turning around. "Close all of the entrances. Turn on the generators and the protective force field Make this city come to life."

"I'm afraid that is beyond my powers. First of all, I don't have the key for segment A," Rick replied, hoping that this would be where it ended.

"Do you mean this key?" Vasilevs took a medallion from an inside pocket.

Rick did not show his surprise and continues, "Secondly, the machine will only obey the person with the correct genetic code."

"What does that mean?"

"The machine recognizes who belongs to the generation of citizens that lived in the city before their birth." Rick did not mention the descendants of Spanidis, such as himself. "I am an outsider for it. You and the soldiers are not. Why don't you do it all yourself?"

Vasilevs jutted his jaw and told him through gritted teeth, "I can't. You must help me. Come on!"

Rick fell silent for a while and suddenly understood that Vasilevs was too stupid to solve a simple problem. He found it funny that this man managed to get thousands of people together, arm them and get them to follow him. Rick was about to say something, but the soldiers suddenly exclaimed as one, as if they were terrified and started to back away towards the exit from the hall, staring at Vasilevs in horror.

Rick turned to the Landmaster, who growled, "What's going on here?"

"A monster..."

"A monster..." the soldiers kept repeating.

"A monster!"

The faces of the soldiers showed a genuine and honest terror, as if they had seen something for the first time in their lives that was so terrifying that it made them forget about their strength and skills. The soldiers turned and ran, as if they were issued an order.

"Halt!" Vasilevs shouted at their backs, pulling out his blaster.

He managed to gun down two of them before the others disappeared in the tower.

"Disgusting vermin!" Vasilevs shouted, spittle flying from his mouth. "Pathetic cowards! I will kill you all!"

His lips trembled and his hands shook from the stress as his wild eyes flitted around the hall.

"So that's it," Rick calmly declared. "You don't have an army anymore."

Vasilevs turned to him sharply.

"How..." he hissed, "...how can we protect ourselves from this evil? Why are people losing their minds?"

"I don't know," shrugged Rick.

"What a strange disease. It affected people a long time ago, when everyone lived in peace and harmony."

"I never believed in the supernatural, but I'm ready to do it now, if only to escape this fate."

"It won't help," came from the darkness of the hall.

Vasilevs raised his hand with the blaster again and Rick turned towards the voice. Paul stood in front of them, with Lucio and Black Ant standing to his side, with the other soldiers from their group nowhere to be seen. Rick worked out what happened to them. They became sick. Paul and Lucio's clothing, and even that of Black Ant was spattered with blood and their faces were tired but firm. They managed to survive and come down and looked at Rick as if they had seen a ghost.

"My commander?" Lucio finally ventured, after carefully examining the Landmaster.

"Yes," Vasilevs replied with irritation. "It's me. I see that you lost a lot of your men. Report. Should I go up top?"

"No, my commander!" Rick automatically stood to attention, but could not resist and stared at Rick again.

"This is not a ghost, this is Rick from Omicron and he is alive," Vasilevs addressed their concerns. He turned to Paul.

"Where were you off to?"

"The lower levels."

Vasilevs nodded with satisfaction, glancing over at Rick.

"Onwards then, my warriors."

No one got the chance to make a move. A growing clamor came from the tunnels into the hall. Everyone exchanged anxious glances.

"What now?" Vasilevs shook his head questioningly.

"Run!" Paul and Rick exclaimed simultaneously.

They headed to the nearest elevator.

The sound coming from the tunnels kept growing — it was the stamp of a thousand possessed feet and the roar of a myriad voices.

Rick was the first to run into the cabin and he looked back. Paul, Black Ant and Vasilevs followed, with Lucio bringing up the rear. Lucio tripped by the doors and fell inside, sliding along the floor on his belly. Rick activated the panel and the closing door cut them off from the hall which had filled with the possessed in a few moments. Rick was genuinely scared. For some reason he knew that had they not managed to get out of there they would have been torn to pieces without the strange speeches that he got to hear before.

The cabin slowly crept downwards and Rick wanted the descent to last as long as possible. He was overcome by a feeling of emptiness and any desire to discover the secret of the city disappeared. All efforts were in vain when madness was all around.

The noise of the maddened crowd kept coming down form above as the cabin descended but eventually started to get quieter.

"They will get through," Paul confidently declared.

"They will," Rick nodded, sitting down on the floor and scowling from the pain in his foot. "But not immediately. We have some time to spare."

Black Ant sat down near Rick and smiled. Rick smiled back, patting the boy on the shoulder.

"Everything will be all right."

Black Ant nodded.

The lamp flickering under the ceiling buzzed, burning brighter for a moment and abruptly went out.

"Switch on your torches," Vasilevs ordered.

"Wait," Rick leaned on Black Ant's shoulder as he rose to his feet.

"He's right," Paul agreed. "There could be others around. The main thing is not to hurry or make too much noise."

Vasilevs was about to disagree, but suddenly noticed the Chorda flickering orange behind the wall.

"This is an energy line," Rick explained. "It pierces the whole citadel. If the line is charged there is enough light. You just need to get used to it."

They passed and empty level and were now descending through a space illuminated with light coming from below. It turned out that the Chorda began in a pool filled with a jelly that shone orange. The elevator took them onto a maintenance catwalk and stopped. Rick opened the door and stepped outside, with everyone following him in silence.

"What is this place?" Lucio whispered.

"My citadel had a launch panel here," Rick replied. "The units of a spaceship launch device are above us."

"Space... what?" Lucio could not repeat his words.

"It doesn't matter." Rick looked around and understood that everything was arranged differently in this citadel. The maintenance catwalk circled the level above the pool. "We are not quite in the place we should be in."

"What's wrong?" Vasilevs asked warily.

"The command center is somewhere off to the side. That's because when the engines start up, the incandescent gases will burn everything alive on the levels below. They will even melt metal and rock."

"So where should we go?" Vasilevs and the rest watched Rick patiently.

"We must examine the exits from the balcony. Paul, look for signs and inscriptions that show the direction of the command center. Anything that is related to controlling sector A."

They split up. Vasilevs went with Rick, while Paul and Lucio who deliberately took Black Ant with them went in the opposite direction.

Rick limped along, reading the writing on the walls, but it was all just minor things they did not need, with the exits leading to all sorts of laboratories, maintenance rooms and reservoirs. They had walked along half of the circumference of the sector border in this way, when Rick stood stock still, not believing his eyes. "Portal to the Center of Directory A" was written on the sign. He re-read it and carefully examined the opening that had some barely noticeable feeder lines on the sides and whispered happily, "I think we found it."

"Are you sure?" Vasilevs asked.

"Yeah."

Vasilevs called the others, who were on their way along the catwalk on the other side and stepped into the corridor.

Blinding light burst from the floor of the corridor behind him. Rick shut his eyes, backing away inadvertently and saw that Vasilevs was already gone and only a shining curtain of light blocked the opening. Paul and Lucio were rubbing at their eyes as they tried to restore their eyesight from being temporarily blinded. Black Ant kept fearfully trying to get close to Rick, who heard a familiar humming noise and the crackle of electrical charges through the irritated cries of his companions.

"Mother Darkness," Rick whispered when he understood what was going on.

The whole catwalk was filled with rollers that had appeared from the side passages.

V

RICK TRIED TO STEP through the curtain of shining light, but ran into a solid barrier. He hit it with his fist, making it ripple with light, but could not make it do anything else.

It was a force field — the technology of the ancients in action. But why did the field prevent a descendant of Spanidis from entering the corridor?

He heard the report of blasters behind his back. Rick turned around and stood still, almost without breathing and covered Black Ant with his body. What could they do and where should they run?

Paul and Lucio poured blaster charges at the silvery spheres. However, the defensive fields of the rollers reflected the shots, which did not stop Lucio from another attempt when it was time to reload his battery. Paul stepped behind his back and looked down over the railing, hoping to find an exit and save himself. No, jumping would be a bad choice as it was too high up and they would fall to their deaths.

Rick felt Black Ant pulling him by the hand. He turned around to see the boy pointing at the shining shield and the receding silhouette of Vasilevs behind it.

"Over there?" Rick asked in surprise. "But it doesn't let me through!"

Black Ant poked himself in the chest with his fingers and put his hand into the opening, easily going through the energy curtain.

"You can go through?"

Black Ant nodded and stepped into the corridor, turned around and brushed his curly hair back from his temple.

"Now that's a surprise", Rick thought as he looked through the green shine of the force field. The boy had a socket in his head just like Book of Faces. What was he planning?

Black Ant started to make shapes with his hands, trying to explain something, but Rick could not understand anything. The boy then just waved his hand, turned around and disappeared in the darkness of the corridor. Rick did not even have time to call out to him.

Well, at least someone had saved himself. He felt a little sorry that Vasilevs managed to get away, but now he had to think about himself and decide what to do.

"Rick!" Paul stepped up to him. "Where did the boy and the Landmaster go?"

Rick had no time to answer as Lucio let out a wild scream — lightning arced towards him, his hair standing on end and his eyes shining with a white glow, as smoke poured out of his mouth and ears. Lucio shook for a while, as branching electrical charges danced all over his body and then suddenly stopped as he fell to the floor, charred like an ember from head to foot.

The spheres slowly rolled towards Rick and Paul. One of them sped up and cut them off from the opening where Vasilevs and Black Ant had gone.

"I never thought that I would die in such a

stupid way," Rick said.

"I have no intention of dying yet," Paul replied, about to jump from the catwalk.

He stepped towards the railing, but a roller quickly moved there and got in his way.

"Well, that's that," Rick chuckled. "You're too late."

"I'm happy that you're having fun," Rick retorted angrily.

"Not at all." Rick took him by the shoulder and turned him so he would face him. "You've really grown up, Paul. It's a shame that you don't share my beliefs, but..."

The humming of the spheres and the crackling of the charges suddenly stopped. A deafening silence fell and Rick and Paul could not believe what was happening. They looked around stupidly, not understanding what was going on. But then, when the spheres suddenly cracked at the top like the eggs of a gigantic spider to show humans sitting in the seats inside. Paul growled with fury and raised his blaster.

This was unbelievable. Rick expected to see anything but people controlling the rollers.

"Stop!" he shouted at Paul, but it was too late, as he shot blaster charge after blaster charge as the roller pilots ran to escape. "Just stop it!"

Rick grabbed Paul's arm when he was

about to finish off one of the running men who had fallen to the floor and tore the blaster from his hands after elbowing him in the shoulder.

"They're not worthy it!"

"Have you lost your mind? They nearly killed us! I want to have revenge!"

"No!"

Rick took a step back, shouldering the blaster.

"Ah, so you're in league with them," Paul bared his teeth. "You deliberately brought us here so they could kill us. Is that it?"

"You idiot! That's not how it is."

"Yes it is!"

"I'll prove it to you, damn it!"

Rick spat angrily and turned to the man who tried to run away, who had already sat up, drawing his legs in and fearfully observing their argument.

"Who are you? Why did you want to kill us? Why are you murdering people on the highways and flyovers? What's your mission?"

The roller pilot was very young and he opened his mouth soundlessly, so terrified that he could not utter a single word.

"Answer me," Rick stepped towards him, aiming straight at his head, "or prepare to die."

"Put your weapon on the floor," an imperious voice sounded from behind them.

Rick and Paul turned around. Armed men in white jumpsuits stepped out of the corridor that had been protected by the force field. They were armed and they lined up in a semicircle. The Landmaster, his face grim, but his spirit unbroken, followed them. He was pushed towards Paul and Rick. Rick understood that resistance was futile and threw his blaster on the floor. A tough-looking gray-bearded man with a silvery chain and a medallion on his neck stepped forward and spoke.

"You stopped your friend, saving many lives. I am a civilized man, so I would like to thank you for that."

Rick nodded curtly.

"But you still wanted to kill Nathaniel. Is that fair?"

The stranger called the youth over and ruffled his hair. Once he understood that Rick had no intention of answering, he continued.

"You are barbarians that entered here without permission. You somehow found out the access codes for the transportation cabins and overcame the energy barriers. And then you sent a saboteur to turn off our network!"

"What have you done to him?" Rick breathed out as he realized that they were talking about Black Ant, who somehow turned off the power supply of the spheres.

"We had to isolate him."

"Where is he? Why didn't you bring him here?" Rick did not like the sound of the word "isolate". The stranger could have put a different meaning to it.

"Don't worry, he'll live." The graybeard pushed the youth towards the armed men saying, "Go, my son, talk to him when he comes to."

"You won't be able to." Rick finally noticed the resemblance between the stranger and the youth. It was his son. "The boy that you isolated can't speak."

"There are many ways to speak to a bearer of implants."

The graybeard moved the hair back from his temple, showing a round disk by his ear which flashed with the weak light of a diode.

"Now then," he caged his fingers. "Why did you come here?"

"We were looking for shelter," Vasilevs replied.

"You're lying." The graybeard glanced at him indifferently.

Commander Fritz suddenly stepped out from among the row of men in white jumpsuits and nodded at Vasilevs. For some reason he was also wearing white.

"I would not advise anyone here to lie," the graybeard added. "We were watching everyone."

Hans and Margaret, who Rick had considered dead stepped forward to stand by Fritz' side. They were joined by Igor from the cluster of the fords and they were all wearing white jumpsuits.

"There is no place for barbarians in the Enclave of the last men of Atlantis," the graybeard declared.

"Do you even know what is going on up top?" Paul exclaimed. "The possessed are about to break in here any minute now!"

The graybeard shook his head and sneered ironically.

"Foolishness. The Enclave is impregnable. We will resist anyone that dares to cross our borders."

"Oh yes," Rick nodded. "Will you manage to repair your spheres in time?"

The grin disappeared from the face of the graybeard.

"Barbarians," he hissed. "Get out of here while you still live!"

Vasilevs breathed heavily and stepped forward.

"You!" He poked Fritz in the chest. "How could you? I know you for so many years!"

Fritz stayed silent, looking at Vasilevs with indifference.

"Information, Landmaster," the graybeard

patiently replied. "The one who had information owns the world."

"So you think that you are in control of the city?" Rick asked him. "You don't even control the core. The city changes, but it's not you changing it. You don't even have an idea about what's happening. You don't have access to the real information. You have probably tried to understand by reading chronicles, instructions, reference manuals and studying diagrams. But you understood nothing. The defensive programs recognize you as civilian citizens. You probably managed to alter some of the algorithms using the keys you found." He nodded at the corridor behind their backs. "You reconfigured the defensive programs but never worked out the purpose of the Citadel. You definitely don't know why the landscape of the city changes. You don't know why the Ancients built such complex architecture and gigantic mechanisms."

The people led by the graybeard looked at Rick in surprise, who added before they could get themselves together, "This is why I am here. Let me through to the lower levels and I will try to find the answers."

"That is forbidden," the graybeard glanced at the railing. "The holy font lies there."

"You seem civilized, but you're exactly the same," Rick spat.

"Go away." The graybeard came to. "There's no place for you here. Be quick, before I change my mind."

"No!" Margaret raised her hand. "Me and Hans are against this. We want to hear this young man out."

"Me too," Igor said, joining them.

The graybeard, glanced at Fritz, who nodded, saying, "I also want to know what he has in mind. Information above all!"

To add to this, some ancient mechanisms creaked far away and the catwalk shook. It seemed that the whole city murmured in complaint, like a gigantic animal that had woken up after a long hibernation.

"What?" the graybeard managed to mutter, before Margaret interrupted him.

"We have all seen Rick the outsider before and we all spoke to him. He is special and his thoughts are special. If he got this far, let him tell us about his goal and give him a chance to reach it."

"Get ready to run," Vasilevs suddenly whispered as he stepped up to Rick.

He looked back and nodded at Paul.

Rick was about to tell them his thoughts and his plans but he suddenly noticed that the armed men behind the back of Margaret, Hans, Igor and Fritz suddenly raised their weapons all at once. Their blasters crackled with charges and Vasilevs pushed the four leaders at them, opening up the way into the corridor. Paul and Rick ran into the opening.

"Don't stop!" Vasilevs shouted behind their backs, when he noticed that Rick had a pronounced limp and slowed down. "Take the first turning on the left, then on the right and keep going straight."

They turned as he ordered and heard more blaster shorts and a scream of pain.

"I'm fine," Vasilevs shouted when Rick looked back. "Keep going!"

A minute later, they were in a corridor filled with light that had rooms with transparent walls on both sides. Rick worked out that these were experimental laboratories. He had no time to read their names on the signs. Vasilevs shouted that they needed to run into the last one on the left. It turned out that this was the medical block that Rick was familiar with from Thermopolis. Black Ant was lying down there with Nathaniel by his side, who had a visor of black plastic over his eyes for some reason. He was moving his hands around as his lips moved soundlessly.

Black Ant's head was covered in wires and complex graphs appeared on the monitors in front of the bed, flashing numbers and glyphs.

Nathaniel heard the noise, but he did not

have time to take the visor off before Vasilevs grabbed a cleaver with a jagged edge from the instrument shelves and put it to the throat of the youth, shouting for Rick and Paul to step away from the entrance.

A few moments later, armed men appeared by the entrance. They let the graybeard into the laboratory and stepped back when Vasilevs demanded, still holding their weapons up.

"Now then, civilized one," Vasilevs began, "are you going to be more agreeable now?"

Rick appreciated the tactics the Landmaster used. He originally thought that they were just running away, but it turned out completely different. He turned to the shelves and started to open them and look for painkiller injectors. Paul stared at him in surprise and whispered, "What are you doing?"

"Look for long white instruments like this one, they have green markings."

He showed Paul an injector.

"You are wounded and you can't get out of here," the graybeard pronounced.

Rick injected himself with the painkiller and then the physical activity stimulant and turned back towards the door. Vasilevs was grimacing and he had a charred hole in his side. Things were not looking good. Rick stepped up to him and glanced back asking, "Paul, what's going on?"

"Here," Paul gave him two injectors.

Rick chuckled as he watched the graybeard grind his teeth with anger and gave Vasilevs a huge dose of the painkiller.

"Find the sealer," he asked Paul. "It's a device that looks a bit like an injector, but it has a wider end and it must have yellow markings. You know how to read, so you'll manage."

"You won't get out of here anyway!" the voice of the graybeard wavered.

"Sure about that?" Vasilevs stared at him with his bloodshot eyes. It looked like the medicine worked too quickly and in a way different to what Rick expected.

The Landmaster swayed and nearly slashed the throat of his hostage.

"Be careful!" the graybeard squealed.

"Why don't you go away and let us go," the Landmaster managed to get over his medical intoxication. "Then the boy might stay alive."

"We're at an impasse. I can let you through, but there are possessed above who will break in here as soon as we open the gates."

"Show us the way downwards!" Vasilevs growled.

"But... but..." the graybeard gasped for air. "I don't know it."

He glanced back, looking for support from

his armed clan-mates, who nodded.

"There is a way," a voice with a metallic timbre sounded from the ceiling.

Rick, Vasilevs and Paul stared upwards in surprise and then looked at each other. The voice did not seem to surprise the graybeard.

"Who's speaking?" Vasilevs asked warily.

"It's me, Black Ant. Rick, are you there?"

"Yes!" Rick looked at the motionless boy on the operating table, gradually realizing how he communicated with them. "Are you talking to us through the Network?"

"That's right!" Black Ant's voice was full of joy. "I never even knew about these capabilities, this is amazing, Rick!"

"We need to get out of here. How do we go down?"

"Only inside the Axis, Rick. The Axis, which you're used to calling the Chorda isn't just a pillar of energy; it's also a path between the levels."

"How do we get inside?"

"The Landmaster has a medallion. You need to match the symbols on the key against similar symbols and the Axis will open up the way for you."

Rick looked at Vasilevs, who shook his head.

"I don't get it," Vasilevs replied.

"I think I do, though. Paul, have you found the sealer?"

"Here you are."

Rick took the sealer from him. He told Vasilevs to hold on as it would hurt and put the device against the wound in his side. Vasilevs gritted his teeth, bravely going through the pain that went through the barrier of painkillers. He grabbed Nathaniel more tightly and told the graybeard to get out of there with the rest of his people before the cleaver in his hand twitched suddenly.

The armed men obeyed, which made Rick think. Something else was going on here. Nathaniel was definitely valuable to them, but what was it? Rick looked at the plastic visor that had covered Nathaniel's eyes and then looked at Black Ant, who was engulfed in wires.

"Black ant, you said that the Network had amazing capabilities, didn't you? You have access to them. Who else has access to the hidden sections?"

"Nathaniel. He explained how everything works to me, but I haven't figured it all out yet. There's a complex architecture here and many new things which I don't quite understand, but I'm learning fast."

Everything became clear. Nathaniel was able to work with the Network better than the graybeard and the others.

"Why was it Nathaniel who taught you?" Rick wanted to check on another of his thoughts.

"Because a young mind is more flexible in perceiving virtual reality." Black Ant realized that he used an unfamiliar word and clarified, "Virtual reality is the space inside the Network."

"Thank you, Black Ant! Look after yourself!" Rick took a bag out of the cabinet and put the sealer and a few briquettes of nutritious concentrate from the neighboring shelf inside. Then he said, "We're done, let's go."

This was exactly what the Landmaster had been waiting for, so he pushed Nathaniel towards the exit. The graybeard backed away into the corridor.

"What was he talking about," Paul asked. "What is the space inside the Network?" Book of Faces told us about the Network and about connecting to it, but I did not understand anything then or now."

"Paul, we'll talk about it later."

Rick hurried after Vasilevs into the corridor. They repeated their journey in the company of the graybeard, coming out onto the catwalk which led around the hall with the holy found and the pillar of the Chorda in the middle.

"How do we come down into the hall?" Vasilevs asked irritably.

"Here," the graybeard took two steps away from the passage and placed the medallion that he had on his silvery chain against the wall. An opening leading into a secret cabin opened in the wall.

"Another elevator," Rick shook his head.

"You're coming with us," Vasilevs pointed his cleaver at the graybeard and pushed him into the cabin after Nathaniel.

They descended and came out into the hall.

"No," the graybeard shook his head, "we can't go over there! There is no way we are going there..."

"Oh yes you will," Vasilevs bared his teeth and pushed Nathaniel forward.

Rick and Paul climbed onto the border of the glowing pool, look at each other and stepped upon its surface in silent agreement. It turned out to be as hard as stone.

"I understand that this is the font!" the Landmaster exclaimed and climbed up, dragging the hostages with him. "Forward, soldiers! To glory!"

Rick and Paul approached the Chorda.

"What next?" Paul asked.

"The medallion," Rick turned to Vasilevs.

He gave Rick a suspicious look but then quietly took the medallion out of his pocket and gave it to Rick.

"Paul, look for the symbol with three circles superimposed on each other with many glyphs inside," Rick instructed and started to carefully examine the symbols on the surface of the pillar.

"I found it!" Paul exclaimed a minute later.

Rick walked around the pillar and stared at the place that Paul indicated. Yes, it was correct. He turned the outer ring on the medallion, making the position of the glyphs similar to the image on the pillar, and then the middle ring until the parts formed the correct pattern.

"By the sky gods!" Vasilevs swore. "How did you guess?"

"He saw the picture from above," Paul answered for him, talking about the way they watched the city rings turn when they had climbed to the top of the tower. "I saw it too, but didn't know that the medallions had hidden features."

"From above? Ah, who cares, what next?" Vasilevs asked impatiently and gave the confused graybeard a dirty look, as he warily stood around nearby.

"Next?" Rick was overcome with excitement — he was about to get the answers to all his questions. "Let Paul open it."

Rick offered him the medallion, which Paul placed against the pictogram on the pillar. The key quickly sunk into the niche that opened up.

Patterns of light crawled to the side of it and then blinding rays emerged as a wide portal appeared in front of them. The shining light around it gradually went dim. Vasilevs let go of Nathaniel, took a look inside the portal and recoiled.

"There's a chasm in there!"

Without pausing to think, Rick pushed him in the back, making him fall into the portal, grabbed Paul hard by the hand and stepped inside after him.

An instant later, the portal closed before the graybeard managed to stick his head inside.

Ш

THEY WERE SLOWLY descending into the viscous depths of an open space. Rick could not help but notice how funny their poses and faces looked. He was sure that he looked no better.

The eternally stern Vasilevs was now milling around with his eyes wide like a child that fell into a pool of water. On the other hand, Paul was looking around in amazement and his face reflected the intense thought processes going through his head.

"What's happening? Where are we?" Vasilevs finally asked after he stopped swing his arms about and let the space around him carry him downwards.

Rick moved his hands a little to change the position of his body, glanced downwards and answered, "We are inside the pillar."

"I don't need you to tell me that!" Vasilevs growled. "I just don't understand why we are falling so slowly!"

Rick explained that a force field the nature of which he did not understand himself was acting on them and that he had decided to trust Black Ant, so there they were, descending.

"Then where exactly are we right now?" Vasilevs asked.

Paul turned and moved closer to the wall. The place that he touched with his finger went yellow. Then Paul put his palm against the wall. The yellow spot started growing. Paul slid his palm upwards and the wall suddenly slowly split apart, as if it was a piece of cloth that had been cut.

"Oh... You... Why?" Vasilevs asked.

Rick was also a little afraid, but then Paul suddenly climbed through the hole he made. Vasilevs quickly hurried after him and Rick joined them without pause.

All three of them rolled onto a hard surface head over heels. Vasilevs was the first to spring up, raising his cleaver, but silence and abandonment surrounded them. They were in a large oval hall that had an impressive sized teardrop-shaped machine at its center. It was in some ways similar to one of the silvery arrows that Rick once got to travel in, but that was the end of the similarity.

Rick looked back over his shoulder. The pillar was missing. Amazingly, there was only a spiral shaped stream of multicolored dots chained one after another. The stream rose from the floor and disappeared inside the ceiling.

"What is this place?" Vasilevs gave Rick and Paul a questioning look each.

Rick looked around and saw a terminal by the wall. At least that was something. It would be good if the ancient device worked.

He approached the terminal, blew the dust from it and touched the screen. The startup menu flickered with green rows of lettering. Rick went through the options, approving and confirming a series of connections. Lamps lit up with soft light around the perimeter of the hall. It was not all of them, but they did work.

Vasilevs cried out in awe behind his back. Rick turned around and saw Paul, who was observing his work with the terminal. Paul looked back as well. Part of the wall nearby lit up with light, with the many cells built into the surface projecting a three-dimensional diagram of the city with the tower rising in the middle. The name "ATLANTIS" was displayed in silvery lettering below.

Rick and Paul approached the hologram. Vasilevs stretched out his hand and touched sector P, making the diagram change its scale and significantly grow in size. At first, the Landmaster stepped back, but then excitedly declared, "That's the home sector of the Division in fine detail! That's incredible!"

Rick touched the sector marker with his fingers and the diagram returned to its previous size. He went to the interactive menu, selected "Current Status" and activated it. "Gaia Program. Status: Hibernation." appeared above the city.

"What does it say there?" Vasilevs excitedly asked, looking at Rick. "Come on, tell me!"

Rick entered a request for a status description, read the message it produced and replied, "The city landscape is changing, but the process was launched by a machine, not by humans. It's an automatic program. There was a similar one active in my citadel and it was called "Chronos.""

"So what will happen when these changes in the landscape are complete?"

"I don't know," Rick shrugged. "Let's try and find out."

He went into the menu again and studied

the different options for a long time. Finally, Rick found a sub-menu with the description of the "Gaia" program. He tried to open it, but the diagram blinked again and bright red letters saying "Access Denied" appeared above it.

"That shouldn't be happening," Rick said, frowning.

"What if we try this with a different device?" asked Paul and nodded at the terminal.

Rick walked up to the terminal and again spent a while digging through the menu and after some complex manipulations to find the right section the result was the same: "Access Denied."

Then, Rick ordered Paul to perform exactly the same actions, but the terminal did not react to his touch and refused to give him access to the program. After this, they offered Vasilevs to try it, but it did not work with him either.

"Very strange," said Rick, looking downcast. "The machine does not request a password or demand for a code to be entered. It simply denies access."

"Is it broken?" Vasilevs suggested.

"No," Rick shook his head.

"Do you remember when the protective field was not letting you into the corridor?" Paul asked and Rick nodded. "And then, when we were in that brightly lit room where the Landmaster took the boy hostage, you said that the graybeard had reconfigured the defensive systems. Maybe it's like that with this too?"

"We should have dragged those bastards along with us!" Vasilevs punched his own hand in disappointment. "We would have fixed everything quickly by now."

"No," Rick shook his head again. "I assure you, they never went down this far. Paul, you're right, someone set up a block here, but someone else did it."

When he heard these words, Vasilevs drew his cleaver from his belt and decided to walk around the hall.

"The Chronos program kept my citadel in hibernation," Rick thought out loud, as he dug around in the Settings menu. "It was a standby mode in which Thermopolis could spend hundreds or thousands of years until a man intelligent enough to start up a new program and sent a loaded transport ship into space came along."

"Wait... So you were not lying to us when you were talking about the launch panel, the incandescent gases and..."

"It was the honest truth. Do you know what outer space is?"

"I read about it in the ancient books we have in the Retreat."

"Good. Well, the city of Thermopolis, where

I grew up, has flown away, but Thermopolis was filled with everything it needed. The citadel here is empty, but it is surrounded by a city with everything it might need. It is probable that the "Gaia" program is active here and that someone had launched it in the past. However, it is automatically going into hibernation now. If that is what's happening, there must be an important reason for it... Damn it!"

Rick slapped the screen, when he saw the "Access Denied" message again.

"Maybe it really is the machine itself that's broken?" Paul repeated Vasilevs' idea.

"I doubt it, as the consequences would be different. If there was an error in the program, there would be a chain of rapid changes to the city landscape, but everything is planned and subject to the logic of the program in our case. If one of the machines had broken down there are always backups, like the hologram behind our backs. It's a completely different device where we could also enter the right menu."

"Look at that," Vasilevs returned and called out to them, pointing at the diagram of Atlantis. "What's going on?"

The core, middle ring and several segments of the outer ring glowed red. A few seconds passed and the red segments of the outer ring went blue. Segment C in the core also went pale for a moment and then filled with the color blue.

"I don't think I like this," Vasilevs said.

As if in confirmation of his words, a thundering noise came from afar and a slight vibration rolled along the floor.

"So maybe we should move somewhere else? Why don't we look on the diagram?" Paul suggested and stepped towards the hologram.

He looked at the three dimensional picture for a while, then swore and told the others, "Everything is so difficult to understand here. I don't quite get where everything is. We need another diagram, better one that shows everything level by level separately, as I can't think about it as a whole."

"Hang on," Rick livened up and came up to the control panel, requesting a report on the process.

That did not require any codes or passwords. A list of changes appeared on the screen. Rick looked at the chronology from the very beginning and exclaimed, "Here it is!"

"What? What is it?" Vasilevs bounded over to him.

"This is where it all started," Rick pointed at segment O and increased the size of the image.

"What?" the Landmaster did not understand. "What's the significance of this?"

"All right, let's have a look," Rick was

visibly animated as he scrolled through the data, commenting on it. "If you look at the intervals, it works out that the hibernation process began just over thirty days ago with one segment. I was there and I saw it all. Those who live in that cluster call themselves fords and they told me that the movements of city buildings do happen but they are very rare. They mentioned an eight year interval. But then, everything happened suddenly. Right, let's keep looking." He scrolled through more data and exclaimed, "Now here, look, the second sector where the hibernation continued was sector N, where everything happened two days later. And then M, again after two days. Then L..."

"The intervals were the same," Paul nodded.

"Yes," Rick agreed and glanced at the confused Vasilevs. "But it was not that way everywhere. See, the segments of the outer ring have already completed their shift. The next stage is the segments of the middle ring, but the intervals are much shorter here. The changes were completed ten hours ago. After that, the segments of the core have been moving once every three hours."

Rick brought up a calculator as a separate hologram and started to punch numbers into it.

"Are you trying to figure out when all of it

will be complete?" Paul asked.

"Yes. Considering the number of segments that have remained unchanged, and there are eight of them, it works out that the hibernation of the core will be complete in... Fourteen hours."

"Ok, stop!" Vasilevs shook his head and clarified, "What exactly will happen to the city in fourteen hours?"

"When we went to the top of the tower, we saw how the outer and middle rings turned," Paul replied quickly. "While that happened, whole quarters were going under the ground, but all that replaced them was a flat surface."

"And what for?" Vasilevs turned his eyes to Rick.

"I think that all the structures in the city do not just go under the ground, they move towards the highways, where they are disassembled into their component parts. It's like when a blaster is taken apart and the stock, the battery with the charges, the firing mechanism and the rest of it to be placed in a warehouse. I hope the gist of it is clear?"

Paul and Vasilevs nodded.

"All of this is somehow laid out in a particular order along the highways that all lead to the tower," Rick finished his explanation.

"What for?" Vasilevs could not resist asking again.

Rick sighed and spread his hands, "I don't know."

"We must stop this," Vasilevs said firmly. "Otherwise the city will completely disappear and I don't want to live under the ground."

"We can't," Rick replied. "We need access to the program. That's the way it worked in my world."

"So what is that?" Vasilevs pointed at the teardrop-shaped machine. "It's not here for nothing."

Rick and Paul stared at the machine.

"What is that?" Vasilevs asked with interest.

Rick was the first to approach the machine. He touched its hull, looking at his own reflection and then walked up to its nearest support. He looked at what was written on the hull and shook his head.

"It can't be!" He glanced over his shoulder. "Come over here. I think that this is a shuttle that can take us into low earth orbit to meet my home ship."

"Thermopolis?" Paul asked.

"Yes."

Rick went forward and activated the control panel on the central support. A hatch opened in the bottom of the shuttle above his head and a stairway slid out.

"Right," the Landmaster said as he appeared behind his back. "So you have decided to run away to this... outer space of yours?"

Rick felt a flutter in this chest — he really did think about his sister and Kyoto and about meeting Maya again. It was really bad to have enemies as allies sometimes.

"Not to run away," he turned to face Vasilevs, "but to return to my friends and relatives."

"Ha, do you think I am that much of an idiot?"

"No."

"I know that is exactly what you think. As soon as we arrive, you will tell your friends that I am an enemy and..."

Rick had already understood what Vasilevs was thinking and he decided against waiting to become his hostage, so he punched him on the chin. It was powerful and well-aimed. The head of the Landmaster jerked, as his eyes faded and he fell onto the steps of the stairs that led into the hatch at the bottom of the shuttle.

"Now turn around, and no sudden moves," he heard a voice say in a controlled but threatening way the side. "Put your hands up."

Rick did as he was ordered. Paul stood two steps away from him, holding a compact blaster in his hand.

"Where did you get the weapon?" Rick asked in surprise.

"I found it in the cabinet when you asked me to find the injectors."

"Paul!" Rick was about to step forward, but then he froze, with his hands raised.

"Don't come near me."

"I know," Rick said hurriedly, "you can pull the trigger. I have no doubt. But I want you to listen to me. Please, listen. I have lost everything that was dear to me, my home and my family. All that I want to do is to go home to those dear to me. Please, let me go. If you want, we can go together and I swear you won't be harmed."

"Do you want to hear the truth?"

"Of course."

"I thought that you would help us. Help us make the city born again and to cleanse it of the possessed."

"It's impossible to save everyone, especially when there's no one left to save. You understand that perfectly well yourself. Stay here if you want, or come with me."

Paul nodded and sneered.

"Rick, your problem is that you have something to lose. And that is what makes you weak."

"Paul! Just don't..."

"Yeah!" he bared his teeth. "You are talking

to a corporal of the Division. As long as one fighter is still standing, the Division exists."

"Don't make me..."

Rick heard a sound behind him, but he had no time to do anything. He felt something hit him on the back of his head and shake the contents of his skull. He felt no pain, he just saw an impenetrable mist in front of his eyes. The last thing that he heard before his consciousness slipped away was, "Good work, corporal."

"Should I finish him off, Landmaster?"

X

THERE WAS A GREAT JOLT and the silence was suddenly shattered by a distant rumble, as Rick's eyes came unstuck.

The fog cleared and he saw a cabin filled with monitors. The lights of indicators shone together like a multicolored rainbow of blossoms. With great difficulty, Rick looked at himself — his hands were tied together with a wire and he was securely fixed to a seat with harnesses. The back of his head felt piercing pain with every movement. The distant roar was coming from somewhere behind his back and he could also feel a light vibration.

Vasilevs and Paul were sitting in the seats in front of him. The Landmaster was patiently questioning his subordinate about the purpose of the buttons and indicators on the instrument panel in front of them. Paul was obediently reading out every word.

"Radar. Odometer. Barometer. Altimeter. Radiation counter. Compartment radiation level. Propulsion system..."

The compartment did not have any glass windows. That was strange. Rick immediately remembered the flying machine in Thermopolis, but everything was different and much more complex here.

"It says, "Launch Capsule" here," Paul's voice rang out.

"What's a capsule?" Vasilevs enquired.

"This ship probably is the capsule."

"Good. Go for it."

"Should I press the launch button, Landmaster? What if we will have no way back afterwards? Are you sure?"

Vasilevs thought for a second or two and then spoke.

"Yes. There are no normal people left in Atlantis anyway, and it's time for us to get out of here. As soon as we arrive in Thermopolis, we can start it all again."

Rick struggled and ground his teeth in

anger, but he could not move from his place. All he did was make his head feel a strong pang of pain.

Paul pressed a button. A piercing short signal sounded and a metallic voice announced, "Attention, this is the Autopilot speaking. Capsule launch activated. The program may only be canceled within the next ten seconds. I am beginning the countdown. Ten, nine..."

The rumble changed to a roar and the vibrations became stronger. Rick struggled again, trying to free his hands, but to no avail. Then he moved his feet, which turned out to be tied as well. Rick could not stop himself from swearing angrily.

"Ah!" Vasilevs heard him through the noise and turned around in his seat. "He's awake now!"

"Five, four..." the autopilot counted down.

"We're going for a ride now!" Vasilevs chuckled.

"Landlord, look at that!"

"The bore has accelerated to ten thousand revolutions per minute," Paul pointed at the central screen.

Rick suddenly realized that everything was completely different to what he had originally thought.

"Stop the launch!" he shouted.

"It's too late!" Vasilevs looked back again.

"We're going back to your home! Be happy that you're still alive!"

"Two, one..."

"Paul!" Rick shouted in desperation. "Cancel the launch!"

Paul was about to stretch out his hand to the panel, but Vasilevs intercepted it, "No!"

"Launch!" the speakers announced.

Paul also shouted something, but his voice was drowned in the roar of the launching capsule. The compartment jolted and leaned forward. Rick was very happy that he was well secured, unlike Vasilevs who managed to hit his forehead on the instrument panel. The capsule kept inclining. His blood stuck to his face and circles appeared in front of his eyes because of the pulsating pain in the back of his head, which made it difficult to watch the central screen.

It was then that Vasilevs, who had managed to pull on the harnesses and fix himself in his seat issued and order, "Corporal, read out the messages!"

"Maximum revolution speed reached," Paul immediately replied.

The screen went black and then lit up with a field separated into quadrants, with a blue dot flashing at the top.

The capsule stopped bending over and started to slide, and the roar behind the aft end of the capsule stopped being low and heavy, gradually changing to a piercing shriek. Then it immediately stopped, changing to a rattling and clanging sound in front.

The capsule started to shake violently. Paul was shouting something to Vasilevs and pointing at the screen, but Rick could not hear him. The rattling sound then changed to an even rustle and a low hum, as the autopilot reported, "Calculated course determined. Depth — ten meters."

Paul and Vasilevs looked at each other. Rick closed his eyes and his shoulders shook, but this was not the shake of the capsule, it was him starting to laugh uncontrollably.

"Fifteen meters," the autopilot reported. "Sandstone located along the course, density of two and a half thousand kilograms per cubic meter."

Rick was now howling with laughter. Even the pain at the back of his head seemed to recede for a while.

"Shut it!" Vasilevs barked and turned to Paul. "Where are we flying to? Answer me, corporal!"

"Flying!" Rick was splitting his sides. "You idiot!"

"Landmaster..." Paul ventured carefully. "We're not flying. We are descending below the ground!"

Vasilevs froze, staring back at him. Paul hurriedly turned away, pretending to study the monitor and the values on the instrument panel. The blue dot on the screen began to slowly descend towards the center of the quadrants on the field, leaving a dotted line behind it. Rick closed his eyes again — the pain in the back of his skull flared up again.

"Where are we going?" Vasilevs asked suddenly.

Paul did not give an immediate reply and only reacted after he was shoved in the shoulder.

"It says... Five hundred meters until the point of destination. The calculated speed is thirty meters a minute. We will be there in a quarter of an hour."

"Where, you moron?" Vasilevs shoved Paul's shoulder again. "Tell me!"

"There's just a message in some unknown language here," Paul muttered.

"So read it!"

"I can't!"

Rick opened his eyes.

"But you know how to read!" Vasilevs roared.

"I don't know these letters! This is another language. Maybe Rick knows it."

Paul looked back for the first time.

"We'll deal with him yet."

The message jumped in front of his eyes, so Rick barely managed to make out some of the letters of the Greek alphabet. He noticed an iota, the hook of the nu and the squiggle of an alpha. All the rest dissolved into a moving line in his eyes.

"I thought better of your corporal!" Vasilevs continued. "But it seems that I was mistaken."

"No, Landmaster, I will surprise you yet!" Paul suddenly replied and quickly ran his fingers along the keys of the control panel.

Vasilevs did not have the time to say anything else when the hum and rattle of the bore suddenly became quieter. The capsule changed its angle slightly, raising its nose towards the horizon. The autopilot reported the recalculation of the time and speed of travel. The noise and vibration soon stopped annoying Rick. The capsule moved through the earth, heading towards and unknown target.

The depth indicator went up to three figures. Rick tried to focus on it, but that made his head spin even more. He did not need to think about where they were heading, but slow down his breathing, have a rest and manage his pain.

He tried to relax and thought about his friends and relatives in Thermopolis, not noticing how his thoughts became slow and fragmented. His body won out in the end and his mind sunk into sleep.

For a while, two voices kept sounding in the darkness. One was low and rough and the other was fresh and clear. The voices sometimes argued with each other. Finally, silence fell and then another sound of the voices, which lasted for only a few moments and quickly got consumed by the monotonous vibration and the humming of the engine.

The capsule growled as it methodically chewed up the earth, but Rick could no longer hear it as he dreamed of his native Thermopolis.

He saw his sister and Kyoto. He talked to Maya.

ч

"GET UP!"

Rick felt someone kick his leg and opened his eyes. Vasilevs towered over him, leaning on the armrests of his seat. Judging by the position of his body and the instrument panel behind his back, the capsule was laying on its side.

"We have arrived," Vasilevs announced gloomily.

He measured Rick with a hateful glance.

"How deep are we?" Rick asked hoarsely.

"Five hundred meters," Paul replied and got out of his seat.

"The message," Vasilevs reminded. "Show it to him."

Paul bent over the panel again, pressed a pair of buttons and a single Greek word appeared on the screen.

"What is this?" Vasilevs pointed.

Paul pressed some buttons on the panel and the metallic voice of the autopilot read it out over the speakers, "Hierusalem."

"Jerusalem," Rick corrected him. "I know as much as you do, believe it or not. This name probably means something else, because the ancient city which bore this name is unlikely to be underground. There is only one way to find out the truth — coming outside and seeing for ourselves."

"All right then," the Landmaster said calmly and unfastened the buckle holding down the harnesses on Rick's chest.

Rick almost fell onto the floor. Paul caught him in time, helped him to sit down and started to cut through the wires which immobilized his arms and legs.

"What's outside?" Rick asked with interests. "How much oxygen is there? Can you bring it up on the screen?"

"Just a moment."

Paul cut off the ties and returned to the panel to press some buttons. Rick raised his eyes — eighty percent oxygen.

"We can breathe. That's already good."

He started to rub at his numb hands and feet and managed to soon get up. However, his injured foot immediately reminded him of itself. The Landmaster used a painkiller injector on himself and gave the second one to Rick so that he would not have to deal with his wound. The medicine worked quickly and all three of them went outside.

The capsule lay at the bottom of the cave that had some kind of weakly phosphorescing mineral in the walls. Rick took a look around and noticed light coming from afar, but Paul was even faster.

"We probably need to go that way," he said, pointing in the direction of the light.

"Pass the weapon to me, corporal," Vasilevs held out his hand and Paul reluctantly gave his blaster to him. "Keep your eyes peeled."

They headed towards the source of the light. The cave was clearly man-made, with its level floor, smooth walls and vaulted ceiling. Following two dozen paces, the floor inclined steeply. It was good that they discovered a stone stairway, otherwise they would have had to descend without ropes at a really acute angle.

When the three of them reached the bottom, they saw another cave, which looked more like a hall with a gigantic silvery-yellow sphere in the center. It seemed that its surface was opalescent as it constantly changed color. The sphere exuded heat.

They all stopped opposite the sphere as they could not go any further. It seemed to Rick that he had seen the light play like this before, but he could not remember where. Paul also examined the glowing surface with interest. Vasilevs sniffed, as if he could smell something beyond the obstacle.

"It looks like a force field," he suddenly said.

Rick immediately remembered that it really was a protective shield which was almost like the one at the entrance to the corridor from the catwalk where Vasilevs run away from them as soon as the rollers came out of all the other passages.

He raised his hand, about to touch the surface, when Vasilevs shouted at him to stop and said to Paul, "Go first, corporal."

Paul only hesitated for a minute, nodded and resolutely stepped forward, disappearing behind the obstacle.

Unlike the defensive curtain that they came

across up top, Rick and Vasilevs did not see a washed out silhouette or hear any foreign sounds coming from the sphere.

Vasilevs gave Rick a meaningful look, so he stepped after Paul.

He was shrouded in fog. His head began to spin slightly, while he felt a prickling in his finger and pain in his injured leg and head. However, as soon as his sight was clear, the pain went way and Rick cried out in amazement. He found himself in a spacious and well-lit hall with a podium in the center. There were rounded steps leading up to the top of the structure. It was perfectly clean here. Rick had never ever seen such cleanliness.

Paul was already rising up the steps, when Vasilevs called out to him as he passed the barrier.

"Be careful, corporal!" he whispered. "Follow me."

Bending down a little and looking around all the time, he quickly crept up the stairs. Paul followed close behind.

Rick shook his head in annoyance, but followed after them. When they had almost reached the top, he noticed how Paul and Vasilevs stopped, not daring to look over the edge and waited for him. The three of them then quickly stepped out onto the top of the structure and froze as they stared at the old man sitting behind an oval table.

Holograms flickered over the table, as well as the blueprints of some sort of complex buildings and devices with diagrams and graphs by their side. Noticing the newcomers at last, the old man turned away from the holograms and waved his hand, immediately collapsing the light show above his table.

Rick, Paul and Vasilevs stepped towards the table simultaneously. The old man observed them with interest, moving his intelligent and colorless eyes from one of them to another. He was clean shaven and his shoulder length gray hair was gathered into a neat ponytail. The old man wore a loose toga, gathered with a golden ring upon his shoulder.

Rick had a feeling that the old man had been waiting for them.

"Keep your hands where I can see them," Vasilevs demanded, aiming his blaster at the old man. "What is this place? Answer me."

"The only nano-silicon bio-molecular replicator in the world," the old man calmly replied and smiled sadly.

Vasilevs frowned, because he did not understand what was said, but calmed down because he realized that he was deep under the group in an extremely clean place, which contained nothing apart from a table, for some reason.

Paul did not understand the words either, but the word "replicator" was familiar to Rick as he had come across it in the educational program that he had completed when he was still back in Thermopolis. However, he still could not understand the meaning of this combination of words as he lacked knowledge.

"We have come from Atlantis," he said.

"I know."

"Did your defense systems tell you?" Vasilevs stepped forward. "I see that this is so. Why are you sitting down here? Why don't you use your replicator and stop the madness up top?"

The old man kept looking at him with the same interest and sad smile. He suddenly sniffed and asked, "Do you think I could?"

"I think so," Vasilevs glanced back at Paul, as if looking for his support, but then immediately got himself together and his face became stern. He continued, "You're the scientist and you know better, of course. I still think that you have the power to impose order upon the city."

"I would like it to be so," the old man sighed.

"What?" Vasilevs began to be angry. "There

is nothing you can do at all? Sitting here in your pristine replicator..." He turned in his place. "There isn't even anywhere to spit! Can't you do anything?"

"You are very excited," the old man raised his hand. "I beg you, there is no need to get so stressed out."

"This is called a compact blaster," Vasilevs thrust the weapon under the old man's nose. "It can kill, all I need is to aim and pull the trigger."

"Yes. But what is the point of killing?" the old man was genuinely surprised.

"Are you making fun of me?" Vasilevs asked aggressively.

"Not at all. I am sorry if I hurt your feelings."

"Landmaster," Paul dared to interrupt. "I think that this man knows a lot and that he would be useful. He's going to answer all of our questions anyway. Isn't that right?"

He turned to the old man, who nodded with a serene expression on his face.

"Yes, you're right," Vasilevs agreed. "Ask him about everything."

"My name is Paul and I am a corporal of the Division. This is my commander, Landmaster Vasilevs. And this is Rick, he's... Anyway, that's not important."

"Pleased to meet you," the old man replied.

"To be honest, I knew who you are. My name is Nivan. I haven't interacted with anyone alive for a long time. I am not used to people at all now. I just observe them more and more."

"All right. Now then..." it was Paul's turn to throw sidelong glances as he searched for support, but for some reason, he looked at Rick instead of Vasilevs. "We need your help."

"I will help you in any way I can."

Paul was completely lost, with no idea what to ask. It was then that Rick spoke.

"What is the "Gaia" program?"

"It's a program for the colonization of Earth-type planets," Nivan answered without hesitation.

"Colonization... You mean the settlement of other planets?" Rick waited for the old man to nod and then asked, "What for?"

"That's an odd question," Nivan chuckled. "Humanity has long used up the resources of the Earth. We needed to find a new place and a new space for life. Humanity had too many ongoing problems that demanded its attention so it could never solve its greatest one — the demographic explosion, which led to an increase in our biomass and became critical for the ecology of the Earth. We are locusts that have consumed the field."

"What about Uranus then?" Rick moved on

to the next question. "What is that?"

"That's the interstellar flight program," Nivan smiled. "The two programs are directly connected."

"I thought that Thermopolis was the only citadel for a long time," Rick scratched the top of his head quizzically. "Until I came across the ruins of another tower and then found Atlantis and its inhabitants. Was Thermopolis not enough?"

"Thermopolis was only a step sideways on the way to the abyss," the old man said. "Much more was required to avoid falling into it." He moved in his chair, waved his hand and a hologram of the bust of the great architect appeared above the table. "Archimedes Spanidis, the creator of Thermopolis. It was his achievement that there was more than one citadel built on earth."

Nivan waved his hand again and the hologram disappeared. He put his fingers together into the shape of a dipper and a small dip appeared in the table and the covering melted in that place like wax, spinning into a little whirlwind and growing, sculpting a very standard plastic glass, which filled with water just as unexpectedly.

Before the amazed eyes of the newcomers, Nivan unhurriedly downed the water, put the glass aside and continued.

"Six more towers were constructed after the first one. Spanidis did this to preserve the variety of Earth's civilizations. European culture, Slavic world, Asia and Africa and the worlds of the peoples of Latin and North America. The towers were practical clones of each other in terms of structure and content, fulfilling several functions at the same time. They were a living space, a place of learning and a seed of the human race in case humanity died out and even six of the seven towers would be destroyed. You must agree, it is better to have seven chances than one, even though their number did not reach seven in the end."

Everyone nodded their agreement.

"Three functional modes were built into the towers," Nivan moved his hand to call up a diagram again, which was an exact copy that they had seen on the underground level where they found the capsule. "One of them is stasis, or hibernation, the other is the spaceship mode and the third is the colonizing city mode. As you could easily have guessed, the three are attached to the Chronos, Uranus and Gaia programs, which were named after ancient Greek gods. In that way, every tower was not just an intergalactic transport model, it was also a transformer. A device which could change depending on the current situation and the active program.

This was Mahsood's idea. He was a rich young man that had ordered the building of the first citadel and died from a terrible disease. The scale of his plan is beyond imagining. Only a very wise and far-sighted man could have thought of something like that. It is twice as incredible considering his young age. Before he died, Mahsood left his last instructions regarding the project to save humanity to the architect. It turned out that the rich Arab had financed breakthrough scientific projects. His group of companies was involved in the development of advanced technologies, such as renewable energy, new types of fuel, gravitational studies, neural networks, bio-electronics, molecular engineering, artificial intelligence and many other things." "All of these developments," Nivan spread his hands, "have made it possible to build the tower and this shelter and have allowed me to keep a healthy mind and spirit for such an unexpectedly long time. Of course, the research was top secret and it would not have been good for the leadership of other countries to know about it..."

He suddenly coughed, picked up the glass again as it quickly filled up with water and drank it down.

Rick used the break to add, "There was no information about this in the Thermopolis archive. I also didn't manage to get access to the data here in Atlantis."

"That's right," Nivan put his hand over the glass, pushed down and it dissolved into the surface of the table. "This is confidential information which is only for the keepers of the project. All of this was set up in the interests of security. Security is paramount."

Paul and Vasilevs glanced at each other and then at Rick when they heard these words. This was a strange coincidence, as the graybeard up top explained things in a similar way.

"So, this means that the towers can turn into spaceships and cities?" Rick confirmed/

"Yes."

"But how is this possible?" Vasilevs asked in surprise.

"Believe me, the human mind is capable of creating great wonders. Mahsood's chemical engineers created a universal construction material that Spanidis' builders used in the architecture of the towers. Basically, all that remained was to construct the building themselves and that was it."

"But then, how does a tower turn into a city," Vasilevs frowned. "I have seen this tower and the city around it with my own eyes."

"The first thing you need is technology. Everything is controlled by automatic processes and active programs that transform the tower when required. Look at this." He called up a menu for all to see. "The requisite code is entered into the computer and the program is selected. Additional options can be entered, such as a greater or lesser number of residential modules, increasing the size of food synthesizer reservoirs or adding a parking zone or a hydroponic zone instead. Anything that's required. The machine then starts to form the blocks in the tower, as it has the standard blueprints already loaded. Everything was planned to create a mobile world suitable for autonomous existence, a technological universe. You must understand that much of what was meant to be done was not. The last citadel was not completed, while the one that Rick saw had been destroyed. The project," and here he shook his head with regret, "is still unfinished."

"It turns out that there are four of them left in total?"

Nivan nodded.

"And who are the keepers of the project? Are you one of them?"

"That's right. My duties are to monitor the current state of the towers and to keep in touch with the keepers on location."

"So who was the keeper of Thermopolis? Is he still on location or did he fly away with the ship?"

"You don't know him. Once upon a time, this man violated the instructions and wanted to fix everything, so he went up into Thermopolis, joined the council of one of the clans and got killed as part of an internecine war."

"That's a shame," Rick sighed sadly and lowered his eyes. A moment later, he looked up again and asked excitedly, "Then could you explain what happened to Atlantis?"

"The Gaia program was activated in Atlantis after the first wave of madness. This citadel contains the culture and peoples of the so-called European world. The transformation of Atlantis went quickly and without issues — the contents of the tower were transferred onto the plain. The rings and the segments were established in accordance with the blueprints. Drones built agglomerations outside the perimeter — sanctuary cities that imitated the settlements of the ancient world. The landscape that was created is a matrix that can be grown layer by layer and ring after ring can be built as much as the population requires. Canals and roads can be laid and new agglomerations founded, connected to each other changed and added to. The balance of the consumption and use of energy is calculated to the smallest detail. Atlantis existed for a long time. It was dynamic in its development. And then..."

"Another explosion of insanity," Rick said. "One of the people from the outer settlements told me about this."

"Yes. A new focus of the disease appeared for the first time in many years."

"Why?"

"That is unknown. Any perfect system created by man always has an imperfect part," Nivan nodded sadly. "Which is man himself."

"You knew this!" Rick suddenly got angry. "You could have..."

"No. We do not have the right to involve ourselves with the affairs of the polises. Everything must happen as it does."

"So this is why you silently watched your world disappear." Rick shook his head in despair. "Watched people dying. So this is your mission? Just sitting there and watching?"

The old man sat there quietly, then sighed and told him, "When the Mindstorm virus appeared again, we were ready. We knew that humanity was vulnerable and that no one was immune to the disease. In the case of a new epidemic, Spanidis left an encrypted message, which needed to be opened and the instructions acted upon. It said what the Mindstorm virus actually was."

"Where did he find out the truth?"

"That is unknown. It remains a secret."

"So what is the Mindstorm virus, Keeper?"

Nivan suddenly let out an unpleasant, grating laugh.

"Haven't you understood yet? Insanity is the reverse of sanity."

"You're going to stop laughing at us now!" Vasilevs raised the blaster.

The old man's face changed, as he raised his hands and asked, "Please calm down. I will explain everything. A defensive mechanism activated. Nature used a fail-safe because we are part of it. It turned off our sanity. We were so stubborn and methodical at destroying the biosphere, that the law of system preservation made nature take our main weapon away from us. That's all it is. The population was reduced to a safe minimum."

"Does that mean that the process has started anew?" Rick asked.

"No."

"Why?"

"Tell me, what is memory?"

Vasilevs started to look gloomy. This conversation, which he did not understand very well was obviously beginning to irritate him. Paul shrugged. Rick decided to stop trying to be clever and listen to the old man.

"Now then, memory is the ability to store information," Nivan continued. "Over time, the accumulated information is layered and lost. We think that we have lost what we forget, but that isn't so. The information remains in our heads but we lose our path to it. Everything that we remembered over the course of our lives remains here," he touched his temple with his finger, "in our heads. The purpose of the new wave of the Mindstorm virus is not to rid you of your mind, but to awaken it and take it to a new level. The Mindstorm virus has increased the mnemonic abilities of the afflicted and they remembered everything they knew and what their ancestors knew before them. The Mindstorm awakened collective memory in people."

"So this is why I sometimes almost lost my consciousness and seemed to hear voices," Rick understood.

"Yes, those fits are unavoidable. We are now remembering everything that disappearing humanity managed to create in its entire history. The diseased are not insane. They are awakened. While we are still hibernating, but on our way to the awakening."

"But..." Rick looked at Paul and then at Vasilevs. "What about the fits of pain and aggression?"

448

"It's a threshold. Some are strong enough to go over it, while others are not. Many are balancing on the edge right now," a cunning sneer formed on Nivan's face.

"All right." Rick frowned yet again, as he sorted through what he heard. "Then why is Atlantis going into hibernation?"

"The machines can't recognize the awakened as humans and make the logical conclusion that they are enemies. The machines are just not programmed to deal with the awakened. This was a serious oversight, which can become fatal. But who knew that everything would happen this way?"

"A city without people must be sealed," Paul suddenly said.

"That's exactly what is happening here."

"Stop this," Vasilevs demanded coldly. "I know that you can do it."

The old man's face went hard as he leaned forward and snapped, "That's impossible! Only Spanidis and his descendants..."

"That's it, the games are over!" Vasilevs exploded. "You're going to listen to me now, understood?"

The Landmaster flushed red. His eyes suddenly went wide as his face streamed with sweat. Something was definitely wrong with him.

"Do you understand?" Vasilevs screamed,

spraying spittle. "Where is the button? Show me and I'll press it myself! How do we get to Thermopolis? What's going on in the other towers, where are they? Answer my questions, you old bag of bones!"

Vasilevs was slowly bending over, as if he was held down by a great weight. His head was pushing down into his shoulders and his hands trembled. His voice was hoarse and the sentences became short and fragmented.

"Bastard!" Vasilevs pulled him by the collar, running out of breath. "It's all your fault! All of it!"

Nivan did not look at him anymore, as his eyes turned towards Rick and Paul.

"You must understand the future of humanity. Its future is in your hand. I waited for this moment for a long time and hoped for a miracle, but there is no more time to wait. This is happening everywhere. We must..."

There was the report of a blaster. The charge hit the old man in the chest, piercing his body and the back of the chair, which made the blood spray onto the white floor in a myriad of misshapen blotches. Nivan's head tilted back, his mouth opened and his eyes closed.

Vasilevs threw the blaster away, let out a wild scream and fell to his knees, swaying from side to side. He was caught by the Mindstorm. A moment later he hit his face on the floor and went quiet.

Paul was frozen in a stupor. Rick ran up to the old man, who was barely breathing as his end was near.

"Rick," Nivan said hoarsely. "I was an agent in Thermopolis once."

"What?"

"Initiate the Jericho protocol."

The old man exhaled loudly, arced his back and went still.

"Hey, Rick!" Paul called out as he got himself together. "Look!"

A three dimensional picture of Atlantis with a view from above rotated above the table.

The outer ring was no more and even the roads were gone. The middle ring was sinking underground at an unbelievable speed. The streets disappeared, whole quarters were folding in on themselves, water-filled canals were getting covered with protective screens and the flyovers and ramps were going underground. The city was disappearing before their eyes, only leaving a bare plain divided into quadrants.

Rick touched one of the core sectors, zooming the picture in. Human figures were climbing the roofs of the buildings that had not yet been deconstructed, but the transformation had reached the core as well. Rick and Paul quietly watched the changes in the landscape. It was only now that they knew the secret of Atlantis and they did not know if they could turn the lifeless plain into a flowering city again.

Vasilevs' terrified scream made them both flinch and tear themselves away from observing the hologram. The Landmaster stood on his knees and looked at them with horror.

"Beasts!" he spat out. "Monsters!"

A thread of spittle hung down from his twisted mouth onto his chin and hung there. His face was burning as his eyes radiated fear and blood flowed out of his broken nose.

"Away! Get away from me!" He waved his hands around and then started to crawl backwards to the edge of the platform.

Paul stepped after him.

"Leave him," Rick called out. "Your Landmaster is not the commander of his own mind anymore."

Paul slowly turned around.

"You're right." He still had a look over his shoulder and waited for the Landmaster to get to the edge and roll down the stairway. "I don't need Vasilevs anymore. His rank now transfers to the last soldier of the Division!"

Rick had an unpleasant premonition as he looked at Paul intently.

"We don't want conflict, do we?" Paul said.

"We're on the same side, isn't that right?"

"Which side?" Rick spat out through his teeth.

"Enough!" Paul bent down and picked up the blaster. "That's the end of Atlantis. We're now going to establish communication with the remaining towers, assess the situation and declare our hegemony. Power is in our hands now. All the agents and keepers in the towers will obey us now. Look at what this old man did to our world! It's time to establish a new order and develop and apply a clear plan for salvation."

"Is that it? So what are you going to say to the keepers? Hi, I'm Paul from Atlantis and you must obey me now?"

"You're mocking me! We are intelligent enough to rule the people."

"You didn't understand. Such tactics are pointless."

"And why is that?"

"Nobody is going to obey you," Rick chuckled. "You also forgot about the Mindstorm."

"What, did you believe what the old man said? It's ridiculous!"

"What about Vasilevs? And Gareth? What about the dozens of those who we saw in the streets? They are all changing to a new level. We will have to as well."

"I don't believe it! That is impossible!"

"What about Black Ant? He was possessed once, but then he regained his sanity in front of your eyes! It was him that brought us here."

Paul gritted his teeth as he had no reply. Rick touched the table with his hands and felt a prickling in his fingers, a special feeling as if the surface stretched out after his hand. He imagined the program module in his head and the menu opened up above the table.

"What are you doing?" Paul shouted.

Rick selected the correct section and calmly replied, "I am initiating the Jericho protocol."

"What is it?" Paul angrily raised the hand holding the blaster and aimed at Rick's face.

"Our future."

"You're lying! You don't even know what you're doing! Is that what that decrepit old man told you?"

Rick made no reply, but continued to use his mind to work with the program, looking for the most important thing — the part of the code that Nivan spoke about where the fatal mistake was written. The part which would give hope to humanity.

"Rick, stop!" The hand with the blaster shook. "No!"

Paul's face was contorted with pain. His eyes became bloodshot and veins stood out on his forehead.

"You're exactly the same!" he exclaimed. "You're a demon from the wastelands!"

"No, Paul." Rick continued going through the code and filtering through terabytes of data, making it appear above the table. "You're just awakening."

"I hate you! I hate you!"

Rick was no longer afraid of him shooting. He learned how to control the replicator. The only thing he was afraid of was that his strength would run out before they had the time to launch the program.

"Die!" Paul shouted.

The blaster popped. But the charge did not penetrate the wall which appeared in the way.

Rick swayed as the effort to create the wall made his head spin.

"Rick? Rick, where are you?" he heard from behind the wall which separated Paul from the table. Next, there was an angry shout, "I will still find you! Just you wait!"

Rick found the part of the program he needed. He opened the dialog, confirmed his identity, closed the "Genetic code confirmed. Source: Thermopolis" message. He opened a new window, ran his eyes along the tabs and found the one labeled "Emergency Protocols."

"Armageddon Protocol, Sanctum Protocol..." his lips moved by themselves as he pronounced the names. "Here it is — Jericho Protocol."

The main thing was going without pause, because if he hesitated he might start doubting and death would be assured. Rick mentally activated the program and exhaled with relief.

That was it. He did it.

"Here you are!" Paul exclaimed as he found his way around the wall. "I will..."

Rick commanded the replicator to push the invader outside the sphere. The wall suddenly exploded in a cloud of shards. Paul waved his hands when his legs grew into the podium which extended quickly beyond the bounds of the platform.

"I hate you!" he heard as Paul was thrown away from him.

"Paul!" Rick shouted to him. "Draw! Draw this world!"

Z

THE SUNLIGHT REFRACTED through the lens of the protective dome and stroked the skin on his face with it warmth. Once he got used to the blinding light of day, Rick opened his eyes wider. This place was unfamiliar to him, a bare plain with structures strewn around here and there.

Rick looked up at the clear sky and tiredly lowered himself to the ground.

All of his power went on replicating himself on the surface. Of course, it sounded wildly improbable, but he had managed to do it. He could not move any further though, as he needed a serious rest. His sight swam before his eyes — it seems everything was not as good as he thought at the beginning.

A drawn out droning sound came from the distance. The sound was familiar and it kept to one note. This was the sound of an electrical engine, Rick realized He soon heard the sound of wheels and the droning sound became quieter.

Rick noticed a large shadow nearby. His eyesight returned for a moment and he saw a rather large vehicle with a covered bed, a real truck. Something was written on the side, but the fog rose in front of his eyes again and Rick powerlessly fell onto his side.

The only relief was that this was not the possessed.

A strong pair of hands carefully took him by the shoulders, raised him up and supported his back.

"Can you hear me?" a male voice said.

Rick nodded with difficulty.

The man who asked the question had a strong accent.

"Can you see me?"

"No," Rick gasped. "Who are you?"

"We came from the Tower of Peace. I am Doctor Xi Jiang."

Something pricked Rick's shoulder. He guessed that it was the needle of an injector. An instant later, his head became clear and the fog lifted from his eyes so he could see the face of the man that came to help him. The man was wearing black armor, with a helmet on his head with its visor raised and a red cross in a white circle on his shoulder.

The man's companions looked the same, but they had weapons in their hands and different signs on their shoulder that Rick could not yet make out. He was also surprised by an unusual pungent smell.

"You have blood," Xi Jiang noticed.

He stretched towards Rick to wipe his face, but Rick drew back because the arm of the doctor suddenly started to undulate like a tentacle and an inhuman green flame burned in his eyes.

Dozens of bright spots shone and faded before his eyes. Rick closed his eyes for a moment, as he felt a pang of sharp, burning pain and when he opened his eyes, the terrible creature was still staring at him and did not look human at all.

That's when Rick started shouting, "Don't

come near me! Don't... Don't..."

The pain started to consume him and tear him apart. He wanted to smash his own head so that the brain would leak out. Rick jerked and hit a barrier and tried it again. His conscious mind came back for a moment and he shouted, "Kill me! Please kill me!"

The monsters surrounded him on all sides and mumbled incomprehensibly in a language only they could understand. Rick tried to tear himself away and did it this time, running away without looking where he was going, swinging his fists at the air and growling curses. He was using all his might as he spat out his lungs, he screamed, tearing his vocal chords until something sharp pierced his chest.

The pain suddenly went away, leaving a silent emptiness, where his fading consciousness continued to rage. Rick was no longer able to move and the world constricted into a bright spot. Soon, it also went out, sinking his mind into impenetrable darkness.

Aurora! Maya! I really wanted to come back...

End of Book Two

Want to be the first to know about our latest
LitRPG, sci fi and fantasy titles from your favorite
authors?

Subscribe to our NEW RELEASES newsletter:
http://eepurl.com/b7niIL

Thank you for reading *The Secret of Atlantis!*
If you like what you've read, check out other LitRPG novels
published by Magic Dome Books:

Dark Paladin **LitRPG series by Vasily Mahanenko:**
The Beginning
The Quest

The *Dark Herbalist* LitRPG series
by Michael Atamanov:
Video Game Plotline Tester
Stay on the Wing
A Trap for the Potentate

The Neuro **LitRPG series by Andrei Livadny:**
The Crystal Sphere
The Curse of Rion Castle
The Reapers

The *Way of the Shaman* LitRPG series
by Vasily Mahanenko:
Survival Quest
The Kartoss Gambit
The Secret of the Dark Forest
The Phantom Castle
The Karmadont Chess Set
Shaman's Revenge
Clans War
The Hour of Pain (a bonus short story)

Galactogon **LitRPG series by Vasily Mahanenko:**
Start the Game!

Phantom Server **LitRPG series by Andrei Livadny:**
Edge of Reality
The Outlaw
Black Sun

Perimeter Defense **LitRPG series by Michael Atamanov:**
Sector Eight
Beyond Death
New Contract
A Game with No Rules

In order to have new books of the series translated faster, we need your help and support! Please consider leaving a review or spread the word by recommending *The Secret of Atlantis* to your friends and posting the link on social media. The more people buy the book, the sooner we'll be able to make new translations available.

Thank you!

Till next time!